'This is the magnificently told journey of a free African girl turned into a woman and slave. It is authoritative and brilliant . . . unrelenting, dramatic and lyrical storytelling'
Austin Clarke, author of *The Polished Hoe*

'Aminata is a heroic figure, a little larger than life, residing within and outside of history. You can never forget this character. She embeds herself in your heart'
Toronto Star

'A powerful indictment of the way in which so many innocent victims were robbed of everything dear to them'
Yorkshire Evening Post

'Hill's elegant voice will leave you spellbound'   *Essence*

'The ebb and flow of Aminata's fortunes is gripping stuff, with the horrors inflicted upon her and her people brought to life almost matter-of-factly – and all the more engaging for that'   *Daily Mail*

'Magnificent, epic . . . one of the great heroines of modern literature . . . not only heartstopping and brutal, but also . . . of great humanity'
Tahmina Anam, author of *A Golden Age*

'Truly compelling . . . It is Hill's ability to observe the multifaceted issue of race with sensitivity, compassion and a keen sense of justice that makes *The Book of Negroes* not just a good book, but a great one – worthy of every honour it is sure to receive'   *Montreal Gazette*

Lawrence Hill was born in Ontario, Canada of a black father and a white mother. He is the author of, among others, a memoir, *Black Berry, Sweet Juice: On Being Black and White in Canada*, and *The Deserter's Tale: the Story of an Ordinary Soldier Who Walked Away from the War in Iraq*, as well as two other novels. His third novel, *The Book of Negroes* (published in the US as *Somebody Knows My Name*) was a no.1 bestseller in Canada, and won the 2008 Commonwealth Writers' Prize for Best Book. He lives in Burlington, Ontario, with his wife and five children.

For more information on Lawrence Hill and his books, see his website at www.lawrencehill.com

Where Bound	Negros Names	Age	Description
St Johns River	Jack Hyde	50	Almost past his Labour
"	Dick	38	Stout Fellow
St Johns River	Corn.l Moss	30	D.o likely
"	Tho.s Brinkerhoof	34	Very short Ordina.y Man
"	Peter Bean	32	Likely fellow
"	Anth.y Gillman	46	Stout short fellow
"	George Black	40	Stout fellow
"	Betsy Black	35	Ordinary Wench
"	W.m Black	14	Fine boy
"	Sam	30	Stout Fell.w
"	Luke Spencer	25	D.o
"	Abigail his Wife	26	Stout Wench, small Child
"	Bill Pigott	28	Stout fellow
"	Pompey Chase	28	D.o
"	John Vorce	36	D.o B
"	Dian	20	Stout squat W.th small Child
Port Roseway	Peter Johnson	35	Stout Fellow
"	Judith Johnson	27	Ordinary Wench
"	Tho.s Danvers	45	D.o Fellow

THE BOOK OF
NEGROES

Lawrence Hill

BLACK SWAN

TRANSWORLD PUBLISHERS
61–63 Uxbridge Road, London W5 5SA
A Random House Group Company
www.rbooks.co.uk

THE BOOK OF NEGROES
A BLACK SWAN BOOK: 9780552775489

First published in Canada by HarperCollins Ltd
Published in the United States as *Someone Knows My Name*

First published in Great Britain
in 2009 by Doubleday
an imprint of Transworld Publishers
Black Swan edition published 2010

Historical documents courtesy of The National Archives, London
(ref: PRO30/55/100, pp. 37, 38)

Addresses for Random House Group Ltd companies outside the UK
can be found at: www.randomhouse.co.uk
The Random House Group Ltd Reg. No. 954009

The Random House Group Limited supports The Forest Stewardship Council
(FSC), the leading international forest certification organisation. All our titles
that are printed on Greenpeace approved FSC certified paper carry the FSC
logo. Our paper procurement policy can be found at
www.rbooks.co.uk/environment

Typeset in 11/13pt Giovanni Book by Falcon Oast Graphic Art Ltd.
Printed in the UK by CPI Cox & Wyman, Reading, RG1 8EX.

2 4 6 8 10 9 7 5 3 1

For my daughter and kindred spirit,
Geneviève Aminata

I have set before thee life and death,
the blessing and the curse.
Therefore choose life.
—Deuteronomy 30:19

So geographers, in Afric-maps,
With savage-pictures fill their gaps;
And o'er unhabitable downs
Place elephants for want of towns.
—Jonathan Swift

Book One

And now I am old

{LONDON, 1802}

I SEEM TO HAVE TROUBLE DYING. By all rights, I should not have lived this long. But I still can smell trouble riding on any wind, just as surely as I could tell you whether it is a stew of chicken necks or pigs' feet bubbling in the iron pot on the fire. And my ears still work just as good as a hound dog's. People assume that just because you don't stand as straight as a sapling, you're deaf. Or that your mind is like pumpkin mush. The other day, when I was being led into a meeting with a bishop, one of the society ladies told another, "We must get this woman into Parliament soon. Who knows how much longer she'll be with us?" Half bent though I was, I dug my fingers into her ribs. She let out a shriek and spun around to face me. "Careful," I told her, "I may outlast you!"

There must be a reason why I have lived in all these lands, survived all those water crossings, while others fell from bullets or shut their eyes and simply willed their lives to end. In the earliest days, when I was free and knew nothing other, I used to sneak outside our walled compound, climb straight up the acacia tree while balancing Father's Qur'an on my head, sit way out on a branch and wonder how I might one day unlock all the mysteries contained in the book. Feet swinging beneath me, I would put

13

down the book—the only one I had ever seen in Bayo—
and look out at the patchwork of mud walls and thatched
coverings. People were always on the move. Women carrying water from the river, men working iron in the fires,
boys returning triumphant from the forest with snared
porcupines. It's a lot of work, extracting meat from a
porcupine, but if they had no other pressing chores, they
would do it anyway, removing the quills, skinning the
animal, slicing out the innards, practising with their sharp
knives on the pathetic little carcass. In those days, I felt free
and happy, and the very idea of safety never intruded on
my thoughts.

I have escaped violent endings even as they have
surrounded me. But I never had the privilege of holding
onto my children, living with them, raising them the way
my own parents raised me for ten or eleven years, until all
of our lives were torn asunder. I never managed to keep my
own children long, which explains why they are not here
with me now, making my meals, adding straw to my
bedding, bringing me a cape to hold off the cold, sitting
with me by the fire with the knowledge that they emerged
from my loins and that our shared moments had grown
like corn stalks in damp soil. Others take care of me now.
And that's a fine thing. But it's not the same as having
one's own flesh and blood to cradle one toward the grave.
I long to hold my own children, and their children if they
exist, and I miss them the way I'd miss limbs from my own
body.

They have me exceedingly busy here in London. They say
I am to meet King George. About me, I have a clutch of
abolitionists—big-whiskered, wide-bellied, bald-headed
men boycotting sugar but smelling of tobacco and burning
candle after candle as they plot deep into the night. The
abolitionists say they have brought me to England to help
them change the course of history. Well. We shall see about
that. But if I have lived this long, it must be for a reason.

Fa means father in my language. *Ba* means river. It also means mother. In my early childhood, my *ba* was like a river, flowing on and on and on with me through the days, and keeping me safe at night. Most of my lifetime has come and gone, but I still think of them as my parents, older and wiser than I, and still hear their voices, sometimes deep-chested, at other moments floating like musical notes. I imagine their hands steering me from trouble, guiding me around cooking fires and leading me to the mat in the cool shade of our home. I can still picture my father with a sharp stick over hard earth, scratching out Arabic in flowing lines and speaking of the distant Timbuktu.

In private moments, when the abolitionists are not swirling about like tornadoes, seeking my presence in this deputation or my signature atop that petition, I wish my parents were still here to care for me. Isn't that strange? Here I am, a broken-down old black woman who has crossed more water than I care to remember, and walked more leagues than a work horse, and the only things I dream of are the things I can't have— children and grandchildren to love, and parents to care for me.

The other day, they took me into a London school and they had me talk to the children. One girl asked if it was true that I was the famous Meena Dee, the one mentioned in all the newspapers. Her parents, she said, did not believe that I could have lived in so many places. I acknowledged that I was Meena Dee, but that she could call me Aminata Diallo if she wanted, which was my childhood name. We worked on my first name for a while. After three tries, she got it. *Aminata*. Four syllables. It's really not that hard. *Ah–ME–naw–tah*, I told her. She said she wished I could meet her parents. And her grandparents. I replied that it amazed me that she still had grandparents in her life. Love them good, I told her, and love them big. Love them every day. She asked why I was so black. I asked why she was so white. She said she was born that way. Same here, I replied. I can see that you must have been quite pretty, even though you are so very dark, she said. You would be prettier if London ever got any sun, I replied. She asked what I ate. My grandfather says he bets you eat raw elephant. I told her I'd never actually taken a bite out of an elephant, but there had been times in my life when I was hungry enough to try. I chased three or four hundred of them, in my life, but never managed to get one to stop rampaging through villages and stand still long enough for me to take a good bite. She laughed and said she wanted to know what I really ate. I eat what you eat, I told her. Do you suppose I'm going to find an elephant walking about the streets of London? Sausages, eggs, mutton stew, bread, crocodiles, all those regular things. Crocodiles? she said. I told her I was just checking to see if she was listening. She said she was an excellent listener and wanted me to please tell her a ghost story.

Honey, I said, my life is a ghost story. Then tell it to me, she said.

As I told her, I am Aminata Diallo, daughter of Mamadu Diallo and Sira Kulibali, born in the village of Bayo, three moons by foot from the Grain Coast in West Africa. I am a Bamana. And a Fula. I am both, and will explain that later. I suspect that I was born in 1745, or close to it. And I am writing this account. All of it. Should I perish before the task is done, I have instructed John Clarkson—one of the quieter abolitionists, but the only one I trust—to change nothing. The abolitionists here in London have already arranged for me to write a short paper, about ten pages, of why the trade in human beings is an abomination and must be stopped. I have done so, and the paper is available in the society offices.

I have a rich, dark skin. Some people have described it as blue black. My eyes are hard to read, and I like them so. Distrust, disdain, dislike—one doesn't want to give public

16

notice of such sentiments. Some say that I was once uncommonly beautiful, but I wouldn't wish beauty on any woman who has not her own freedom, and who chooses not the hands that claim her.

Not much beauty remains now. Not the round, rising buttocks so uncommon in this land of English flatbacks. Not the thighs, thick and well packed, or the calves, rounded and firm like ripe apples. My breasts have fallen, where once they soared like proud birds. I have all but one of my teeth, and clean them every day. To me, a clean, white, full, glowing set of teeth is a beautiful thing indeed, and using the twig, vigorously, three or four times a day keeps them that way. I don't know why it is, but the more fervent the abolitionist, it seems, the more foul the breath. Some men from my homeland eat the bitter kola nut so often that their teeth turn orange. But in England, the abolitionists do much worse, with coffee, tea and tobacco.

My hair has mostly fallen out now, and the remaining strands are grey, still curled, tight to my head, and I don't fuss with them. The East India Company brings bright silk scarves to London, and I have willingly parted with a shilling here and there to buy them, always wearing one when I am brought out to adorn the abolitionist move-ment. Just above my right breast, the initials GO run together, in a tight, inch-wide circle. Alas, I am branded, and can do nothing to cleanse myself of the scar. I have carried this mark since the age of eleven, but only recently learned what the initials represent. At least they are hidden from public view. I am much happier about the lovely crescent moons sculpted into my cheeks. I have one fine, thin moon curving down each of my cheekbones, and have always loved the beauty marks, although the people of London do tend to stare.

I was tall for my age when I was kidnapped, but stopped growing after that and as a result stand at the un-remarkable height of five feet, two inches. To tell the truth,

I don't quite hit that mark any longer. I keel to one side these days, and favour my right leg. My toenails are yellow and crusted and thick and most resistant to trimming. These days, my toes lift rather than settling flat on the ground. No matter, as I have shoes, and I am not asked or required to run, or even to walk considerable distances.

By my bed, I like to keep my favourite objects. One is a blue glass pot of skin cream. Each night, I rub the cream over my ashen elbows and knees. After the life I have lived, the white gel seems like a magical indulgence. *Rub me all the way in,* it seems to say, *and I will grant you and your wrinkles another day or two.*

My hands are the only part of me that still do me proud and that hint at my former beauty. The hands are long and dark and smooth, despite everything, and the nails are nicely embedded, still round, still pink. I have wondrously beautiful hands. I like to put them on things. I like to feel the bark on trees, the hair on children's heads, and before my time is up, I would like to place those hands on a good man's body, if the occasion arises. But nothing—not a man's body, or a sip of whisky, or a peppered goat stew from the old country—would give anything like the pleasure I would take from the sound of a baby breathing in my bed, a grandchild snoring against me. Sometimes, I wake in the morning with the splash of sunlight in my small room, and my one longing, other than to use the chamber pot and have a drink of tea with honey, is to lie back into the soft, bumpy bed with a child to hold. To listen to an infant's voice rise and fall. To feel the magic of a little hand, not even fully aware of what it is doing, falling on my shoulder, my face.

These days, the men who want to end the slave trade are feeding me. They have given me sufficient clothes to ward off the London damp. I have a better bed than I've enjoyed since my earliest childhood, when my parents let me stuff as many soft grasses as I could gather under a woven mat. Not having to think about food, or shelter, or clothing is a rare thing indeed. What does a person do, when survival is not an issue? Well, there is the abolitionist cause, which takes time and fatigues me greatly. At times, I still panic when surrounded by big white men with a purpose. When they swell around me to ask questions, I remember the hot iron smoking above my breast.

Thankfully, the public visits are only so often and leave me time for reading, to which I am addicted like some are to drink or to tobacco. And they leave me time for writing. I have my life to tell, my own private ghost story, and what purpose would there be to this life I have lived, if I could not take this opportunity to relate it? My hand cramps after a while, and sometimes my back or neck aches when I have sat for too long at the table, but this writing business demands little. After the life I have lived, it goes down as easy as sausages and gravy.

Let me begin with a caveat to any and all who find these pages. Do not trust large bodies of water, and do not cross them. If you, dear reader, have an African hue and find yourself led toward water with vanishing shores, seize your freedom by any means necessary. And cultivate distrust of the colour pink. Pink is taken as the colour of innocence, the colour of childhood, but as it spills across the water in the light of the dying sun, do not fall into its pretty path. There, right underneath, lies a bottomless graveyard of children, mothers and men. I shudder to imagine all the Africans rocking in the deep. Every time I have sailed the seas, I have had the sense of gliding over the unburied.

Some people call the sunset a creation of extraordinary beauty, and proof of God's existence. But what benevolent force would bewitch the human spirit by choosing pink to light the path of a slave vessel? Do not be fooled by that pretty colour, and do not submit to its beckoning.

Once I have met with the King and told my story, I desire to be interred right here, in the soil of London. Africa is my homeland. But I have weathered enough migrations for five lifetimes, thank you very much, and don't care to be moved again.

Small hands were good
{BAYO, 1745}

NO MATTER THE TIME OF LIFE or the continent, the pungent, liberating smell of mint tea has always brought me back to my childhood in Bayo. From the hands of traders who walked for many moons with bundles on their heads, magical things appeared in our village just as often as people vanished. Entire villages and towns were walled, and sentries were posted with poison-tipped spears to prevent the theft of men, but when trusted traders arrived, villagers of all ages came to admire the goods.

Papa was a jeweller, and one day, he gave up a gold necklace for a metal teapot with bulging sides and a long, narrow, curving spout. The trader said that the teapot had crossed the desert and would bring luck and longevity to any who drank from it.

In the middle of the next night, Papa stroked my shoulder while I lay in bed. He believed that a sleeping person has a vulnerable soul and deserves to be woken gently.

"Come have tea with your mama and me," Papa said.

I scrambled out of bed, ran outside and climbed into my mother's lap. Everybody else in the village was sleeping. The cocks were silent. The stars blinked like the eyes of a whole town of nervous men who knew of a terrible secret.

Mama and I watched as Papa used the thick, folded leaves from a banana plant to remove the teapot from three burning sticks. He lifted the lid that rose on mysterious hinges and used a whittled stick to scrape honey from a comb into the bubbling tea.

"What are you doing?" I whispered.

"Sweetening the tea," he said.

I brought my nose near. Fresh mint leaves had been stuffed into the pot, and the fragrance seemed to speak of life in distant places.

"Hmm," I said, breathing it in.

"If you close your eyes," Papa said, "you can smell all the way to Timbuktu."

With a hand on my shoulder, my mother also inhaled and sighed.

I asked Papa where, exactly, was Timbuktu? Far away, he said. Had he been there? Yes, he said, he had. It was located on the mighty Joliba River, and he had once travelled there to pray, to learn and to cultivate his mind, which every believer should do. This made me want to cultivate my mind too. About half of the people of Bayo were Muslims, but Papa was the only one who had a copy of the Qur'an, and who knew how to read and write. I asked how far it was across the Joliba. Was it like crossing the streams near Bayo? No, he said, it was ten times the distance a man could throw a stone. I couldn't imagine such a river.

When the tea was strong and sweet with the gift of the bees, Papa lifted the steaming pot to the full height of his raised arm, tipped the spout, and poured the boiling liquid into a small calabash for me, another for Mama and a third for himself. He didn't spill a drop. He set the teapot back on the embers, and warned me to let the drink cool.

I cupped my palms around the warm calabash and

said, "Tell me again, Papa, about how you and Mama met."

I loved to hear the story about how they had never been meant to set eyes on each other, Mama being a Bamana and Papa a Fula. I loved how their story defied the impossible. They were never supposed to meet, let alone come together and start a family.

"A lucky thing for strange times," Papa said, "or you would not have been born."

JUST ONE RAIN SEASON BEFORE MY BIRTH, Papa had set out with other Fulbe men from Bayo. They had walked for five suns to trade their shea butter for salt in a distant market. On the way home, they gave a little pouch of salt to the chief of a friendly Bamana village. The chief invited them into the village to eat and rest and spend the night. While eating, Papa noticed Mama passing by. She was balancing on her head a tray of three yams and a calabash of goat's milk. Papa drank in her smooth walking gait, level head, lifted chin, the arch of her back, her long, strong legs and the heels of her feet, dyed red.

"She seemed serious and dependable, but not to be trifled with," Papa said. "I knew in an instant that she would become my wife."

Mama sipped her tea and laughed. "I was busy," she said, "and your father was in my way. I was going to help a woman who was ready to have her baby."

Mama had no children yet, but had already brought many babies into the world. Papa found Mama's father, and made inquiries. He learned that Mama's first husband had disappeared many moons earlier, shortly after they had married. People assumed that he was either dead or kidnapped. Papa's wife—to whom he had been betrothed before he or she were even born—had recently died of fever.

Mama was brought to meet Papa. This interrupted the

catching of the baby, and she told him so. Papa smiled, and noted the muscles at the back of her legs as she turned to go back to her work. Negotiations continued about how to compensate Mama's father for the loss of a daughter. They settled on six goats, seven bars of iron, ten copper manillas and four hundred strung cowrie shells.

These were troubled times, and without all the turmoil, the marriage between a Fula and a Bamana would not have been permitted. People were disappearing, and villagers were so concerned about falling into the hands of kidnappers that new alliances were forming among neighbouring villages. Hunters and fishermen travelled in groups. Men spent days at a time building walls around towns and villages.

Papa brought Mama to his village of Bayo. He made jewellery with fine threads of gold and silver and travelled to bring his goods to markets and to pray in mosques. He sometimes returned with the Qur'an or with other writings, in Arabic. He claimed that it was not the place of a girl to learn to read or write, but relented when he saw me attempting to draw words in Arabic with a stick in the sand. So, in the privacy of our home, with nobody but my mother as a witness, I was shown how to use a reed, dyed water and parchment. I learned to write phrases in Arabic, such as *Allaahu Akbar* (God is great) and *Laa ilaaha illa-Lah* (There is none worthy of worship except God).

Mama spoke her native Bamanankan, a language she always used when the two of us were alone together, but she also had picked up much Fulfulde and learned some prayers from Papa. Sometimes, while I watched, a gaggle of Fulbe women would bump elbows and tease one another as Mama bent over with a sharpened stick and scratched *Al-hamdulillah* (Praise be to God) in the earth, to prove to the village women that she had learned some Arabic prayers. Nearby, the women pounded millet, using heavy wooden pestles that were long like human legs and smooth like baby skin and hard like stone. When they flung their pestles against the mortars full of millet, it sounded like drummers beating out a song. Once in a while, they paused to sip water and examine their calloused palms, while Mama repeated the words she had learned from Papa.

By the time I came along, Mama was respected in the village. Like the other women, she planted maize and millet, and collected shea nuts. She dried the nuts in a woodfired kiln and pounded them with her pestle to extract the oil. Mama kept most of the oil, but set aside some of it for bringing babies into the world. Mama was always wanted when a woman was ready to bring a child to light. Once she even helped a donkey stalled in labour. She had a peaceful smile when she was happy and felt safe, a smile that I have thought of every day since I was ripped away from her.

When my time came, I refused to enter the world. Papa said that I was punishing my mother for conceiving me. Finally, Mama summoned Papa.

"Speak to your child," she told him, "for I am growing weary."

Papa placed his hand flat on Mama's belly. He brought his mouth close to her navel, which bulged like an unbloomed tulip.

"Son," Papa said.

"You don't know that we have a son in here," Mama said.

"If you keep taking so long, we just may end up with a goat," Papa said. "But you have asked me to speak, and I am thinking of a son. So, dear Son, come out of there now. You have been living the good life, sleeping and clinging to your mother. Come now, or I shall beat you."

Papa claimed that I answered him from the womb.

"I am not a boy," he told me I said, "and before I come out, we must talk."

25

"Then talk."

"To come out right now, I require hot corn cakes, a calabash of fresh milk, and that fine drink the unbelievers tap from the tree—"

"No palm wine," my father cut in. "Not for one who fears Allah. But I can bring cakes when you have teeth, and Mama will supply the milk. And if you are good, one day I shall give you the bitter kola nut. Allah doesn't mind the kola."

Out I came, sliding from my mother like an otter from a riverbank.

AS AN INFANT, I TRAVELLED on my mother's back. She slid me around to her breast when I cried for food, and passed me among villagers, but usually I was swathed in red and orange cloth and rode low down on her back when she walked to market, pounded millet into flour, fetched water from the spring and tended to births. I remember wondering, within a year or two of taking my first steps, why only men sat to drink tea and converse, and why women were always busy. I reasoned that men were weak and needed rest.

As soon as I could walk, I made myself useful. I collected shea nuts, and scrambled up trees to fetch mangoes and avocadoes, oranges and other fruits. I was made to hold other women's babies, and to keep them content. There was nothing wrong with a girl as young as three or four rain seasons holding and caring for a baby while the mother did other work. Once, however, Fanta, the youngest wife of the village chief, slapped me when she found me attempting to make a baby suckle me.

By my eighth rain season, I had heard stories of men in other villages being stolen by invading warriors or even sold by their own people, but never did it seem that this could happen to me. After all, I was a freeborn Muslim. I knew some of the Arabic prayers, and even had the proud crescent moon carved high into each of my cheeks. The crescent moons were to make me beautiful, but they also identified me as a believer among my Fulbe villagers. There were three captives—all unbelievers—in our village, but even children knew that no Muslim was allowed to hold another Muslim in captivity. I believed that I would be safe.

My father said it was so, when I came to him with all the stories that the village children chanted: somebody, some night, was sure to snatch me from my bed. Some said it would be our people, the Fulbe. Others warned about my mother's people, the Bamana. Still others talked of the mysterious toubabu, the white men, whom none of us had ever seen. *Put those silly children out of your mind*, Papa said. *Stay close to your Mama and me, don't go out wandering alone, and you will be fine.* Mama wasn't quite as confident. She tried to warn him about travelling such long distances, to sell his jewellery and to pray in mosques. Once or twice, at night when I was supposed to be sleeping, I heard them arguing. *Don't go travelling so far*, Mama said, *It's not safe.* And Papa said, *We travel in groups, with arrows and clubs, and what man would test his strength against me?* Mama: *I have heard that before.*

Mama took me along when women were at their biggest, ballooning from within. I watched her quick hands loosen umbilical cords from babies' necks. I saw her reach inside a woman, with the other hand firm and pushing outside the womb, to turn the baby around. I saw her rub oil into her hands and massage a woman's private parts to relax her skin and prevent it from tearing. Mama said that some women had their womanly parts cut up and put back together very badly. I asked what she meant. She smashed an old ceramic pot of no value, pushed apart the pieces, discarded one or two, and then had me try to reassemble it. I managed to stick some pieces together, but they were jagged, and stuck out and didn't quite fit any longer.

"Like that," Mama said.

"What happens to a woman like that?"

"She might survive. Or she might bleed too much and die. Or she might die when she tries to push out her first baby."

Over time, I watched how Mama helped women have their babies. She had a series of goatskin pouches, and I learned the names of all her crushed leaves, dried bark and herbs. As a game, to test myself, I tried to anticipate when Mama would encourage a woman to ride out all the shaking in her belly. From the way the woman moved, breathed and smelled, and from the way she let out a guttural, animal-like sound when she was at the height of her convulsing, I tried to guess when she would start to push. Mama usually brought along an antelope bladder full of a drink made from the bitter tamarind fruit and honey. When the woman cried out in thirst, I would pour a little into a calabash and pass it along, proud of my service, proud to be dependable.

After Mama caught a baby in another village, the mother's family would give her soap and oils and meats, and Mama would eat with the family and praise me for being her little helper. I cut through my first rope of life at the age of seven rains, holding the knife fast and sawing on and on until I made it all the way through the resistant cord. One rain season later, I was catching babies as they slid out. Later still, my mother taught me how to reach inside a woman—after coating my hand with warm oil— and to touch in the right spot to tell if the door was suitably wide. I became adept at that, and Mama said it was good to have me along because my hands were so small.

Mama began to speak to me about how my body would change. I would soon start bleeding, she said, and around that time some women would work with her to perform a little ritual on me. I wanted to know more about that ritual. All girls have it done when they are ready to become women, she said. When I pressed for details, Mama said that part of my womanhood was to be cut off so that I would be considered clean and pure and ready for marriage. I was none too impressed by this, and informed her that I was in no hurry to marry and would be declining the treatment. Mama said that no person could be taken seriously without being married, and that in due time, she and Papa would tell me about their plans for me. I told her that I remembered what she had said earlier, about some people having their womanly parts torn apart and put back together improperly. She carried on with an implacable confidence that left me worried.

"Did they do this to you?" I asked her.

"Of course," she said, "or your father would never have married me."

"Did it hurt?"

"More than childbirth, but it didn't last long. It is just a little correction."

"But I have done nothing wrong, so I am in no need of correction," I said. Mama simply laughed, so I tried another approach. "Some of the girls told me that Salima in the next village died last year, when they were doing that thing to her."

"Who told you that?"

"Never mind," I said, employing one of her expressions. "But is it true?"

"The woman who worked on Salima was a fool. She was untrained, and she tried to do too much. I'll take care of you when the time comes."

We let the matter drop, and never had the chance to discuss it again.

* * *

IN OUR VILLAGE, THERE WAS A STRONG, gentle man named Fomba. He was a *woloso*, which in my mother's language meant captive of the second generation. Since his birth, he had belonged to our village chief. Fomba wasn't a freeborn Muslim, and never learned the proper prayers in Arabic, but sometimes he kneeled down with Papa and the believers, facing in the direction of the rising sun.

Fomba had muscled arms and thick legs. He was the best shot in the village. Once, I saw him take sixty paces back from a lizard on a tree, draw back his bow and release the arrow. It shot right through the lizard's abdomen, pinning it to the bark.

The village chief let Fomba go hunting every day, but released him from the tasks of planting and harvesting millet because he never seemed able to grasp all the rules or techniques, or to know how to work with a team of men. The children loved to follow Fomba about the village, watching him. He had a strange way of holding his head, tilting it way off to the side. Sometimes we gave him a platter of empty calabashes and asked him to balance it on his head, just for the pleasure of watching the whole thing slide off and crash to the ground. Fomba let us do that to him time and again.

We teased Fomba mercilessly, but he never seemed to mind us children. He would smile, and put up with rude taunts that would have gotten us beaten by any other adult in Bayo. On some days, we would hide behind a wall and spy on Fomba while he played with the ashes of a fire. This was one of his favourite activities. Long after the women had done their cooking and we had eaten millet balls and sauce and finished using soap from the ashes of banana leaves to clean the pots, Fomba would bring a stick to the fire and poke around in the ashes. One day he trapped five chickens in a fishing net. He brought them out one by one, wrung their necks, plucked and cleaned and gutted them.

Then he drove a sharp iron rod through their bodies and set them over a fire to roast.

Fanta, the youngest wife of the village chief, came running from the millet-pounding circle and smacked him about the head.

It seemed strange to me that he didn't try to protect himself. "The children need meat," was all he said.

Fanta scoffed. "They don't need meat until they can work," she said. "Stupid *woloso*. You have just wasted five chickens."

Under Fanta's gaze, Fomba kept roasting the chickens, and then pulled them out of the fire, cut them up and handed the pieces to us. I took a leg, burning hot, and grabbed a leaf to protect my fingers. Warm juice ran down my chin as I sucked the brown flesh and crunched the bone to suck out the marrow. I heard that night that Fanta told her husband to beat the man, but he refused.

One day, Fomba was sent to kill a goat that had suddenly started biting children and acting like its mind had departed. Fomba caught the goat, made it sit, put his arm around it, patted its head to calm it down. Then, he drew a knife from his loincloth and sliced the neck where the artery was thick. The goat lay still in Fomba's arms, staring like a baby at him as it bled ferociously, weakened, and died. Fomba, however, hadn't positioned himself cleverly, and blood ran all over him. He stood in the middle of the village compound, ringed by mud homes, and called out for hot water. The women were pounding millet, and Fanta told the others to ignore him. But Mama had a soft spot for Fomba. I had heard her once, at night, telling Papa that Fanta mistreated the *woloso*. I wasn't surprised when Mama took leave of the millet pounding, grabbed a prized metal bucket, poured in several calabashes of hot water and carried it over to Fomba, who lugged it into the bathing enclosure.

I thought the bucket was magical. One day, I snuck into

Fanta's round, thatched home. I found the bucket and brought it into the better light by the door. It was made of smooth, rounded metal, and reflected sunlight. The metal was thin, but I was unable to bend it. I turned it upside down and beat it with the heels of my palms. It swallowed sound. The metal had no character, no personality, and was useless for making music. It was not at all like goatskin pulled taut across the head of a drum. The bucket was said to have come from the toubabu. I wondered what sort of person would invent such a thing.

I tried lifting and swinging it by the looping metal handle. At that moment, Fanta came upon me, ripped the bucket from my hand, hung it from a peg in the wall, and popped me on the side of my head.

"You came into my house with no permission?"

Slap.

"No, I was just . . ."

"It's not for you to touch."

Slap.

"You can't beat me like this. I'll tell my father."

Slap.

"I'll beat you all I want. And he'll beat you again when he hears that you were in my home."

Fanta, who had been planting millet in the boiling sun, had beads of sweat on her lip. I saw that she had better things to do than to stand there hitting me all day. I ducked and ran out of her home, knowing she would not follow.

PAPA WAS ONE OF THE BIGGEST MEN IN BAYO. It was said that he could outwrestle any man in our village. One day, he crouched low to the ground and called for me. Up I climbed onto his back, all the way to his shoulders. There I sat, higher than the tallest villager, my legs curled around his neck and my hands in his. He took me outside the walled village, me riding high up like that.

"Since you are so strong and can make such beautiful jewellery," I said, "why don't you take a second wife? Our chief has four wives!"

He laughed. "I cannot afford four wives, my little one. And why do I need four wives, when your mother gives me all the trouble I can manage? The Qur'an says that a man must treat all his wives equally, if he is to have more than one. But how could I treat anyone as equally as your mother?"

"Mama is beautiful," I said.

"Mama is strong," he said. "Beauty comes and goes. Strength, you keep forever."

"What about the old people?"

"They are the strongest of all, for they have lived longer than all of us, and they have wisdom," he said, tapping his temple.

We stopped at the edge of a forest.

"Does Aminata go wandering off alone this far?" he asked.

"Never," I said.

"Which way is the mighty Joliba, river of many canoes?"

"That way," I said, pointing north.

"How far?"

"Four suns, by foot," I said.

"Would you like to see the town of Segu one day?" he said.

"Segu on the Joliba?" I asked. "Yes. If I get to ride on your shoulders."

"When you are old enough to walk for four suns, I will take you for a visit."

"And I will travel, and cultivate my mind," I said.

"We will not speak of that," he said. "Your task is to become a woman."

Papa had already shown me how to scratch out a few prayers in Arabic. Surely he would show me more, in good time.

"Mama's village is over there, five suns away," I said, pointing east.

"Since you are so clever, pretend I am blind and show me the way home."

"Are we cultivating my mind now?"

He chuckled. "Show me the way home, Aminata."

"Go that way, past the baobab tree."

We made it that far. "Turn this way. Take this path. Watch out. Mama and I saw three white scorpions on this path yesterday."

"Good girl. Now what?"

"Ahead, we enter our village. The walls are thick and as high as two men. We come in this way. Say hello to the sentry."

Papa laughed and saluted the sentry. We approached the chief's rectangular house, and passed the four round homes, one for each wife.

"Let me know when we pass Fanta's house."

"Why, Papa?"

"Perhaps we should stop in and drum your favourite bucket."

I laughed and slapped his shoulder playfully and told him, in a whisper, that I did not like that woman.

"You must learn respect," Papa said.

"But I do not respect her," I said.

Papa paused for a moment, and patted my leg. "Then you must learn to hide your disrespect."

Papa walked on, and soon, two women came upon us.

"Mamadu Diallo," one called out to Papa, "that is not the way to educate your daughter. She has legs for walking."

My father's real name was Muhammad. But every Muslim man in the village was thus named, so he went by Mamadu to distinguish himself.

"Aminata and I, we were having a little chat," Papa told the women, "and I needed her ears close to my mouth."

The woman laughed. "You spoil her."

"Not a chance. I am training her to carry me the same way, when I am old."

The women bent over, slapping their thighs in laughter. We said goodbye, and I continued to direct Papa past the walled enclosure for bathing, past the shaded bench for palavering and past the round huts for storing millet and rice. And then Papa and I came upon Fanta, who was pulling Fomba by the ear.

"Stupid man," she said.

"Hello, Fourth Wife of Chief," Papa said.

"Mamadu Diallo," she said.

"No salutations for my little girl today?" Papa said.

She grimaced and said, "Aminata Diallo."

"And why are you dragging poor Fomba thus?" Papa said. She still had the man by the ear.

"He led an ass to the well, and it fell in," she said. "Put down that spoiled girl, Mamadu Diallo, and help us fetch out the ass before it soils our drinking water."

"If you let go of Fomba, who needs his ear, I shall help you with the ass."

Papa let me down from his shoulders. Fomba and I watched Papa and some other men tie vines around a village boy and send him deep into the well. The boy in the well wrapped more vines around the ass, and was hoisted out. Then Papa and the men hauled out the ass. The animal seemed undisturbed, and on the whole less bruised than Fomba's ear.

I wanted my papa to teach me how to tie vines around the belly of a donkey. Maybe he would teach me everything he knew. It wouldn't hurt anybody if I learned to read and write. Perhaps, one day, I would be the only woman, and one of the only people in my entire village, to be able to read the Qur'an and to write in the gorgeous, flowing Arabic script.

* * *

ONE DAY, MAMA AND I WERE CALLED from our millet pounding to attend a birth in Kinta, four villages away in the direction of the setting sun. The men were weeding the millet fields, but Fomba was told to fetch his bow and a quiver of poisoned arrows and to walk with us for our protection. When we arrived in Kinta, Fomba was given a place to drink tea and rest, and we went to work. The birth stretched from the morning into the evening, and by the time Mama had caught the baby and swaddled him and brought him to his mother's nipple, fatigue had gripped our bones. We took some millet cakes in hot gumbo sauce, which I loved. Before we left, the village women warned us to stay off the main trail leading from the village, because strange men—unknown in any neighbouring villages— had been spotted lately. The villagers asked if we would like to stay the night with them. My mother refused, because another mother in Bayo was expecting her baby at any time. As we prepared to leave, the villagers gave us a skin of water and three live chickens bound by the feet, along with a special gift of thanks—a metal pail, like the big washing bucket Fomba used the day he killed the goat.

Fomba couldn't carry a thing on his head because his neck was always bent to the left, so Mama told him to carry the pail, into which the chickens were stuffed. Fomba seemed proud of his acquisition, but Mama warned him that he would have to surrender it when we returned to the village. He nodded happily and set out ahead of us.

"When we get home, can I have the pail?" I asked.

"The pail belongs to the village. We will give it to the chief."

"But then Fanta will get it."

Mama held her breath. I could tell that she didn't like Fanta, either, but she watched her words.

We walked under a full moon that blazed in the night sky and lit our path. When we were almost home, three hares dashed in front of us, one right after the other, disappearing into the woods. Fomba set down his bucket, lifted a throwing stone from a flap at the hip of his loincloth and cocked his arm. He seemed to know that the hares would scurry back across the path. When they reappeared, Fomba pegged the slowest hare in the head. He stooped to pick it up, but Mama held him back. The hare was thick around the middle. Mama ran her finger along the body. The rabbit had been pregnant. It would make a fine stew, Mama told Fomba, but next time he saw rabbits streaking across the trail, he should sharpen his aim and take the fastest one—not the female lugging babies in her belly. Fomba nodded and draped his swollen prey over his shoulder. He stood up and resumed walking, but suddenly bent his neck even further to the side and listened.

There was more rustling in the bushes. I looked for another sign of the hares. Nothing. We walked more quickly. Mama reached for my hand.

"If strangers come upon us, Aminata—" she began, but got no further.

From behind a grove of trees stepped four men with massive arms and powerful legs. In the moonlight, I could see that they had faces like mine, but with no facial carvings. Whoever they were, they came from another village. They had ropes, leather straps and knives, and an odd, long piece of wood with a hole at one end. For an instant, they stared at us and we looked at them. I heard the click of fear at the back of Mama's throat. I longed to run. Never could one of those thick, clumsy, loud-breathing men catch me whirling and dashing and sidestepping among the trees, flying down the forest paths just as quick as an antelope. But Mama had the water skins balanced on a platter on her head, and I had some pineapples balanced over mine, and in the instant that I hesitated, wondering what to do with those platters, worrying that the fruit would tumble to the ground if I moved too awkwardly, the men encircled us.

Fomba was the first among us to move. He grabbed the man with the odd stick, locked one arm around his neck and hit him on the head with the chicken bucket. The man stumbled. Fomba grabbed his neck with one hand and twisted it, hard, to the right. A gurgling sound escaped the man's throat before he fell. Fomba turned and reached for me, but another man came up behind him.

"Fomba," I cried out. "Watch out!"

But before Fomba could turn, he was clubbed in the back of the head. He crumpled to the ground. The rabbit carcass slipped off his shoulder. I hadn't imagined that a man of his size and strength could fall so quickly. A man bound Fomba's hands, slipped a knotted rope around his neck and picked up the rabbit. But Fomba did not stir.

Mama shouted at me to drop the fruits and run. But I couldn't move. I couldn't leave her. She faced the men and called out like a warrior: "Curses of the dead upon you. Let us pass."

The men spoke in a strange tongue. I thought I recognized the words *girl, young* and *not too young*—but I wasn't sure.

Mama switched to Fulfulde. "Run, Daughter," she whispered, but I couldn't. I just couldn't.

She was holding her birthing kit, and still had the water skins balanced on her head. She was carrying too much to flee, so I stayed beside her. I could hear her breathing. I knew that she was thinking. Perhaps she would start shouting, and I would join her. Our village was not far. Someone might hear us. Two men grabbed Mama and knocked down her water skins. Another man grabbed me by the arm. I flailed and kicked and bit his hand. He pulled it free. He was angry now and breathing harder. When he lunged for me, I kicked with all my might and got him where his legs came together. He groaned and stumbled, but I knew I hadn't hurt him enough to keep him down. I turned to run to my mother, but another man tripped me and pinned me to the ground. I spat dirt from my mouth and tried to wriggle free, but I had no strength against the one who held me.

"This is a mistake," I said. "I am a freeborn Muslim. Let me go!" I said it in Fulfulde and I said it in Bamanankan, but my words had no effect, so I started screaming. If any villager happened to be out at night, perhaps he would hear. Someone bound my wrists behind my back and slipped a leather noose around my neck, which he tightened just to the point of cutting off my breath so I couldn't scream and could barely breathe. Gagging, I waved wildly at the men. The noose was loosened enough to let me breathe. I was still alive. *Allaahu Akbar*, I said. I hoped that someone would hear the words in Arabic and realize the mistake. But nobody heard me. Or cared.

I craned my neck to look up from the ground. Mama broke away from one man, slapped at his face and bit his shoulder, then grabbed a thick branch and belted him in the head. He paused, stunned. Mama charged the man who held the strap around my neck. I pulled against it, straining toward her even as it choked me. But another man intercepted her, raised high a big, thick club and brought it swinging down against the back of her head. Mama dropped. I saw her blood in the moonlight, angry and dark and spilling fast. I tried to crawl to her. I knew what to do about spilling blood. I just had to get my palm against the wound, and to press hard. But I couldn't crawl, or wriggle, or move an inch. The captors had me firmly now, the leash tightening once more around my neck. They forced Fomba and me up, and we had no choice but to follow.

I struggled against the leash to look back over my shoulder, and saw that Mama was still on the ground, not moving. I was slapped hard in the face, spun forward and shoved in the back. Over and over and over again I was shoved, and I had to move my feet.

Other than in her sleep, I had never seen Mama motionless. This had to be a dream. I longed to wake up in my bed, and to eat a millet cake with Mama, and to admire the way she dipped her calabash in a clay jar and brought out the water without spilling a drop. Soon, for sure, I would be free from these evil spirits. Soon, I would find my Papa, and together we would run back to Mama, wake her before it was too late, carry her into the cool walls of our home.

But I was not waking.

The longest cry rose from my lungs. The men stuffed cloth in my mouth. Whenever my pace slowed, they shoved me again in the back. We walked so fast that I had trouble breathing. They removed the cloth but showed me, with angry hand signals, that they would stuff it back in my mouth if I made a sound. On and on they made me walk, further from my Mama. Smoke hung in the air. We were circling outside my village. The drums of Bayo rang out warnings of danger. I heard popping, over and over. It sounded like branches cracking from trees. The drumming stopped. Through a gap in the woods, I could see the flames. Bayo was burning.

Five more strange men joined us, leading three captives—also yoked— toward us. From one man's wide-legged gait in the light of the moon, I recognized my father.

"*Fa*," I called out to him.

"Aminata," he shouted.

"They killed *Ba*." The man holding my strap smacked my face.

"You are less than porcupine shit," I hissed at the captor, but he didn't understand.

I watched my father. The other captives struggled against their ropes, but my father walked upright and tall, rubbing his wrists together until they slid free. He jabbed his fingers into a captor's eyes, pulled the knife from his hands and sliced through the strap around his own neck. When another captor rushed forward, Papa plunged the knife deep into the man's chest. The captor seemed to sigh, stood long enough for my father to remove the knife, and dropped dead.

I wanted my *fa* to flee and to find *Ba* on the trail leading away from Bayo. If there was still life in her, I wanted him to save her. While shouting broke out among our captors, Papa ran to me. He slashed at the man holding my yoke, cutting deeply into his arm. The man slid down and moaned in agony. Two men jumped my father, but he flung them off. He stabbed one, then the other, and was circling three injured men. Then one of the captors hoisted an unusual, long, rectangular stick. He pursed his lips and pointed the stick at my father from a distance of five paces. Papa stopped where he was and held up his palm. Fire exploded from the stick and blew Papa onto his back. He turned his head to look for me, but then his eyes went blank. The life gushed up out of Papa's chest, flooded his ribs and ran into the waiting earth, which soaked up everything that came out of him.

There were two new male captives. I didn't recognize them. They came from different villages, perhaps. I looked at them pleadingly. Their eyes sank. Fomba dropped his head. The male captives could do nothing for me. They were all tied at the hands and yoked by the necks. To resist was suicide, and who but my own father and mother would fight for me now, and fight to the death?

My feet felt stuck to the ground. My thighs felt wooden. My stomach heaved up against my chest. I could barely breathe. *Fa* was the strongest man in Bayo. He could lift me with one arm, and send sparks flying like stars when he pounded red iron with his mallet. How could this be? I prayed that this was a dream, but the dream would not relent.

I wondered what my *ba* and *fa* would tell me to do. *Keep walking!* That was all I could imagine. *Don't fall.* I thought of my Mama walking in Bayo with her soles dyed red. I tried to keep their voices in my head. I tried to think about drinking mint tea with them at night, while my mother laughed and my father told melodious stories. But I could not feed those thoughts. Each and every time, they were starved, flattened and sucked out of my mind, and replaced by visions of my mother motionless in the woods and my father, lips quivering while his chest erupted.

I walked, because I was made to do it. I walked, because it was the only thing to do. And that night as I walked, over and over again I heard my father's final word. *Aminata. Aminata. Aminata.*

Three revolutions of the moon

I LIVED IN TERROR THAT THE CAPTORS WOULD BEAT US, boil us and eat us, but they began with humiliation: they tore the clothes off our backs. We had no head scarves or wraps for our body, or anything to cover our private parts. We had not even sandals for our feet. We had no more clothing than goats, and nakedness marked us as captives wherever we went. But our captors were also marked by what they lacked: light in their eyes. Never have I met a person doing terrible things who would meet my own eyes peacefully. To gaze into another person's face is to do two things: to recognize their humanity, and to assert your own. As I began my long march from home, I discovered that there were people in the world who didn't know me, didn't love me, and didn't care whether I lived or died.

Eight of us were taken captive outside Bayo and neighbouring villages. In the darkness, Fomba was the only one I recognized. I stumbled forward, and didn't notice for hours that the yoke was rubbing the skin of my neck raw. I could not stop thinking about my parents, or what had happened to them. In one moment, I could not have imagined life without them. In the next, I was still living but they were gone. *Wake now*, I told myself. *Wake now, sip from the calabash by your sleeping mat and go hug your mama.*

43

This dream is like a set of soiled clothes; step out of them and go see your mama. But there was only an unbearable nightmare that would not end.

While we walked through the night, others were attached to our string of captives. In the morning light, I noticed Fomba walking with his head down. And then I saw Fanta. There was no sign of the chief. Fanta too was yoked about the neck. Her eyes darted left and right, up and down, peering at the woods and evaluating our captors. I wanted to call out to her, but she had a cloth stuck in her mouth and a rope holding it in place. I tried to meet her eyes, but she would not greet my glance. My gaze fell to her naked belly. The chief's wife was with child. I guessed that she was five moons in progress.

We walked with the rising sun behind us, and came to a great and busy river. Finally, they unyoked and untied us and let us rest at the edge of the water. Four men stood guard over us, with firesticks and clubs.

Perhaps this river was the same Joliba said to flow past Segu. As my father had described, it was farther across than a stone's throw. It was full of canoes and men rowing people and goods. Our captors negotiated with the head boatman, and we were bound by the wrists and tossed into the middle of the canoes. Six oarsmen rowed my boat. Between the steady rocking of the rowers' arms, I watched the other canoes gliding over the water. In one, I saw a horse. Regal and entirely black but for one white circle between the eyes. As the oarsmen rowed, the horse held perfectly still.

At the other side of the river, we were untied and let out. The swampy air stank. Mosquitoes feasted on my arms and legs. They even attacked my cheeks. Our captors paid the oarsmen with cowrie shells. I felt a cowrie in the sand, under my toes, and scooped it up before they yoked my neck again. It was white, and hard, with curled lips ridged like tiny teeth, the whole thing as small as my thumbnail.

It was beautiful and perfect and, it seemed, unbreakable. I rinsed it in the water and put it on my tongue. It felt like a friend in my mouth, and comforted me. I sucked it fiercely, and wondered how many cowries I was worth.

We were lined up in a coffle of captives, attached by the neck in groups of two or three and made to walk. A boy, perhaps just four rains older than I, walked beside us, checking captives, letting us sip from a water skin, passing us scraps of millet or maize cake, a mango or an orange. The boy kept glancing at me when the older captors were not watching. He spoke Bamanankan, but I ignored him. He was bony and seemed to be made entirely of shoulders, elbows, knees and ankles. He strode along with an awkward, uncoordinated gait. Pasted to his face was a permanent smile, for which I distrusted him utterly. There was no reason to smile. There were no friends to make. One did not smile at enemies. I told myself this, but suddenly doubted it. My father, I remembered, had told me that a wise man knows his enemies, and keeps them close. Possibly, this boy who kept looking at me, wide-eyed and innocent, was an enemy. Or he was just a stupid, smiling, curious boy who amused himself by walking alongside our coffle, with not a clue in his head about what he was witnessing. I did not appreciate his gaze when I was naked. I did not want to be noticed, seen or known by anybody, in my present state. Surely I would get free. Surely this would end. Surely I would find a way to flee into the woods and to make my way home. But at such a moment, without a scrap of clothing on my back, I couldn't possibly run to any person who knew me. I was too old to be seen like this. My breasts were not far from budding. My mother had said that I would soon become a woman. This was no way to be seen. I nearly made myself crazy, wondering how to escape my own nakedness. To where could a naked person run?

We now had ten or so captors, all with spears, clubs and

firesticks. They seemed to speak a language vaguely like Bamanankan. I knew they were not Muslims, because they never stopped to pray. At night, we were herded under a baobab tree. Our captors paid five men from a nearby village to stand guard over us. Still attached neck to neck, we were made to help gather wood, build a fire and boil yams in water, with nary a pepper to give the meal bite. The gruel was watery and tasteless, and I couldn't eat it. The boy who kept his eye on me brought me a banana. I took it and ate it, but still refused to speak with him.

"You," Fanta called out. "Bayo child. Daughter of Mamadu, the jeweller. Give me that banana. Throw it, here."

I finished the banana, dropped the peel and said, "I only had the one."

"Speak to that boy who gave it to you. I see him watching you."

"He has no more food."

"Insolent children are beaten. I always told Mamadu Diallo that he was too free with you."

I felt my anger spiralling. I wanted desperately to escape her taunts. "Leave me alone," I said.

"And your Bamana mother," she sneered.

"I said leave me alone."

"Taking you with her to see all those babies being born. Ridiculous."

"I didn't just see them. I caught them. And who do you think will catch yours?"

Fanta's mouth fell open. There. We were even. But then I felt ashamed at what I had said. My father had told me to hide my disrespect. And my mother never would have used a woman's pregnancy against her. Fanta grew silent. I imagined her shame at having to push out her baby while our captors watched.

We were roped above the ankles, in pairs, and our neck yokes were removed so that we could lie down under the baobab tree. I was attached to Fomba, who allowed me to settle down next to Fanta. I touched her belly. She glared at me, but softened as she felt my hand calm and still over her navel.

"Come near, child," she said. "I can feel you shivering. I spoke harshly because I am hungry and tired, but I won't really beat you."

I huddled against her and fell asleep.

Someone was rubbing my shoulder. At first, I dreamed it was Fanta, ordering me again to fetch her a banana. But my eyes opened and I was no longer dreaming, and there was Fomba, come to tell me that I had been crying aloud in my sleep.

My moans were spooking the guards, Fomba said, and they were threatening to beat me if I didn't give them peace. Besides, he said, my legs were twitching madly. He lay next to me, patted my arm, and said he would not let them hurt me but that I must sleep correctly.

The men who had captured me had taken Fomba's hare, skinned and gutted it and roasted it over a fire. None of the rabbit meat—or that of the chickens soon slaughtered and cooked—came to my mouth. I lay on my back and stared up at the stars. In happier times, I had loved to watch them with my parents. There was the Drinking Gourd in the sky, with its brilliant handle. I wondered if anyone in Bayo was watching it, at that moment.

Fomba had fallen back to sleep. Doing my best not to tug at his feet, I stood to pray. I had nothing to cover my hair, but proceeded anyway. With my head down, I put my thumbs behind my ears. *Allaahu Akbar*, I said. I placed my right hand over left and began to say *Subhaana ala huuma wa bihamdika*, but I got no further. A captor came and struck me with his stick and ordered me back onto the ground. Eventually, I fell asleep.

The next morning, between first light and sunrise, I tried again to pray, but another captor struck me with the rod.

The next night, after another thrashing, I gave up the prayers. I had lost my mother. My father. And my community. I had lost my chance to learn all the Qur'anic prayers. I had lost my secret opportunities to learn to read. When I tried to mumble the prayers in my head—*Allaahu Akbar. Subhaana ala huuma wa bihamdika. A'uudhu billaahi minash shaitaan ar-Rajeem*—it wasn't the same. Praying inside the head was no good. I was worse than a captive. I was becoming an unbeliever. I could not praise Allah properly, without prayer.

WE WALKED FOR MANY SUNS, growing slowly in numbers, lumbering forward until we were an entire town of kidnapped peoples. We passed village after village, and town after town. Each time, people swarmed out to stare at us. Initially, I believed that the villagers were coming to save us. Surely they would oppose this outrage. But they only watched and sometimes brought our captors roasted meat in exchange for cowrie shells and chunks of salt.

Some nights, when they had us lie down in fields, our captors paid village women to cook for us—yams, millet cakes, corn cakes, sometimes with a bubbling, peppered sauce. We ate in small groups, crouching around a big calabash, spooning out the hot food with the curved fingers of our right hands. While we ate, our captors negotiated with local chiefs. Every chief demanded payment for passage through his land. Every night, our captors bartered and bickered well into the evening. I tried to understand, in the hope of learning something about where we were going, and why.

The boy who worked for our captors came back many times to offer me water and food. I watched and listened as he tried to convince the head captors that children should be freed from the coffle and allowed to walk alongside the bound adults. After a few days the leather strap was taken off my neck. I nodded to the boy in thanks.

There was a little girl who walked beside her yoked father, holding his hand for most of the day. She was very young, perhaps only four or five rains. Sometimes, when she pleaded with him, he carried her. One time, the girl tried to catch my attention, and to play peekaboo with her hands and eyes. I turned away from her. I couldn't bear to watch them together, and did my best not to listen to them talking. Everything about them reminded me of home.

The boy who travelled with the coffle often fell into step beside me. His name was Chekura. He was as thin as a blade of grass, and as ungainly as a goat on three legs. He had a star etched high on each cheek.

"Your moons are beautiful," he said.

"You are from the village of Kinta," I said.

"How did you know?"

I pointed at his cheek. "I've seen those marks before."

"You've been to Kinta?" he asked.

"Yes. How old are you?"

"Fourteen rains."

"I bet my mother caught you," I said.

"Caught me doing what?"

"Being born, silly. She is a midwife. I always help her."

"You lie." He persisted in his disbelief until I named some of the women from Kinta who had recently had babies.

"Yes," I said, "my mother surely caught you. What's your mother's name?"

"My mother is dead," he said, flatly.

We walked silently for a while, but he remained next to me.

"How could you do this to us?" I finally whispered. He said nothing, so I continued. "My mother and I came to your village. I know it by the two round huts, the high mud walls, and the funny looking donkey with one ear torn and the other streaked with yellow."

49

"That was my uncle's donkey," he said.

"So have you no honour?"

After his parents died, he told me, Chekura had been sold by his uncle. For three rains now, the abductors had used him to help march captives to the big water. So that meant that we were heading toward big water too. I could think of only three reasons: to drink, to fish or to cross. It had to be the third reason. I wanted to ask Chekura about it, but he kept talking about himself. He said they told him that they might let him go one day soon, but they also warned that if he didn't mind his orders, he would be sent away with the other captives. Chekura wore a forced smile on his face. He smiled so much that I thought the corners of his mouth would form lasting creases. He smiled even as he told me that his uncle had never liked him, and that he had beaten Chekura often before finally selling him to man-stealers. Part of me wanted to hate Chekura, and to keep my hatred simple and focused. Another part of me liked the boy and craved his company—any conversation with another child was welcome.

Fanta was often in a vile mood, and disapproved of me speaking to Chekura. She tried to order me to walk beside her, but I usually refused to do so.

"He's not from our village," she said.

"His village isn't far from ours, and he's just a boy," I said.

"He works with the captors," Fanta said. "Don't tell him anything. Don't talk to him."

"And the food he brings, that I sometimes share with you?" I said.

"Take the food," she said, "but don't talk to him. He is not your friend. Remember that."

The next day, while I was chatting with Chekura, Fanta flung a pebble at me.

"That woman holds her head high," Chekura said.

"Her neck is chafing," I said. "Tell your leaders to release

50

Fanta and the other women from the yoke. They will not run."

"I will speak to the others," he said.

A day later, Fanta was let loose of her neck yoke, but her ankle was roped to that of another woman. Fanta and I began to walk side by side, but never at the front of the coffle, so we wouldn't be the ones meeting snakes or scorpions, nor at the back, for fear of being whipped if we slowed the pace.

"Here in the middle is safest," Fanta whispered. "This is where my husband would tell me to walk."

"What happened to him?" I whispered.

"When I was carried off, he was fighting two men," she said.

"And the village?"

"Half of it was burning."

Fanta pressed her lips together and turned her face away, and I knew better than to ask another question.

We passed scores of villages. I heard the beating of tam-tam drums, saw buzzards circling lazily in the sky and caught the smell of goat meat riding in the breeze, but there was no rescue. There weren't even any objections from villagers.

One day, as we were passing a village, a man was taken from a walled enclosure and led to our captors. He was bound at the wrists, and was followed by children who watched the villagers negotiate with the captors. Finally, in exchange for copper manillas and salt, the captors took the man and yoked him to the last person in the coffle. The children began taunting the new captive. As the clamour grew, some of the bigger boys threw stones and rotting fruit peels at us. A stick flew into my thigh, drawing blood. I gasped and swallowed the cowrie shell that I had been keeping in my mouth for company. I choked as it made its way down, and ran behind Fomba for protection. Fomba did his best to block the flying objects and shouted at the boys to stop. Stark naked, hair matted and filthy, head held angled to the side, hands waving wildly, he was quite a sight. He was hit by a few stones and mangoes before the coffle leaders chased away the boys and hustled us from the village.

I could not understand why we had been the amusement of those village boys. True, the children of Bayo—myself included—had teased Fomba all the time. but we had never hurt him. We had never yoked him by the neck, or deprived him of food. I had never seen captives passing outside our walled village. But if we had seen men, women and children yoked and forced to march like *woloso*, only worse, I hoped that we would have fought for them and freed them.

That evening, Chekura brought a calabash of water and some soap made from shea nuts, and offered to help clean the wound on my thigh.

"I can do it," I said.

"Let me help," he said, aiming a thin stream of water so that it ran over my cut.

"Why do the children in the villages taunt us?" I asked.

"They are only boys, Aminata," Chekura said.

"And all these villagers who sell goods to the captors and stand guard over us at night? Why do they help these men?"

"Why do *I* help them?" he said. "What choice have they?"

"They were not all sold by their uncles," I said.

"We do not know their stories," Chekura said.

The next day, when we passed a town, I felt relieved that nobody came out to throw stones or hurl insults. A few women bearing fruits and nuts clustered around our captors, and one of them watched me carefully, followed me for a moment, and then walked beside me. She removed the platter from her head and handed me a banana and small sack of peanuts. I could not understand her words, but her voice sounded kind. She placed her dry, dusty hand on my shoulder. It was such an unexpected gesture of kindness that my eyes filled with tears. She patted my shoulder, said something in an urgent tone and was gone before I had the chance to thank her.

I HAD MY FIRST BLEEDING during our long march. I tried to calm myself by thinking that I wouldn't live much longer, and that my humiliation wouldn't last long. Cramps shot through my belly. In my nakedness, it was impossible to hide the blood running down my legs.

When Chekura approached me, I hissed at him, "Go away."

"Are you ill?"

"Go away."

"Have some water." I sipped from his skin of water, but refused to acknowledge him.

"Have you been cut?"

"Are you stupid?"

"I can help you."

"Leave me alone." He walked beside me for some time, but I was silent. Finally, he turned to walk away. As he did, I called out, "When we stop tonight, find me a woman from a village."

He nodded and kept going.

We settled for the evening on the outskirts of a village. Chekura disappeared. Later, two women walked up to my captors, pointed at me and had an animated talk. They gave the captors some palm wine and then came up to me.

The women chattered in a language I could not under-stand. One woman tugged my hand. I looked toward Chekura, who nodded that I was free to go. The woman led me by the hand while the other followed. We left the captives, who were settled under trees, and wandered past a sentry and inside a walled village. I saw a well, some round storage huts and some rectangular homes with mud walls similar to those of Bayo. The women led me behind a small home. Evidently, it belonged to the woman who had taken me by the hand. They brought me a cauldron of warm water and let me wash myself. When I was done, they led me inside, where it was cool, and had me sit on a bench. I looked for signs of knives or other instruments, wondering if they meant to do something to me, now that my womanhood was emerging. Just as my terror was reaching such a peak that I looked to see if anybody was blocking the door to prevent my escape, another woman came in carrying a blue cloth. She gave it to me, and signalled for me to wrap it around myself. It was long and wide enough to reach around my belly and backside. I felt so much better, and safer, with my privates covered. Suddenly I was hungry, and I realized that the shame of nakedness had kept my appetite at bay. Now that I was decent, they invited me to sit and eat with them, chatting at me all the while. *Take the food.* This I heard my mother saying to me, from the spirit lands. *Take the food, child. These women won't hurt you.*

They gave me some goat meat with malaguetta pepper, dripping in a hot peanut sauce. It was delicious, but rich. I could feel my stomach revolting, and could only eat a little. They pressed a pouch of peanuts into my hand, as well as dried, salty strips of goat meat. They kept chattering at me, and I assumed they were asking about my family and my name. I answered in my own language, which made them shriek with laughter. Finally, they led me back to my captors. They seemed to be negotiating, offering, cajoling, but they could make no headway with the men in the group, who shook their heads and waved the women off. The women came back to me, squeezed my hands and touched the moons on my face. They told me something over and over again that I could not understand, and turned and left. I wished that I had been allowed to stay with them. I settled again under a tree, guarded by my captors, and felt too confused to sleep. I had no idea whether the people of the next village would show brutality or kindness.

The coffle increased in size daily. Every morning, when we were roused and made to start walking again, there were two or three new captives. Only the women and children were allowed to walk without neck yokes. At night, when the men were released from the yokes so they could lie down and sleep, guards watched our every movement. My feet formed blisters, grew painful and became leathery and calloused. Fomba showed me the soles of his feet after a long day's walking. They were yellowed and thick and tougher than goatskin, but also dried and cracked. He was bleeding between his toes. I convinced Chekura to get me some shea butter at a village, and one night, while Fanta clucked in disapproval, I rubbed the butter into Fomba's feet.

"Daughter of Mamadu and Sira, I thank you," he said.

I didn't know who his parents were. I didn't know his family name. "You are welcome, Fomba," was all I said. He smiled and patted my hand.

"Daughter of Mamadu and Sira, you are good."

Fanta clucked again.

"Wife of Chief," Fomba said, addressing her. "Puller of ears."

I broke into laughter. It was the first time I had laughed in a long time. Fomba smiled, and even Fanta saw the humour in it.

"Is there any shea butter left?" she said.

Fomba rubbed some into her feet, and she promised to never pull his ears again.

I WAS WALKING ONE DAY BEHIND A YOKED MAN who swerved without warning to the left. I had no time to react, and my foot sank into something wet and soft. Something like a twig cracked under my heel. I let out a scream. Under my foot was the body of a naked, decomposing man. I jumped away and ripped leaves from the nearest branch. In a frenzy, I wiped a mass of wriggling white worms from my ankle. I was shaking and wheezing. Fanta took the leaves and wiped my foot and held me and told me not to be afraid. But my hysteria escalated, even though Fanta barked at me to calm down, and I could not stop screaming.

"Stop it right now," Fanta said. She grabbed me, shook my shoulders and clamped a hand on my mouth. She twisted my chin around until our eyes met.

"Look at me," she said. "Look. Here. In my eyes. That is no longer a man."

My lungs began to settle down. As they stopped heaving, I was able to breathe more easily. Fanta took her hand off my mouth. I did not scream again.

"It's just skin and bones," she said. "Think of a goat. It's just a body." Fanta put an arm around me until my trembling subsided.

From that point on, snakes and scorpions were not the only things to watch out for on the increasingly well-worn path. Soon we were stepping over at least one body a day. When captives fell, they were untied from their coffles and left to rot.

We WALKED THROUGH AN ENTIRE REVOLUTION of the moon, and then through another. Along with the coming and going of the moon, I now had my own body to mark passage of time. Between one bleeding and the next, I encountered more villages, more captives sold into our coffle and more guards to tighten the knots around our ankles at night.

When people ask about my homeland now, they all

seem to be fascinated by dangerous beasts. Everybody wants to know if I had to run from lions or stampeding elephants. But it was the man-stealers that I had to worry about most. Any man or woman who disrupted the coffle was beaten severely. And anyone who tried to escape was killed. Wild animals were the last thing on my mind. One night, however, as we settled under a cluster of trees, a baboon raced out of the bushes. Its shoulders and haunches swung riotously, and it shot straight like a bee into our midst. We stood and yelled. The captors yelled too. The baboon swept up the small girl who had been walking for two moons with her father and stole away with her, tearing back into the bushes. Even after she was out of sight, I could hear the girl wailing. The father jumped to his feet, crying for help. Chekura cut through the rope around the man's ankle and ran off with him in pursuit of the baboon.

They were gone for a long time. Long enough for us to eat our food glumly, waiting for news of the girl. We heard the father wailing before we saw him, and then we saw Chekura and the man descending a hill. The father was carrying his inert daughter in his arms. Her neck was open and bright red. The captors did not tie him back up. They let him dig a shallow grave for the girl. He covered her up with the soil, got down on his knees and wept uncontrollably. It was the first time that a man had cried in my presence. The distress made my stomach heave. It wasn't right to see a grown man sobbing. It seemed impossible that his daughter had been taken from him so abruptly. I found it unbearable to contemplate his pain, yet I could not escape the sound of his agony. Although I was allowed to walk freely with the coffle in the daytime, I was tied up at night. I tried to focus on other things around me—the palm trees, the rocks, the outline of high mud walls around a village in the distance, a rabbit hopping in the moonlight. The other captives also turned away from the grieving father.

The others eventually fell asleep, but I could not stop thinking about the man and his daughter. When I could no longer hear his sobs, I looked for him in the darkness, but the place beside the grave was empty. Finally, I noticed him approaching a tree some twenty paces behind us. Up and up he scaled, pulling himself onto one branch after another. The tree was taller than twenty men stacked one above the other, but the man kept climbing.

I willed him to climb back down. I prayed that he would come to his senses. Perhaps his wife was dead too, but one day he might be free again. One day he might find another wife and have another daughter. I stood up and stared and hoped. A captor noticed me, and then hollered at the father to come down. Still the man kept climbing. The captives heard the shouting and awakened and saw what was happening, and moved—bound as they were in pairs, by the ankles—away from the tree. At the top, the father climbed all the way out on a branch jutting from the trunk. He howled one last time and dropped through the air at an astonishing speed. Never had I seen a body fall from such a height. I turned away just before he struck the ground, but I heard the *thud* and I felt the vibration run under my toes. Our captors refused to bring him to his daughter, or to bury him or even to touch the body. They were unwilling to acknowledge this act of self-destruction. On their orders, we walked for a good spell through the night and finally settled under another set of trees far removed from the bodies of the father and his child.

OUR OVERLAND JOURNEY CONTINUED for three cycles of the moon. One day, our captors stopped at a fork in the path and saluted a new breed of man. Skin speckled, like that of a washed pig. Shrunken lips, blackened teeth. But big, and tall, and standing like a chief, chest out. So this was a toubab! My fellow captives' eyes widened to take in this strange creature, but the villagers on the path didn't react at all. I realized that they had seen toubabu before. He joined our captors at the head of the walk. He was tall and gaunt and bearded and thin lipped, and he had crust around his eyes. He spoke a few words in the language of the captors.

I caught Chekura's eye, and when he came up beside me, I asked, "Where is the toubab from?"

"Across the big water," Chekura said.

"Is he a man or an evil spirit?"

"A man," Chekura said. "But he is not a man you want to know."

"You know him?"

"No, but you don't want to know any toubab."

"My papa said, fear no man, but come to know him."

"Fear the toubab."

"How can he breathe, with a nose so thin? Do those nostrils admit air?"

"Do not look at the toubab."

"He has many hairs."

"To look directly at the toubab is a mark of defiance."

"Chekura! There are even hairs growing from his nostrils."

"Walk carefully, Aminata."

"Are you my captor or my brother?"

Chekura shook his head and said no more. I had heard that toubabu were white, but it was not so. This one was not at all the colour of an elephant tooth. He was sand coloured. Darker on the forearms than on the neck. I had never seen wrists so thick boned. He didn't have much of a backside, and he walked like an elephant. *Thump, thump, thump.* His heels struck the earth with the rudeness of a falling tree. The toubab was not barefoot like the captives, nor in antelope-hide sandals like the captors. Thick shoes rose past his ankles.

The toubab kept a chain about his neck, and at the leather belt around his waist he had an object covered in glass that he often consulted. He shouted and waved his hands angrily at our two lead captors. Under his supervision, the captors promptly brought the women and me back into neck yokes. Fanta was placed directly ahead of me in the coffle. One end of a wooden yoke was fastened around her neck and the other around mine. The yokes were bound fast at the back of our necks, and no amount of tugging could get me free, or accomplish anything other than to rub my skin raw.

While the toubab watched, our captors led three more captives into the coffle. A new woman was brought to us. She too was big with child. She was placed between Fanta and me. It wasn't a bad change. Fanta often muttered complaints, which made the days seem long, and the new woman was shorter, closer to my height, so it was easier to walk with my neck attached to hers. That night, when I came to rest under a tree, she lay on her side and I could hear her laboured breathing.

I settled in beside her.

"*I ni su,*" I whispered, Good evening. These were my first words to her, in Bamanankan.

"*Nse ini su,*" she replied, in Bamanankan.

I asked if she would have her baby soon. Very soon, she told me.

"This is a bad time," she said. "I wish the child would wait."

"The child doesn't know our woes," I said. "Do you think it will be a boy?"

"Girl. And she doesn't want to wait."

"How do you know it's to be a daughter?"

"Only a petulant little girl would come at such a bad time. Only a girl would defy me. A boy would not defy me. He knows that I would beat him."

This woman made the time pass. I liked her. "And you would not beat a girl?"

"A girl is too wise. She knows how to avoid a beating."

"Then why is she defying you now?" I asked.

"You are very clever. What is your name?"

I told her.

"I'm Sanu," she said.

"Sleep in peace, Sanu," I said, yawning.

"Yes, girl woman. Sleep in peace."

In the morning, we were yoked again. Once more, I was placed behind Sanu. She moaned as she walked, and I could tell, by the way her soles slapped the ground, by the way she pushed in her backside to relieve the tension in her lower back, by the way she let her hands ride on her hips while she walked, that before long, she would have her baby. As the afternoon progressed, she began to slow the coffle.

"She will have her baby soon," I said to Chekura.

"What do we do about that?"

"I have helped at births. My mother and I bring babies to the light. It is our trade. Our work. Our way of life."

Sanu spoke. "The child is right. I am ready."

"There is a village ahead," Chekura said. "I will have them stop there."

Chekura moved ahead to the front of the coffle and spoke to his superiors. We settled under a grove of trees. Chekura came back, with an older captor and the toubab, and he released us from our yokes.

I spoke to Chekura only: "The woman and I will settle quietly under that big tree, over there. Leave us alone, but bring me one woman to help. I will need a sharp knife that you have cleaned properly. And water. Go to the village and get three gourds of water, one of which should be warm. And some cloth."

The toubab held a firestick by his side. He stared at me. He spoke to the older man, who spoke in yet another tongue to the younger man, who in turn spoke to me. "He asks if you know what to do."

"Yes," I said. "Bring me the things I need."

Fanta had turned her back and walked away. Another girl, just a few rain seasons older than I, was sent to help. At least she did what I told her. When the warm water came, she poured water over the knife and cleaned it properly. She arranged for the woman to lie down comfortably, with bundled leaves under her head, and some furs and skins under her body, keeping her off the ground.

Our captors stood and watched. Thinking of my mother and what she would do, I opened my palm wide, and shoved it at them with elbow locked and arm straight. They raised their eyebrows, and the toubab stared at me again. He muttered something to one of the captors, who passed it on to another captor, who asked me in Bamanankan if I was sure that I knew what I was doing. I gestured once more for them to go, and this time they retreated.

I rubbed Sanu's shoulders and back with shea butter. "You will be a fine mother," I said to her, and she smiled gently and told me I would make my mother proud.

Sanu told me about her husband and her two other babies. She described how she had been taken captive while carrying food to the women who were working in the cassava fields, pulling the roots from the ground. With the baby so full inside her, she had chosen not to fight.

I encouraged her to keep breathing steadily, even when the contractions shook her. She dozed off momentarily.

When she awoke, Sanu said, "I am ready now, child. If we live, I will name her Aminata. After you."

The moon was blazing again, and I could feel heaviness in the air. Dampness. A big wind flailed about like a child in a tantrum, but Sanu was silent and still.

The baby came out head-first, just as it should have, and

the rest of the body slid out into the world. I tied the slippery cord off at the belly and hacked through its thickness. The baby started bawling. She had huge, swollen female parts—even this I could see in the moonlight. I got the baby wrapped and warm and up against the mother's nipple, and then I waited for the afterbirth and helped bring that out. It was the fastest birth I had ever seen.

"Aminata, my baby," Sanu said.

I didn't know if it was wise to name a child so quickly, or to name it after me. Perhaps it would bring bad luck to name a child after someone in such danger. But Sanu was set on the idea. I was touched to see her gentleness as she turned the baby and brought her close to a nipple.

The tiny Aminata began to suck on her mother with such intensity that one might think she had already been doing it for months, and Sanu and I touched fingers. Tears sprang from Sanu's eyes, and that unlocked all the sadness within me. I heaved and shook and cried until my eyes were emptied, and Sanu's tears rolled steadily down her cheeks as she held still and fed the baby. It was bad luck, I knew, to cry when a baby was born.

In the morning, we were tied again. With cloth that Chekura had brought, Sanu slung the baby low on her back. Blood from her childbirth coursed down her legs as we climbed and descended mountain paths and crossed valleys and forests full of kola-nut traders.

To pass the time, since I was walking directly behind her, I watched the baby Aminata. When her head bounced around too much, I called out to Sanu to tie her up tighter. The baby had little tufts of softly curled hair at the back of her head, and I spent hours imagining how this little girl would someday grow her hair, comb it and braid it. For two days, I lost myself in daydreams while staring at the tiny baby bundled up close against her mother.

On the third day of walking after Aminata's birth, the

coffle slowed at the crest of a hill. Although the morning was still young, the sun was already hot. I took my eyes off the back of Aminata's head and looked out at the world again.

What I saw seemed impossible.

Over to my right, where the path led, the river flowed fast and wide. It was wider than ten stone throws. At the shore of this angry river waited many canoes, each with eight rowers. I had never seen so many boats and rowers. To my left, the water expanded into eternity. It heaved and roared, lifted and dropped. It was green in some parts, blue in others, forever shifting and sliding and changing colour. It foamed at the mouth like a horse run too hard. To my left, water had taken over the world.

The captors led us to the shore. The toubab shouted directions as the captors released our yokes and shoved us into the middle of the canoes. It confused me to see them force Chekura into my canoe. The rowers were naked, other than loincloths, and they reeked of salt and sweat and dirt. Their muscles glistened in the sun. The canoes pulled smoothly over the water as the river widened, until I could not make out the details on the distant shore. As we left the land, a captive in the boat next to mine struggled to his feet, bellowed and rocked his canoe. Two huge oarsmen stopped rowing and bashed him mightily with their oars. Still he kept struggling. When the canoe began to pitch, they dropped their oars and quickly threw the captive out into the fast-moving waters. He thrashed and sank and was gone.

We were rowed through the morning. The sunlight reflected off the water and burned my eyes. The river widened so dreadfully that all I could see of the land was that it was mountainous to my left and flat to my right. Chekura sat in the canoe, unbound but among us, and he whispered to me as we travelled.

"You are one of the lucky ones," he said. "A big boat is

64

waiting, and nearly full. All of you will be sold and will travel across the water in very short time."

"Lucky?" I asked.

"Others will have been waiting on that ship for moons. Dying, slowly, as it fills. But you will not have to wait."

A horrid smell wafted along with the breeze. It smelled like rotting food. It smelled like the waste produced by a town of men. I scrunched up my face.

"The smell of the ship," Chekura said, his voice trembling. "We will soon be parted."

"Walk gently among your captives, Chekura. One will be sure to have a knife, and be waiting for you to make one false step."

"And you, Aminata, beware of your own beauty, flowering among strangers."

The foul-smelling breeze smacked us again. "How could anything flower, or even live, in that kind of stench?" I said.

Chekura's lip quivered. The boy who had been smiling through three revolutions of the moon was now frowning. I never had a brother, but now he seemed like one.

"Where will they take us now?" I whispered.

"Across the water."

"I won't go."

"You will go or you will die," he said.

"Then I will return."

"I have taken many men to the sea," Chekura said, "but not once have I seen one return to his village."

"Then I will sleep by day and walk at night. But listen to me, friend. I will come back. And I will come home."

THE CANOES PULLED UP TO A WHARF by an island, where I saw a castle on a hill. More toubabu and men of the colours of my homeland swarmed about, loading goods and leading people. We were marched up a steep path and behind the building. I noticed that Chekura was still with us. Ahead lay two penned areas, side by side, bordered by sharpened stakes jutting out of the ground to the height of two men. The captors pushed open the gates and shoved the men into one pen, and the women and children into another. I looked back for Chekura, but he was gone. I couldn't see Fanta either. Perhaps I could find Sanu, with her baby. There they were, twenty steps to my left. I wasn't bound any more, so I ran over to be with them.

Two toubabu with firesticks guarded my penned area, but men of my homeland also stood ready with clubs, knives and firesticks. Locked inside this pen, naked and sore and bleeding, we stood tight together in sandy soil that stank of urine and feces.

We waited and watched as the sun edged across the sky. They brought us boiled millet and dumped it in a trough. Some of the women picked at it. I couldn't bring myself to do so, but when we were passed calabashes of water, I did drink.

Women from my own homeland washed us with cold water and rubbed palm oil on our skin, to make us look shiny and healthy. Inside our pen, homelander women who were clothed and cold-eyed dragged one female captive to a corner, where toubabu and homelander men stood waiting with a metal device heating over glowing embers. I looked away, but heard the woman screaming as if someone had torn off her arm.

I vowed not to give them the pleasure of my pain. But when my turn came, I surrendered to their coarseness and their stink. They dragged me to the branding corner. Their wounding metal was curved like a giant insect. As they brought it toward me, I defecated. They aimed a finger's length above my right nipple, and pressed it into my flesh. I could smell it burning. The pain ran through me like hot waves of lava. The people who had been pinning me down let me go. I could think only of heat, and of pain. I could not move. I opened my mouth, but no sound came. Finally, I heard a moan escape my lips. Arms around me. Another woman's scream. And I was gone.

When I awoke, I was unsure how far the sun had moved in the sky, or if it had moved at all. Then I slept again. I thought I dreamed that Chekura was touching my hand. Big men were grabbing him, pinning him as he cried out in protest. When I awoke again, my chest was still burning. The heat twirled and danced under the ugly, raised welt on my chest. All the other women had the same welt.

I couldn't sleep that night. When it began to rain, I stood. At least a good rainfall would clean me. I liked the cool water running down my face. It was good to see the mud sliding off my legs, but I cupped a hand over my raw wound to protect it. The rain felt soothing until the thunder rolled in and the lightning began lighting up the sky. Water fell on me as if it were being dropped from a hundred buckets, and the thunder boomed in the night, echoing over and over again in the mountains. The rain kept up with such fierceness that I prayed for it not to sweep us all into the big river below. In the women's pen, some twenty of us huddled together in the storm. I held Fanta with one hand, Sanu with the other. The noise was such that it drowned out the crying of Sanu's baby. When the explosion from the clouds ceased, we found ourselves in a field of mud up to our ankles. We spent the whole night standing.

IN THE MORNING, MY WOUND STILL BURNED. Fog hung over our pen. As the sun rose, the thick vapours cleared and the day became bright. Homelander women in clothes and sandals dumped more boiled millet into the trough. Still and tired, we stared at the food. I imagined that we would be left to stand there until our hunger overcame our disgust.

But the gate swung open. We were all hurried out of the pen and back down the path to the water. We were tied and tossed into the bottoms of the canoes, and rowed straight out into the widening water. A wave splashed up against my canoe and smacked me in the face. I thought I would welcome the long drink, but I gagged and choked and then vomited the burning water. Salt. Each wave stung the cuts on my feet and the welt on my chest.

I dreaded the big boat up ahead, growing larger with each oar stroke. In size, it dwarfed a twelve-man canoe, and it stank worse than the pen they had put us in on the island. The boat terrified me, but I was even more afraid of sinking deep into the salty water, with no possibility for my spirit to return to my ancestors. Let them do what they wanted with my body—on land. Then, at least, my spirit would travel, and I would return home to my ancestors, and I would no longer be alone.

The oarsmen kept paddling us over the rolling waves. We slid up to the side of the toubabu's boat. It was a huge and strange affair with poles towering like palm trees. On the deck above, faces stared down at us. Homelander faces and toubabu faces, all working together. Waves smacked against the giant sides of the boat, which rose and fell but seemed mysteriously pinned to one spot in the water.

One of the captives screamed and rocked and struggled, but his feet and wrists were tightly bound with vines, and finally he was clubbed until he fell silent. Men and women shook and trembled. I grew quiet, and calmer. "*Fear no man*," father had said, "*and come to know him.*"

Something bumped our canoe. It was another small boat, pulling up beside ours. Among the bound men and women, I saw Chekura. His face was bruised and his expression defeated. His head was slumped. What a stupid boy. He should have fled on land, near Bayo, where he knew the forests and the people. He should have fled long before they turned on him. I did not call out to him. I clenched my teeth and looked out over the water at all my people tied in canoes and being pushed, prodded and pulled up a long plank rising along the great wall of the ship. I turned back to see my homeland. There were mountains in the distance. One of them rose like an enormous lion. But all its power was trapped on the land. It could do nothing for any of us out on the water.

We glide over the unburied

ONE DAY, IF I EVER GOT HOME, perhaps they would make an exception and allow me to become a *djeli*, or storyteller. At night, in the village, while the fire glowed and the elders drank sweetened tea, visitors would come from afar to hear my curious story. To become a *djeli*, you had to be born into a special family. I used to wish that I had been, for the honour of learning and retelling the stories of our village and our ancestors. Early in life, a child born into the *djeli* family would be taught the story of the crocodile who carried off five children, and of the man who was so rich that he had seventeen wives but so cruel that each one ran away, and of the first time that a man in our village returned from Timbuktu with the mysterious Qur'an in his hand. It was said that when a *djeli* passed away, the knowledge of one hundred men died with him.

When I was carried up the ladder and dropped like a sack of meal on the deck of the toubabu's ship, I sought comfort by imagining that I had been made a *djeli*, and was required to see and remember everything. My purpose would be to witness, and to prepare to testify. Papa was not supposed to show his daughter how to read and write a few lines in Arabic. Why did he break the rules? Perhaps he knew that something was coming, and wanted me to be ready.

On the ship and in all the years that have followed, I have thought of how much my parents planted in my mind in the short time we had together. They made sure that I learned how to cultivate a millet field. As a young child, I was just as quick and capable as an adult when it came time to seed. I knew how to dig with my right heel in the soil, drop seeds in the little hole, cover up the hole with the toes of my foot, move on a step and do it again. I knew how to pull weeds, and I understood that you hoed the soil so that the rain, when it came, would kiss the soil and marry it—not kiss it and run away. Yes, I knew how to cultivate a millet field, and I had been shown that the mind had to be grown.

A series of coincidences saved my life during the ocean crossing. It helped to be among the last persons from my homeland to be loaded onto that vessel. It also helped to be a child. A child had certain advantages on a slave vessel. Nobody rushed to kill a child. Not even a manstealer. But, also, the child's mind has elasticity. Adults are different— push them too far and they snap. Many times during that long journey, I was terrified beyond description, yet somehow my mind remained intact. Men and women the age of my parents lost their minds on that journey. Had I been twice the age of eleven, my mind might also have departed.

On that slave vessel, I saw things that the people of London would never believe. But I think of the people who crossed the sea with me. The ones who survived. We saw the same things. Some of us still scream out in the middle of the night. But there are men, women and children walking about the streets without the faintest idea of our nightmares. They cannot know what we endured if we never find anyone to listen. In telling my story, I remember all those who never made it through the musket balls and the sharks and the nightmares, all those who never found a group of listeners, and all those who never touched a quill and an inkpot.

THE SHIP WAS AN ANIMAL IN THE WATER. It rocked from side to side like a donkey trying to shake off a bundle, climbing on the waves like a monkey gone mad. The animal had an endless appetite and consumed us all: men, women and babies. And along with us came elephant teeth, sacks of yams and all manner of goods that working homelanders hauled up in nets.

Above the cries of the captives and the shouts of the toubabu and the working homelanders, Sanu's baby wailed on and on. It seemed to sense our fate. It howled and gasped and cried again. Goosebumps covered my arms. I fought to keep myself from screaming. Instead, I choked on the stink of the ship and vomited. For a while, the nausea was a distraction.

Around my right ankle, I had an iron claw which was attached to a claw clasped around Sanu's left ankle. Beside her was Fomba, chained to another man. Person by person, we were hauled on board and added to the growing chain. One captive broke loose before they could clap the iron around his ankle and jumped out into the angry water. He was naked, except for one red bandana around his neck, and I felt sorry to see the man's head and bandana bobbing in the water. I had hoped that he would get his wish and sink to a quick death. But homelanders working on the deck pelted the poor man with oranges, and other homelanders in the canoes followed the trail of raining fruit. They scooped the man out of the water, smacked him about the head, and sent him into the arms of a giant homelander standing on the ladder outside the ship. The giant carried the man right back onto the deck and held him until his ankle was clasped.

Trembling in the wind, I feared that I would faint. I tried

to steady myself and to keep from falling, because captives who went down on their hands and knees were beaten until they stood. I tried to calm myself by imagining a mother soothing a hysterical child. *Look about*, I imagined my own mother telling me. *Look about, and do not fear.*

Homelanders were hauling barrels up onto the deck. One of them fell through a hole in a net, crashed to the deck and burst open, spilling water over our feet. Amid the hauling and the shouting and the clasping of claws around captives, I was able to see a pattern. A toubab in fancy dress and another man were moving along a long line of captives, inspecting them one by one. Once inspected, the captives were sent down into the stinking belly of the ship.

The toubab was a tall, skinny man with hair the colour of an orange. The hair fell straight down from the sides of his head. On top, he was bald. He had blue eyes. I couldn't have imagined such a thing, before I saw it. The same blue as river water on a sunny day. The toubab's helper looked neither darkskinned nor light, neither toubab nor homelander but a blend of the two. This helper had yellow-brown colouring, and a scar running in a raised ridge of flesh from one eye all the way to his mouth. It wasn't a mark of beauty. It was a knife mark.

When they reached me in the line, the helper pinched my arms. He grabbed my cheeks roughly to force my mouth open. The orange-haired toubab stopped him, and stepped forward. He signalled for me to open my mouth, and reached inside with a hairy index finger. I gagged. He ran his hands along my neck and shoulders, touched my back and made me move my elbows and knees. While the toubab inspector worked on me, the helper smacked Fomba in the face. Fomba's mouth hung half open, lips unmoving, eyes as wide as mangoes. The helper smacked him again and mumbled something in a language vaguely like Bamanankan. Something about bending his head down. Fomba said nothing. He did nothing. The helper cocked his arm back again.

"Fomba," I called out. "Bend your head."

Fomba looked to me, and bent his head.

The helper and the inspector turned to face me. "You speak Maninka?" the helper said.

"Bamanankan," I answered.

"And you speak his language too?"

"Fulfulde," I said.

The helper and the inspector conferred in the toubab's language. I looked again at the toubab inspector. He had a firestick attached to one hip, a sword attached to the other and pinched nostrils. I listened to the strange words flying between them. Then the helper switched to Maninka and, to my surprise, the inspector understood.

Using baby words so that the man would understand, the helper said, "She speaks his language, and she speaks Maninka."

The inspector gestured for another toubab and pointed at my chains. The other toubab ran up, bent down, jammed a piece of metal into the iron loop around my ankle, and released me. The helper pulled me over to Fomba.

"Tell him to open his mouth and not to bite," the helper told me.

I told Fomba what to do. The toubab inspector stuck his finger in Fomba's mouth, tested the teeth and seemed to find them solid.

"Tell him not to move," the helper said. The inspector tapped his ribs and saw Fomba wince.

"Broken?" the helper said.

"Fomba, look at me again. Do your ribs hurt?" Fomba mumbled an almost inaudible "yes," but instinctively I changed his answer when I translated it for the assistant. It seemed safer to lie. "He says he is fine, and that the ribs don't hurt too badly."

The orange-haired toubab looked in Fomba's ears and inspected every other part of him—even his penis, which he picked up and tugged. Fomba's mouth opened wide, but no sound came out. The inspector spoke to the other toubab, who stood beside me and used a quill to scratch symbols on thin parchment. The hand moved the wrong way across the parchment, leaving nothing but senseless symbols. They were done with Fomba. Two homelanders pulled up a heavy door lying flat in the floor. It grew wide like a crocodile's mouth and kept widening, until it was lifted straight up. The stench of human waste rose from it in thick clouds, and with it the cries of grown men. Fomba and the man chained to him were shoved down the hatch and out of sight. The door was slammed shut. The toubab inspector turned to me. He spoke, but I couldn't understand.

Pointing at Sanu and her baby, the assistant said to me, "Toubab asks if you are the one."

"Say again?"

"Are you the one who caught that woman's baby?"

I wondered how they knew. I wondered what else they knew about me. I nodded.

The inspector asked me a question. I didn't understand. He asked again. I picked out the word *rains* in Maninka.

"Eleven," I said.

"Walk long time?" he asked.

"Three moons," I said.

"Where mother?" he asked. I said nothing. He pointed at Sanu. "Mother?" he asked again. I shook my head from side to side. He pointed at Fanta, who stood next to Sanu. "Mother?" Again, I shook my head.

"What are you saying to him?" Fanta called out. I tried to ignore her, but she shouted out that I must not speak with the evil man. The helper took a step in her direction, but the toubab inspector pulled him back.

"No mother?" the inspector asked.

I stood silently and said nothing.

The helper and the inspector examined Sanu. She and her baby, who was now sleeping, were sent off. I wished I could go with them.

While toubabu men led Sanu away, the helper pulled me over to Fanta and let me go. I stood, with no arm or foot held, bound or clasped in irons, and looked out over the side of the ship. I could have run and jumped, but I weighed my fear of the water against my fear of the ship, and stood motionless.

"Open your mouth," the helper told Fanta. The inspector stood there waiting.

She mumbled in Fulfulde that the helper was a horse's ass. He sensed the insult and drew back his hand. She stood before him, unflinching, defiant.

"No speak Maninka," I said.

"Tell her to open her mouth, and no biting," the helper said.

I told her.

"Never," Fanta said to me. "They are going to eat us, anyway."

I did not want to see Fanta beaten, and I feared that they would punish me for her disobedience.

This time, I did not plan the words. They just came out of my mouth. "He says he will hurt me if you don't," I said.

Fanta opened her mouth. The inspector looked at her teeth, poked at her round belly and told me to tell her to open her legs.

"They say to open your legs," I said.

"Never," Fanta said.

"Baby soon," I said to the toubab inspector.

"Baby when?" he asked.

"One moon," I said.

The inspector hesitated. He made noise when he breathed. It was a whistling, wheezing sound. I wondered if his small nostrils were blocked. His mouth held black teeth, and I caught a glimpse of his gums, flaming red like turkey wattles. He was an ugly man who seemed to be rotting from the inside out, but I spotted no hurting intentions in this man's eyes. I took another chance.

"Baby one moon," I repeated. I rolled my hand over Fanta's big belly. "Big mama. Big mama. She say you eat her."

The toubab inspector did not understand. The helper explained.

"No eat mother," the inspector said. He and the helper held their bellies and laughed. "Work. Work toubabu land. No eat." The orange-haired toubab man lowered his hands. The inspection was over.

The helper jumped in again. "He is not going to boil her. She will work for toubabu. All of you will work."

It struck me as unbelievable that the toubabu would go to all this trouble to make us work in their land. building the toubabu's ship, fighting the angry waters, loading all these people and goods onto the ship—just to make us work for them? Surely they could gather their own mangoes and pound their own millet. Surely that would be easier than all this!

I pointed at the toubab inspector and asked the helper, "What does he do?"

"Medicine man," the helper said.

"You talk too much to them," Fanta said.

"He says they won't eat you," I said.

"Who says?"

"Toubab."

"What did he say?"

"That you will have to work."

"Why should I work, if they will eat me anyway? Listen to me, child. We will all be boiled and eaten."

More toubabu men took Fanta away. But I was made to stand next to the medicine man, and to explain the helper's instructions to Fulbe captives. One by one they were sent below. When I was the last captive on the deck of the ship, my bravery left me. The toubabu had used me, and now they were going to kill me. I could barely keep myself from falling to my knees, but I thought about my mother and my father outside my village and I kept standing. Warm urine ran down my legs, which made me burn with shame.

The medicine man passed me a calabash of water. "You help me," he said.

I drank but said nothing.

"You help me, and I help you."

I had no idea how he could help me, or what I could do for him. I wished I had been sent away with Sanu and Fanta. I watched the working homelanders leave the ship, climb into the canoes below and row away. They were allowed to come and go, but we, the captives, were to be taken away. Of that I was sure.

THE MEDICINE MAN'S HAND rested on my shoulder. He was saying something I couldn't understand. The helper explained that I was to go with them down into the ship. He led the way. The medicine man grabbed my arm and took me down steep steps into a dark, stinking hold. I choked at the stench of human waste. I imagined the biggest lion of my land—as big as the lion mountain on shore, but living and breathing and hungry. It seemed as if we were being taken straight into its anus. The lion had already rampaged through the villages and swallowed all the people live, and was now keeping them stacked and barely breathing in the faint light of its belly. Up ahead, the assistant held the portable fire that threw light into the shadows. The medicine man also carried fire in a container. Everywhere I turned, men were lying naked, chained to each other and to their sleeping boards, groaning and crying. Waste and blood streamed along the floorboards, covering my toes.

Our corridor was nothing but a narrow footpath separating the men to our left and right. Piled like fish in a bucket, the men were stacked on three levels—one just above my feet, another by my waist and a third level by my neck. They could not lift their heads more than a foot off the wet, wooden slabs.

The men couldn't stand unless they stooped—chained in pairs—in the narrow corridor where I walked. On their rough planks, they had no room to sit. Some were lying on their backs, others on their stomachs. They were manacled at the ankles, in pairs, the left ankle of one to the right ankle of the other. And through loops in these irons ran chains long enough for a man—with the consent of his partner—to move only a few feet, toward the occasional cone-shaped bucket meant for collecting waste.

Men grabbed at me, begging for help. I recoiled from their scratching fingernails. One inmate bit the helper on the hand. The helper clubbed the man on the head.

The men called out in a frenzy of languages. They called out Arabic prayers. They shouted in Fulfulde. They hollered in Bamanankan, and in many other tongues I had never heard. They were all shouting for the same things: water, food, air, light. One hollered over and over that he was chained to a dead man. In the flickering light, I could see him striking the motionless body attached to him, foot to foot. I shivered and wanted to scream. *No*, I told myself. *Be a djeli. See, and remember.*

"Sister, sister," one man said.

He spoke with an authority that I could not ignore. He spoke like my father. I saw a face that was taut and tired but full of purpose. He was on the highest of the three levels, so his face came close to mine.

"Sister," he whispered hoarsely, in Bamanankan. "Where are you from?"

"Bayo, near Segu," I told him.

"We have heard of you. Are you the one who catches babies, but is still a child?"

"I am not a child. I have seen Eleven rains."

"What is your name, Eleven Rains?"

"Aminata Diallo."

I told the helper that somebody ten rows back was attached to a dead man. He went with two toubabu men to fish him out. They rattled chains, grunted, rattled more chains, and finally pulled out a man by his feet and dragged him through the slop. My head spun and my knees weakened, but I couldn't let myself fall in filth like this. The cries of the men rang in my ears.

"Pass by here every chance you get," said the man issuing orders like a father. "Without the helper listening. Gather information and bring it to me. I am Biton, Chief of Sama. I too am Bamana. Speak to me. Tell me everything. Do not forget. Do you hear me, child?"

I gulped and nodded. "I was not supposed to be stolen," I blurted out. "I am a freeborn Muslim."

"We have all been stolen," he said. "When the time is right, we shall rise up. But for now, child, you must get us water."

"We leave soon," I said, pleased that I could offer him something.

"How do you know?"

"I heard, outside. We leave very soon."

"Good," he said. "Some of us have been in here for moons, and we are dying of the heat. Do you speak the toubabu's language?"

"No. But I speak Fulfulde too and know some prayers in Arabic."

"Learn the toubabu's language," he said, "but do not teach them ours." The medicine man was pushing me from behind. Biton spoke once more: "Eleven Rains. Aminata Diallo! Remember your Bamana chief."

We struggled ahead. It was slow-going in the dark. After a brief spell, another hand reached out and took my wrist. I was about to slap it off, but when I turned, I saw Chekura.

"Aminata," he whispered.

"Chekura," I said.

"You do not hate me for bringing you here?" he asked.

"It is too hot in here for hate," I said.

"You will not tell anyone what I did? Before they trapped me?"

"No. I want you to live."

He repeated my name over and over, and then added, "I must hear you say it. Please. Say it. Say my name."

"Chekura," I said.

"Someone knows my name. Seeing you makes me want to live."

I wondered if there was a way for me to bring him water. "Now we must all live," I said. "Who wants to die in the anus of a lion?"

My expression, *anus of a lion*, raced through the stacks of men. Biton heard the phrase and gave off a deep, booming laugh that echoed inside the hold. He shouted out the phrase, and the man next to him repeated it. Those who spoke Bamanankan called out. One man asked the question, and all the others answered.

"Where are we?" the one said.

"Sister says the anus of a lion," two men called back.

"I say where are we?" one called.

"The anus of a lion," more men called back.

One man asked, "Who is the sister who visits us?"

"Aminata. I am from Bayo, near Segu on the Joliba."

In the darkness, men repeated my name and called out their own as I passed. They wanted me to know them. Who they were. Their names. That they were alive, and would go on living.

"Idrissa."

"Keita."

And so it went. I looked for Fomba, and finally saw him. I called out his name. He stared at me blankly. Not a word escaped his lips. "It's me, Aminata," I whispered. Nothing. He would not speak. I touched his cheek but he did not even blink. I wanted to lay my head down beside this great, strong man who had turned silent and empty, but the medicine man grabbed my arm and pointed ahead.

The helper unlocked a wooden partition and slid it back, revealing a new room filled with about twenty women captives and a handful of infants. The women were not chained, but they had little room to move. In the middle of the hold, there was more headroom, so the women were standing there, although the taller ones had to stoop. I had to edge and twist myself about to get through the group. Women whispered their names to me and asked where I was from.

A hand gripped me firmly by the elbow. It was Fanta's. "Stay away from those toubabu, for they will eat you," she said.

I wriggled free and spun away from the crowd. I heard a baby begin to wail and I moved through the cluster of women until I found Sanu. She held my arm.

"I need water or there will be no milk for the baby," she said.

I touched my fingers to hers.

The medicine man pushed past me and headed up the stairs. The helper stopped, turned with his burning light, and said, "This is where you stay, unless we tell you to come up. Take this spot, near the stairs," he said. "If you leave this spot, I will beat you. If you stay in this spot, I will save the beatings for the others."

I stared at him defiantly. I saw the assistant raise his arm. I don't recall him hitting me. I only remember falling.

*   *   *

I AWOKE IN THE DARKNESS with my mouth tasting foul. I felt rocking, as if I were on a donkey that had drunk palm wine. My stomach was sick again, and sore, and empty. I tried to stay motionless and go back to sleep. But the rocking persisted and a voice came to me. I opened my eyes. The medicine man. I stirred on the rough wood and felt a sliver cut my hip. I raised my head as much as I could—just a foot or so—and slid out onto the floor, where I could stand. My hips ached. Dried waste caked my feet. My teeth hadn't been cleaned. I felt my womanly bleeding gush out of me and detested having to stand before this hairy toubab.

The medicine man grabbed my hand and pulled me up the steps. We came out of a hatch separate from the one serving the male captives. Out on the deck, daylight burned my eyes, and I had to shut them. When I opened them again, I saw that our ship was gliding over open water, with not an oarsman in sight. Waves brought the ship up and down, up and down. Above me, linens on upright poles beat like the wings of flying monsters. I could see no land. No canoes with homelanders. We were lost in a world of water. I thought that the toubabu must possess a fearsome magic to steer this ship across the endless desert of water.

The medicine man pointed to a water bucket. I crouched and rinsed myself. I had cuts everywhere: face, hips, thighs, ankles. The mark on my breast was too sore to touch, or to wash. The salty water stung and burned my skin. Still, it felt good to sluice off all that muck. As I cupped water and splashed myself, I watched other homelander women crouching around food buckets. Down on their haunches, they used their fingers to eat a gruel of mashed-up beans.

The medicine man gave me an empty cocoa-nut shell, and pointed to a bucket of fresh water. I scooped out some water and sipped cautiously. No salt. I drank it fast. Fanta came up to me.

"Give me that," she said, pointing at the cocoa-nut shell. "I didn't get enough."

I handed it over. While Fanta drank, the medicine man gave me a long, sand-coloured cloth. I fumbled to cover myself, and was almost as relieved as I had been to drink.

Fanta dropped the cocoa-nut shell. "Women before children," she said, snatching the cloth from me and wrapping it around herself.

The medicine man exhaled through crooked teeth, but said nothing. I wasn't sure what sort of man he was, but he did not appear inclined toward beatings. At that moment, however, I wished that he had smacked Fanta hard in the face and given me back the cloth. Instead, he let her keep it and motioned for me to follow him through the women's area on deck and through a door.

The medicine man led me into a separate compartment for the male captives. Many were chained along the edge of the ship. Some called out to me by name, and I greeted each one who did so. I came up to Biton, the chief from below. He stood with his shoulders back and head up.

He smiled. "Aminata Diallo." He said my name fiercely. He said it with pride. I liked to hear it said that way. It made me stand a little straighter.

"Chief Biton," I said.

"You have been away for more than a day. Why have you taken so long to come see me?"

I said I had been sleeping, but had no idea it had been that long.

Biton stared at the bruise on my face. "Stay up here if you can," he said. "The more time you spend below, the faster you die."

The medicine man asked me, in baby Maninka words, if there were dead men below. I looked at Biton, but he hadn't understood. I repeated the question in Bamanankan. Biton said there was one dead man and that

84

the fellow chained to him couldn't get up to the deck to eat or drink.

"One dead man," I told the medicine man. He didn't understand. I held up one finger, and pointed below.

The medicine man needed two men to help him. I pointed to the irons binding Biton to a man named Poto. The medicine man reached into a fold in his pants, drew out a set of thin metal keys, selected one, inserted it into the leg irons and freed the men. While ten other home-landers watched, he returned the metal to his pocket, took along two other toubabu with firesticks and led the two homelanders down the hatch.

I joined Fomba, who was eating. "Good?"

He shook his head to indicate no.

"Feet hurt?" I asked him. He nodded. He wouldn't look at me but he took my hand and wouldn't let go. I sat with him, feeling the ship pitch. Biton and Poto emerged from the hatch, dragging up a dead man. They stood, staring at one another and then at me. The medicine man waved them over to the side of the deck and gestured furiously to them to throw the man over. Linens were flapping madly in the wind, and I could not even hear the body hit the water. I wondered how many of us would end up in the deep.

I grabbed the medicine man's arm, pointed to Fomba, tried to tell him that the man was strong and would do his bidding, if only he could be released from those awful leg irons. The toubab had no idea what I was talking about.

"Don't bring him into it," Biton told me, pointing at Fomba.

"Why?"

"He can't even speak. His mind is departed. We need the toubab to trust men who are of use to us."

"He is from my village," I said.

"We are all from a village, child. I will see to it that he is not harmed." Biton stood still to make it easy for the medicine man to put him back in shackles. "Come see me soon, Aminata."

The orange-haired toubab put his hand under my arm and pulled me along behind him, stopping to examine the chains of a few homelanders. From the next line, I heard my name whispered.

"Aminata."

It was Chekura. His hair was matted, he had bruises on both cheeks, and his feet were caked with filth. At the moment, however, he didn't seem to care. He whispered in Fulfulde so that Biton could not understand: "Watch out for that man. He wants to be our leader. But he could get you killed."

Biton was a man, and Chekura still just a boy. Biton was far bigger and more powerful, and homelanders already listened when he spoke. Chekura had aided my captors, but still I wanted to trust him. He had walked with me for three moons. Chekura came from a village near mine, and spoke my father's language. I sensed that Chekura would protect me if he could. But I had seen what firesticks could do, and Chekura was likely to die if the homelanders revolted. And then who would help me? I did not know who to trust. I wondered what my father would say. Chekura or Biton? His answer brought me little comfort. *Keep your eyes wide and ears open*, he said, *and trust no one but yourself.*

Holding me by the arm, the medicine man led me down a new set of stairs. He pushed through a crowded room where men slept in hammocks slung from beams over-head. We passed a cook working by a huge pot, then through a narrow space lined with doors. The medicine man opened one of them and we entered a small room. He shut the door. It was just the two of us in there. It was a relief to be away from the fetid sleeping quarters and away from the crowded deck. But alone with the toubab in his room was not a good place for me.

He yawned, stretched his arms and removed a jacket. His shirt was yellow around the armpits and he gave off a sharp smell. He sat on the bed. It was a wooden platform raised above the floor and covered with a lumpy cloth bag stuffed with straw. He motioned for me to sit. I remained standing. He banged the edge of the bed. I sat, uneasily, wishing some others were with me. In this situation, Fanta would know what to do.

The medicine man uttered a toubabu word, pointing where I sat.

"Bed," he said, over and over, waiting for me to point and say the same.

"Bed," I said, and he seemed happy.

He struck his own chest, thumb pointing toward his breastbone, and repeated another word. "Tom," he said many times.

"Tom," I repeated.

Then he pointed at me. I said my name. He scrunched up his face.

"Aminata," I said once more.

But he pointed at me and said something else. Over and over. He wanted me to repeat it.

"Mary," I finally said. He pointed to me again, and I did it too. I used my thumb, just like him. "Mary," I said softly. I pushed the word through my lips and told myself it would be the last time I would ever say it, or his name.

He jumped up and clapped his hands. "Mary," he said, over and over.

I got up too. I wanted to be with the women again. But he put his hand on my shoulder and pushed me back down, leaning his face too close to mine. There were orange hairs on his chin, and huge whiskers shooting out from his ears and his face. On the side of his face, near his ears, hair grew as thick as his thumbs. He crossed the floor of his room, rummaged through a trunk, and brought out some red cloth. It was wide and long and made of soft linen. He draped it over my arm. I jumped up and wrapped it around my backside and privates, knotting it at the hip. He seemed to marvel at my knot, and at the speed of my hands. After making me sit once more on the bed, he left the room.

Opposite the bed was a small hole in the wall. I went over to look, and caught a fine spray of mist on the face. We were riding over calm waters. I could hear the gentle flapping of the ship's linens, but a strange new sound came from behind me. I stood still. Although the door had not opened, I was sure somebody was watching me. My heart pounded. I spun around. Nobody. Nobody at all. And then the sound came again, from a corner of the room. There, on another table, was a metal cage. Inside was a blue and yellow parrot with a nasty beak. Its wings rustled. I jumped back. It was only moving on its perch. It could not escape, and it could not get me, for it was locked in that cage just as surely as I was locked in the ship.

It put its head to one side, as if to get a better look at me, and suddenly uttered a string of words. I could not understand a thing. The bird was not singing. It was speaking. And it did not use a homelander language. The bird spoke the toubabu's language.

Beside the cage was a dish with nuts. I bit into one. It tasted full, and rich. I put two more in my mouth and chewed them. The bird looked at the nuts and at my mouth. Back and forth it looked, squawking wildly. I dropped the nuts. Next to them was a yellow fruit with a thick peel, about half the size of my fist and pointed at the ends. I bit into it. It was bitter, so I put it down.

I turned when the door opened.

"Oh oh oh," the medicine man said. He came up to me and inspected the yellow fruit with my teeth marks. He reached for his belt and pulled a knife from a sheath. I backed to the bed and pressed my lips together to keep from crying out. But he did not point the knife at me.

Instead, he sliced the fruit into sections, took some light brown crystals from a jar and sprinkled them on the fruit. He raised a section to his mouth, bit into it and sucked the flesh away without eating the peel. He gave a section to me. I raised it to my mouth, sucked, and gagged on the sourness. The medicine man put on more crystals. I sucked again. My mouth danced with taste, and I was suddenly aware of my hunger and thirst.

He had brought me two cocoa-nut shells. One held water, and the other, boiled yams with palm oil. I ate the yams too fast, drank the water as if someone might steal it, and then felt my stomach threatening to revolt. The boat was rocking again on the waters.

"Food," he said, pointing at what I ate.

I repeated the word.

"Hungry," he said, tapping his belly.

I tried to say that.

He tapped the surface on which I was sitting once more. I remembered the word.

"Bed," I said.

He smiled and indicated that I should lie down. This did not seem like a good idea, but I had no place to go. The ship was a mystery. If I broke free and ran from the medicine man, I wouldn't even know how to find the homelander women. And even if I did, I would have to sleep again in the stinking hold of the ship. He pulled a woven cloth over me, stroked my shoulder, and repeated, "Mary."

His hand slid under the cloth and moved lower down my back. I turned sharply and drew the cloth over my body. I lay face down, legs clamped together. He slipped his hand onto my back again. I turned over, sat up and hissed at him.

"Don't do that, or my father will return from the dead to strike you down," I said. "I have just eleven rains."

The toubab had no idea what I was saying, though he

must have sensed my anger and fear. When some animals smell fear, they attack all the more fiercely. But the medicine man turned away sharply, head in his hands. After a moment, he reached for a white object on a table and clutched it to his breast. It was an oddly simple carving, with one stick running down and the other across. He pressed this to his chest, mumbled something softly and covered me with the cloth. He patted my shoulders and kept mumbling. His hand did not drift down my back again. I stayed rigid, lying on my back so I could watch him, incommunicative. Finally, I must have fallen asleep.

I awoke in the darkness. I had been shoved over to the far side of the bed, right up against a wall, and I was not alone. Beside me two figures, one atop the other, rocked back and forth. Both breathed loudly. One had a high, protesting, frightened voice. She was a homelander woman, gasping and uttering words I could not understand. She was underneath. The medicine man lay on top of her, grunting and pushing, up and down, up and down. I pressed myself flat against the wall and closed my eyes. I knew that a man was never to touch a woman like that, unless she was his wife. Even if Papa had not taught me parts of the Qur'an, I would have known that.

"Aaaaah," the toubab sighed. The bed grew still.

I felt the medicine man's weight fall into the space between the woman and me, while she gasped and cried. Eventually his breathing slowed and so did hers. I watched their chests rise and fall in the night for a long time, until I too must have fallen asleep.

I awoke with light streaming through the window. The medicine man was gone. The woman was gone. I pulled the red cloth tight around me. The window was shut. On the table beneath it, I found some cowrie shells and three hard metal objects. Not even the thickness of a lady-bug, they were round like my thumbnail, but bigger. They were silver coloured. I bit into one of them, but it would not give. A man's head was sculpted into one side of each object.

OVER THE NEXT DAYS, the orange-haired toubab showed me how to get out of the cabin and go up on the deck, and where to find compartments there for the male and the female captives. The women could visit the men's area, but the men remained chained and couldn't leave theirs. Armed sentries were posted to keep them to their small patch on the deck.

By day I moved freely on the deck, but at night I was expected down in the medicine man's room. He showed me how to care for his bird. I was to cover the birdcage with a cloth at night and to remove it in the morning. I had to clean out the cage, feed the bird nuts, and give it any other treat that the toubab brought into the room. Banana. Cooked meat. Yams, millet, rice. That bird ate anything. When the medicine man wasn't around, I ate the food myself. The bird squawked when I ate the nuts, so I gave him some of them. If I ever made it back to Bayo, the people would never believe me. *The toubab medicine man loved a bird. Let it perch on his arm. Loved it so much he taught it to speak the toubabu's language.* I could only imagine their reaction. They would throw things at me and howl in laughter and talk about it for two moons straight. *Tell me again about the man and his bird.*

The medicine man never tried to touch me when the bird was watching. First, he made me slip the cloth over its cage. There are men whose eyes burn with the intention to hurt, but this toubab had weak, blue, watering irises—even when the bird could not see us. Whenever he put his hand on my shoulder or back, I gave a sharp shove and an angry shout. He would recoil like a kicked dog and begin to read from a book that he kept in the room. He read out loud. It sounded as if he was saying the same words, over and over again. Oddly, in those moments, he would give me whatever I asked for. Food. Water. Another arm's length of cloth from the wooden trunk in his cabin. Or one of his mysterious metal discs with a man's head sculpted into one side.

THE TOUBABU BROUGHT THE HOMELANDER men up from their hold in small groups every day. I would see them emerge from the darkness, stumbling, wincing in the blazing sunlight and covering their eyes with the crook of their arms. Confined in their little compartment on deck, the men were given water and food, and sometimes allowed to wash themselves. I saw one older man tumble over face-forward as he attempted to wash himself. He could not get up. His ribs were showing and he looked utterly spent. A homelander woman—also older, and also weak—was tending to him, caressing his forehead and tipping a calabash of water to his lips. Four toubabu pushed her aside and seized him by his knees and armpits. He sagged in their arms, and barely had the strength to resist. The woman screamed and pleaded and tried to loosen the toubabu's fingers. They bumped past her, lugged him to the side of the ship and threw him over.

In the next days, the woman's sadness was so great that nobody wanted to stand near her on the deck, or crouch beside her at the food bucket. From Sanu, I heard that one day the woman would not come up on the deck any longer. After two more days, she was no longer moving. She was carried out and thrown into the deep, the same as her man. Nobody fought or pleaded for her. And nobody wanted to speak of her, when she was gone. I asked Fanta if she thought the woman had died, at least, before they took her out of the hold.

"Shh," she said, and turned away.

* * *

92

As THE DAYS WENT BY, I saw that the more the women were free to move about, the more they risked. Fanta told me that I was a fool to go with the medicine man. She said she would rather sleep by the shit buckets in the hold than in the bed of a toubab. She usually stayed in the hold, and because she was so big with child, the toubabu let her do so. But I didn't have much choice, and many of the other women were made to spend nights, or parts of nights, with the toubabu leaders. The medicine man took a woman into his bed every few nights. He had three or four favourites, and made me stay in the bed even when he had a woman. I would push myself up against the wall and plug my ears and hum loudly and try to ignore the heaving and vibrations. I knew that almost as soon as his body quit shuddering, he would fall into a short sleep. The woman would get out of bed as gingerly as she could, and rustle around the medicine man's room, sometimes pulling an object out of a storage box and slipping it inside her wrap. The toubab would wake with a start, get up, give the woman some food or water or coloured cloth and send her out.

In his room at night, the women never looked at me or met my eyes. I understood that I was not to speak to them. I would never tell that the homelander women stole whatever they could from the boxes brought daily in and out of the medicine man's cabin. I saw iron files disappear inside cloth wraps. I saw one woman take an orange with his consent, wait for him to turn his back, pick a nail off the floor and plunge it deep inside the fruit.

Up on the top deck of the ship, I heard the women talking. They said that the grand chief of the toubabu was built like a donkey and never gave the women anything but the stink of his body. The women said that hair covered his neck, his back and even his toes. Fanta just grunted, warning that one of us would surely end up in his stomach, right next to his hairball.

After ten days at sea, the toubabu removed the irons from some of the men allowed up on deck, but reshackled them later when they were pushed back down the hold. Biton encouraged me to learn all the toubabu words that I could, so that I could give him information. And he was always telling me to take objects from the medicine man's cabin.

"If Biton loved you like a father," Chekura warned, "he wouldn't try to put you in danger. Tell him you can't find anything."

FOMBA STAYED SILENT AND CHAINED. I knew that Biton had told me not to ask for favours for Fomba, but I couldn't bear looking at the raw skin and the blood on his ankles. He wouldn't even complain to me. I got the medicine man to understand that Fomba could be trusted to be let out of chains and slop the food from the cooking pots into the buckets. I also managed to get a waistcloth for Fomba. But after that, it worried me to see women sometimes approaching Fomba and passing him objects when the toubabu were not looking. *Keep away from trouble*, I imagined my father telling me, *and stay safe*.

I saved food from the medicine man's cabin for Fomba, Chekura, Fanta and Sanu, passing it to them on deck. One day, when I brought Chekura an orange, he ripped it apart, slurped out all the guts, and threw the remains overboard. He had juice and pulp all over his lips and face, and he looked like a child just learning to eat with his own hands, but he didn't care. He was bursting with news.

"Fomba may not speak, but he sure can use his hands."

"What did he do?"

"Down in the hold, he brought out a nail and snapped off his shackle. Biton thought it was a fluke. Fomba closed it back up, and snapped it off again. Biton tried to do it, but couldn't. All night, he tried to open his own shackle with the nail. Couldn't do it. Called over Fomba, who did it for him in an instant."

ON DECK ONE AFTERNOON, before the captives' meal, the toubab chief showed up carrying the carcass of a picked-over chicken. He tossed it into the thick of the male captives. The men kicked and fought for the remains, licking and sucking what they won, combing bones for scraps of meat and crunching them for marrow. Another chicken carcass was thrown into their midst, and once more the men wrestled. The sailors doubled over in laughter, then threw in another.

Biton was among the group of homelanders on deck. I heard him issuing orders, and saw the men stop fighting and back away from the third carcass. Biton picked it up and threw it back at the toubab chief.

"You don't dare kill me," Biton shouted. "I'm too valuable."

The toubabu had no idea what he was saying, but they whipped him anyway. Ten lashes, on the back. I watched the first lash tear into his flesh, and then I went to the medicine man's room. I couldn't bear the sight of Biton being whipped.

The next day, he was back up on deck, walking stiffly but without complaint. From that day forward, Biton was the undisputed chief of the captives.

THE HOMELANDERS HATED NOTHING MORE than being made to dance over a whip that the assistant raked over the deck. One day, when the toubabu's helper had taken ill and left a toubab sailor in charge of the whip, I began to sing a song while we danced, naming all the people I saw. I tried to name every single face, and give the name of the person's home village. Already, I knew a few.

"Biton," I began, "of Sama."

"Chekura," I sang, "of Kinta. And Isa, of Sirakoro. Ngolo, of Jelibugu. Fanta, of Bayo." The homelanders' spirits picked up, a little. When I sang out a name, a man or woman would clap if I got it right, and the others would call it out, once. When I got a name wrong or didn't know it, the person would clap twice and dance a little with me and sing out his or her name and village. Everybody took to this activity, and on other occasions when we were made to dance, homelanders took turns calling out the names and villages of the people around them. Some of the others were able to count out as many as fifteen names and villages, but after several days I could call out the names of almost every person I saw.

Biton made us sing the naming game and dance so lustily that the toubabu would come closer to admire us. The toubabu assembled in their natural order, with the toubab chief, his second in command, the medicine man and other leaders in the front of the other toubabu. Biton would do a dance himself and sing for us all to hear.

He began with a question, which he made to sound like a song. *"Is the toubabu's helper here? Please tell me that, my friends."* "No," someone sang back, *"the helper is not here."* *"Look again, my friends, to be sure,"* he called out. And when he was reassured that the helper was not present, Biton stepped up his dance and sang some more: *"This one, with the hairs just on his chin, is Second Chief. He operates the ship. He lives. And this second one, with the belly as big as a woman with child, he is Toubab Chief, and he dies. But first, we wait for Fanta's baby."*

WE HAD BEEN ON BOARD for a full cycle of the moon. Homelanders were dying steadily, at a rate of one or two a day. The dead were shown no respect. The splash of a man or woman hitting the water horrified me more each time and insulted the spirits of the dead. It was worse, to my way of thinking, than killing them. I listened for the splash, even though I dreaded it, but the one thing that disturbed me even more was not hearing it at all. To me, silent entry suggested that the bodies were sinking into oblivion. At night, my dreams were haunted by images of people falling from the edge of Bayo, disappearing without warning and without sound, as if they had walked blindfolded over the edge of a cliff.

Toubabu sailors died too, on board. I saw some of them, sick and dying, on days when I followed the medicine man around. They had gums rotting and overgrown, spit full of green phlegm, black spots breaking out on their skin, and open sores that stank terribly. When a toubab leader died, he was thrown overboard with his clothes on. When a toubab sailor died, he was stripped of his clothing and tossed to the sharks that trailed us like water vultures. Sailors tossed all sorts of garbage overboard daily—pails of shit, split barrels disgorging rotten food, swollen rats—but it got so that every time I heard a splash, I feared the worst.

There were no children my age on board. There was no one to play with. Other than a few babies, it was just men and women. I was lucky not to be confined with the others in the hold, but too often there was nothing for me to do. Alone in the medicine man's cabin, sometimes I would sleep to pass the time. Or I would amuse myself by throwing peanuts at the parrot, or teaching it words such as *the toubab will pay* in Fulfulde. And I staged conversations between my parents. I would have them argue, back and forth, about me. *She will sleep with the women, in the hold. No, she won't, it's better to leave her with the toubab because he's harmless. Harmless? Is he harmless with the women, at night?* When that sort of conversation made my head pound, I would steer the subject toward home. *You spend too much time visiting women in other villages and we haven't planted enough millet. The women complain every time you avoid going to the fields with them. I am not visiting women. I am catching babies, and I bring home chickens and pots and knives, and once I even brought a goat. I don't care about your stupid women in the fields. Do they plant chickens, out there? Do they plant goats?*

One evening on the top deck, Fanta told me that her belly was in convulsions and that she was ready to have her baby. I signalled to Chekura, who was just being led back down into the hatch for the evening with the other men. He nodded when he saw me point to Fanta, cup my hands together and thrust them out from my lower belly.

I had been coming and going every day between the deck and the medicine man's cabin below, and nobody had dared stop me because I belonged to him. This time, I brought Fanta with me. It was the first time she had descended into the toubab's living space. She saw the cooking pot for the toubabu leaders, and said, "We should kill them before they boil us all."

In the medicine man's room, I covered the bed with extra cloths and brought close a pail of water. I hoped this birth was going to be fast.

"I could be here all night, if this takes a long time," Fanta said. "And I will not spend the night in bed with any toubab. I will die first. Or he will."

I put my hand on her shoulder and told her to think about the baby. She grunted.

"I stopped caring about that a long time ago. No toubab will do to this baby what they have done to us." A shiver ran through my body.

I had to get away from Fanta for a moment. I had to collect myself, so I did what the medicine man had shown me before. I took a wide metal wash bucket from the room, stepped out for a moment and motioned to the junior toubab working at the cooking fire to throw two red-hot iron bricks into the bucket. I returned with them to the cabin. Inside, Fanta was pointing at the bird with her mouth wide open.The bird was squawking at her. I tossed it a few peanuts and hung a sack over the cage to make it shut up.

"Don't give food to that thing," Fanta said. "Take the food for yourself. Give it to the others. Or give it to me."

"I have to feed this bird or it will die. And if it dies, the medicine man—"

"I know, I know," she said.

I dumped several pails of water into the metal bucket and got Fanta to step in. She crouched, careful to avoid the red metal.

"I haven't had warm water like this since we were back in Bayo," she said.

"Hmm," I said.

"Do you do this?"

"Sometimes."

"Does he watch you?"

"Yes."

"Touch you?"

"He has tried, but I won't let him."

"You can do that?"

"He stops when I look in his eyes and speak fiercely."

"He's a weak toubab. And the weak die first."

I did not dare ask which weak people Fanta had in mind. Homelanders or toubabu?

Fanta relaxed a little. I watched her ride out a few convulsions. She finished with the bath, dried herself off with a cloth I handed her, shivered and climbed onto the bed.

"Do you call him anything?" Fanta asked.

"Who?"

"The medicine man. Do you call him by a name?"

"He has a name. Sounds like 'Tom.' "

"Do you call him that?"

"No. I never call him anything. I just speak to him. No name."

"Good."

The convulsions shook Fanta for some time, but eventually they diminished and she fell asleep. During that time, the medicine man came into the room. His arms flew up. He looked shocked.

"Baby," I said. "Catch baby." He had taught me these terms.

"No."

I stood up. Looked him in the eyes. This was the only way. It had worked when I pushed his hands away from me, and I hoped it would work now. "Catch baby," I said again, and in Bamanankan, said firmly, "Go. Mother sleep."

"When?" he asked.

"Catch baby soon," I said.

He removed an orange from his pocket and unsheathed from his belt a long knife with a handle made from elephant tooth. Then he sliced open the fruit, set the knife and fruit down on a small table and indicated to me that Fanta and I could eat the food. He turned, picked out another cloth from his trunk and left it near Fanta's feet. My eyes fell on the knife. The medicine man had forgotten it on the table. He drank quickly from a bottle, stuffed it back under the cloth in his trunk, gathered a few more things and left the room.

I sat on the bed and waited for Fanta to wake. She snored. I thought about teasing her later, and telling her that she sounded like a wild boar. When she finally awoke, she sat up quickly, looked around and remembered where she was. She moaned and lay back. Her breathing was speeding up. I rubbed her back.

"You need to know something," she said.

"No one will be eaten, so stop thinking about that now," I said.

"In just a rainy season or two, you were about to become my husband's next wife," Fanta said.

My mouth dropped, and I yanked my hand away from her. "That's a lie."

"That's why I never liked you," Fanta said. "You were so young, not half-way a woman yet, and I knew that one day you would be my husband's favourite." Beads of sweat had broken out on her forehead, but I did not move to wipe them. "I would have made your mother leave you at the door," Fanta continued, "and as soon as we were alone, I would have given you a royal beating. I would have made you pay."

"I don't believe you," I said. "My father and mother never would have agreed."

"No? What do you think a jeweller would tell the village chief? Wouldn't it be better to accept and to negotiate good terms?"

"I don't believe you."

"Don't you want to know what you went for?"

"No."

"One day you will hate people just like me. You won't have that childish look on your face that makes everybody want to love you and clap their hands with pride that a little runt like you can already catch babies. You know what, Aminata? Anyone can have a baby, and any idiot can catch one."

I was so angry that I didn't know what to say. I wanted to stab her with the knife. I wanted to rip her hair out. I wanted to scream and shout that she was a liar and that my parents would never have let me go to that old man. Even if he was the chief. But I knew I couldn't hurt her, and I couldn't scream. My mother had taught me well. When you catch a baby, you are calm. The mother may behave like a tyrant or a wild child, but you cannot. When you catch a baby, you are not yourself. You forget yourself and you help the other. I gulped. I swallowed. I wondered if what Fanta had said was true. Sadness had been welling inside me during three moons overland and more than one moon in this stinking toubabu's vessel, and now it burst. Tears shot from my eyes and my breath grew short.

I heaved and sobbed and stood there useless, while Fanta lay back and watched and waited. I shook terribly for a few moments, both feet planted beneath me, eyes shut, fists clenched. I swayed, and rocked, and finally settled down. I had nothing to do but to appeal, as I hadn't in a long, long time, to God. *Allahu Akbar*, I mumbled. God is great.

"Don't waste your time on that any longer," Fanta said. "Can't you see that Allah doesn't exist? The toubabu are in charge, and there is only madness here."

Perhaps it was true. Maybe Allah lived only in my land, with the homelanders. Maybe he didn't live on the toubabu's ship, or in the toubabu's land. I said nothing. I tried to shove all the things Fanta had said into a little room in my mind, and I tried to close the door. I imagined my mother's voice, calm and capable. *We have a baby to catch.*

Fanta's body started shuddering again. I offered to check with my hand to see if she was ready, but she refused. The contractions began rolling hard and long and often, and I left it to Fanta to decide when to push. I would not guide her. I would offer her water, and hold her hand, and wait for the chief's wife to make up her own mind about what to do next.

She pushed for a long time, and then she lay back and rested. Something seemed to grab her body again, and she pushed once more. She rested again, then pushed so mightily that I could smell her bowels moving. "Now," Fanta said. She pushed three more times. I saw hairs on a head starting to part her, but the baby wouldn't come yet. She pushed once more, and the head came all the way out, blue and purplish and light coloured and specked with bits of whiteness and blood. Fanta pushed again, and out came the shoulders. The rest slid out quickly: a belly, a penis, legs, feet. I used the toubab's knife to slice the cord, then I wrapped the baby and gave him to Fanta. The baby cried, and Fanta let it howl good and long before allowing it to root for her nipple. She was not a proud mother, but an angry one. I tried to settle Fanta comfortably on the bed, but she pushed me away.

I turned my back and squatted over the waste bucket. The baby started to scream again and I whirled around to see Fanta unsteady on her feet, standing across the room. She flipped the hood off the birdcage, opened up the wide door and grabbed the bird by the beak. Its claws flew up and raked her, and she cursed, but she kept on.

"Stop," I called out.

Fanta ignored me. She had the medicine man's knife in her hand. She stabbed and stabbed until the claws stopped scraping at her and the body stopped quivering. She threw the mess back in the cage, closed the door, and covered it with the hood. After wiping the knife clean, she wrapped herself, and slipped the knife inside cloth. Then she picked up her bawling baby and shoved its face against her nipple. Fanta and the baby eventually slept again, but I stayed awake, fearing what was going to happen when the medicine man returned and took the hood off the birdcage. But the little window showed light, and there was no sign of the medicine man.

I woke Fanta and the three of us went up on deck as the day was breaking. A pale moon hung low in the sky, at the very moment that the upper tip of a ball of fire crested the opposite horizon. Trouble was coming when the moon and sun shared the same sky.

The medicine man saw the baby and sang out words of pleasure. He patted me on the shoulder. He took a step toward Fanta, but the look in her eyes stopped him. Fanta was now steady on her feet. I thought about how she had walked for three moons with a growing baby in her belly, and about how she had sliced open that parrot even as it kicked and clawed and cut her wrist. The sun cleared the horizon. Now it was a furious ball of red. The moon began

103

to fade in the sky and I had the feeling that it was leaving me to fend for myself.

The orange-haired toubab was so pleased with the baby that you would think he had pushed it out himself. He sent off some toubabu sailors, who returned with the toubab chief and the assistant. The three of them spoke. After taking instructions, the assistant spoke to me, but I could not understand. The assistant repeated himself. I realized that the medicine man wanted me to call out to the men below. I was to tell them that Fanta had had her baby.

A toubab drew up the door to the men's hold. I took a few steps down into the darkness. I could barely see.

"A son for Fanta," I called out in Bamanankan.

"Louder," the assistant told me.

I called out again, and then in Fulfulde.

I expected that the men would give a cheer, and that when they came up, we would all be made to dance over the whip raking the deck. But there was no movement. No sound. Not even the whispering of men. I heard the clinking of metal on metal. On the assistant's command, I called out once more. There was still no response. I climbed back out onto the deck.

The medicine man conferred again with the toubab chief and the assistant. Two sailors and the assistant were sent down into the hold with clubs, firesticks and burning light. Down through the hatch they went. I heard the assistant shouting on his way down the hatch that Fanta had had her baby and that the men could come up and dance with the women. A toubab sailor was sent off to fetch the women out of their hatch.

Somebody touched my elbow. I spun around. It was Sanu, holding her own baby in her arms. The baby was sleeping. Sanu stepped over to hug Fanta, but Fanta stared at her stonily. Sanu stepped back and stood again near me. The other women—some coming from their own

104

hold, others from the toubabu leaders' cabins—began to cluster around us.

At that moment, homelander men began charging out of the hold. They moved so swiftly that it took the two toubabu guarding the hatch a moment to grasp that the men were not shackled. The guards were thrown down into the hatch, into the hands of the rising men.

The toubabu began to blast away with their firesticks. Some of the homelanders took shots in the face or chest and fell right back against the surging tide of men, while others pushed through the hole and ran free on the deck. Some twenty or thirty men managed to escape the hatch before the blazing firesticks became so intense that every man who showed his chest was shot back into the hold.

Biton flew past me with an iron file in one hand and his ankle shackles in another. He jabbed one toubab in the eye with the file, and smashed another in the face with the shackles. One homelander used rusty nails to poke out the eye of a sailor. The toubabu leaders kept up an onslaught with their firesticks.

All around me, shots rang out and men and women cried. I backed myself against the ship's railing. I saw a woman jump onto the back of a toubab sailor, clutching him like a monkey and using her fingers to claw at his eyes. Homelander men and women screamed, as did some toubabu. Other toubabu shouted orders. Their firesticks were deadly, but it seemed to take the toubabu time to use a firestick more than once. With knives and hammers and nails and enraged hands, the homelanders struck more quickly.

A few steps to my left, I saw Fanta crouching. At first, I thought she was injured or exhausted from the birth. She was doubled over, and the baby was wriggling on a cloth beside her. As I watched, Fanta reached inside her wrap. I heard the baby give a little cry. I saw his heels kicking. Fanta brought out the knife from the medicine man's room, placed a hand over the baby's face and jerked up his chin. She dug the tip of the knife into the baby's neck and ripped his throat open. Then she pulled the blue cloth over him, stood and heaved him overboard. I retched and felt my body grow limp, but I couldn't take my eyes off her. Fanta ran behind the medicine man, who was pointing his firestick in another direction, and plunged the knife deep into the back of his neck. He started to turn, but sank to his knees. I saw his eyeballs bulging, and he fell forward, arms out, toward me. Blood streamed from his mouth. His eyes seemed fixed on me. I could not bear to look into the eyes of the dying man, and I hoped that he would die quickly.

I was tackled from behind. Now, for sure, I would die. *Allahu Akbar*, I mumbled, crashing to the deck. But no hand went around my neck, and no knife plunged into my ribs. It was Fomba who was lying over me. Blood spilled from his arm onto my face. He jumped up again. He had a hammer in the hand of his injured arm and used it to smash the skull of a toubab who was pointing a firestick at Biton.

I was too terrified to move. I watched Fanta run over to Sanu, who was crouching on the deck, clutching her baby and trying to avoid the mayhem. I could see Fanta gesture madly at Sanu and try to pull her baby away. Sanu held on to her child, but Fanta pulled it again, pushing and shoving and finally striking Sanu on the nose. Sanu fell back. Fanta grabbed the bawling baby by the leg. I tried to get up. I had to get over there. I had to make Fanta listen to me. But before I could move, Fanta had the baby by the ankle and was holding her upside down. I couldn't understand what kind of madness had overtaken her. Fanta stepped toward the railing and heaved the baby out over the waiting waters. Sanu jumped up. Her mouth opened, but I couldn't hear her voice over the firing weapons and the cries of the homelanders and toubabu. Sanu climbed up onto the railing and followed her baby into the sea.

Now Fanta attempted to climb up on the railing, but a toubab tackled her, slammed her onto the deck and began to beat her. Beside me, one homelander had a sword rammed deep into his gut. He tumbled over me, covering me, bleeding on me, pinning me. I was stuck underneath him and couldn't get up. Two men streaked past me and jumped overboard. I cringed at the double splash. A woman jumped overboard. And then another. I tried to push the man's dead weight off me. Impossible. Biton fought with the toubab chief, whose firestick had stopped working. The toubab chief swung his firestick. Biton ducked, grabbed the toubab's foot, pulled him down. Another homelander with a hammer smashed the toubab chief's skull. Once, and the toubab chief kept moving. twice, and he was still. The homelander was covered in blood. I couldn't tell whose it was. Two toubabu closed and secured the hatch. A sailor fought Chekura, and sliced his arm with a knife. Chekura fell, clutching his shoulder, but Fomba stepped up from behind. He grabbed the sailor by the hair, snapped back his head, locked his other hand onto the man's crotch and flung him overboard. Fomba was clubbed in the back of the head with the butt of a firestick, and he went down hard.

One homelander used a wooden feeding tub to bash out the brains of a toubab sailor, but his chest was then blown open. I couldn't bear to watch the cascading blood. Two sailors passed armloads of new firesticks to the toubabu, who blasted at every homelander still fighting.

Two more homelanders were shot, and fell. I closed my eyes for a moment. I could hear no more battle cries of attacking homelanders. Now none of us was left standing. There was only moaning and wheezing and the sound of firesticks exploding. Then came the sound of angry metal clanking, as the toubabu clamped us all in irons. Fomba was shackled. Chekura was bleeding but not so badly as to be thrown overboard, so he too went into irons. Biton had been beaten savagely, and had a rag stuffed in his mouth, and irons were already on his foot. I saw the bodies of three toubabu sailors, plus that of the medicine man and the toubab chief. I felt numb. With such a mess of bodies, bleeding, unconscious or dead, I couldn't tell how many homelanders had been killed and how many had been lost to the sea.

The toubabu stumbled about with clothes ripped, hair loose and faces wild, bleeding. One toubab began shouting at all of the others, who moved where he pointed and did what he said. The toubabu locked up one homelander after another. I too was ironed. The metal bit into my ankle. But I was still alive. Now I just had to be still.

I looked up from the iron clasp around my foot. A huge sailor with pants down around his knees held Fanta flat on the deck. He pinned her two wrists with one thick hand, and as his manhood swung about like a long, hard tongue, he slapped her with his free hand and lowered himself onto her. Fanta spat up at him. She bit his wrist so hard that he pulled away. Another toubab used a wooden pail to smack the head of the man on top of Fanta. The attacker gave up and rolled off Fanta and kicked her. She was put in irons, and a cloth was stuffed in her mouth to keep her quiet.

I watched the toubabu throw the dead homelanders overboard. Over screeching protests, they also grabbed the badly wounded homelanders and heaved them over the railing. When the homelanders went overboard, they cried out again. Seven or eight toubabu lay crumpled in every imaginable position of death: face down, face up, on their sides, hanging over beams and railings. The toubab chief and the medicine man were left lying on their backs, as dead as I could have wanted them. *Allahu Akbar*, I mumbled to myself. But maybe Fanta had been right. Maybe God was impossible here.

* * *

THE TOUBABU DID NOT EXECUTE BITON. They hoisted some homelanders up by their thumbs and whipped them, and let them down only after they had died. But they only did that to the men who were weak and lame, and of little value to them. I thought they would kill Fanta or perhaps all the women, but they didn't even do that.

After the revolt, they kept us shackled at all times. We were brought up in small groups to watch the whippings. We were made to eat and drink, and then were sent back below. No washings. No clothes. No treats. No women in the rooms of the toubabu leaders. Sailors were sent below with firesticks and clubs. They pulled out the dead bodies, and they collected all the clothing and unused weapons they could find.

Each rising sun saw more people die. We called their names as they were pulled from the hold. *Makeda, of Segu. Salima, of Kambolo.* Down below, at least, I couldn't hear bodies hitting the water. Although the hold was dark and filthy, I no longer wanted to see the water, or to breathe the air above.

After what seemed to be several days, the toubabu started bringing us back up on deck in small groups. We were given food and a vile drink with bits of fruit in it. We were given tubs and water to wash ourselves. The toubabu burned tar in our sleeping quarters, which made us choke and gag. They tried to make us wash our sleeping planks, but we were too weak. Our ribs were showing, our anuses draining. The toubabu sailors looked just as ill. I saw many dead seamen thrown overboard without ceremony.

After two months at sea, the toubabu brought every one of us up on deck. Naked, we were made to wash. There were only two-thirds of us left. They grabbed those who could not walk and began to throw them overboard, one by one. I shut my eyes and plugged my ears, but could not block out all the shrieking.

Some time after the noise ended, I opened my eyes and looked out at the setting sun. It hovered just over the horizon, casting a long pink path across the still water. We sailed steadily toward the beckoning pink, which hovered forever at arm's length, always close but never with us. Come this way, it seemed to be saying. Far ahead in the direction of the sun, I saw something grey and solid. It was barely visible, but it was there. We were moving toward land.

When they brought us back up on deck the next morning, I could see it again. It was much closer now. Land. Trees. A coastline. And even closer than the coast, there was a small island. I could see it clearly now. No trees, but sand and a huge, square barricade. That was where we were heading. They released our chains. Chekura appeared by my side, with barely more meat on him than a stripped bone.

"I am sorry, Aminata."

"We have lost our homeland," I said. "We have lost our people."

"I am sorry for what I did to you."

I looked at Chekura blankly. That he had once worked for the manstealers was the last thing on my mind. "I am cold, and I can't even pray. Allah doesn't live here."

"We still live, Aminata of Bayo," Chekura said. "We have crossed the water. We have survived."

And so it happened that the vessel that had so terrified us in the waters near our homeland saved at least some of us from being buried in the deep. We, the survivors of the crossing, clung to the beast that had stolen us away. Not a soul among us had wanted to board that ship, but once out on open waters, we held on for dear life. The ship became an extension of our own rotting bodies. Those who were cut from the heaving animal sank quickly to their deaths, and we who remained attached wilted more slowly as poison festered in our bellies and bowels. We stayed with the beast until new lands met our feet, and we stumbled down the long planks just before the poison became fatal. Perhaps here in this new land, we would keep living.

Book Two

And my story waits like a restful beast

{LONDON, 1803}

WHEN I WAS VERY YOUNG, Papa used to tell me that words fly on wild winds from the mouths of sly people. When the winds pick up, he said, sand blows into your ears and bites your eyes. Storms build overhead like a lake with a spout, but you can't see or hear. Only when you are safely sheltered, Papa said, can you tell which way the wind is blowing. Only from the calm, he said, can you see how to protect yourself from trouble.

So now I am in London, taking a break from twelve men and their swirling words. I sit alone in a separate room, spooning bees' honey into my hot tea. Down the hall, I can hear the laughter of the leading abolitionist. A man who frequently removes his wig to scratch his scalp, he stands short and fierce like an exclamation mark. With me, however, he must appear solicitous. He opens his arms wide, as if to comfort me with his ample belly. His name is Sir Stanley Hastings, but I think of him as the jolly abolitionist. In his musical and enthusiastic voice, he has been telling me that his wife and children have pledged to do without sugar in their tea. God willing, he says, no one in his family will drink from the blood of slaves. He says that what we really need—what would stop this trade dead in a minute—is an invention to stain all sugar products with red dye. Now he gesticulates like a man at the pulpit. Let the colour of blood spoil every teacup in the nation, he says, and our battles will be over.

They bring me out from my quiet time. Suffocating me with empathy, the jolly abolitionist asks if I feel ready to continue. Decisions must be made, and they must be made soon. Hear hear, the other men echo as they smile at me. We need to know if you will support our plan, Sir Hastings says, peering at me over crumpled manifestos.

The abolitionists call me their equal and say that we all conspire to end tyranny against mankind. "Then why—" I begin to ask. But they don't let me finish. I hear whisperings about property and compensation and the rule of law. I observe the massaging of palms and the interlocking of fingers. Believing I am deaf, Sir Hastings murmurs to his neighbour that I can't be expected to grasp the details in their complexity. He turns back to me once more.

Your story is one of virtue, he says.

Survival has nothing to do with virtue, I reply.

I am referring to your dignity and courage, he says. We need a human face for our fight, and here you are. A woman. An African. A liberated slave who has risen up, self-taught. For twenty years, he goes on, British parliamentarians have extinguished every abolitionist fire. But this time, he says, a woman like you could make all the difference.

The tension makes me tired. I do not care to fight. When I lower my voice, they all lean forward. I say, I can't speak to your Parliament or meet your King without addressing the bondage of my people.

The men keep pressing. Any talk of outright abolition will unite planters, shippers, traders and insurers. Can I not see that it is men of property who vote in Parliament?

But I am too old for cleverness. I cannot speak against the slave trade without condemning slavery, I say. Make the arguments that you must, I tell them, and let me make mine.

Forcing a smile, Sir Hastings says the british people are still haunted by the bloody slave uprisings in St Domingue. Nasty business, all that butchering of white men. The most we can ask, he says, is to stop the trade.

Even if you destroy every slave ship, I say, what remains of the men and women already in bondage? What remains of the children who were born to them but belong to others?

The men turn to John Clarkson, the man who gives me lodging. It is plain to see that he has little standing among these men. He is too vocal with his ideals and is never mentioned in the newspapers. But he is the one Englishman with whom I have journeyed, and he is the one who brought me to the abolitionists. He does his best but cannot convince me.

So we are stuck with this problem. The abolitionists keep plotting. Already, there are talks of hearings into the slave trade. And one day, when the hearings are done, they will introduce yet another bill in Parliament. They say they can win this time, and I do want them to prevail. Their way is better than the alternative, but their way is not enough.

The abolitionists may well call me their equal, but their lips do not yet say my name and their ears do not yet hear my story. Not the way I want to tell it. But I have long loved the written word, and come to see in it the power of the sleeping lion. *This is my name. This is who I am. This is how I got here.* In the absence of an audience, I will write down my story so that it waits like a restful beast with lungs breathing and heart beating.

John Clarkson whispers that they cannot go on exhausting me like this. The abolitionists all rise from their chairs. We have finished our talks for the day. The men come to me one by one, full of handshakes and salutations.

One man asks if I have enough to eat, and if English food is not offensive to my palate. I reassure him that my palate has not been offended. A fellow with a bushy moustache offers distractions from inevitable boredom. There is an astounding display of African mammals and reptiles in town, he says. It is all the rage in London. Have I seen it? I have no great feelings for creatures preserved in alcohol, but I don't want to insult the good man. No, I tell him, I haven't been out that way.

Sir Hastings takes his turn: Then what, dear God, do you do all day? Are you not disoriented by the commotion of mongers, horses and carts? His mouth drops when I say that no such commotion compares to that in the belly of a slave ship. Another abolitionist asks about the thieving street urchins of London. Do they not trouble me? I am of no interest to street urchins, I reply, but at the corner of old Jewry and Prince a ragged old African man stands under a hat sculpted in the shape of a ship. Sometimes I give a few pence when the hat man extends his palm. The abolitionists howl in concert: I must take great care, they say, not to be duped by London's idle connivers. No disrespect intended, they say, but rascals and layabouts have the black hearts of highwaymen.

I step toward the door. One persistent chatterer pleads with me to say how I spend my time. I volunteer that I have someone who takes me to the library. He has a chuckle over that. I can imagine heads turning, he says.

Don't laugh, John Clarkson says a little too sharply, I bet she has read more books than you.

At the end of each meeting, the abolitionists bring out little gifts. At the last meeting I received a book, a newspaper and a piece of hard yellow candy with two peanuts inside. This time, Sir Hastings presents me with a new quill and a glass inkpot decorated with swirling lines of indigo blue. I love the smoothness and the heft in my hand. I rub the surface but the indigo is buried deep in the glass. Englishmen do love to bury one thing so completely in another that the two can only be separated by force:

peanuts in candy, indigo in glass, Africans in irons.

Standing too close and bumping into one another, the abolitionists escort me from 18 Old Jewry Street. Down the stairs I go and out into the heart of London. I take hold of the offered arm, and John Clarkson walks me back to his house. He lives nearby. These days, it takes me time to cover two city blocks. People stream by as we inch along, but that does not matter. I am still upright and I am still walking.

Back in John Clarkson's home, I will have a bit of bread with some sharp Cheddar. I like all foods with voices: mangoes, malaguetta peppers, boiled ginger with honey, rum. John Clarkson's wife was quite scandalized when I first asked for it. *Rum?*

After a snack and a nap, I hope to pick up my quill. If I live long enough to finish this story, it will outlive me. Long after I have returned to the spirits of my ancestors, perhaps it will wait in the London Library. Sometimes I imagine the first reader to come upon my story. Could it be a girl? Perhaps a woman. A man. An Englishman. An African. One of these people will find my story and pass it along. And then, I believe, I will have lived for a reason.

They call me an 'African'
{SULLIVAN'S ISLAND, 1757}

WE WERE BROUGHT TO AN ISLAND just off the coast of the toubabu's land. There were about one hundred of us left. We were all placed inside a square barricade. Toubabu stood as sentries at the gate and patrolled inside with clubs and firesticks, but mostly we were left alone to wonder what would now become of us.

It seemed to me that we had travelled to the other side of the sun. On this side of the world, the sun was worn out and not to be trusted. My fingers grew thick and numb every night and throbbed every day as the sun climbed the sky. My ears were cold. My nose was cold. Like the others, I had been given a rough cloth barely long enough to wrap around my backside. I shivered at night on the sandy earth, and one morning I awoke to find smoke trickling from my mouth. I thought my face had caught fire. I thought that someone had bedevilled me during the night, or branded my tongue. I waited for the burning. I prepared to scream. I held my breath. No smoke. I breathed. Smoke again. It came from within me. No burning. Just smoke. The smoke in my breath continued until the sun began to climb the sky. And then I noticed that others, too, had smoke mouths in the morning.

Most of the other homelanders were gaining strength

every day. But here on this tiny island, my bowels issued streams of brown water. My body was giving up.

Biton came to sit by me one morning. "You crossed the big river, child. Don't die now."

I blinked. I had not the strength to answer. He stayed by my side, patting my hand.

Twice a day, without fail, the toubabu placed buckets of food and water just inside the gate. They always left enough for all of us. Fanta poked around in the rice and yams and picked out bits of meat that she said smelled like pork. She and I wouldn't touch them, but the others ate them readily. I sipped water but had lost my appetite. I felt that I would sooner die than eat pork. Still, Biton came to me each day and told me I must eat. He balled some rice on his fingertips and brought it to my face.

"Look," he said. "No pork in this rice. To live, child, you must eat."

Fanta muttered that pork had contaminated the entire bucket of food, but Biton shooed her away and brought the food to my lips. I was too weak to protest.

On days that I couldn't lift myself up off the ground, Chekura brought me food and Fomba brought water. Fanta said she would pull my ear if I didn't move again, but even in my illness, I did not want her to mother me. Nobody spoke of the revolt or the killings, but I could not forget the things Fanta had done. We, the survivors of the crossing, broke off into little groups to eat and to sleep and to spend our days waiting together. I found myself with Biton, Chekura, Fomba and Fanta and a young woman named Oumou. At night, the six of us slept close together, for comfort, but I did my best to avoid lying next to Fanta.

The toubabu left us cold water for washing and brought us bowls of oil to rub on our skin. They dropped off food buckets twice a day and kept their distance from us. But they watched who was eating and rubbing oil and who was not, and they threatened to club any captive

121

who resisted. Chekura offered to rub the oil into my dry, cracked skin. Fanta stood between the two of us and said she would take care of it. I preferred Chekura's gentler manner, but had not the will to object.

"So now they fatten us," Fanta said, oiling my shins, "and we know what that means."

I tried to pray in Papa's way. I thought that if I could find my way back to Allah, someone might rescue me. By now, the people of Bayo and other villages would know what had happened to me. They could put together enough men to overwhelm the captors with firesticks, trace my steps, and come save me. Bent down, with head lowered, I turned toward where the sun rose. I turned in the direction of my homeland. Come save me. Someone, please come save me. I began the ritual prayers. But biton forbade me, hand on my shoulder, stern and unmoving. Biton said that just a day earlier a man had been beaten for praying in my manner. I was not to pray. Not to expose myself to beatings. In my state, he said, I would never survive a beating. First and foremost, he said, I had a duty to stay alive.

"Remember your mama and your papa," he said. "You carry them in your heart. Listen to them. They will tell you what to do."

"And all those people who jumped overboard, had they not mamas and papas?"

"Turn your mind from the ship, child. It is nothing but a rotting carcass in the grass. The carcass has shocked you with its stink and its flies. But you have walked past it, already, and now you must keep walking."

"Do you think they will come for us?"

Biton helped me back up on my feet and looked at me with darkening eyes. "Who?"

"The homelanders. Our people."

Biton looked out toward the water. I followed his gaze, and noticed that the ship that had brought us was no longer there. It must have sailed away in the night.

"No, child," Biton said, "they will not come."

I told myself that Biton didn't know about these things. He didn't pray. He had no knowledge of Allah. He had to be wrong. But perhaps he could help me in another way.

"One day, when we are strong again, could you take me back across that river?"

"Do you know the thickness of a rabbit's foot?"

"Yes," I said.

"That's how close we all came to dying. Only six moons ago, I taught the boys in my village to wrestle. None of them could beat me. And now I am already old. Too old for the thing you ask. And you are too young to think of it."

"One day," I said.

"Today you live, child. Tomorrow, you dream."

Once or twice more, I recited the ritual prayers in my head. *Allaahu Akbar. Ashhadu Allah ilaaha illa-Lah. Ash hadu anna Muhamadar rasuululah*. It wasn't the same as praying at home in a quiet spot with all thoughts of the world behind me. At home, even during the Ramadan, when we fasted during daylight for a full cycle of the moon, praying came easily. But in the toubabu's land I couldn't pray by myself. Praying inside my head felt lonely and futile. As the nights came and went, thoughts of Allah faded.

We ate on Sullivan's Island around communal buckets. On our third day, Fanta would not stop glaring at Fomba during a meal. He scraped some food up into his palm and wandered off to eat alone. Biton stood abruptly, followed Fomba and brought him back with a hand on his shoulder.

"He eats with us," he said in Bamanankan, and made me explain it to Fanta. He said it didn't matter if Fomba and certain others were slaves in our homeland. Here, in the toubabu's land, we would eat together. We would reveal no differences. The toubabu were to know nothing of us.

123

Fanta kicked over the bucket. "I was not to be a captive," she muttered. "I am freeborn."

A BUNCH OF US HUDDLED TOGETHER to sleep on the cold, hard sand. Biton. Fanta. Chekura. Fomba. Oumou. A few others. And me. Never in Bayo had I seen numerous men and women all sleeping together. It never would have been tolerated. But here on this island, pooling our warmth in a nest of bodies gave us comfort.

I awoke one night to see the stars on fire. I missed the feel of Oumou's warm leg over mine, and the sound of Biton snoring. Chekura was there. Fomba was nearby. Fanta, unfortunately, was right beside me. But Oumou and Biton were gone.

I rolled over and sucked in my breath. There they were. Biton and Oumou! Just a few steps away. They were riding each other, gasping, thrusting their loins one into the other. They were locked together like dogs. I heard the sound of wet flesh slapping. It made me think of the medicine man taking the women always at the same time of day: after eating and after firewater, but before sleep. At home with my parents, sometimes I had to rise in the night to relieve myself. But first, I had to look. Mama and Papa might be together, rocking and heaving just like Oumou and Biton. Now I couldn't get up. I would have to lie still. I would shut my eyes and hope they would stop soon, and wish I never saw it again.

In the morning, when I awoke, Oumou and Biton were back among us, and nobody said a thing.

A SHIP CAME TO THE ISLAND. The toubabu began to round us up, starting with those of us who still had fluids draining from our bodies. My body wanted to drop. It wanted nothing other than to spread out and be cradled by the earth itself. Straw. Grass. Earth. Sand. I was beyond caring. Any sort of bed would do. But they forced me up on my feet and made me bend over. I feared that they would burn my flesh again, but lacked the strength to fight. They pushed my head lower, pulled out my hips and slid a plug of grass deep into my anus. It stung and brought on sharp cramps, but I could not expel the thing. I was made to stand straight again. They made each of us remove the rough cloth we had been given and throw it into a raging fire. We were led onto a ship and sailed across the water, toward the land that was in view.

An unmistakable stink blew in with the wind. I smelled it before I turned around. Another ship from my homeland. I could barely make out the people bunched together on the deck. Their ship drew slowly toward the island we had just left. I felt relieved that I would not have to look into their eyes, or to confront their misery. I hoped I would never meet them.

The toubabu gave us each another bit of cloth, just as rough as the first. I put my arms through it and pulled it down over my head. The coarse material scratched my skin, but it didn't hurt as much as the white rope that they bound around my wrists. Planks were laid from the ship to a wharf, and we walked down into the toubabu's land.

Never had I seen a place so crowded or strange. I saw toubabu boys and toubabu men, straight-haired and yellow-toothed, walking, riding horses or sitting in carts. Some wore rags and others fine layers of cloth with thick boots.

Strangest of all, I saw homelanders everywhere carrying goods, sweating and shouting. In their voices I sometimes heard notes of joy and play. No shackles bound their wrists or ankles, but not one of them fought or tried to run away. Some of the working homelander men wore nothing but breeches. The homelander women took their time on the streets, parading their backsides and sporting coloured head scarves. I could not take my eyes off the reds and oranges and blues that ran and swam in those scarves. Some of the women laughed with the toubabu. I saw one toubab man place his hand on the backside of a home-lander woman. She smiled at him, open mouthed.

Toubabu boys laughed and threw pebbles at us. On the street, on steps, on porches, on top of wooden buildings and on horsedrawn carts, people yelled and stared. The world had gone mad.

I saw a toubab woman. She held a round object over her head for shade. Her hands were as white as bones. No. Not bones. Not possible. Her hands were the colour of scrubbed elephant teeth. I looked again. That wasn't skin. It was something else, covering her hands. It looked soft and delicate. How I longed for that material. Perhaps it would save my fingers from feeling cold and swollen through the nights.

The toubab woman looked straight at me. Cheeks, pink and fat. Lips, thin and pale. Her eyes made me think of a rock-strewn river, with deep, dangerous water calling out to me, *Jump in, child. Jump right in. It won't hurt.*

Our eyes met. The woman's hand flew up to her mouth. I could feel my scalp itching where the hair had fallen out, the running sore on my knee and the plug of grass that choked my backside. I wished to become the woman who was growing inside me, to find my dignity and never have it stripped from me again.

I stepped in a hole and lost my balance. Even with his hands bound, Chekura managed to use an arm to keep me from falling. "Aminata! Walk correctly. Walk!"

Everywhere I looked, I saw goods. Sacks of grain, stacks of corn, hay for horses, piles of nails, cows and pigs being led across streets. No goats. But chickens everywhere, bunched together five or more, feet strung, hanging upside down from the same rope, carried along by boys or by homelanders.

The streets and gutters were filled with waste. Rotting fruit, dead cats, human feces and green meat, all of it picked over by fat-bellied, big-winged birds of death that circled and spun and looped in the air. I thought they eyed me too as they flew past, and I imagined they were thinking, *In good time we'll get you too.*

In my homeland, the towns I knew were set up in a circle so everybody could be together. In this place, people walked off in all directions, taking dusty roads running either side by side or at sharp angles to one another. I didn't believe I could ever find my way in such a place.

We were herded into an open space in front of a building made of wood, built to the height of five grown men. So many people were packed into the space that I thought it was a market. I looked around for piles of squashes, salt or shea nuts, but saw only people—my people—bound and roughly clothed. Chekura was pulled away from me, and so were Fanta, Biton and most of the others. I called out to Chekura, but the sounds of shouting men drowned out my voice. The healthy captives were shoved into one large circle, and into another circle went the rest of us—those who limped or bled or had gone blind or had ribs protruding like half-built ships. Somebody nudged me. I looked back. It was Fomba. His eyes were glassy, and he walked off balance, head cocked far to the side. It seemed that the toubabu already knew that Fomba was not quite right.

"Fomba," I said. He looked at me. He raised his tied wrists so he could nibble a fingernail. His mind had left him, but I could bring it back. "Don't lean like that. Straighten your head." If he looked valuable, perhaps he would be spared a beating, or worse.

Two toubabu men stood on a platform. The healthy captives were led up to them, one by one. Most of them stood with shoulders slumped and heads down while the toubabu shouted. When the shouting stopped, they were

127

taken down from the platform and led out through the crowd.

When Biton was brought up onto the platform, he held his chin up. He had a cut on his shin and a scar on his face, but he stood tall and straight. His skin was oiled and shiny. I hated that he had to stand there like that with all eyes turned on him. A toubab lifted up Biton's cloth to look at his shrivelled penis. He dropped the cloth back into place and tested a bicep. When the shouting grew loud, Biton looked around and caught my eyes. He opened his mouth. *Aminata Diallo*, he said. I couldn't hear a thing over the noise of the crowd. But I saw his mouth move and I knew he was saying my name.

Two toubabu stepped up on the platform, prodded Biton's cheeks, made him open his mouth, and stuck their fingers inside. They poked him everywhere, and then left the platform. The din increased. One toubab broke into nasal singing. He stopped as quickly as he had started. A man in the crowd shouted, and the first toubab picked up where he had left off. More men shouted. The song stopped and started, over and over, and so it went until Biton was led off the platform, into the thick crowd.

One by one, the captives were brought up on the platform. I called out to Chekura when he stood before the crowd, but he could not hear me. I hoped that he would stand as proudly as Biton, but he couldn't manage. He stumbled. He reared back when someone reached into his mouth. The toubabu roared in laughter. After more shouting, Chekura was dragged off the platform and out of my sight.

The toubabu men used the same quills and inkpots that the medicine man had shown me on the boat. I stared at one man as he wrote. Left to right. Left to right. Others did it the same way. Had they all learned to write backwards? The man caught me looking at him, stared at me hard, for a moment, and turned away so that I couldn't see. Other men passed rounded pieces of metal back and forth. Some were shiny, others dull. They didn't look as attractive as cowrie shells or copper manillas.

In the dirt by my feet, I noticed a glittering piece of metal, about three times the size of my thumbnail. I managed to squat, get it between my fingers, and stand up again to examine it more closely. I saw a man's head on one side—the same head I had seen in the medicine man's room. I put the metal between my teeth. Too hard to break. Perhaps it could be pierced. If a hole could be made, through it, perhaps a tightly woven thread of grasses could be slipped through, so that the thing could hang off a wrist, or a neck. Still, it would be ugly. I could not imagine what gave this thing value.

I heard more shouting and looked back to the platform. Fanta was now up before the crowd. She spat when they made her open her mouth, and kicked when they tried to inspect her womanhood. The people laughed and threw pebbles. When Fanta cried out, they stuffed a rag in her mouth. She choked, and they pulled it out. She screamed again and they stuffed it back in. A man cupped her breast. She scratched his face and drew blood. Her hands were tied behind her back. I hoped that she would stop resisting before somebody hurt her badly. When she kneed another man in the face, the crowd roared again. He smacked her cheek, and somebody else bound her ankles. Of all the homelanders brought up to the platform that day, Fanta was the only one who had her mouth stuffed, wrists bound and legs tied. She seemed to be begging them to kill her, but they were having too much fun for that. When the toubabu finished laughing and shouting, they carried Fanta off the platform.

All the healthy captives were gone. Many of the toubabu were gone. Under the guard of clothed homelanders who didn't speak our languages, the rest of us waited in the square. The sun moved a distance across the sky, and we had no water or food or place to sit. There were about fifty of us: older captives, younger ones, the sick and the frail ones, the ones with broken limbs and missing teeth and watery, whitened, useless eyes. Some of us could stand on our own. Others couldn't, and either leaned against the building or fell down. While we waited, a homelander released my bound wrists, but Fomba remained tied up. Fomba managed to sit down, push his back up against a tree and fall asleep. I sat too, but was sure I would not be able to sleep with the toubabu circling around me.

The next thing I knew, I was awakened by a young homelander who was prodding me with a stick. With his thumb, he signalled for me to get up. Now there were far fewer toubabu and captives in front of the building. All of the captives around me were sick, bleeding or blind; one or two, like Fomba, were glassy eyed and with minds gone. There were only about thirty of us. There was far less noise than before. None of the toubabu were shouting or laughing. There were no toubabu women left watching.

Two young homelanders, each holding the end of a thick wooden pole, pushed us apart, separating us an arm's length from each other. We were refuse captives, and we were lined up in one long row. The space in front of us was cleared away. Toubabu and working homelanders stood to one side of us or the other, except for a group of five toubabu men who stood facing us at a distance of some thirty paces. The five toubabu formed a row, and were separated by equal distances. Each man was holding a rope and standing behind a line that had been scratched in the ground.

A toubab to the side shouted out a few words and held a firestick above his head. He pointed it up. We, the refuse captives, were spread just a little farther apart. The toubab with the firestick would have to kill us one by one. *Please let me go first*, I prayed.

The toubab let off a report so loud that it made me lose

control of my bowels. I had not even a moment to ponder my own humiliation as the grass plug and my own waste flowed out of me. The toubabu raced forward, ropes in hand, pushing and shoving as they tried to grab captives and sling ropes around them. A man grabbed me. He tried to tie me up. Another man knocked him back, and tied his own rope around my waist. He pulled me closer to his stinking chest and tightened the rope, which bit into my skin. Fixing a knot, he stepped on my toes, set all of his weight down on my right foot. I shrieked. He stepped back. I wondered if my bloody toes were broken. Now that a rope was fastened around my waist, I was left standing alone.

An old homelander woman—I saw her, and wondered how she had survived the crossing—was knocked down. I caught a glimpse of Fomba, sitting on the ground, elbows around his knees, palms over his ears, eyes shut, rocking back and forth. The same man who had tied me up was tightening a rope around Fomba. It took three men to get him up. He sagged in their arms. Dead weight, but not dead. A man ripped Fomba's hands off his ears and screamed at him. Others crowded in. I couldn't see him any more. We, the refuse captives, were now all roped and bundled.

The toubabu men with ropes began moving away from the building with groups of two, three or four ailing captives. A toubab grabbed the rope around Fomba's waist, pulled him to me and led us both away from the building and down a dusty lane. I looked left and right for Chekura, Biton and Fanta, but could catch no glimpse of them or any of the healthy captives.

Fomba walked just a few steps to my side. His eyes were open, but he didn't see me, or anything, or anyone. The toubab stepped on my toes again. I cried out. Fomba's head swivelled around. His eyes came alive, and he stared at me. Now he saw me. My voice seemed the only thing that could pull him from that trance. Now I felt shame. In Bayo, he was meant to serve us. But now he needed me.

"Are you all right?" I asked.

He smiled.

"If I find any water," I said, "I'll give you some."

Fomba opened his mouth, but nothing—not one sound—came from his lips.

After walking for some time, we were brought to a young working homelander who was standing by a horse and cart. Waiting with him were two bound captives—one man and one woman. I didn't know them. They had not come off our ship, and looked stronger and healthier than I. I whispered a few words to them, but it was clear that they could speak neither to me nor to each other.

The toubab rearranged us, placing us in single file, separating us by five paces and attaching us with new ropes, waist to waist. Fomba, in the front, was attached to the back of the cart. The second man, who looked like he wanted to run, was placed behind him. The young woman was placed ahead of me, and I saw her looking left, right and behind as I was tied up in the last position. The toubab climbed up on the cart and tapped his horse with a rod. The horse began walking, the cart started moving, and we had no choice but to move forward.

WE WALKED ALL DAY. NO WATER. No food. No breaks to pee. If you had to go, you had to do it and keep walking with the urine running down your sore legs and burning your broken skin. Sometimes to one side, I glimpsed the big water. But mostly it was trees, and land, and the endless path, and swamps on my left. I had not seen such wet ground, with grasses and reeds growing straight out of the water, in my homeland.

Moss draped from the trees like loose clothes. The wheels on the back of the wagon turned, and I watched them for hours, turning, moving, not breaking, not giving. The wheels fascinated me, and I tried to imagine my legs were like that, rolling on and on and on in the sun. The working homelander walked near to us with his head down, like a beaten dog.

When we stopped at night, they left the ropes knotted around our waists but let us lie on the ground. I took the space next to the woman who had been walking in front of me. We looked freely into each other's faces, and I felt relieved to find friendly eyes. The homelander working for the toubab got a fire going and boiled up cornmeal mush. He ladled it out in calabashes that made me ache terribly for my homeland, and gave us water. We were pointed to the open ground. I sat down and stretched out.

The woman and I lay down beside each other, and she put her arm around me. I felt grateful for her warmth and comfort even though I never could have asked for it. Her language was unfamiliar, so we pointed to exchange names. Tala. That was her name. We pointed at the bucket, and traded words for food. And water. And the moon. And the stars. To learn the woman's language, I had only to lie down with her.

I dreamt that I was walking through a forest in the toubabu's land. The toubabu and their working home-landers were taking me far away from the town. We walked through the early morning mist. Rabbits cut across the path. *Hurry*, I thought, speaking to them in my mind, *or somebody will catch and cook you*. I called out the warning to one passing rabbit, which was heavily pregnant. Rather than slipping into the bushes, the creature stopped and turned and stared at me long and hard, until I saw that she had my mother's eyes. For some time, she hopped along ahead of me, showing me the way, letting me know that I should stay on the path, reassuring me that I was travelling properly. I walked on and the toubabu transformed into hunters from my village. We heard drumbeats from the forest, shouts from the village women washing clothes by a stream. The rabbit turned into my mother, balancing a slain rabbit on a platter on her head. We had just caught a baby and we were returning home.

When I awoke the next morning and our march continued, I looked left and right for signs of people from my village. On the beaten track and in the fields, there were homelanders everywhere. I had never imagined it would be so. I had expected that I would be all alone, one homelander in a sea of toubabu. But everywhere I looked, homelander men and women passed us. Some were in chains. Others in ropes. Still others walked free, entirely unescorted. With all these homelanders about on foot—I could see that they outnumbered the toubabu—surely my captivity would not be allowed. Someone would come to rescue me. But this was a strange, strange world. I could not make any sense of it. Not a single homelander fought or shouted or ran. They showed no resistance at all. Not one of them took any notice of me.

When Tala and I encountered others from our land, we called out in our various languages. Usually, nobody would respond. But during our first full day of walking, Tala recognized a man. He was about my father's age, and he was off to the side of the dirt path, with a small group of chained homelanders who were resting in a field. He, too, was overseen by a toubab and by a working homelander. The man was tall and gaunt. It was clear by the bald patches in his hair, by his hungry look and wobbly posture that, like us, he had recently come off a ship. She shouted at him, and he shouted back. Tala ignored the obvious warnings from our own toubab leader and kept calling out to him. She and the man appeared to be naming people. *Wole. Youssouf. Fatima.* They howled out as fast as two humans could speak. They traded every bit of information allowed in the brief time they had. The man continued to call out to Tala as we grew more distant, until his shouts were no longer audible. Tala yelled back at him. Finally, when she could no longer hear the man, she fell sobbing to the earth and our little chain was forced to stop.

The toubab man got off his wagon and marched toward her, but I waved at him, pointing to my own chest and then to Tala. I got down on my knees and spoke gentle sounds into Tala's ear. I took her hand, pulled her up, nodding at the toubab and tugging her in the direction of the path that lay ahead. The toubab returned to the cart, and his homelander helper came to walk beside us. He wore smooth leather moccasins, a sleeveless linen shirt and coarse pants with a rope knotted at the waist. I wondered who he was and where he had come from.

"Where are they taking us?" I whispered to him.

He looked at me without expression on his face, and said a few incomprehensible words.

Homelanders in this new land were always on the move. As we walked, I saw a toubab leading a packed mule and four homelander men and five women. The women had cloth bundled and balanced on their heads, babies slung against their backs, and each was carrying an assortment of pots and pans. The men had nothing on their heads or backs, but they were walking, drenched in sweat, each on the corner of a large bed frame. They were walking along the side of the road, and we passed them because they moved slowly. They were not hurrying, but they were working hard, and as we walked past I tried again, making eye contact with one of the women farthest from the toubab.

"Fulfulde? Bamanankan?" I whispered. "Do you speak my language?"

She was brown and short and wide-hipped, and looked like she knew how to bring a baby into the world all by herself. She looked right through me and kept on walking.

To pass the time, I studied people's faces and tried to speak to them whenever the toubab with the firestick couldn't hear. As people passed by, I looked to see who had tribal marks, and how the women kept their hair. Braided? Rowed? Bunched? Covered? I watched to see if any homelanders looked like people from my village. Many of those we passed did not appear to come from my homeland at all. I wondered where they were born, and how they got here.

On our second day of walking, I saw a woman approaching. I could tell by the way the pail was balanced near the front of her head, and by the way the baby was slung low on her back, that she was a Bamana.

"*I ni sógóma,*" I cried out as she came near, *Good morning.*

The woman stopped in her tracks. "*Nse i ni sógóma,*" she answered, *And good morning to you.* "Child!" she continued in Bamanankan, "you are but a bag of bones. Whose daughter are you?"

"I am Aminata Diallo, the daughter of Mamadu and Sira, from the village of Bayo, near Segu, and we have been walking two suns in this land."

"I am Nyeba, daughter of Tembe, from Sikasso, my child, here now for five rains. You are very strong to have survived the crossing."

"Where am I going?" I said.

The toubab got off his cart and walked angrily toward me.

"Go," Nyeba said, "or you will be beaten."

"Where can I find you?"

"If you are lucky, you will find some people in the fishnet."

"The fishnet?" I asked.

The toubab cuffed me on the head and shouted until Nyeba walked away. I was cuffed once more, and after that, dared not even look back over my shoulder. On I walked with the others. All of my sorrow was coiled in the very organs of my body, wanting to explode but with nowhere to go.

We came to a river the width of a stone's throw. We waited half a day. Eight homelanders came to fetch us in a long canoe carved out of two trees. We were untied and led into the canoe. The toubab climbed in with us but left the homelander and the horse and cart behind.

The bare-backed men dug long oars into the water, pushing off the bed of the river and out toward an island, not far away. Cords of muscles rippled under their skin, but several had the crisscross scars of the lash across their backs. Fomba watched the homelanders closely as they dipped their oars in the water. He seemed fascinated. He nudged a homelander, grunted and grabbed an oar. The working men watched and laughed as Fomba struggled to stand balanced and pull with the oar at the same time. But Fomba quickly found the rhythm. They let him keep using the oar, and sang a low song in unison as they worked. It was the most mournful melody I had ever heard, bubbling out of troubled and weary souls. I believed they too must have survived the water crossing. How else could they sing like that? I nudged the one who had given his oar to Fomba.

"Bamanankan?" I whispered.

"Maninka," he answered, without moving his head. "Learned from my mother. She was from Africa."

"From where?"

"Africa. Your land."

I stared at him excitedly. I wanted to leap into his arms. He raised his head casually. He bore no tribal marks. He looked to make sure that the toubab wasn't watching.

"What is the fishnet?" I asked.

"It is how we find each other, passing messages from one to another to still another."

"Where are we going?" I asked.

"To work on an island. Stay by the women and learn from them."

"You have no marks on your face."

137

"Those are country marks. They are fine moons, child. But I don't want that."

"Why?"

"I was born here. In this land, we don't use country marks."

"Were others born here too?"

"Yes. But we say that the ones who survive the great river crossing are destined to live two lives."

I didn't want to live two lives. I only wanted my real life back. "Why have they done this to me?"

"You were taken from Africa to work for the toubabu."

"Africa," I said. "What is that?"

"The land of my mother. The land you come from."

"They call it Africa?"

"Yes. If you were born there, they call you an African. But here they call all of us the same things: niggers, Negroes. They especially call us slaves."

"Slaves?" I said.

"Slaves. It means we belong to the buckra."

"And who are the buckra?"

"The men who own us."

"I belong to nobody, and I am not an African. I am a Bamana. And a Fula. I am from Bayo near Segu. I am not what you say. I am not an African."

"The toubab is watching us."

"Where is he taking me?"

He seemed to give me an admiring look. "You are like my mother. Your mind is fierce like a trap. But now you must eat and learn and make yourself valuable. The toubab is still watching. We must stop talking."

"I am a freeborn believer," I said. "*Allaahu Akbar.*"

He seized my forearm violently. "Stop," he whispered.

I gasped and looked into his face. Anger had clouded his eyes. His fingers were like claws, squeezing tighter and tighter.

"You must never pray in that manner. It is dangerous,

and the toubab will correct you with the whip. The toubab will correct us all." The man who had called me an African dropped my arm, seized the oar from Fomba and returned to his rowing.

We glided over some reeds and pulled up to an island. Fomba and I were the first to be led off the boat. We stumbled through a swamp and up onto dry land, and were met by a homelander with a firestick who took us away.

Words swim farther than a man can walk

{St. Helena Island, 1757}

I WOULD HAVE BEEN ABOUT TWELVE when I arrived on Robinson Appleby's indigo plantation. I believe it was the month of January, 1757. The air was cold, and around my waist I had nothing but a bit of rough osnaburg cloth. It bit into my hip, leaving it red and raw, and the toes of my left foot were bleeding. Two of them felt broken. I could barely walk. As I stumbled into a big yard in front of a white home bursting with importance, it occurred to me that I couldn't even balance a platter of food on my head. Entrusted to me, oranges or bananas would have gone crashing to the ground.

Into the yard I limped, Fomba at my side. I gaped at the many men, women and children. I saw dark brown skin like mine, and I saw light brown. Among the children and babies, I saw some who had skin of the faintest brown, and others who were as washed out as the buckra. And then there were the heads. Cornrows. Bunches. Braids. Bald heads. Heads with patterns shaved through tight hair. Heads with scarves of the brightest colours. Red. Orange. My gaze locked onto a yellow scarf and I wondered if I might ever have one too.

It must have been a Sunday, the day of my arrival. Women were tending to a pot over a fire. A big pot, but only three sticks burning. A long, slow stew. An aroma rose on the wind. Meat. Vegetables. Peppers. It was my first encounter in half a year with food that smelled good. One man was sitting on the ground, crosslegged, with his back up against another man who sat on a bench, legs wide. The man on the ground bent his head, and the one above slid a long knife along the back of the neck, shaving off the hair, rinsing the knife in a calabash of water, shaving again. I was so tired that I could barely stand, but I remember thinking, *That man has a knife and he's not even using it. If he's got a knife and still can't run, what will become of me?*

Among all these Negroes was one toubab with a long jacket buttoned down the front. He had a sharp nose, a thin chin, and hair as straight as parchment. Sunlight reflected off the buttons on his long coat, and his breeches were made of a smooth, shiny material. With legs apart and feet planted wide, he looked like he owned the world. Beside him a straw-haired woman dipped a quill in an inkpot held by a Negro and began to write into a book. Left to right. Left to right.

The toubab chief had a Negro helper who was dressed better than the others of our colour and who stood with the aid of a cane. The Negro helper signalled to Fomba to bend down, and inspected his face and chest. With his cane he tapped Fomba's shins, ribs and back, and then he turned to me.

The helper peered into my eyes. He was issuing an order. I saw a single gap between his lower front teeth. I couldn't understand. The toubab came forward, ripped the cloth away from my waist and motioned with his hands. He wanted me to spread my legs. All the other Negroes were watching. I stood motionless. The signal came again, but I could not move. I could not submit to one more inspection. The toubab slapped me, and I fell. I stayed on my back, thinking that he would have to exert himself to bend over and keep striking me on the ground. The Negro

141

raised his cane. I drew my arms around me and closed my eyes. I heard a voice. It was the toubab barking an order. When no blow came, I opened my eyes and saw the cane drop slowly to the Negro's side. The toubab crouched low and I looked into his eyes. Blue. Moving up and down my body. Lingering. It wasn't the welt on my chest that drew his eyes. It was something else. I felt my own nakedness acutely in that moment, knowing that he was evaluating the buds on my chest. He said something else, and the Negro with the cane crouched down low as well. Now they were both yelling at me.

A woman's voice cut through the din. I saw a red scarf, a neck as dark as mine, a broad nose, a flash of teeth. The woman had a small cloth tucked into her clothes at the waist. I saw her rub her hands once on the cloth, and heard her sing abuse at the Negro with the cane. Her mouth let fly a thousand words. They flowed together like soup, and it didn't seem possible that anyone could understand her. The Negro and the toubab took a step back and the big woman scooped me up in her arms.

Up and down I bumped against the woman's biceps. I could hear the breath whistling out of her nostrils as she carried me, but she did not speak. At the far end of the clearing, we came to a series of homes with mud walls and thatched roofs. The woman manoeuvred her broad body through a doorway. Inside, two men were standing in a damp room, bent over and laughing and clapping hands. The woman put me down on my feet, but held me by the arm so I wouldn't fall. The men fell silent and motionless. It was as if they had never seen anything like me before.

The men backed out of the tent as if retreating from a miracle, and the woman led me to a bed of straw. She covered me with a blanket and brought a gourd of water to my lips. I took a sip. Her eyes were deep brown and hard to read. She didn't look like she would die anytime soon. I felt safe in her presence, and fell into a sleep more profound than any I had known for many moons.

Sometimes I was aware of the sound of the woman fussing with a collection of calabashes. Their hard leathery surfaces tapped each other musically, almost like toy drums, and made me dream of home. I knew vaguely that I was being propped up and made to drink. A warm, wet cloth moved across my face. One time I heard a bird singing in the pitch black of the night. For whom, I wondered, was it chirping? Maybe it was calling to me. A warm body slept beside me. I liked the smell of the woman and felt reassured by her snoring, the deep life inside her singing out.

When I emerged from my long sleep, I had a rough gown hanging from my shoulders. The woman who had been sheltering me in her bed took me by the hand to greet all the people living under the thatched roofs. The men stared at me in wonderment, sometimes touched my wrists and spoke words that I did not know. The women clasped my shoulders, hugged me, used their fingers to trace the moons on my face, laughed insanely and brought me calabashes of water, boiled cornmeal, sometimes meat. I sniffed the meat and turned away. Pork. The big-armed woman who slept with me snatched a chicken from a pen, held it by the feet, pointed to my mouth. Yes, I nodded, I would eat chicken. But no, I waved my finger, pointed at the big animal with the snout in the mud pen. Not that. Not pork.

Three men emerged from a hut, and I saw that one was Fomba. His eyes grew wide, and I ran to him. He felt sturdy and strong; he felt like he had been eating. He opened his mouth and tried to say my name, but no sound emerged.

"Fomba," I told the woman. "He is Fomba, from my village of Bayo."

She smiled. She didn't seem to worry or wonder about what I was saying. And I knew why. I knew exactly why.

She was a Negro, but she was not a homelander. She was from this place. This place was her home. It was not for her to understand me. It was for me to understand her. I could go nowhere and understand nothing until I could learn to speak with this woman. I knew that I would have to learn for myself, but also for Fomba.

When we got back to our own sleeping place, the woman sat me on a stump outside the door and spoke slowly to me. She gripped my hand in a palm twice the size of mine. She had broken nails, calloused fingers and skin creased like a dried riverbed. She tapped my hand, slid her finger along my rib cage and sat her palm on my shoulder. She dug a finger into her own breast, said "Georgia," and opened her hands toward me.

"Aminata," I told her.

Three times, Georgia made me repeat it, but the best she could do was to say "Meena." In this new land, I was an African. In this new land, I had a different name, given by someone who did not even know me. A new name for the second life of a girl who survived the great river crossing.

THE MOONS CAME AND WENT. The air was warming up, growing heavy. Mosquitoes hummed angrily, landing in my ears, stinging my calves and back and neck.

We had to work "albees albees albees," as Georgia said. "Albees," I came to see, meant until we had done our work, six days out of seven. There were hogs to feed and kill. There were hens to pester for eggs, soap to make from ashes and lye, and clothes to wash and mend. Robinson Appleby, the toubab chief, was away most of the time, and his woman rarely joined him on his visits to the plantation. When Appleby was gone, another toubab lived in the big house and watched over our work. *Overseer* was one of the first words I learned. But not more than a moon or two after Appleby had left, the overseer died and

144

Appleby returned. When he left a few days later, Mamed—
the Negro with the hitting cane—was in charge. Mamed
had two helpers. All of them had firesticks, clubs and
whips. Most of the time there was nobody on the
plantation but fifty Negroes, watched by a Negro overseer
and his two Negro assistants. There was not a toubab in
sight, but still nobody tried to escape the island.

Georgia took me everywhere she went, talking all the
time, naming every thing she did. She gathered long
grasses and wove them into baskets. When men brought
her possums, she skinned them. When others brought her
turtles, I watched her put them in soup. The shells came
off easily after she boiled them. Georgia was forever
gathering leaves, berries and roots. "Elderberry," she said
one day, examining a tall leafy plant with white, bunched
flowers. Back at her cooking pot, she brewed the leaves in
hot water and kept the liquid in a calabash. She stewed the
flowers in hog fat and stored that concoction in a ball-
shaped gourd with a thin neck. The gourd came from a
collection of calabashes of every size and shape that hung
from sticks and nails in the walls of her cabin. "Elderberry
flowers and lard," she said, over and over, until I could
repeat it. One day, she smeared this concoction on the
open sore festering on the foot of a man who came to her
home. He gave her a gourd of his own, filled with a strong-
smelling liquid. She drank a big gulp and opened her
mouth, as if exhaling fire. "Likker," she said.

I repeated every word that came from Georgia's mouth.
After one or two moons, I was accustomed to the way she
spoke. As it became possible for me to follow her speech,
and to talk to her, I came to see that she was teaching me
two languages. It was like Maninka and Bamanankan—
different languages, but related. One sounded a little like
the other. There was the language that Georgia spoke when
alone with the Negroes on the plantation, and she called
that Gullah. And there was the way she spoke to Robinson

Appleby or to other white people, and she called that English. "Bruddahtief de hog" was Gullah, and "brother done steal the hog" was the way to say it to the white man. "De hebby dry drought 'most racktify de cawn" was one way to speak, but I also had to learn to say "The long drought done spoil the corn." "De buckra gib we de gam; demse'f nyam de hin' quawtuh" was Georgia's normal way of speaking, but I also had to learn to say it another way: "The white people done give us the front quarter, they done eat the hindquarter themselves." *Buckra* was the Negroes' word for white people, but, Georgia warned, I was never to call a man "white."

"You call a white man white, he beat you black and blue."

"So what do I call him?" I asked.

I was to call the man who owned this farm "Master Apbee," Georgia said, explaining that when he spoke to me, he would say "Master Appleby." His wife was to be called "Missus," or "De Missus."

The lessons and instructions were never-ending. Appleby had the first name of Robinson, but I would surely be beaten for addressing a buckra by his first name. If I didn't know the last name, "Master" or "Missus" would do. I was never to look a buckra in the eye when he spoke to me, nor to act like I knew more than him. It was equally foolish to act stupid, Georgia said. The best approach was to follow the buckra's conversation like a well-trained dog. I was to do my utmost to keep away from Appleby, especially when I was alone. Finally, Georgia said, I was never to forget that the buckra did not know Gullah. They understood only their own way of speaking. I was never to teach a buckra a single word or expression that the Negroes used. And I was never to let on that I understood too much of the buckra's way of speaking.

Georgia was clearly pleased that I had learned to speak so quickly. She started taking me to other women and men

146

on the plantation, so she could boast about my progress.

"She done learn so fast," she said. "Zing zing zing. Words fly out her mouth like eagles."

I laughed. I did love to hear that woman talk. Every time she opened her mouth, she said something astounding. Something in her way of speaking made life tolerable.

"Honey chile," she said to me one day, "why don't Fomba speak?"

I said that he had lost his words on the big ship.

"He done crossed the river with you?"

"Yes."

Georgia nodded and put her hands on my shoulders. "You done cross the river, and your head is on fire. But grown man done cross the river and shut his mouth forever." Georgia seemed to be thinking about it, making sense of it all. She crossed her arms and put her hands in her armpits. "You all done cross one nasty shut-mouth river."

I didn't tell Georgia that Fomba had been the village *woloso*. I didn't want anybody to know. "He works good," I said. "Strong like an ox."

"I know," Georgia said. "Yesterday he done lift a hog off the ground and string him up in a red oak to bleed. Work for three men, but he done string the hog up lonesome."

I wanted Fomba to live. I worried about him being unable to speak. On this plantation, I learned that there were two classes of captives. There were "sensible Negroes," like me, who could speak the toubabu's language and understand orders. And there were the other ones. The insensible ones. The ones who couldn't speak at all to the white man, and who would never be given an easier job, or taught an interesting skill, or be given extra food or privileges.

I thought that if it were widely understood that Fomba could lift and string and bleed a hog by himself, perhaps he would be taken care of and left in peace. I understood enough about him to see that he became distraught when people confined him. But when he was free to throw quicklime in ponds to stun the fish and scoop them out, he did well enough. In those moments, he was capable and strong. I hoped desperately that he would stay that way. Around me I wanted only the strong.

ONE DAY WHEN THE MOSQUITOES were particularly hostile, Mamed interrupted my work at the washtubs with Georgia and told me to come with him.

"Ain't no call for pesterin' her," Georgia said. "She busy as a bird wit' nest."

Mamed pushed her aside and grabbed my wrist in an iron grip. It felt like the clamp of a leg iron on the slaving ship.

Georgia dropped her arms to her sides and called out, "You'll have to mess with me if you lay a hand on that girl."

Mamed headed behind the shacks, pulling me along. Something about his knee—the right one, on the same side that he kept his cane—didn't bend properly. But it didn't keep him from moving fast, and he certainly wasn't lacking in strength. His breeches were cut off at the knees, and the muscles in his lower legs slid and slithered like snakes. His silver hair was not curled as tightly as mine, and he had lighter skin than most people on the plantation.

When we were out of Georgia's sight, Mamed let go of my wrist and led the way through the woods. We came to a clearing. I saw a large thatched roof suspended on long poles, without walls or floor. The roof was just for shade, and under it were rectangular vats made of cypress. There were six of them, in two rows of three, and they stank of urine. In each row three vats were placed side by side, but each elevated at a slightly different height. Pipes ran from vat to vat.

Mamed handed me pine needles and a brush. He showed me how to climb into the vats, dip the brush in lye and water and scrub the wood. Then he watched to see if I followed his instructions. It was hard work, but I showed him that I learned fast and would do the job well. I had no wish to anger him.

At night, I asked Georgia why I was cleaning the vats.

"For indigo," Georgia said.

"Indigo," I repeated.

She said it had something to do with dye for buckra clothing. I couldn't understand what brushing an empty wooden vat had to do with clothes. She explained that while I was working with Mamed, she and the men were hauling stumps from a patch of land. "Snake-biting, bee-stinging, bug-crawling no-good dirty work," Georgia said.

Day after day, Mamed brought me back to clean. One day I looked up from scrubbing and saw Appleby walking toward me. Mamed shouted that I had missed a dirty spot on the vat, and he whacked me with his cane. I felt Appleby's eyes resting too long on my body and I was relieved to have the osnaburg cloth, no matter how rough, wrapped around me. Appleby soon left us, and my work continued with no more lessons from Mamed's cane.

When he was alone with me, overseeing my cleaning work, Mamed did not use the Negro language. He spoke in the buckra way. I wondered if it had something to do with the way he looked. He was much lighter than me, but darker than a buckra. I wondered about his parents, but dared not ask a word.

Eventually, Mamed began to leave me alone to scrub off the muddy stains. "Clean to here," he would say, marking a spot on a vat. When he came back, he would check to see if I had reached the target mark. To avoid beatings with the cane, I hurried to do the work quickly and kept myself company by imagining encouraging words from my father. What a difference a father would make. A father to speak to me in my own language, to show me how to avoid being hit with a cane or having my wrists pinched in a big man's hand, to show me how to be in this new land. I ached for someone who knew everything about me and knew exactly how to guide me. Inside my own head, I tried to hear the sound of my father's low and steady voice while his fingers lit gently on my arm. *This is what they want, Aminata, and this is how to survive. Chickens, for example. They don't bleed them in this country. You just lop off the head and rip out the guts. Avoid the pork, if you can, but don't worry about it too much. You are in a new land now. Do what it takes to stay alive. I am watching over you, Daughter. I use the stars for eyes, and I see you in this new land. You crossed the big river and you must keep on living.*

Mamed came back to check a few times a day, nodding grudgingly and occasionally bringing water or food. After seven days of work, the vats were finally cleaned to Mamed's satisfaction.

In our bed at night, Georgia told me she had heard Mamed saying that I did good work.

"Where is he from?" I asked.

"He is just a Negro," she said, "born here in the Carolina low-country."

I stopped for a moment, listening to how she said the word. She made it sound like "Ky-ly-na." While I was thinking about how she had stretched out each sound in the word, almost pausing as she went, Georgia whispered another detail.

"Mamed's mama pure African."

"She is?" I shouted.

"Hush up, chile."

I grabbed her wrist and whispered, "Mamed's mama is African?"

"Uh-huh."

"Where is she from?"

"Let go my hand, girl."

150

I released her wrist. "But where is she from?"

"African is African and that's all I know."

"Is his mama alive?"

"Dead and gone long ago."

"Did you know Mamed's mama?"

"Never done meet her, but that ain't all," Georgia said.

"What ain't all?"

"Mamed's daddy was a buckra. Had his own plantation on Coosaw Island."

"His daddy living?"

"Daddy just as dead as mama."

"But how come Mamed is a slave?"

"Overseer," Georgia said.

"Isn't he a slave too?"

"Uh-huh, but more uppity than you 'n' me."

"But his daddy was a buckra?"

"True as day," Georgia said.

"Then why is Mamed a slave?"

"Got a slave mama, then you is slave. Got a slave daddy, then you is slave. Any nigger in you at all, then you is slave as clear as day."

I was going to ask how Mamed came to our plantation, but Georgia already had the answer ready.

"When Mamed's mama done passed away, the buckra daddy done sell him to Master Apbee."

I fell silent for a while, but could not sleep. It seemed absurd that I should be scrubbing wooden vats, washing clothes and slitting the throats of chickens for a man who didn't even live with us. How did it come to be that he owned me, and all the others? I wondered if he owned me at all times, or only when I was working for him. Did he own me when I slept? When I dreamed?

Georgia was snoring hard, but I couldn't stop myself from tapping her arm.

"Hunh?" she said.

"What is a slave?"

"Don't wake me up with foolish questions."

"How exactly does that man own us?" I asked.

"In every way."

"And if we don't?"

"Don't what?"

"Don't work."

"If you don't work, you die," Georgia said. "Buckra man has things to grow and houses to build, and if you don't do his work, you die."

"Before we was done here. Before the Negroes. Before the Africans. Who did the work?"

"I was having myself a good dream," Georgia said. "Why are you messing my head with all this talk? Who, what, where. Gal, I am smacked down tired. I got tree stump pulling all through my bones."

I lay on my back and pressed my lips shut. Perhaps another time I could ask all these things. Now that I knew how to converse with her, my mind was spilling over with questions.

Georgia shifted away from me in the bed, stayed that way a moment, then let out a snort and turned back to face me. She slapped my hand teasingly. "In your land, do Africans yap all the time?"

"No more'n you," I said. "When you get going, you yap like a dog wit' tail caught fire."

Georgia laughed and got up to relieve herself in the bucket outside the door. When she came back to bed, she said, "Your African mouth is like a galloping horse. Slow down and steer, honey chile, or you will hit a tree. Now let me sleep before I beat you black and blue." She patted my back once, but then turned and was soon snoring again.

It took me some time to fall asleep, but I felt comforted by the sounds that she made and by the way her warmth swam across our bed.

*   *   *

ONE CHANGE OF THE MOON later, Mamed led a group of Negroes—including Georgia, Fomba and me—down to some farmland. While he watched, we planted seeds. It was just like back home. I would dig with my heel, drop a seed in the hole and cover up the hole with the toes of the other foot. I could see that Mamed was impressed with my ability. The men used long hoes, though, and could move much faster.

We sang with the people who worked near us, and Georgia often took the lead. While we dug soil, planted seeds, covered the holes and did it again, each of us working in our own row, Georgia would sing in a low, plaintive voice. I never knew where all of Georgia's songs came from. Sometimes she just sang them straight, and at other times she waited for us to respond at the end of each line. In those moments of singing together, we would slide into a rhythm of planting seeds with each response.

On our last day of planting, while we dug the hole, Georgia sang out a line: "*Had a big ole daddy but he done gone.*"

And we dropped down the seed and called back, "*Big ole daddy but he done gone.*"

Fomba, who was working in the row to my left, dropped his seed too, even though he didn't sing. We covered up our holes, stepped forward and paused for a moment. Then, as Georgia sang again, "*He pull ten stumps in da burnin' sun,*" we dug another hole. Down dropped our seeds, and with the others I called out, "*Ten stumps in da burnin' sun.*"

With the next line about to come from Georgia, I readied my foot to dig. She began to sing and I put my foot down on a snake. It slithered and hissed and coiled, tongue flickering. I screamed. Fomba flew to my side, sliced down with his hoe and severed the snake's head. Before I could say a word of thanks, he picked up the head with one hand and the quivering body with the other and tossed them away.

"Country fool," Georgia said, giving him a shove. She ran to where Fomba had thrown the snake and retrieved the body.

That night she skinned the snake and rubbed oil on the skin, kept oiling it for days. Eventually she dried off the oily skin and wrapped it in two rows around her Sunday washing hat—a wide-brimmed, straw-woven affair with a green and blue peacock feather jutting out at an angle.

"Snake or master, same ole thing," Georgia said. "Wear his clothes, it bring good luck."

It only took fifteen days for plants to start pushing up out of the sandy earth. Under Mamed's close watch, I used a bucket to water them, and they shot out of the ground. When they started showing thick leaves, Mamed assigned me to ten rows of plants each day. My task was to remove all grasshoppers. I was under the strictest orders not to damage the leaves, nor to disturb their faint layer of powder. I was merely to lift the bug off gently, squish it, drop it in a bucket and keep moving from plant to plant. Mamed watched over the leaves as if he knew them individually and couldn't bear the thought of sharing them with the insects. Ten rows a day, for days on end, I cleaned those plants as they grew higher.

MASTER APPLEBY'S BIG HOUSE was cleaned by a Negro woman who worked with a baby slung on her back in the African way. She lived with her baby in a mud home apart from the others and she didn't speak much to anybody. Not long after I had become comfortable in speaking Gullah, I went to join the woman while she was working in her own little garden.

"Evening, Cindy-Lou," I said.

She grunted and kept pulling weeds.

"Y'all hold your baby in the African way."

She grunted again, but offered no words.

"Fomba and I come from the same village," I said. "In Bayo, we wrap up our babies just like—"

"I's from dis here land and jes' now I is stakin' beans, so doan be telling me nothing 'bout Africa."

When we were in bed later that night, Georgia scolded me. "Doan be running your mouth on Africa," she said. "You walk by a nigger with shut-mouth lips, or you walk by a white man on a horse or on his arse, doan be carrying on about back home an' all. Ky-ly-na buckra beat the Africa clean out of you."

The next night, while Georgia was watching me eat and declaring that I now had "meat on my bones," Appleby came into our home. He was a tall man, clean shaven, and he wore tight-fitting pants and fine leather riding boots. I knew not to trust him, but wanted—from a safe distance—to learn more about him.

I tried to follow every word as Appleby spoke with Georgia. He said something about a woman having problems on another island.

"Work all night, no work tomorrow," Georgia said.

"Morning only," Appleby said.

Georgia wouldn't budge. When he gave in, she demanded that he bring her a mortar and pestle, "babe size," from Charles Town. Appleby agreed. Georgia gathered a cloth bag holding her potions, liquids and plants and then she grabbed my hand.

"Just you," Appleby told her.

"She go with me."

"Hurry, then."

Walking as quickly as Georgia could manage, we tried to match Appleby's long strides. Georgia breathed loud, like something was stopping up her nose. We came up to a plantation Negro named Happy Jack, who was waiting with two horses and a cart. Georgia and I climbed onto the back of the cart and bumped along until we came to a pier.

There, we were guided into a canoe—a hollowed-out cypress log with two others fastened beside it. Negroes from another plantation stood upright in the canoe and used poles to push Appleby, Georgia and me across the water. The whole time we were in that canoe, Georgia asked the oarsmen questions. She spoke very fast, and it was clear not only that Appleby didn't understand, but that he wasn't even listening. Where was old Joe? Georgia asked. And Quaco? And what had happened to Sally, after they took her away from St Helena Island? I could follow most of what the men in the canoe said to her. We arrived at another island, and were taken by horse and cart to a hut where a woman was crying out.

Before going in, Georgia spoke to the buckra man on this new plantation. "Master, give me pipe and tobacco," she said, "and two yards of red Charles Town cloth."

"You can have two pipes and tobacco and not a thing more," he said.

Georgia nodded, and the two of us entered the hut.

A woman was lying on a bed next to three burning candles. Georgia asked the new buckra man for cloth and three calabashes of warm water and shooed him and Appleby away. From her pouch, Georgia brought out a stopped gourd of oil.

"Sit by her head and talk," Georgia said.

While Georgia rubbed her right hand in oil, spread the woman's legs, and slid her fingers inside, I looked into the woman's eyes and asked her name. She didn't answer. "What your name?" I asked again. No response.

"She done ask your name," Georgia called out. Still no answer.

The woman looked scared. When I tried Bamanankan, the woman's eyes grew wide. When I tried Fulfulde, words rushed out of her.

Georgia nudged me with her elbow. "Good thing you're here, chile."

156

The woman's name was Falisha, and she said she had crossed the big river only a few moons ago. Falisha gripped my hand and arched her back.

"Take fast little breaths when it hurts," I said.

Georgia placed my hand on Falisha's womb. In one spot, and another, and another. She asked if I felt anything.

"Two babies," I said.

Georgia's mouth fell open. "How you know that?"

"I done tell you before. My mama done teach me to catch babies."

"Could use your mama right here," Georgia said. "This woman can die."

All through the night, Falisha rode through waves of pain. But between convulsions, she talked and talked as if she had not spoken to another soul for months. She said she had two children at home. She had been abducted with her husband, but he had died crossing the water. I didn't want to hear about that and didn't ask any questions, hoping that she would tire and be silent, but Falisha just kept on speaking. Her other children had seen three and five rain seasons. She had no idea where they were now, or who was caring for them. I felt relieved when she stopped talking and let out a long, low moan. It came from far back in her throat.

Falisha didn't wait for instructions. She pushed mightily of her own accord and, after several tries, out came the head. She pushed again and the shoulders and butt and little feet came out. Georgia wrapped the baby and had me hold it. It had a tiny, squished nose and a rooting mouth. I wondered how much time would pass before this tiny creature would understand that he was not free to live as he wanted.

Falisha was taking shallow breaths.

"A boy," I told her.

Falisha smiled faintly but she had no energy to speak.

"You have still another baby to come," I told her.

The first baby started to cry.

"Good, he is breathing," Falisha said. "I die now. You take my baby, Fula girl. I die now."

"Nobody dies," I said. "You have another baby inside you."

Falisha slept for a while. I held the baby tight against me until he settled to sleep.

"You all sure talk mumbo-jumbo," Georgia said.

"Fulfulde," I said.

"Foo-what?"

"Our language," I said. "Fulfulde."

Georgia shrugged. She lit a pipe and smoked tobacco.

I didn't want to wake the mother or the sleeping baby, but I had been wanting for days to ask Georgia a question. Whispering, I said, "I been wanting to find a man named Chekura."

Georgia looked at me intently. "You too young for a man."

"He ain't my man," I said. "We done cross the big water together. He is like a brother."

"Brother," she snorted. Seeing me stare so seriously, Georgia softened. "If he is in the low-country, the fishnet will pull him up."

"The fishnet," I repeated.

"We got our ways," Georgia said. "Niggers got mouths like rivers. Our words swim the rivers, all the way from Savannah to St Helena to Charles Town and farther up. I done hear of our words swimming all the way to Virginia and back. Our words swim farther than a man can walk. When we find someone, up he comes in the fishnet."

"He's not really a man," I said. "Just a boy, and his name is Chekura."

"If he nearby, I find him in the fishnet. Or maybe he find you."

Georgia used her thumb to stuff tobacco in her pipe. "You smoke?"

I shook my head. "Believers don't smoke."

"Believers?"

I pointed up. "Allah."

"What you talking about, girl?"

"God," I said.

"What God got to do wit it?" Georgia said.

"God say no smoke. Our book say no smoke."

"Don't be talking books. Buckra man not like that at all."

I was completely confused. I had seen the medicine man reading books by lamplight in his room on the ship.

"What God got to do wit it?" Georgia repeated.

"God say no tobacco," I said.

"Huh!" Georgia slapped her thighs. "Master Apbee got God, he smoke. Two niggers on our plantation talking all the time about Jesus this and Jesus that, and they smoke. Some of us got God and some of us don't, but ain't a nigger in Carolina don't love tobacco."

I didn't know how to tell Georgia that palm wine and tobacco were not allowed, but that kola nuts were fine. I hadn't even seen a kola nut since leaving my homeland. The Qur'an was just too complicated to explain.

The baby started crying. Georgia took him from me and squished his rooting mouth up against Falisha's nipple. The baby sucked furiously. "That'll get her going," Georgia said.

Sure enough, Falisha awoke and pushed again. The second baby came quickly then. A girl. Discoloured and motionless.

Georgia cut the cord and listened for the breathing that didn't come, the heart that didn't beat. Then she wrapped the baby completely.

"And the second one?" Falisha asked.

"She is dead," I said.

"A girl?" Falisha said.

"Yes."

"I always wanted a girl." Falisha stretched her hand across her eyebrows, covering her face, and she lay completely still.

I stroked her hair for a moment, but Falisha did not move or respond. I stood up to take some air outside. The stars were brilliant that night, and the cicadas were crying in endless song. If the sky was so perfect, why was the earth all wrong?

Georgia came out to get me. "We got to move. Buckra coming soon. The second baby is our secret. Nobody knows. Falisha had only the boy. You hear? You tell her too."

Georgia bundled up the dead child and put it under her clothes. We left the son on Falisha's breast.

By the time we arrived back at the Appleby plantation, light was creeping into the eastern skies. We paused at our door for a moment. When we were sure that all was still, Georgia took me deep into the woods to bury the dead twin. Afterwards, we returned quickly to our bed.

"I never seen someone from Africa learn so fast." Georgia stopped to touch my hair. "But watch out, girl. You know too much, someone kill you."

"I ain't killable," I said.

"You were sure 'nuf half-dead when I scooped you out the yard,"Georgia said, "but I sure is glad you living now."

THE WEATHER GREW WARMER and more humid. With the meat on my bones that made Georgia so proud, my womanly bleedings also returned. The heat reminded me of home, but the dampness weighed on me like a wet blanket. I saw the first of many rainstorms. Late in the afternoon, puffy clouds started darkening. Long before the day was done, the light suddenly changed as if evening had come instantly. Lightning cracked, the thunder grew louder and then the skies exploded. Georgia grabbed me away from the washtub.

"Lightning fry you up like bacon," she said, pulling me into her home and putting her arm around my shoulders. "Hope the roof gwine hold."

It wasn't just rain. It was like a thousand buckets of water pouring down at the same time. Two trees blew over. Lightning split another one. Our roof held, but another caved in. We heard the shouts of Negroes running from the destroyed house, seeking cover in another. After a short time, the onslaught ended as quickly as it had begun. The sky cleared, the clouds blew away and the coolness brought by the rain turned to steamy vapours in the sun.

Georgia took me along whenever she was asked to catch babies on the plantation or on neighbouring islands. About one out of three babies died in childbirth or soon after, and a number of the mothers died too. I loved being with Georgia, but despised having to face sickness and death. Georgia didn't want to leave me alone on the plantation—she said I wasn't safe without her by my side—but I pleaded to be allowed to stay when she knew ahead of time that an expecting mother was already ill.

It wasn't just mothers and babies who died. Lots of others died, including buckra and adult Negroes. They died of fevers, with their bones on fire. Georgia told me that the buckra feared the vapours in the low-country swamps. In the hottest half of the year, which Georgia called "sick season," Appleby stayed away almost entirely.

Georgia was known all through the low-country islands for baby catching and doctressing. Every time buckra or Negro overseers from other plantations came asking for her services, she insisted on some form of payment. The one thing she craved—more than rum, tobacco or bright-coloured cloth—was Peruvian bark. Appleby or other plantation owners had to bring it to her from the Charles Town market, and they complained of its great cost.

Sometimes Georgia had to trade as much as ten baby catchings for one pouch of the bark. When she got it, she dried it, ground some of it in her handsized mortar and pestle, didn't allow a grain of the dust to be lost and kept it in a leather pouch, hanging from a wooden beam overhead in her home. Other bits of it, she chewed. She offered some to me, but it was too bitter for my liking. Apart from me and Happy Jack, whom she occasionally took into her bed, Georgia defied any Negro to enter her home. She didn't want anybody messing with her powders and roots, especially the Peruvian bark, which she said was the best treatment for fever.

Georgia kept pouches in various shades of blue. She made me remember every detail. In the blueblack pouch went thyme, for speeding delivery and bringing away the afterbirth. In the deep-water-blue pouch went jimsonweed, which she kept as a secret weapon to bring on madness. She gathered pine-needle clusters in a sky-blue pouch and used them to make tea for stuffy noses. In a light blue bag went sweet fennel and anise seeds, for windy disorders.

"What's this?" Georgia would say, testing me.

"Plantain and horehound mixture, for snakebites," I said.

"Good. And this?"

"Pennyroyal, for insects."

"Don't tell no buckra about how fast your head work, girl," she said. "They take you straight to the river and drown you."

Not long after we planted the indigo, Georgia announced that she was going to make me very sick, but only to ensure that I wouldn't die later. She said we needed time, and that this was the good time to do it. There was sickness going around the country, she said. In Charles Town. In the low-country. In crowded areas. The sickness came and went, she said, and when it came it took many lives. Georgia said she had learned from an old low-country woman how to prevent the pox.

"I fix you up so it don't kill you," she said.

I told her that I didn't want a knife touching any part of my body.

"Just a little piece of your arm," she said.

Still I refused.

"Look here," she said, baring her shoulders and back. I saw numerous pockmarks. "That's all you get. Some of these marks. I make you sick so that you don't die."

"When?"

"Now. You got time to get better before indigo harvest."

"But Mamed will beat me if I don't work," I said.

"Mamed knows. Years back, I done fix him up against the pox."

I started to cry. She grabbed my jaw.

"Stop that now. I fix you up like you my own family."

Using a sharp knife, Georgia made a cut in my forearm. I was expecting the worst pain imaginable, but it was a quick cut, only an inch long and not too deep. Into the cut, she pushed a bit of thread that she said had come from another man that she had made sick in the very same way. She closed up the cut and placed elderberry lard over it.

"Is that it?" I asked.

"For now," she said.

"No more cutting?"

"No more cutting. But sickness comes soon."

"When?"

"'Bout seven days."

Georgia made me stay put in her little home. I could not go out. I had to eat inside, and use the waste bucket inside. I nearly went out of my mind with boredom. I was feeling fine, and there was nothing to do. I argued with her about sitting all day in the dark, damp hut, but she insisted. Then the fever came. My bones

163

and back felt like they were splitting. It subsided quickly.

"Now can I go?" I asked.

"You not done yet," Georgia said.

The fever came back. I had a headache so bad that I had to lie down and cover my eyes against the light. When I leaned over the bed to vomit, I saw one of my teeth fall into the pail. Within a day, sores began to fester in my mouth and nose.

"It will smell so bad that you hate yourself," Georgia said, "but don't worry. It will pass. The smell will go away. Don't you pay it no mind."

Sores started breaking out on my body. The ones on the soles of my feet stung the most. They gave off such a stench that I was ashamed to be near Georgia. I couldn't bear the smell of myself.

"I knows the smell. I am used to it. You got good sores," she said.

"What do you mean, 'good'?" I asked. My voice was barely a whisper. I could not get out of bed. I wanted to die.

"The sores are apart. One here. One there. Not together. Not touching. And you only have ten of them. Ten is good."

I remained sick for nearly half a cycle of the moon. The blisters turned to scabs. I promised myself that if I ever got better, I would never complain—not even to myself— about having to work hard in the sun, or having to work for the buckra. My strength began to return, and eventually turning in the bed became less painful. Then I was sitting again, moving around the cabin and able to eat a bit of dinner. When the last scab fell off, Georgia said I was better.

"Go out and get some respiration," she said. "You be working again soon enough."

She checked me over and over that summer. "You got off easy. Just a few pockmarks and none on your face."

I said I was relieved about that.

"Pockmarks on your face a good thing, chile."

"Why?"

"You need something to ugly you up. You're like a flower now, and that ain't good."

GEORGIA WAS RIGHT. I was well in time for the indigo harvest. The night before it began, Georgia and I lugged buckets from a storehouse and set them outside the other Negroes' doors.

"What is that for?" I asked.

"Piss," Georgia said.

That night, all fifty slaves on Appleby's plantation stood or squatted over the buckets to urinate. And the next morning, Georgia and I hauled each stinking one down to the vats that I had scrubbed so carefully in the spring. By the time we were finished hauling, Mamed and all the others were assembled. Mamed gave orders, but everyone but Fomba and I knew exactly what to do. Mamed set Fomba to chopping down the indigo plants close to the ground. Fomba couldn't follow the instructions. Mamed pulled him to the side, put another man in his place, and then told me to bundle the indigo stems and leaves in my arms and put them in the vats.

"Not so fast," Georgia said, panting to keep up with me. on the outskirts of our busy group, I saw Appleby. He had been gone for a few months, and I had stopped thinking about him.

"Master Apbee watching," I whispered, "and Mamed said hurry."

"Not that much. It too hot. You got to last all day. You got to do this nice and easy."

The indigo scratched my arms badly. I was in a hurry to get it away from my skin, so I dumped it quickly into a vat. Mamed's cane crashed across my leg. I was furious that

165

Mamed had hit me again, especially after I had worked so hard to clean the vats earlier in the spring. In that moment, I wasn't afraid of him. I was only angry.

Mamed grabbed my arm. "Smooth walking," he said. "Hurry, but don't run. The indigo is like a sleeping baby. Walk smooth, so it doesn't wake."

I tried to shake loose of his grip, but he held on to me.

"Look," he said, pointing to the leaves in Georgia's arms. "See that fine powder?" I saw the trace of dust on the leaves. "You shake the leaves, the dust falls off. We work for the dust. The dust is what we want. Smooth walking. Gentle with the plants."

I looked fiercely at Mamed, but then I noticed Appleby watching carefully. The flies and mosquitoes buzzed around us, getting into my ears and hair. Two Negroes used the cedar boughs to fan Appleby, and four more fanned the vats to keep the insects from landing.

"Gentle," I repeated. "Gentle."

Mamed let go of my arm and I slid back into the flow of work, moving as he'd told me. An hour later, Appleby pulled me aside.

"You. Meena."

I was surprised that he knew my name. I gazed down at my feet, as Georgia had taught me.

"You sensible nigger?"

"Yessir."

"You learn fast," he said.

"Just sensible, Master Apbee."

"How old are you?"

"Twelve years," I said.

"What can you do?"

Georgia had prepared me for this question. "Make soap and slop hogs," I said.

"Is that all?"

"No, sir."

"What else can you do?"

I saw Georgia watching. "Hoe fields," I said. "Clean vats, catch babies."

"How you learn that?"

"Done learn it from Georgia," I told Appleby.

"Girl, what are these marks on your neck?"

"Dunno, Master."

"Girl, you had the pox?"

"Dunno, Master."

"Keep working and listen to Georgia," he said.

"Yes, Master."

Appleby turned away from me and back to Mamed. "She'll turn out fine next season," he said, and left for the big house.

Returning to work, I helped let the stinking liquid run into the second set of vats, to which were attached long, forked poles. At the end of each pole was a bucket with the bottom cut out. Georgia showed me how to use the pole to stir the liquid. I had to stir violently and consistently. I stirred one vat, and right next to me Georgia stirred another. My arms burned with fatigue, but Georgia stirred on and on. When I had to rest, Georgia stirred her vat with one hand and my vat with the other. I slapped at the mosquitoes and resumed stirring. Eventually the liquid in the second set of vats began to foam. Mamed added oil from a separate leather bucket. When blue mud formed at the bottom of the vats, the water was drawn off into a third set of vats.

"This here is what we want," Georgia said, pointing to the mud in the second vat.

While the mud dried, Georgia and I waved the cedar boughs to keep the flies away. Mamed and the men scooped the mud into heavy sacks and hung them up so the liquid could drip out. Then we used wide, flat paddles to spread out the mud in a drying shed. It was hard to keep from choking on the stink when we formed the mud into cakes and loaded it into wooden casks.

We worked from darkness in the morning until darkness at night. In the yard outside our home, Georgia and I kept a fire burning under a huge cauldron of water. Before we went to bed, no matter how late it was and no matter how much our arms ached, we scooped out buckets of water, carried them off to the woods, and washed ourselves clean under the stars.

"What they do with all that mud?" I asked.

"Turns the white man's clothes blue," Georgia said.

"That mud is for their clothes?"

"Last time he came by, Master Apbee was wearing a blue shirt. Ain't you seen it?"

I told her I didn't remember.

"Fifty niggers pull piss out of mud for Master Apbee's shirt," she said. Georgia grumbled about all the hard work during the harvest, but she too was drawn to the indigo. Because Georgia tended to Mamed's sores and cuts, he let her take small quantities of indigo leaves and one or two pouches of mud. Georgia could make a paste from the leaves to ease the hemorrhoids that women developed while straining to push out their babies, but she also used the mud for her own experiments.

"Here I is, a grown woman messing with mud," she said, snorting and laughing.

I sat on my haunches and watched as Georgia stirred water into indigo mud in a big gourd. "Can't say why I like it so. When I was just knee high, I had a blind dog. He was a pretty dog, never bit a soul, and stone blind. Couldn't see a thing. But I didn't know any more than that dog. Stick in the mud was all I saw. I just loved to poke that stick in the mud."

Georgia left some cloth to soak in the gourd. By the next morning, the cloth had turned a light shade of blue. When she pulled it from the gourd and held it up in the sun, the cloth looked like it had been cut out of the sky. While we worked, she set the cloth back in the liquid. When she

168

stretched it out again it was darker, more purple, like my favourite flower in the woods—blue-eyed grass. Georgia shook her head and dunked it again. This time it turned the colour of a night sky with a full moon glowing.

"There," Georgia said, and set it by the fire.

When Georgia's hair was finally covered by the dried, dyed cloth, I paused to admire the shade of indigo above the wrinkles by her eyes and the corners of her mouth. It seemed that both the scarf and the face had soaked up the wisdom and the beauty of the world.

For weeks we harvested and processed indigo. On the last day of our work, I dropped a sack of indigo mud. It fell onto the ground and was completely spoiled. Mamed grabbed my arm fiercely, his fingers pushing into my tired muscle.

"*Allahu Akbar,*" I cried out without thinking. I feared Mamed would beat me for uttering a trace of the forbidden prayer, but he released my arm and stepped away. "*Allahu Akbar,*" he murmured so that only I could hear.

He motioned for me to follow him to the edge of the woods.

"How did you learn those words?" he whispered.

"From my father."

"He spoke Arabic?"

"In prayer." I watched his cane, which was still by his side. "Are you going to beat me again?"

"For what?"

"For saying the words. For saying I had a father."

"No. I am not going to beat you."

The tiny reassurance allowed the anger to come flooding out of me. "Stop grabbing me. It hurts. You leave marks on my arms."

"The hard work ends today," he said. "The harvest is over. This evening, after you have eaten, come see me."

I could not forget the sensation of Mamed's fingers digging into my skin. Perhaps, however, there was something to learn from the man who spoke the same words as my father. Georgia was teaching me how to survive in the land of the buckra, but maybe Mamed could teach me how to get out.

Mamed lived in the last of the slave huts. It was located at one of the far ends of our horseshoe-shaped arrangement of homes. Twice as big as the others, Mamed's home had thick walls made out of lime, sand and oyster shells. Although Georgia and I had a mud floor, Mamed built his wooden floor off the ground. We had a door but no window, but he had both. Our space was just big enough for a bed and a stool and room to "get out the door," as Georgia liked to say, but Mamed had room for two stools, a fireplace with a chimney, a little table and a shelf lined with books.

It was pitch dark outside, but Mamed had a candle burning. His bed was made with wood, raised well off the ground and covered with straw and cloth. He had extra blankets.

I looked around the cabin and inched closer to the door.

"I brought you here to talk," he said, speaking in the style of Appleby. "Shall I teach you to speak like the buckra?"

"I dunno."

"I could teach you. Do you understand it?"

"Some."

"You are afraid I will hurt you," he said.

I held my words. When Master Appleby looked at me, his eyes roamed all over my body. Mamed was staring at me, but straight into my eyes, as if he sought to evaluate and understand me. Mamed scooped up a stool and brought it over to me.

"Sit," he said.

The seat, worn smooth, had been polished with oil. It rested on four solid legs, connected by crossbars fitting into grooves in the wood. It was simple, elegant, and made me think of home.

"Where did this come from?" I asked.

"I made it."

"How?"

"From a cypress log."

"It's beautiful."

"When you have time, you can make things of beauty. Even here, in the land of the buckra."

"Is this your land?"

"Do you mean, am I an African or a Negro?"

I nodded. Mamed patted the stool and waited while I lowered myself slowly onto it. His father had been a buckra plantation owner from Coosaw Island, and his mother the daughter of a Fula chief, he said. Mamed's mother had learned to read from her master. He had promised to free her, and Mamed too, one day. She remembered a few prayers from her homeland, and taught them to Mamed along with every single thing that the buckra taught her.

I liked hearing his story and I liked his melodious voice. He had nicks and cuts all over his arms, but now he didn't seem like an overseer with a raised cane. He seemed like a different man—like a man who was willing to teach.

If Papa had lived and crossed the river with me, he would have been encouraging me to learn. But I dared not ask Mamed the thing I wanted. If he knew so much, I wondered, why was he still on Appleby's plantation? He saw the question in my eyes.

"A horse fell on my leg when I was young, made me lame, and now I am also too old to run," Mamed said.

"Where do Negroes run?" I asked.

Mamed studied me carefully, locking his fingers together. He said they hid among the Indians or they went south to live with the Spanish. But he didn't want to hide with the Indians or live in Fort Musa with the Spanish. He liked sleeping in the same bed every night and having a garden to tend.

"You accept your life this way?" I said.

Mamed coughed uncomfortably. "I stay here and live well. This is the best that I can do. Nobody knows the indigo work better than me—and Master Appleby knows it."

Mamed said he had made a deal with Appleby. If Mamed managed the plantation and kept producing good indigo mud, he could eat what he wanted, organize his home the way he wanted, and get extra supplies from Charles Town as well as books every year from Appleby. But he was to keep his home locked, and not to show the books to any person or to teach any Negro how to read.

I nodded again.

"I was not planning to teach reading to anyone. But I have seen the brightness of your eyes."

So much had been taken from me that was mine by rights—my mother, my father, my land, my freedom. And now I was being offered something I might never have received. I was afraid to reach out and take it, but even more afraid to let it go.

"I have wanted to read forever," I said. "Since before I crossed the big river."

"The buckra do not call it a river. They call it a sea. Or an ocean. They call it the Atlantic Ocean."

"The Atlantic Ocean," I repeated.

"You mustn't tell anybody about the things I teach," Mamed said.

"I promise."

"No one must know," he insisted.

I met his eyes and calmly nodded.

Our first lesson began with the pronunciation and spelling of my name. Mamed was the only person in South Carolina who ever asked for my whole name. He spoke it properly, and then he taught me how to write it. But on the plantation he would always call me Meena.

* * *

172

GEORGIA WAS WAITING when I climbed into bed.

"Did that man mess with you?" she said.

"No."

"What he want?"

"Just talk."

"Menfolk don't just talk."

"Just talk was all."

Georgia let a moment pass. "When you were 'just talking,' Miss Meena, someone came for you."

"Came for me?" I jumped out of bed. Already in this day, the impossible had become possible. "Someone came to take me home?"

"Sit down, girl," Georgia said. "It was just a boy. Size of a little man, but he nothing but a boy."

I climbed back into bed. "What boy?" I asked, quietly.

"He asked for you in that African name. He is called something just as funny. Something like—"

"Chekura?"

"That's it. That's his name."

I jumped up again, shrieking.

"Shush up, girl, before you wake the dead or someone worse."

I lowered my voice but I wouldn't let go of Georgia's hand. "How did he look?"

"Like a layabout. A wastrel. I don't like the look in his eyes. Too African. That's what you made me drag up in the fishnet?"

My excitement gave way to an ache. I felt crushed to have missed him.

"He be back, honey chile. He just over on Lady's Island. Not far at all. He come for you again, just like a hungry dog."

WE WENT THROUGH A SECOND CYCLE of indigo harvesting. The work was just as hard, but when our daily tasks were done

173

we were free to cook, garden or mend clothes, and left alone without any buckra to disturb our days. Sometimes, when nobody was looking, I would climb high up a tree in the woods and practise reading the words that Mamed had written out for me. Once I could manage "cat," "dog," "lion," "water," "father" and the like, I moved on quickly to new challenges. Mamed knew how to keep my interest. He said he was doing it as his mother had done for him. One day it was "The dog ate the cat." Then it was: "The cat ran from the barking dog." And then it was: "The barking dog chased the cat up the tree and the birds flew out of the nest." The language came together like pieces of a secret, and I wanted more of it every day.

When the reading lessons were done, sometimes Mamed would explain how things worked on Appleby's plantation, and at other times he asked me questions.

Fomba had not uttered a sound since he came to St Helena Island. His inability to follow instructions during the indigo harvest infuriated Mamed, who asked me about him one night.

"What did he do in your village?"

"Hunted, and we ate whatever he killed."

"Good hunter?"

"The best," I said. "He could kill a rabbit with one throw of a stone."

Within a few days, Mamed had arranged for an experienced Negro to help Fomba build a canoe out of bamboo. They bound it tight with water reeds and cut down a long sapling to use as a pole. They also fashioned a paddle out of cypress wood. Fomba learned the ways of the boat just as if it were part of his body. Almost overnight, he was paddling or poling the boat along the waterways and creeks of the low-country islands, tossing down nets and pulling up shrimp, crabs and fish. Mamed released Fomba from all indigo jobs on the understanding that he would return every afternoon with whatever fish he had netted. Fomba did even better than that. He brought back squirrels, possums, wild turkeys and turtle eggs for Mamed and the rest of us. Everybody so enjoyed his additions to the cooking pots that they began to accept that Fomba would make himself useful if he was left to work alone.

GEORGIA COMPLAINED ABOUT MY STUDYING but she liked having the cabin to herself in the evenings. When I walked toward Mamed's place, I would often pass Happy Jack as he walked to our cabin to see Georgia. He was the only man I knew who could walk, whistle and whittle a stick at the same time. He often brought her flowers picked from the woods, which he kept bunched up behind his ear to keep his hands free for the whittling.

One night when I returned from studying, Georgia had news for me. "Happy Jack and I were rolling and heaving and hot and bothering, having ourselves a right good time, and in walks that big-mouthed African. Happy Jack jumps up and runs out. There goes my man. And I am left looking at this meatless African. He keeps saying your name. I could have slapped that boy three days into next week."

"Where did he go?"

"I don't know, but I hope it's far away. The way that boy run his mouth—"

I raced into the woods behind our cabin and called his name. He was hiding behind a grove of trees. I flew into his arms. I hugged that boy until I felt him growing hard against me. I pulled back suddenly. The words came spilling out of me in Fulfulde. I had to know where he was living and where he had been and what he had seen and I wanted to know it all, at once.

Georgia came up to us from behind and said she would be back at sunrise. No, Chekura said, not sunrise. I was struck to see that he did not speak the Negro English nearly as well as I. Georgia didn't care to stand around listening to translations, so I quickly explained that he had to be back where he belonged before sunrise. She shrugged and went off to find Happy Jack.

Chekura let his eyes fall over me, and I stood proud before him. I learned that the buckra who ran the plantation on Lady's Island was gone for the sick season, so Chekura was free to wander at night. During this season, Chekura said, dozens of Negroes could be found at night, roaming and boating, trading poultry for rice, vegetables for gourds, rabbits for rum, exchanging news of brothers and sisters and wives and children, sinking the fishnet and pulling it back up. Chekura had found Africans all over the low-country islands: there were two Fulbe on Edisto, a Bamana on Coosaw, and three Eboes on Morgan.

Chekura said he could not believe how quickly I had learned the Negro language. I whispered proudly that I was secretly learning to read.

"I have something for you," he said. He pulled a cloth from his sleeve, folded it in a square and presented it to me as if it were a traditional gift of kola nuts in our homeland.

It was a red-striped handkerchief. I clutched it, smelled it, rubbed it on my face and then tied it up around my hair.

"You look beautiful in it," he said.

I held his arm again. I wanted to feel him next to me and I craved finding him next to me when I woke up there in the morning. I tried to think of how to tell him that I wasn't ready for the thing he wanted, but he saw my hesitation and saved me from having to speak. He had to leave, he said, so he could slip back onto his plantation before his absence was noticed.

* * *

CHEKURA WAS ONLY ABLE TO COME see me once a month or so. I longed for his face, and his voice, and the very smell of him that reminded me of home. It excited me to think that he knew me, and knew of my past, before this life in Carolina. We held each other longer each time he came to visit. Something stirred deep down in my belly and between my legs. But I didn't trust those feelings. I wanted to hold on to his voice and the sounds of my village in them. He seemed prepared to talk just as much as I needed. He did not press the other matter.

THE MOONS CAME AND WENT, and in the colder season when there was no indigo to plant or harvest, Appleby was frequently with us. He returned to the plantation around the time I had spent a full year on St Helena Island, and opened up his big house. Several of the Negroes had to work night and day to get his house back in order, and to start cooking up meals for him and his wife. She only stayed for a while, then he took her back to Charles Town and returned alone.

One morning in the cold season, Appleby came to our home.

"Georgia. Get a move on. I've got a man waiting to take you to catch a baby on Lady's Island."

Georgia swept up her bag with one hand and grabbed my arm with the other.

"No," Appleby said to her. "This time it's just you."

I gave Georgia a pleading look.

"She goes with me," Georgia said.

"Enough backtalk," Appleby said. "You've got to go now."

AFTER GEORGIA WAS GONE, Appleby led me into the big house. I wanted to look at all the strange objects inside, to touch the books and to smell the foods cooking in the kitchen. But I had no time. And I knew that it would not be allowed. Still, I hoped any little distraction might give me a chance to think of a way to escape. The cook gave me a long look and left. A man who cleaned the floors of the big house watched me too for a moment, and left.

"Think I'm stupid?" Appleby asked.

"Master?" I said.

Appleby pushed me down a hall and into a room, ripped off my wrapper, tore my red-striped handkerchief in half and flung me onto a bed.

"Who's that boy sniffing after you?"

"No boy, Master."

He slapped me. "He ain't one of mine. Who is that boy?"

"No boy, Master."

He clamped one hand on my mouth, pinned me down with his chest and began unbuttoning his trousers with his other hand. His skin pressed down on mine. I could feel his wet skin, sweating. And he stank.

"Who owns you?" he said.

"Master."

"I say who owns you?"

The wiry hairs on his chest scratched my breasts. The stubble on his cheeks bit into my face.

"Master, please don't—"

"Don't you tell me what to do," he said.

I gasped and pushed but could not get out from under his weight. I thought about biting his shoulder, or a finger, but then he might hurt me even more. Should I lie still, like I was dead, and wait for it to be over? I tried to keep my thighs together, but he yanked them apart with his hands. He owned my labour, but now he was bursting to own all of me.

If only I had had Georgia's birthing oil, it wouldn't have hurt so much. But there was no oil, and the pain was terrible as he plunged deep inside my body where nobody belonged but me. I could not shove his heaving body off me, so I lay as still as I could. I just wanted to live through this, and have it end. Live through it, and have it end. His breath quickened, he gave out a wild squeal and he was finished. When he slid out of me, I felt like everything inside me was draining out.

"African whore,"Appleby said, panting. He stood, pulled up his breeches and disappeared out the door.

My blood was all over the bed. Underneath me, it kept on running. Still I couldn't move, trapped in my own pain and shame.

A figure stood at the door. It was Happy Jack, wearing a cook's white bib. He had a slice of orange in his hand. He stepped forward and stuck the orange in my mouth.

"Take some of the sweetness, chile," he said, trying to get his hands under me.

I began to choke on the orange, so he opened my mouth, pulled it out and tossed it away. He picked me up like a father would lift his own child and carried me outside. I didn't know if I would get there alive, but I knew I was going to Georgia's bed. It was a long walk, and up and down I rose and fell in his arms while Happy Jack took his long, fast strides. The panting of the cook and the wailing of women were the last things I heard.

Milk for the longest nursing

AFTER APPLEBY'S ATTACK, Georgia had me drink a hot potion of tansy and ground-up cedar berries. It gave me awful stomach cramps and made me bleed between the legs.

"Master's filth run out of you," Georgia said, and I was thankful.

I worried about what to tell Chekura, but Georgia advised silence.

"Menfolk don't have to know everything," she said, "and some things they don't need to know at all."

After Georgia healed me, two things helped me avoid more troubles with Appleby: I never left Georgia's side when the master was around, and Appleby bought a new Negro woman named Sally. I was relieved to escape his attentions, but it weighed on me that he had turned to another woman. Just a few years older than me, Sally had a kind face, wide hips and full breasts. She was weak, however, and had trouble keeping up with the others during the indigo planting and harvest. Appleby had his way many times with Sally and might have kept on going, but she and eight others on the plantation died suddenly of the pox. It had taken another woman to save me from Appleby, and only the pox had saved her.

Two years came and went, and it became clear to me

that the Negroes who remained on the Appleby plantation either died there of old age or succumbed much sooner to breathing ailments, fever or the pox. I sought to find a way off the indigo plantation and to discover the route back to my homeland. But there was no quick path to the things that I wanted. Every day, I thought of my parents and imagined them telling me to soak up learning and to use my skills. Robinson Appleby owned my body. For him, I toiled in the stink of the indigo mud under the burning sun and the biting mosquitoes. But it was for my father that I learned as much as Mamed about the preparation of indigo mud, and it was for my mother that I became Georgia's steady helper, catching babies in all the low-country islands.

I knew that I had to understand the buckra to survive among them, so I devoured Mamed's lessons. Soon I could read as well as he, and there wasn't much left for him to teach. It came as a disappointment to learn that Mamed had no idea about how a person could get to Africa. He could only say that he had never heard of a slave returning to Africa, or even trying to get there. None of his books addressed the question, but I read and reread them whenever I was free. The safest place to read was in Mamed's cabin. He never objected to having me there. On the contrary, he protested when I let more than a few days pass without coming by at night to light a candle, sit on one of his cypress stools and keep reading.

The chief advantage of the Bible was its length. Its wonderful stories were endless, and the tales about Abraham and Moses reminded me of accounts Papa had described from the Qur'an. After reading the *Planter's Medicine Guide*, I made the mistake of telling Georgia that the book recommended bleeding as a cure for all sorts of ailments. She said I'd best avoid reading if I knew what was good for me. *The buckra man is plum crazy, gal. Imagine. Letting blood run from a sick man.* Mamed also gave me an almanac by a man who called himself Poor Richard. This writer knew all about securing houses from mischief by thunder and lightning, but nothing about how to get from Carolina to Africa.

Reading felt like a daytime dream in a secret land. Nobody but I knew how to get there, and nobody but I owned that place. Books were all about the ways of the buckra, but soon I felt that I could not do without them. And I lived in hope that one day I would find a book that answered my questions. *Where was Africa, exactly, and how did you get there?* Sometimes I felt ashamed to have no answer. How could I come from a place, but not know where it was?

We were in the middle of the indigo cutting season. Early in the morning, while Georgia was still sleeping, I would run out and throw up in the woods. But not long after this began, Georgia put her hand on my arm while we walked to the fields.

"What you going to do when Master Apbee finds out?"

"About what?" I said.

"About the little one making you sick every morning."

I had been meaning to tell Georgia, but I had wanted to let the secret swell inside me a little longer. I was bursting with pride and purpose. My own baby, by my own man! This was the baby I would keep and love. This baby had come not from a buckra but from a man of my own choosing: an African who knew where I came from and spoke my language and came every month to see me. I had come to depend on Chekura's visits, timed consistently with the full moon and almost entirely reliable during the sick season when it was easier to travel unnoticed at night. We rarely spoke about the journey overland or across the water, but comforted each other with stories in Fulfulde about our early childhoods, and with observations—often in Gullah—of our new world in Carolina. While we talked and laughed and brought our foreheads together to rest one against the other, Chekura rubbed my toes and my soles and the tops of my feet with oil he had coaxed from Georgia, but at first he demanded nothing of me. With the passing moons, his hands travelled beyond my ankles and then past my knees. Finally desire awoke in me like water bursting from a dam. I brought his hungry lips to mine and took him deep inside my body. We had only devoured each other a few times before my bleedings stopped.

"I was going to tell you," I said to Georgia.

"Don't tell me things I already know," she said. "Just tell me what you're going to do with Master Apbee now that Sally's dead and gone."

I didn't know what to say.

"Don't tell him about Chekura," Georgia finally said.

"He already knows," I said.

"He don't know names. If you want that boy to stay alive, don't say his name. And one other thing."

"What?"

"When that baby comes, nurse it till your milk runs dry."

"Why?"

"If you are nursing, maybe Appleby won't take your baby."

"He would take a baby?"

"If you old enough to have a baby, you old enough to know that Master Apbee owns you from head to toe. And anything you make."

I fell silent. Georgia and I had caught two babies on the Appleby plantation, and they were still with their mothers.

"He wouldn't take a baby," I said.

"Child," Georgia said, "evil ain't got no roof." She glanced at my face and put her hand on my shoulder. "Just feed that baby and pray for milk," she said. "Lots and lots of milk. Let everybody see you nursing that baby. How many bleedings you missed?"

"Just two."

"You got a long ways to go, chile. A long ways yet."

LATE ONE AFTERNOON, while Georgia and I were stirring vats full of indigo leaves and manpiss, Robinson Appleby showed up with two visitors. Mamed barked at us to stir the vats faster.

One of Appleby's acquaintances was a well-dressed man who fanned himself to keep off the flies and looked like he wanted to get out of the hot sun. The other man leaned in to get a good look at what we were doing. He was tall, perhaps the age of my father, and he had a beard as dark as my own skin. I kept up beating the water, stems and leaves in the second vat, and when I turned to look, caught the man staring at me. Our eyes met and I promptly dropped my gaze. Was that a smile? I turned back to my work. From a buckra, a smile was a facial gesture I didn't trust. To me, it meant, *I know something you don't know*. I kept on beating the indigo.

"Do you know who this man is?" Appleby asked Mamed.

"No, sir."

"This here is Solomon Lindo," Appleby said. "He's the new indigo inspector for the entire Province of South Carolina."

The man named Solomon Lindo asked Mamed, "What do you have in there?"

"In this beater vat?" Mamed asked.

Solomon Lindo nodded.

"Lime," Mamed said, "urine and water."

"How many inches of sludge you reckon to find on the bottom of this beater vat?" Lindo asked.

"Three," Mamed said.

Solomon Lindo nudged me. I stopped working. "Look at me, please," he said.

Slowly, I turned my face up to him. Unlike Appleby, Lindo had dark eyes.

"And what are you doing?" he asked me.

"Beating this indigo so the air move through it."

"How long do you beat it?" The man spoke English in a way I hadn't heard before. He didn't sound like Appleby at all.

"Till the blue dust come up on the water."

"And then?"

"We stop beating and let the blueness settle down on the mud."

"Do you know what happens if you beat the liquid too long?"

"Dye come out wrong," I said.

Solomon Lindo turned back to Appleby. "You have good people," he said. The three men headed back up to the house.

That night, Georgia and two other women and I were made to help the cook put together a big pot of chicken gumbo. "No pork," Appleby had told us. "I can't give it to the Jew. The man has come all the way from London. Make him the best gumbo in Carolina, 'cause he's grading our indigo."

I wanted to know more about this man who avoided the same food as Muslims. We made enough food for ten Negroes, carrying plates and water and food and drinks, and Appleby and his guests ate most of it. Finally they sat slumped in their chairs in the sitting room, smoking cigars, and drinking coffee with whisky. Appleby sent all of the Negroes out of the big house but me. It was the first time in two years that I had been in his presence without Georgia or Mamed close by. I stood in the middle of the room while the three men looked at me.

"My prize Coromantee," Appleby said to the others. "Just three years here, and perfectly sensible. She helps the others cook. Makes soap. You've seen her handle indigo.

And the most amazing thing is that she doctors pregnant slave women. Got her for a steal in Charles Town. She was wasted away to nothing when she came off Sullivan's Island. I didn't think she'd survive. But look at her now. Could sell her for twenty times what I paid."

"And what would you sell her for?" Solomon Lindo asked, eyeing me quickly.

"No less than twenty pounds," Appleby said.

The third man put down his cigar and stepped up to me. He had a huge belly hanging over his belt, and a big red nose. "How old are you, Mary?" he said.

Buckra men called Negro women "Mary" when they didn't know their names, but I hated it. I kept my eyes down and my mouth shut.

"Girl," Appleby said to me, "this here is William King. He practically runs the slave trade in Charles Town. He asked you a question."

"Fifteen, I reckon," I said.

"You reckon that, do you?" King said.

"Yessir," I said.

"She looks more like eighteen to me," King said. "Any babies yet?"

He was talking to Appleby, so I said nothing.

Appleby suddenly put a drinking glass in my hand and said, "Have some Madeira."

"Don't give her that," Lindo said, taking the glass away. "You'll make her sick. Don't give wine to a child."

"More woman than child," Appleby said.

"She is not far from childhood," Lindo said, carefully.

"I'm the trader," King said. "You stick to indigo, and I'll tell you about nigger women." He turned to me again. "How did you learn about indigo?" he asked.

"Mamed taught me."

King eyed me suspiciously. "Say what?"

Taught. I realized my mistake. *Taught* was a buckra word. Mamed had warned me never to speak proper English to a

186

buckra. "Done teach me," I quickly said. "Mamed done teach me indigo."

Appleby took King off on a tour of the house, but Lindo stayed with me. He scratched his beard. His fingers were long and slender. They were not the fingers of a planter, or an overseer. Perhaps all indigo graders had smooth fingers with clean nails and soft skin.

Lindo wore a tiny cap on his head. It wasn't anything like the bandana that I liked to wear. It covered a small part of the back of his head. He caught me looking at it.

"Know what that is?" he said, touching his cap.

I shook my head.

"Want to know?" he asked.

I nodded.

"Curious girl?" he said.

I kept staring at him.

"It's a yarmulke. I'm a Jew. Know what that means?"

I didn't answer.

Solomon Lindo walked to a desk in the room, pulled out a quill and an inkpot and wrote a message on a piece of parchment. He showed it to me. It read: "Turn around. You will see your mother."

I spun around. Nothing. I turned back. He smiled, broadly.

"Little trick," he said, "but I won't tell anyone."

I stood frozen before him.

"Don't worry," he said again. "I could use a girl like you."

I heard loud conversation just outside the door. Appleby and King returned, drinking from leather flasks.

"So you are pure African," King said.

I nodded.

"Let me hear some African talk," he said.

In Bamanankan, I said that he looked like an evil man.

King laughed. "I don't understand any of that," he told the other men, "but I like to see if they can truly speak one of the languages."

Something burst out of me before I could contain it. "Where do I come from?" I asked.

King smiled at me. He seemed to think this was truly funny. "That's for you to tell us."

"Where is my land?"

"Going back, are you?" King said.

Appleby laughed again.

King stepped over to the desk, opened a drawer, unrolled a large piece of parchment and spread it out. He drew wavy lines and told me that was water. On one side of the lines, he drew a circle, and said that was Carolina. On the other side of the lines, he drew an odd shape, something like a mushroom with the left half of the cap overgrown, and said that was Africa.

He drew a dark circle on the mushroom. "She is from here," he said to the men, pointing to the upper left.

"Coromantee is the best kind of African," King said, "but, my good man Appleby, there weren't any Coromantees on the shipment you got. I can tell just by looking that she's not Coromantee. That's your very finest breed. Good symmetry and a proud bearing. Handsomer than most. So handsome you almost forget they're black."

"She's handsome," Appleby told King.

"No worries, she'll fetch you a fine price. Appleby, my boy, you want to run a class plantation, then get to know your people. Slaves from the Gold Coast or Gambia are best. After that, try picking strong males from the Windward Coast. Mandingoes—there you go, your girl here might be a Mandingo—are gentle but useless when tired. And they tire too damn fast. Then you got your Whydahs, who are cheerful to the point of lusty.

You want one or two of them around, but more and you've got too much dancing and frolicking. You can bet your life that a buck from the Congo will run straight to the Spanish, just as soon as he hears about Fort Musa. Don't buy from the Congo, and never buy a Callabar.

They are the worst. The worst, I tell you, the very worst."

"You can tell them all apart?" Appleby said.

"I didn't get rich by sleeping," King said. "Take my word for it. You end up with an Ibo from Callabar, and soon as you give the man a knife to slit a hog's throat, he'll slit his own, instead. An Ibo is so lazy he doesn't even want to live."

I was bursting with questions but couldn't ask any of them. Where were all these people from? How did King know all these tribes, and who they were? If he knew so much, how could he say Mandingoes tired fast, when I had seen them working all day with the mortar and pestle, throwing and lifting and throwing again for hours at a time to pound millet into flour, or shea nuts into butter?

"Lindo, come with me," Appleby said. "Let's talk about my indigo."

As the two men walked out and the door was shutting, I could see Lindo peering back at me, brows furrowed. I made a move to leave, but the other man blocked my way.

"Know who I am?" he said.

I shook my head.

"William King. I'm the richest trader in Charles Town."

I tried to step around him, but he wouldn't let me past. "You understand rich? Girl, you still sensible?"

I was worried that he might think I had somehow become insensible, and that he would beat me, so the words rushed. "Big house, many niggers, plenty indigo vats."

"Your man Appleby sticks to indigo. I grow rice, too. You think indigo is hard work?"

I nodded reluctantly.

"Indigo is nothing," he said. "Try rice. Some niggers drop dead in one season. Wet work. Wet and hot. Gators, too, swimming right up to where you work. Snap snap and down you go." William King spread his arms and clapped his hands together. I jumped back. "I like a sensible nigger," he said.

I wondered if the door behind him was locked.

"Lindo came to grade the indigo, but I just came out here to see his niggers. I sold you myself and wanted to see how you were working out. Just fine, I see. Only you're not Coromantee. I brought you over from Bance Island, and no Coromantees shipped from Bance that year. Step on over here."

He held out his hand, but I stayed put.

"What is Bance?" I said.

"Don't miss a thing, do you? Bance is where you were sold in Guinea."

The door was probably not locked, but it would be hard to get around this big man to reach it.

William King slid off his waistcoat and unbuttoned himself. I stepped back, and dodged him when he lunged, but he lunged again and pinned me against a wall.

"Stop wriggling, girl. I just want to see how you turned out." His breeches were down around his ankles. His bigness swung like a branch in the wind.

Behind King, the door rattled. I heard Lindo speaking to Appleby.

"Damnation," King muttered, scrambling to fix his breeches.

A MONTH OR SO LATER, Georgia heard talk through the fish-net. The Jew in Charles Town had offered to buy me, but Appleby had refused. I felt disappointed. Going away with Solomon Lindo had to be better than staying on Appleby's plantation. But Georgia said Appleby would never sell me.

"Why?" I asked, weakly.

"Because you are too good. Too valuable. Catching babies and making indigo mud, why would that man want to sell you now?"

190

* * *

MY BREASTS WERE GETTING FULLER. Soon enough, I would be showing. Appleby didn't let his Negroes marry. Some of them jumped the broom secretly, and others just lived together or visited at night. But I had no doubt what my parents would wish, and I told Chekura that I wanted to be married.

We chose the first full moon in August. The idea of our ceremony, no matter how humble, excited me. I wanted to bind my tiny family and keep us together. We wouldn't be able to have a marriage like in my homeland, with village elders and *djeli* to witness the event and describe it to the next generations. There were no elaborate negotiations between parents and villages, and there was no exchange of gifts to compensate my family for losing a daughter. But I insisted that Chekura give Georgia a big present— and he rustled up two chickens, two head scarves, one blue glass jar, a bottle of rum and a pouch of Peruvian bark.

"Where did that crazy boy get Peruvian bark?" she said, over and over again. From that day forward, Georgia decided that she loved Chekura.

The guests showed up with presents and food. Georgia and Fomba had lugged an iron pot out to the clearing ahead of time, and she had a rabbit stew simmering. Mamed brought me a candle and a beautiful stool made out of polished cypress wood. Fomba had whittled a little statue of a woman holding a baby. He had oiled and polished it for days, and seemed unbelievably happy to give it to me. Chekura gave me a comb, a jar of corn oil said to be good for working through kinky hair, a red and gold headscarf, and a beautiful blue wrapper made of soft, smooth cotton—the same material that I saw on buckra visitors when they came to the big house. I gave Chekura a bright yellow wrap that I had received in exchange for catching a baby. Georgia said I shouldn't give him anything at all.

"You is giving yourself to him," she said, "an' the crazy big-mouth African lucky to have you."

We had flutes and a banjo at that frolick. Some of the men and women sang and danced, while others drank rum and smoked pipes. I had stopped praying years ago, but still avoided spirits and tobacco—even the night that Chekura and I married. After we ate, Mamed laid down a broom, had us jump over it, and said that made us man and wife. Chekura and I kissed. We were married, and now my baby would have a proper father. We went back to the hut and held each other and moved together as man and wife and fell asleep in each other's arms. At least, I fell asleep in his.

When I awoke, Chekura was gone—back to his own work on a plantation on Lady's Island.

ROBINSON APPLEBY RETURNED TO THE PLANTATION in December. He sent for me. I arrived, swollen-bellied, on the broad porch that wrapped around his big house. The baby inside me had only three moons to go.

"I heard," he said, nodding in the direction of my belly.

"Li'l baby," I said. I didn't want him to see my pride, but my lower lip was quivering.

He swallowed. He chewed his cheek. He stuffed his hands in his pockets, brought them out, removed a watch from his breast pocket and examined it.

"Who is the father?" he said.

I said nothing.

"I know a boy has been coming to see you."

I looked down so he couldn't read anything on my face. I was hoping that he hadn't heard about the wedding.

"I make the decisions around here about breeding," he said.

He motioned for me with his fingers. I stepped a little closer.

"Fancy clothes these days. Blue wrapper, red and gold scarf. Bet you love those clothes. Let me see that wrapper. Come here. Right here."

I stepped closer.

"Say 'I love my clothes, Master.'"

I said it. "Come out into the yard," he said.

I felt a momentary wave of relief. If we were going to stay outside, there were certain things he wouldn't do. Appleby hollered for Mamed and Georgia to gather every man, woman and child on the plantation. Any who did not come would miss the next three meals and do without any of his little gifts of rum, cloth and salt from Charles Town. Everyone on the plantation formed a big circle around us in the yard. Appleby ordered two women to start a small fire. He made Mamed roll up an empty barrel from the storehouse. Another man was to fetch a shaving knife. A woman had to fetch a washtub and scissors. And Georgia was ordered to bring every shred of my clothing to Appleby, who was standing there by the fire.

When the fire was blazing, the washtub filled and the knife ready, Appleby shouted out that any person who raised a word of protest would suffer the same fate as me, or worse.

"Your clothes," he said to me. When I hesitated, he tore them off and threw them down into the pile that Georgia had brought. "We have a law in the Province of South Carolina," he said. "Niggers don't dress grand."

I made a decision then. He would do whatever he wanted, anyway. I was from Bayo and I had a child growing inside me and I would stand proud.

"Throw them in the fire," Appleby said to me, motioning to my clothes on the ground.

I did not move. Appleby turned to Georgia. He pointed at me.

193

"Georgia. You know I mean business. In the fire or I'll make it worse for her."

Georgia's face was as blank as a skipping stone. She bent over, picked up my clothes and threw them in the fire. Privately, I thanked her. She had burned my clothes but saved my dignity. With all the Negroes watching, I had stood up to Appleby. I had that one victory, and I would remember it.

Now he pointed to the tub. "Get down on your knees and soak your head," he said. I remained motionless. "Last warning. Head in the tub."

I kneeled but, with my swollen belly, couldn't bring my head to the tub.

"Then sit up," he said, and dumped three buckets of water on me. The water ran down my face and neck and over my belly.

Appleby rolled the barrel up to me. "Lean over that barrel."

"No," I cried.

"Do what I say and do it now, or I'll clean out your hut. I will burn everything you have. Clothes, comb, all of it. Georgia too. I will throw her clothes, pouches and gourds in the fire. Everything. You hear?"

I tried to lean over the barrel, but my belly was too big.

He grabbed my hair and pulled up my head. "Then sit up straight," he said.

Still on my knees, I straightened my back.

"You and your secret man," Appleby said. "Aren't you clever? Don't you think I knew you were with child? You and your head scarves. Fancied up like white folks, you put the nigger women in Charles Town to shame."

Appleby stepped behind me and yanked my hair. "What is this?" he shouted.

I cried out in pain.

"What's this?" he said again.

"My hair."

"Not hair," he said, pulling my head back even farther. "Wool." When he pulled harder, I gasped. "Not hair," he said. "Say 'wool.'"

"Wool."

"Say 'I gots wool on my head, not hair.'"

"Gots wool, not hair."

"It is just wool, and you ain't even got a right to it without my say so."

Pressing one elbow down into my shoulder blades and forcing me to stay bent over the barrel, Robinson Appleby began snipping with his scissors. Slivers of my hair began to fall over my forehead and into my eyes. More slivers of hair fell into my mouth, while silent tears ran down my cheeks.

I lost all of the hair that Georgia and I had worked over every Sunday morning. All the combing, oiling, braiding and bunching was gone. When Appleby had finished with the scissors, he soaped my head and drew out a knife.

"You move an inch, your own scalp bleeds," he said.

I heard the Negro women whimpering. I had kept my courage up to that point, but suddenly it broke.

"Master, please—"

He pushed my head back down and rubbed soap and water all over my scalp. Then he began shaving me crudely with his knife, scraping the blade over my head, from the top of my forehead to the nape of my neck. He splashed more soapy water on my head. It burned the cuts on my scalp, ran over my face and stung my eyes. Its bitter taste mingled with the hair slivers on my tongue. He kept me bent over, kept his elbow high up on my back, and drew the knife over and over, always moving backwards on my head. Finally, he tossed more water on my head and forced me to stand. He held a mirror up to my face.

I screamed as I have never screamed before. I didn't

recognize myself. I had no clothes, no hair, no beauty, no womanhood.

"I let you off without a beating this time," he said. "Get out of here, and go put on your osnaburgs. If I catch you again dressing white, I'll shave you like a lamb again and burn every single thing in Georgia's hut."

"Georgia don't live in no hut," I whispered.

"That better not be back talk," he said.

"She has a home. It's a home she lives in."

His jaw dropped. I turned away from him. Head shaven, clothes ripped from me and belly distended, I began walking toward the far end of the yard. It was a Sunday, and people had been doing their washing and cooking. Every man, woman and child on the plantation stood silent and still as I passed by. Fomba had his head down, hands covering his eyes. I touched his arm as I walked by, held in my sobs, and refused to run. It would only add to my shame.

"You don't own that baby any more than you own the wool on your head," Appleby said. "They both belong to me."

I walked on, as smoothly as I could, big bellied and all, and shed not a single tear until I was alone in my home.

I HAD BEEN LIVING ON ST. HELENA ISLAND for four years when my time came. It was March 15, 1761, and I was sixteen years old.

"This is your home now," Georgia said. "For you and your baby, right here in Carolina."

I thought it would hurt Georgia's feelings for me to disagree, so I kept quiet. Where would home be for this child of mine? Africa? The indigo plantation? One seemed impossible, the other unacceptable. For this child of mine, home would be me. I would be home. I would be everything for this child until we went home together. But I

196

didn't say that to the woman who had been caring for me like a mother since I arrived in this land.

Georgia had me wash in a big leather bucket out under the moon. She rubbed my back, and made my skin and my muscles go soft in her hands. In due time I was riding waves inside my own body. When the big waves came, they threw me about. Georgia prepared to slide her hand inside me, but I said no. I wasn't ready. It was still time to wait. And so it went for more hurting and waves and revolting from within my own belly. How could such a tiny child cause such commotion?

I thought of all the babies my mother and I had caught together. I was good at it even by the age of eight, but then had no idea of the pain involved. How could I have known? I heard my own throat growling, like an animal outside of me, and I knew that I was ready. Push . . . .push . . . push.

Georgia said that I ought to rest and try again in a moment. She slipped a salve from the indigo leafs on my hemorrhoids. I rested and sipped some water. Georgia put me in a tub and washed me with warm water. When the waves struck again, I crouched in the washtub and pushed, and out dropped my baby boy.

"Mamadu," I gasped.

"Is that African?" Georgia asked.

"Mamadu," I said again. "It was my father's name."

I put my son right away against my nipple. For a brief time, while he rooted and fed, I felt elated and full of energy. When Mamadu had had his fill of me, Georgia washed him and covered him and fed me water and small quantities of sugar and pieces of banana and orange and corn mush. She put the boy back in my arms. I held him close to my breasts, curled up around him and we slept together.

When I awoke, the women slaughtered some of the chickens that we kept for our own use. Many of the

Negroes ate together that night, coming one after the other into Georgia's home to see the baby and congratulate me. It chagrined me terribly that Robinson Appleby saw the baby before Chekura. Appleby stepped up to my bed and gave me a woven basket. I didn't want him so near, and I didn't want him to touch Mamadu. Georgia slid up next to us, expertly lifted the baby away from me and held him securely in her arms. Appleby lifted the flap of cloth to check my baby's sex, and thankfully turned and left us alone.

I had hoped to see Chekura the very day that our son was born. But he did not come. He knew which moon was mine. My own baby's father didn't show up to meet his son or to kiss me. My father had held me, I was told, the day after I came into this world. So where was the man who had led me to the sea and survived the crossing with me and come back sniffing between my legs and finally put his seed in me and jumped the broom with me under a full moon?

"Men comes and goes," Georgia said. "Doan worry 'bout Chekura. Just give this little man your milk."

THE DAYS CAME AND WENT, but still I did not see my husband.

"Don't you fuss over that," Georgia said. "Your man will come as soon as he can."

One night when Georgia went out to spend the night with Happy Jack, I fell asleep with Mamadu curled up tight next to me in bed. I dreamed that a hand was reaching along my neck, and suddenly the dream transformed into a nightmare: someone was stealing my baby. I grabbed the hand that had touched my neck and bit hard into it, and awoke to the sound of Chekura groaning in pain.

"My dangerous wife," he said, shaking his hand.

"Might be dangerous for you to come around fourteen days after your own son was born."

"You were counting the days, were you? So you love me after all?"

I looked at him tenderly. The nightmare was gone, and my husband had finally come to see us. "Come closer to look at your son."

"That's what I was doing when you bit me." Chekura reached down to pick up Mamadu, who grunted but kept right on sleeping. Chekura put the tip of his finger in the baby's mouth. Mamadu rooted and sucked for it, even as he slept. Chekura smiled broadly and climbed into bed with me.

While the baby slept between us, Chekura explained that he had been kept to his plantation lately. A new overseer was trying to stop the Negroes from midnight trading. Sentries and man-traps were posted all around the plantation. Any Negro man found walking around at night would be shot. Anyone caught in a man-trap would be lashed fifty times. Chekura said the homelanders were preparing to rebel. He said it had taken all of his abilities to escape the plantation unseen. I told him to get back to the plantation well before dawn, and that we could visit when his situation calmed down. I didn't want my husband killed for chasing out at night to see me. I didn't want Mamadu's father harmed for a whim.

Georgia suddenly appeared in the door. "I done heard noise," she said, "so I done come to inspect the nest. And look what bird done flew on in."

"Flying would be mighty fine," Chekura said. "Hard to see the man-traps at night. I done looked for them in the day, to remember them in the moonlight."

"Don't get yourself killed," Georgia added. "Get right back before they find you missing."

"You too, Georgia?" Chekura said. "You throwing me out, just like Aminata?"

I loved it when Chekura said my name. All of it.

"I don't like you," Georgia said, smiling broadly at my husband, "but I reckon you is family now."

Chekura stood up from the bed and walked over to give her a mock kiss. "Ain't you sweet?" he said.

Georgia swatted him away and wandered out to find Happy Jack again.

When she was out of earshot, Chekura said, "You should have waited for me to name him. I was going to call him Sundee."

"That's what we'll name the next one," I said, holding my man's hand. "Come see our son as much as you can," I said, "but don't get caught and don't get hurt."

I WAS GIVEN A WEEK OF LYING-IN TIME, then expected to perform a half-share of work on the plantation. The others did my tasks when I was not energetic enough to work. Georgia made no changes to our home, but she began to spend the nights with Happy Jack. I carried Mamadu in a bright orange cloth slung along my back. His sounds and movements were just like a new kind of language, and I wanted to learn it all so I could give him everything he needed. I nursed him before he was hungry and vowed that I would never let him have a reason to cry. I could even feel him grunting and preparing for a bowel movement, which gave me time to slip him off my back and out of his wrap before he did his business.

But when my son Mamadu was just ten months old, I woke up in the middle of the night to his bawling. I rolled over to bring him close, to relieve his cries and all the pressure of the milk within me. My hand brushed against the bed of woven grasses. The bed. The air. My own body. Nothing else. I opened my eyes. The crying was outside my little room now. Out there in the night. I jumped up, dizzy, confused and full like an unmilked cow, and there I saw Robinson Appleby put my baby into a man's arms up on a carriage. I ran toward them. The driver whipped a horse and the carriage pulled forward. The whip struck again and the carriage sped away. And my baby disappeared into the darkness as fast as a falling star.

I ran to Appleby, beating my hands on his chest. I slapped and hit until he threw me down.

"Bring back my baby!" I shouted.

He laughed in my face.

"Bring him back!"

"Too late. He's sold. Only got me five pounds, but he's a buck, and he'll grow and make his new master a fine profit one day."

Dirt dug into my knees, and milk was streaming from my breasts. I had never before wanted to kill a man. But I would have killed Robinson Appleby then. My heart and my body were screaming for Mamadu. But my baby was gone. Sold, sold, sold. Appleby would not say where.

We dipped the fishnet deep, but no one knew a thing about a baby boy arriving in their midst without his mother. Not on St. Helena or any of the neighbouring islands. He wasn't on Lady's, Coosaw, Edisto or Hunting islands.

"He ain't in the fishnet," Georgia said. "He's long gone. Master Apbee done sold him good."

All the fire and the fight drained out of me. I felt worse than I had felt since arriving in Carolina. Chekura did not come once to see me. I was convinced it was my fault. My husband had turned away because I had lost the son that we had made together. I felt sickness and despair and had no desire to lift a hand. I caught the fever that killed so very many Negroes and even more buckras, but Georgia nursed me back to health. I would have welcomed death, but it merely whistled at my door and blew away.

"If your man ain't coming," Georgia said, "he been done sold or hired out and he just can't come."

But I did not believe her. I refused to work. I would

catch no more babies and wash no more indigo vats. Appleby threatened to shave my head again, but I didn't flinch. My son was gone, my husband wasn't coming to see me any more, and all of my efforts to learn the ways of the buckra had ended in disaster. Georgia grew furious at me for refusing to work, and Mamed said he could only protect me for so long. Appleby beat me, but still I would not work for him. At the onset of the indigo season, I would not plant a seed. I stopped eating. I would not leave my bed.

One morning Appleby barged into the room and dragged me into the yard. I readied myself for a whipping, but he simply uttered an oath—*you stupid no-good Guinea wench*—and sold me to Solomon Lindo.

The shape of Africa
{CHARLES TOWN, 1762}

I MISSED CHEKURA DESPERATELY. My young body was perfect back then, smooth and strong and curved and full. My skin was screaming out to be kissed and caressed. My hands and body were ready to stroke and hold and straddle a man. I woke up at night wet between the legs, aching for Chekura's touch. But I never saw or heard from him, even though I had left word for him with Georgia that I had gone to stay with Solomon Lindo in Charles Town. He could have found me if he wanted me. It caused me no end of anguish to think that if I somehow made it back to Bayo, there would be no baby in my arms and no husband beside me. No child to show from my loins, and no man to stand proudly by me while I told my people about the strange ways of the buckra.

CHARLES TOWN WAS BURSTING WITH ACTIVITY. The moment I arrived in the harbour with Solomon Lindo, I knew from the smell of the rotten foods and human waste that it was the place I had come to five years earlier. I tried to shake the thought from my mind. I glanced at the tall man who was my new owner. I noticed that he was calmly looking at the stalls of food as we entered a market, and that he was humming.

"Do you have other slaves?" I asked.

He flinched. "One other. But my wife and I prefer the term *servant*. And we don't treat our servants rudely. In our home, you will find none of the barbarism of St. Helena Island."

Shrimp gleamed on tables in the sun, crabs were piled high and fish were stacked for sale, but what astonished me most was to see Negro women walking freely with platters on heads and baskets in hands. The women wore head scarves, bright shifts and blazing petticoats. Some had hats with fur around them, others wore bright shoes. They laughed, gestured and bargained. They carried on in rapid-fire language, seemed entirely at home and acted like there wasn't a soul in the world who could do them harm.

"Mister, give me a shilling for oranges." A Negro woman with a baby in her belly and oranges piled in a sack by her feet grabbed at Lindo's trousers, clutching for change in his pockets.

Lindo stepped back but showed no sign of shock. "Give me ten of them," he said.

She waved her finger in his face. "Five for one shilling," she said.

"You gave me ten for that price last week."

"Price done change," she said.

He put a coin in her hand.

She flashed him a smile. "Good oranges, Mister. Always buy from me. Oranges for you and your little woman."

His *little woman*? He said nothing in response. She put the oranges in his sack and sauntered off. I watched as she made her way back into the crowd. A white man in shabby clothes approached her, offering something for her fruit. She spat on the ground and turned away—the shabby man was of no more interest to her than a river rat. Lindo, in his wig and fine clothes, was the only sort of man she wanted.

Lindo looked at me and smiled. "You'll find fruiterers and hucksters all about this town," he said. "They keep some of their earnings, but are still owned by masters."

We headed back into the streets. Jumping to the side to avoid a horse and cart, I stepped in a pile of horse manure. In disgust, I wiped my foot on a cleaner part of the street, which was topped with sand and crushed oyster shells.

"You can wash when we get home," Lindo said. "Just keep one eye on the ground in Charles Town. Always."

When I saw that the next patch of ground was safe for walking, I looked back up. Huge turkey vultures wheeled in the sky, slow-moving and patient.

"It's against the law to kill those birds," Lindo said. "People here value them, because they make off with foul carrion. They clean our streets for free."

"Georgia would boil a big bird like that in soup with onion and yams."

"Georgia?"

"The woman done take care of me on Master Appleby's land."

"Took care of you, did she?"

"Yes, Master. She took care of me."

"You don't have to be afraid to speak properly, Meena," he said. "I already know that you can read and speak well."

"You want me to talk like you? Talk like white folks?"

"English," he said. He paused for a moment while we walked. "I am not a white man. I am a Jew, and that is very different. You and I are both outsiders."

I hoped that he could not see disbelief in my eyes. I didn't want to have any trouble with this man. We walked by a tavern. Loud men spilled out of it, some of them clutching drinks. One of them turned to the side of the building and urinated in plain sight of passersby. Through the door, I could see two Negroes drinking with the white men. It seemed incomprehensible. Women selling in the market, Negroes drinking with white men, and yet here I was—a slave.

"Do I hear two pounds?" a voice called out.

In front of a big building, I saw a white man standing on a platform with an African woman. She was covered with ripped cloth. Her eyes darted left and right, and white foam seeped from her mouth. She waved a hand at something in front of her face, but nothing was there. Men called out more numbers.

"Two," someone shouted

"Do I hear five pounds?" the man on the platform shouted. No one answered. There were guffaws in the group. "Gentlemen, please. I ask only five pounds. Tender care will restore this wench."

Near the platform stood a group of Africans, some barely able to stand and others with pus dripping from sores on their legs. Five of them looked like they would not regret the closing fist of death. I felt my stomach churning, my throat tightening. I looked down to avoid meeting their eyes. I was fed, and they were not. I had clothes, and they had none. I could do nothing to change their prospects or even my own. That, I decided, was what it meant to be a slave: your past didn't matter; in the present you were invisible and you had no claim on the future. My situation was no better now than it had been before. I didn't know where my own child was. I wouldn't even know if his name had been changed. I had lost any hope of finding him. In the five years since coming to Carolina, I had lost much more than I had gained.

Suddenly I missed St. Helena terribly. I missed the touch of Chekura's hand, the evening readings of the Bible with Mamed, and sitting around the soup pot on Sunday afternoons, smelling the fish and the vegetables while Georgia did up my hair. I missed the nonstop crying of the cicadas, which I imagined to be the voices of my ancestors, saying,

We will cry out like this always always always just so you don't forget us.

I looked up from the street and again at the wretched captives. I vowed not to let the noises of the city drown out their voices or rob me of my past. It was less painful to forget, but I would look and I would remember.

SOLOMON LINDO KEPT A LARGE, two-storey wooden home on King Street. On the main floor of the home, he had his office as the official inspector of indigo for the Province of South Carolina. He and his wife lived above and behind the shop.

When we arrived, I wasn't stripped or inspected but was brought inside the big house. Lindo left me standing quite alone. I noticed large windows, paintings of Lindo and a woman, and chairs with sculpted feet. As I was looking at a wooden table with silver vases, a woman entered the room. She was tall, slender, very white and not ten years older than me. She had a cap on her hair, and a yellow gown with a plain petticoat. Her lips and nose were thin, and her eyes blueish with the tiniest hint of orange stars circling her pupils. White people had odd eyes. They had the strangest flashes of colour, and no two pairs seemed the same. The wife of Solomon Lindo had friendly eyes. She did not seem like a person who would use a whip.

"Meena," she said. "Am I saying it right?" She had a high voice, like that of an excited child.

I swallowed. She was the first white person to know my name before we met.

"I am Mrs Lindo. I am so pleased to finally meet you. Mr Lindo told me all about you, so young and bright."

I wasn't sure if it was wise to catch her eyes again, so I bowed my head.

"Do sit, please," Mrs Lindo said. I sat on a pink chair with thick cushions and a rigid back. "It is wickedly hot," she continued. "Something to drink?"

I did not know how to reply, but she spoke as if I were her guest. Back home, to refuse food or drink was an insult of the highest order. I accepted her offer. When I brought the thin glass to my lips, the sweetness grabbed the back of my mouth, as if to say, *we're not going to let you forget this*.

"I hope you like lemon cordial," Mrs Lindo said. She talked about the house, her life, how busy Charles Town was and how much they had been looking forward to my joining them. I understood her words, but did not absorb them. While she went on about a hundred things, I wondered where the Negroes were and when I would be shown my sleeping quarters.

I felt a wave of relief when a Negro woman with a swollen belly appeared in the doorway. I guessed she had about five months to go.

"So," the Negro woman said, "she done take my place?"

"Don't say that, Dolly," Mrs Lindo said. "Mr Lindo and I have already told you that nobody is taking your place."

"Now that I got a baby in my belly, this pretty new girl come and take my place."

"Meena is going to help you with that baby," Mrs Lindo said. "Mr Lindo says that Meena has caught many babies."

Dolly's lip curled in disbelief. "This little lamb? Catch my baby?"

I expected that Dolly would be threatened with a beating, but Mrs Lindo just sighed.

"That's quite enough. Please take Meena to the quarters. And be nice. If not, you will lose your privileges. No going to market, no extra clothes, no taking Saturday off. Is that clear?"

"Yes'm," Dolly said, and I followed her out the door.

BEHIND THE HOUSE, I passed a garden, a magnolia tree, some fruit trees and a live oak. Further back stood a two-storey wooden building. It looked big enough for twenty people.

When we entered I noticed that the floors were planked. No mud, no earth, no water between my toes. I saw candles and a bed with straw on the lower level.

"Who stays there?"

"Self-hire men, when the Lindos need them," she said.

"Self-hire?"

"The Lindos pay them to do work, sometimes. Slaves of other folks, on hire to the Lindos."

I nodded. I thought I understood.

Dolly led me up a flight of wooden steps. There, I discovered an apartment more spacious than anything I had ever slept in before.

"This is my room, but now you gonna sleep here too," Dolly said.

Two beds were built up on wooden planks about a foot off the floor. There was straw bedding on the planks, with blankets thrown overtop. We had so much space that it seemed lonely to have only two people in it. A space like that would be happier with Georgia and two or three other women who could laugh and comb one another's hair.

"I do the cooking," Dolly said, "and I go to market. If you take those jobs from me, they'll throw me out."

"Throw you out? Aren't you their slave?"

"They'll sell me down in Georgia," she said.

"Don't worry. I don't cook."

"Don't cook?" she said. "What kind of woman you is?" She studied me carefully and finally said, "You African?"

"Yes."

"Pure African? From Africa, straight off the ship?"

"I am from Africa," I said.

"Mrs Lindo done say 'pure African,'" she said. I nodded. "I never done meet an African who don't cook and who talks so natural."

I smiled at her. "I like to eat," I said, "but I hate to cook."

"If I hated to cook," Dolly said, "Master Lindo throw me out. You must be good at something else."

* * *

MY FIRST WEEKS IN CHARLES Town were given over to following Dolly around on her errands. Each morning, she set out to buy fruit, vegetables and bread. Dolly liked to get the errands done before the thunderstorms rolled in.

Walking with Dolly in the dusty tracks in town, I often had to jump to avoid being run over by teams of horses. Charles Town stank of horse shit and human shit, of animals rooting through the streets, of people who never bathed and of rotting food strewn in the streets or tossed into the Ashley River. Without even looking at the harbour or casting a glance in the direction of Sullivan's Island, anyone could detect the presence of a slave ship. The odour of the dead and dying lifted into the air, growing so thick that it made you choke.

Walking about the town on business for the Lindos, I would distract myself from the smells by looking at women's clothing. Dolly wore none of the rough cloth that had scratched my skin in St. Helena. She had a finer grade of cotton, frequently dyed in blue or red, and the Lindos gave me some too. Dolly liked to wear a petticoat around her waist, but I preferred to take a yard of cloth that Lindo had given me and to wrap it around me in the African way, knotting it at the hip. Dolly didn't usually bother with a head scarf or footwear while working in "Lindotown," as she called the house, but she wouldn't be caught dead out in the streets without a red scarf around her hair, an orange scarf over her shoulders and a pair of red shoes with big brass buckles. Dolly and I pointed out to each other shoes of all colours, petticoats, silk scarves and white gloves. Dolly so loved buckled shoes that she kept a little collection of the wornout footwear hidden under a loose floorboard in our back house. From time to time, she took them out to dust them and to try them on.

One day, Dolly gestured at a woman in a silk petticoat

and said, "Would you look at that? She is one fine-looking woman, dressed just like the Queen."

"What is the Queen?" I asked.

"Doan you even know 'bout the King and Queen?"

I didn't.

"King George and Queen Charlotte," Dolly said. *Chawlut*, was how Dolly said it.

"What does the King do?" I asked.

"Boss man of the whole land."

"What land?" I asked.

"Any land the buckra got. And she the boss woman." We walked for a minute while I thought about that. Then Dolly leaned toward me and said, "They call her the Black Queen."

"How is that?"

Dolly whispered, "Got some African in her."

I didn't believe her. Nobody would let an African become boss woman of the whole land.

All the market vendors knew that Dolly worked for Lindo. She usually got her vegetables and spices from a Negro who sat alone on a stump that he hauled to market every day on his cart. He went by the name of Jimbo, and he had hair all over his face. A big, thick matting of hair. "He look bad," Dolly said, "but he treat you right."

"Hairy dog," I whispered back to her.

"What Mr Lindo want today?" Jimbo called out to Dolly.

"Best vegetables you got," she said.

"Always de best for Mr Lindo," Jimbo said. "He keep me in business. He is my kind of white man. I give you okra, snap beans, tomatoes and three chicken necks."

"Lindo don't eat your chicken necks," Dolly said.

"I give 'em to you, so you loves me more," he said.

"I been loved already by a runaway dog," Dolly said, laughing and patting her belly, "and I don't need no man no how. Put them necks here in this basket and I'll cook them up for me."

"Who is your little friend?" Jimbo asked.

"Don't ask her African name. I can't say it. We just call her Meena. Nice. Sweet. But she straight from low-country and don't know a buzzard from a bathtub."

"Why sure I know," I said, sliding into the conversation. "Buzzard done drop his business on your head and bathtub what you done need yesterday."

Jimbo slapped his thighs in laughter.

"So what you do, Meena chile?" he said. "What you good at?"

"I am helping Dolly 'cause she getting big as a house."

"Good gal," he said. Turning to Dolly, he worked out the amount due.

"I don't do numbers," Dolly said to me. Turning back to Jimbo she added, "Mr Lindo be by to pay you tomorrow."

As we left the market we saw a white man leading five young Negro boys—all about eight years old with shaved heads and light complexions—along the street. As the boys walked, they danced, sang and clapped. A sixth boy—taller, bigger, about my age—walked behind them with a sign that read: COLOURED QUINTUPLETS. FOR HIRE. HOUSE PARTIES. ENQUIRE WILLIAM KING, WATER STREET.

I spotted William King with his fine clothes and upright posture. He glanced my way but looked right past me. The man who had once sold me to Robinson Appleby now had no idea who I was.

King's coloured quintuplets wrapped chains around their ankles and then danced out of them. They took an orange and tossed it back and forth, always dancing and half the time airborne. Emptying their pockets, they each began juggling three oranges. They sang something crazy, happy and meaningless, something that sounded straight from my homeland, although the words didn't mean anything to me. "*Bokele bokele bo. Bokele bokele bo. Awa. Bokele*

bokele bo." They sang and clapped their hands while the oranges were looping through the air. Then they returned the oranges to a wooden crate, bent over and began walking around and dancing upside down and clapping their feet together as if they were hands.

A young bare-chested white man, perhaps just eighteen or so, ran into their midst and began hollering and dancing with the younger Negroes.

"White folks love these boys," Dolly said.

"Why is that white boy acting crazy?" I said.

"Rum, I expect," Dolly said. "There are fighting men all around town, drinking and waiting to get out and go home."

"Who are they fighting?"

"Each other. The English and the French were killing each other and the Indians too."

I shook my head. I couldn't imagine such a thing. I had never seen white men fighting each other.

"White men fight about any old thing," Dolly said. "Lindo tell me that a long while ago white folks went to killing themselves just because one of them cut off the ear of the other. Jenkins the man got his ear cut off, so they called it War of Jenkins' Ear."

The man who was leading the Negro boys chased off the bare-chested white dancer, and we watched the procession reach the end of the block and turn the corner. Dolly said she had heard that the man who owned the coloured quints made money by renting them out at house parties. I said it seemed strange to me that white people would take Negroes to a party.

"White folks is strange," Dolly said. "They like their party-niggers light, mixed up, mulattoes and mustees. The things they like is strange, and the things they don't like is stranger."

On the way back to the Lindos' house, Dolly had to stop and rest. "My feets shouting loud as a churchman," she said.

I loved the way Dolly spoke. Although she had a different way of speaking than Georgia, she still made me think of folks in St. Helena around a fire at night, poking the logs with sticks and telling stories. I had become entranced by the books of the buckra, but was equally taken by the languages of Negroes—tongues that made me feel at home. As I unfastened Dolly's buckles, the words flew from my mouth.

"Your feets too swole fuh them red shoes," I said.

"Shoes jes' fine an' I ain't swole," she said.

"I done catch babies all over the low-country. You get big wit' chile, yo feets swole up."

"Young thing like you gwine catch my baby?"

"Come five moons," I said.

"Gawd help me. You kill me sure as dog kill cat."

THE LINDOS ATE THEIR MAIN MEAL in the middle of the afternoon. Dolly had to cook the meal and wash up afterwards, but once she got her tasks done she could spend her time as she pleased. She did not have to work on Saturdays, as that was the Lindos' Sabbath, but she was expected to prepare their Sabbath meal the night before. The Jews in Charles Town had taught one of their slaves to butcher meat according to their beliefs, and Dolly stopped by the shop where he worked to pick up meat and chicken. Solomon Lindo and his wife also avoided pork. Perhaps he was right in saying that we were similar. I resolved that for as long as I lived with the Lindos, I would try to take meat in the way that they had it prepared. Dolly and I were often allowed to take the Lindos' leftover food and eat it in our back house, and Mrs Lindo frequently gave us pomegranates, figs and cheese.

The land of Charles Town was shaped like a finger, bordered by the Cooper River on one side and the Ashley on the other. The tides rose and fell twice a day in town, and when the water pulled out, the mud flats could stink to high heaven in the broiling sun. Sometimes animals were found rotting in the flats. On other days the bodies of Africans washed up on shore, or were discovered when the tide went out. Whenever commotion erupted by the waterside, I knew better than to join the crowds. I couldn't bear the sight of the bloated bodies.

One Saturday, Lindo allowed us to go to a fair out of town. Like the very Negroes I had watched with such confusion after coming off the slave ship, Dolly and I walked there without a thought of running away. At the fair, we watched bear-baiting and cockfights, and saw white men wrestling greased pigs while onlookers shouted and laughed and threw coins. The first man to wrestle a pig to the ground got to take it home. Dolly seemed relaxed, but I didn't feel comfortable in the crowd of shouting and drinking white men. I worried that their boisterous happiness could erupt into anger at any minute. If it did, I'd be pressed right among them, just as I had been on the ship.

On the way back through the town, we passed the Sign of the Bacchus punch house. It had a written notice: WHITE NEGRO GIRL, GREY EYES AND WHITE HAIR. I tried to spy her through the swinging doors, but only caught a glimpse of light-skinned Negro women drinking at a counter with white men.

"Buckra like their niggers white," Dolly said. "High yellow, washed out, with just a little taste of African."

I didn't entirely believe Dolly. I remembered Robinson Appleby. And many men stared at me in the streets of Charles Town.

Walking through town, especially on the days that Dolly was too tired to join me, I had found that I had to be careful. In plain daylight, a white man tried to grab me and pull me into a tavern. I wrenched my arm free and ran away. The very next day, a tall Negro man in the fish market put his hand on my breast and tried to pull me by the wrist. "Come to my boat," he said, "I have a gift for you." I fled from him, too.

Solomon Lindo let me grow accustomed to Dolly's routines and learn my way about Charles Town. I grew attached to my new comforts. I slept more and ate better than at any time since I had left my homeland. One day, Lindo called for me to join him in his parlour. He said his wife was out discussing books and music with her friends, but that she knew he had been planning to speak with me. Lindo fixed me a glass of lemon cordial with three pieces of ice—I loved ice more than anything else on those hot, sticky Charles Town days—and looked at me once again.

"I am not sure how you managed to learn to read," he said.

I sat a little more rigidly in the hard-backed chair.

"But I don't have to know," he said. "You are keeping that confidence, and you must keep this one too. I am prepared to teach you to read even more than you can read now."

He asked if I would like that. I nodded. He said that he and Mrs Lindo were going to give me lessons in sums and writing. Charlestonians would not take kindly to any Negro reading, he said, so this would have to remain a secret in the house.

"Yes," I said.

"Dolly says you're not one for cooking," he said.

"That's right, sir."

"Not to worry. I have something else in mind for you. How do you like being a servant in this household?"

"Like it right fine, Master Lindo."

"Good. Then I want you to start paying your own way."

"Paying?"

"There are ten thousand people in this town, and more

216

than half of them are Negroes. You are going to start catching babies in Charles Town."

"Whose babies?"

"The babies of Negro servants," he said, "although I know some Jews who might want to use you too. I'm putting you on the self-hire system."

I sat forward in my chair. "Self-hire?"

"You will work in the mornings on my books, keeping accounts. I'm going to teach you how to do that. And when you are not busy with that, you will start catching babies. With what you earn from that, you are going to start paying me ten shillings a week."

Solomon Lindo began teaching me for two hours a day, early in the morning before his long days of work. He promised to give me a book of my own if I could learn all about money in South Carolina. And he showed me a notice he had placed in the *South Carolina Gazette*: "Skilled midwife. Obedient, sensible Guinea wench. For hire. Enquire of Solomon Lindo, King Street."

"What does 'midwife' mean?" I asked him.

"A woman who catches babies."

"And what is a 'wench'?"

"Woman," he said.

"Is Mrs Lindo a wench?"

He sat up straight. He rubbed his hands, then looked at me directly. "She is a lady."

"I'm not from Guinea," I said suddenly. The anger in my own voice surprised me. I jumped up from the table, knocking over an ink pot. "And I'm not a wench. I had a baby and I would have it now but Master Appleby stole him away. I am no wench. I am a wife. I am a mother. Aren't I a woman?"

Lindo righted the ink pot, patting paper over the spill. He gave me a little smile. "It is only a term for the newspaper. Calm yourself. I will avoid the word if it causes offence. But what's wrong with Guinea?"

He was peering at me brightly. He seemed to be enjoying himself. I didn't like the way his eyes paused on my body.

"Guinea means nothing to me, so how can I be from it? I am from Bayo. It is my village. Have you heard of that?"

"It's a big, dark continent. I don't know it at all. Nobody does. Enough chatting, Meena. We have work to do."

A ledger was a record of what you had. Keeping books meant writing down what you spent and what you earned. That was where things got complicated. Lindo said you could get something in one of two ways. One way was to pay for one item by offering something else in return.

"Like Georgia gets rum or cloth for catching a baby," I said.

"Exactly why I purchased you," Lindo said. "I knew you would catch on fast. I saw the intelligence in your eyes and I wanted to lift you up."

"Lift me up?"

"Give you a chance to use your God-given abilities."

No white person had ever spoken to me like this, and I didn't trust him.

"Do you have a religion, Meena?"

"My father used to pray to Allah," I said, "and I was learning from him."

"So you are a Muslim and I, a Jew. You see, we are not so very far apart at all."

I fiddled with the quill and the ink pot. I did not feel like meeting his eyes. But Solomon Lindo kept speaking.

"Our religions come from similar books. Your father had the Qur'an, and I have the Torah."

It astounded me that Solomon Lindo could name the book my father had shown me, in Bayo.

"In my faith," he said, "it is considered a very good thing to give another person what they need to become independent, and to take care of themselves in the world."

Then why, I wondered, didn't he set me free?

I believe he sensed the coldness in my eyes, because he turned abruptly back to our lessons.

LINDO EXPLAINED THAT I COULD either barter for an object, or pay with copper, silver or gold coins. This confused me. It made no sense to me that someone would prefer to be paid with a useless metal coin than with five chickens or a tierce of corn. Lindo put some coins in my left hand and told me to imagine that I had a live chicken in my right. I was to imagine myself going to market with only these two possessions, he said. A person selling oranges would gladly take my coins, but only a person who needed the chicken would accept it as payment.

"But what if the coins become useless?" I said. "People will always want a chicken, but will they always want an ugly metal disc? It has no beauty and it can't be eaten. If I were selling oranges, I would take the chicken."

Lindo tapped the table. "This is not a debate. It is a lesson. Are you ready to continue?"

I nodded.

We moved on to sums. One shilling plus another equalled two shillings. Two plus two made four. Lindo shuffled the coins quickly on the table. With one shilling, I could buy ten eggs. With five shillings, I could buy fifty. For two hours each morning and six days a week, we reviewed arithmetic. After adding and subtracting, multiplication and division came fairly easily. Solomon Lindo was making my mind gallop like a horse and I loved the challenge of keeping up with him.

Lindo's next lessons concerned all the specie circulating in Charles Town. There was the Spanish eight-reales coin, but it was simplest to call it a dollar. It wasn't British, but silver was silver and it was one of the most common coins in Carolina. He showed me a Spanish dollar that had been cut into pieces. The eight triangular bits were used because there weren't enough small coins. A Spanish dollar was worth six shillings, he said, and began to explain the relationship among pence, shillings, crowns, pounds and guineas. There were copper coins and silver, he said, but the guinea was made of gold.

"Guinea?" I said. "That's the same word you used for my homeland."

They were called guineas, he said, because they were made from gold taken from Ethiopia.

"From where?" I asked.

"Your land."

"I thought you called it Guinea."

"We call it many things," he said. "Guinea, Ethiopia, Negritia, Africa—they all mean the same."

"And you have named your big gold coin after Africa?"

"The guinea. Worth twenty-one shillings."

My mouth fell open. From my homeland the buckra were taking both gold and people, and using one to buy and sell the other.

I didn't feel like learning any more that day, and was relieved to see the lesson end. As we stood and prepared to leave his office, Lindo said, "You will make me good money. And I will see that you are properly clothed and fed. You will be treated better than any Negro where you come from, I can guarantee you that."

"I come from Bayo and I was born free," I whispered.

Solomon Lindo sat back. "I beg your pardon?"

"I was a freeborn Muslim."

"Well, I was born in England. But we are in the Colonies now."

I crossed my arms.

He stared at me for a minute, and said, "You will be free enough. You will be free to make extra money on self-hire, as a midwife. And I will collect a return on my investment. I spent a fortune on you."

I was not a little surprised by the sarcasm of my own

220

words: "And you paid this fortune in coins or chickens?"

Lindo looked stunned. Perhaps such words would not be tolerated. Perhaps I would be terribly beaten. But Lindo shook his head, stroked his beard and began to laugh. It was the first time I had said something to make a white man laugh. But it wasn't at all funny to me.

LINDO TESTED ME FOR SEVERAL DAYS and decided that I had learned all his lessons about arithmetic and coins. As a gift, he gave me a book called *Gulliver's Travels* by Jonathan Swift. My eyes fell across these words:

> *I lay down on the grass, which was very short and soft; where I slept sounder than ever I remember to have done in my life . . . I attempted to rise, but was not able to stir: for, as I happened to lie on my back, I found my arms and legs were strongly fastened on each side to the ground; and my hair, which was long and thick, tied down in the same manner . . .*

I was instantly full of desire to read the book. "It looks as good as Exodus," I told him.

"And what do you know of that?" he asked.

I explained that I had been reading the Bible on St. Helena Island.

"We all talk about the Exodus, did you know that?" he said.

It seemed foolish to say too much, but I could not stop myself from blurting out a question: "What do you mean?"

"What I mean is that Jews and Muslims and Christians all have the story of the Exodus in our religious books," Lindo said. "The Israelites are my people and Exodus is the story of our escape from slavery."

I listened carefully to Lindo, and thought about what he

221

was saying. The discovery was fascinating, yet confusing. Perhaps Lindo could explain why Christians and Jews kept Muslims as slaves if we all had the same God and if we all celebrated the flight of the Hebrews from Egypt.

How much had been paid for me, I wondered, and who had arranged to have me brought to this land? How were the black men who stole me from Bayo tied to the Christians and Jews who traded in slaves in South Carolina? Just as the world of the buckra was beginning to make a little more sense, it was becoming increasingly confusing. Answers only led to more questions.

Lindo interrupted my thoughts. "I have a hunch that an African can learn anything, if given the opportunity," he said. "So let's have an experiment and see how much you learn."

Lindo placed one hand over the other. My eyes drifted to the ring on his finger. *Guinea*, I thought to myself. *Guinea gold. Use me if you must, but I will use you too.*

SOLOMON LINDO HAD VARIOUS FORMS OF INCOME as the official indigo inspector for the Province of South Carolina. He didn't get a salary, but the House of Assembly paid him five hundred pounds a year to calculate how many pounds of indigo were being shipped to Britain, and indigo producers paid him to grade their indigo mud and advise them about how to improve it. I kept his books, delivered his reminders of accounts due, and began, as a result of an advertisement that Lindo placed in the *South Carolina Gazette*, to be asked once or twice a week to catch babies in Charles Town and outlying areas. Lindo gave me the money to buy a cloth bag and healing herbs and supplies from a market vendor. To show that I had the right to travel about town on self-hire, and to avoid being harassed or arrested by buckra, I had to pin to my clothes a six-sided tin badge stamped with my name and the year: *Meena. 1762.*

At the market, I bought elderberry flowers and stewed them in lard to treat the bites of the chiggers—insects that hid in the Spanish moss hanging from the oak trees. I bought the root of cotton, as I was sometimes asked to stop a child from growing inside a woman, the same way Georgia had saved me when I was set upon by Robinson Appleby. I bought the bark from the wild black cherry tree, which I would soak in warm water to help women whose monthly bleedings were too strong. I acquired the root bark of the Georgia tree and the leaves of the American aloe for rattlesnake bites, because sometimes people came in to complain of such matters when I was helping a woman with her baby. Blackberry herbs were good for stomach pains and the runs, and tea made from the white sassafras root could cure blindness. Dogwood, cherry bark and red oak bark were good for tea to help with the fevers that plagued Negroes working in the swampy, dismal air.

After collecting my herbs and roots, I began to venture out to catch the babies of the slaves in town. I learned to negotiate with their owners as boldly as the women who hawked fish in the streets. I had to give Solomon Lindo ten shillings a week, so I began to charge slave owners twelve shillings for catching a baby. I always tried to have several weeks of payment stored up and hidden under a loose plank in the room where I slept with Dolly. Sometimes I earned nothing in an entire week. At other times, I was hired out a few times the same week and brought home one or two pounds. Masters sometimes refused to pay me in coins, but the only other payments I would accept were Madeira, rum, tobacco and high-quality cotton fabric. I knew how much of each were needed to make up twelve shillings, and I could trade them easily for the things I needed.

*   *   *

AFTER LINDO FINISHED OUR LESSONS about arithmetic, coins and keeping ledgers, his wife began to tutor me in the art of writing. Mrs Lindo was happy to have me around, and she was a gentle teacher. She taught me how to write in smooth, flowing calligraphy, made sure I learned how to spell, and taught me how to compose words and sentences. I was desperate to learn the things that my father had begun to teach me years earlier, and I ate up every word of her instruction. *Dog. Bone. Cat. Tree. The dog bit the bone. The cat ran up the tree.* It was easy. It was thrilling. As I progressed, Mrs Lindo left me alone to practise writing on my own. *Ten sea bass cost one shilling in the fish market. Indigo production will increase next year. One day I will go back home.*

When Mrs Lindo determined that I could write to her satisfaction, I began to compose business letters for her husband:

William King, Esquire. Funds are overdue to Solomon Lindo, indigo inspector for the Province of Carolina, 55 pounds sterling for consultation on indigo production and 20 pounds sterling for inspection. Remit payment to Solomon Lindo, King Street. Overdue accounts assessed at ten per cent interest per annum. Your humble servant, Solomon D. Lindo.

As the months passed and I managed to keep up my payments of ten shillings a week, I was allowed to read more and more books that Solomon Lindo brought home from the Charles Town Library Society. I read other books by Jonathan Swift. I read Voltaire. I read *The Shipwreck* by William Falconer. And while the candle burned late into the night in the backhouse room that I shared with Dolly, I read copies of the *South Carolina Gazette*, stopping always to look at the notices about runaway slaves.

*Lusty Negro wench new from the Guiney country, run
away last Wednesday from Goose Creek with a new
osnaburg coat and wrapper and a black striped
handkerchief around her head, insensible, cheek pitted
with the pox. Ten pound reward for return to owner,
Randolph Clark.*

As the time passed in Charles Town, I managed to
acquire a fine red scarf, an indigo wrap, a pouch of
Peruvian bark, and still save ten pounds of silver. I was not
beaten once by Mr or Mrs Lindo, but I missed Georgia and
Chekura terribly, and Mamadu was never far from my
thoughts.

One evening, I had caught the baby of one of the few
free Negroes in town. The mother was barely older than
me, and her man had flown into the room the instant my
work was done to hug her and hold the baby. When I
returned home, I found Dolly asleep with her palm on her
swollen belly. I sat on the edge of my bed, put my face in
my hands and let my grief pour out. Dolly awoke in the
middle of my tears.

"What's the matter, honey chile?" The sympathy in her
voice made me cry even more. Dolly got up out of bed and
came to put her arm over my shoulders. "One day your
man come back and you start all over again," she said.

A FEW MONTHS LATER, I helped bring Dolly's son Samuel
into the world. The three of us lived together in the backhouse, the baby travelling on Dolly's back as she went
about her house chores and sleeping in her bed at night. It
was comforting to have new life in our backhouse, but my
body would sometimes ache at the sound of Samuel
sucking and gurgling.

The Lindos were so pleased with the reports of my baby-
catching that when the time came for Mrs Lindo to have

her first baby, she took me aside for a private conversation. "We've heard about the town doctor,"Mrs Lindo whispered. "He bleeds the women in their labour."

So I helped Mrs Lindo bring a healthy boy named David into the world. To my surprise, the Lindos had the boy circumcised, just as we would have done in Bayo. A few weeks later, Mr and Mrs Lindo brought me into their parlour, offered me a cordial and asked if there was any little gift that I might like to have.

"Gift?" I said.

"Since you have been such a wonderful help to us," Mrs. Lindo said.

I thought for a moment. I asked if I could see a map of the world.

"Why do you want to see a map?" Mr Lindo asked.

"She has read dozens of books," his wife cut in. "She does everything we ask of her. I can't see how it would hurt."

"What do you seek to learn?" he asked.

"I do not know from where I come," I said.

"You came from Africa. You crossed the ocean. We are in Charles Town. You already know these things."

"Yes, but I do not understand where South Carolina is in relation to my homeland."

Mr Lindo sighed. "I don't see why that is necessary."

"Solomon,"Mrs Lindo said, putting her hand on his knee. "Take her to the Charles Town library. Let her see the maps."

He jumped up from the couch, knocking over his drink. "I had to grovel just to be let into the Society," he shouted.

"Solomon, please," Mrs Lindo said.

I took a cloth from Mrs Lindo to clean up the spill and kept my eyes on my work. Mr Lindo had mentioned a few times that Jews had been slaves in ancient Egypt and that his own ancestors had been driven from Spain. He had told me that Jews and Africans could understand each other because we were both outsiders, but even though the man preferred the term *servant* to *slave*, he owned me and he owned Dolly and now he owned Dolly's baby boy. He had a big house in town and he did business throughout the low-country. He wore fine clothes and came and went as he pleased. He could sail to London on the next ship if he so desired.

I thought that Mr Lindo would be embarrassed over losing his temper, but he did not seem able to contain himself.

"I'm good enough to be their indigo inspector, but can I vote in their elections? The Anglicans won't even have me on their library board."

I kept my eyes on my hands but could hear the tremor in Mr Lindo's voice.

Mrs Lindo reached up, took her husband's hand and brought him back to sit beside her. "Nobody has to grovel," she said calmly, placing her hand on his arm. "You don't have to ask to borrow the map. Just go in and look at it."

"And Meena?" Lindo asked.

"Take her with you. She's your servant." Mrs Lindo giggled. "Take a fan, Meena. Keep the flies away during his consultations."

THE CHARLES TOWN LIBRARY SOCIETY kept its books and maps in a room on Union Street. The keeper of the books sat at a desk at the entrance. He glanced at me quickly and turned away, as if from something distasteful.

"Ah yes, Mr Lindo," he said. "I'm afraid we don't allow Negroes here."

"Mr Jackson, don't you have a brother in the indigo trade?"

The library man carefully closed a book on his desk. "I'm sure nobody will object this one time, Mr Lindo."

"Good. We need some books by Voltaire, and your most recent maps of the world."

The keeper led us to a table at the far end of the room, brought us two of Voltaire's books and some rolled maps, and left us alone.

"Keep that fan going," Lindo said.

"He's not watching."

"Use it anyway," he said, "it's hot in here."

While I fanned him, Solomon Lindo untied a string around a large scroll.

"I have never seen so many books," I said, looking around and wishing that women and Negroes were allowed in the library.

"They have a thousand books," Mr Lindo muttered, "and I paid for half of them."

"Where are we?" I asked, pointing at the map.

"This is British North America," he said, indicating a mass of land.

On the edge of the land, right up against a huge swathe of blue named the Atlantic Ocean, Lindo put his finger by a dot, beside which was the name *Charles Town*.

"And here," he said, "is Africa." Across the blue sea, I saw a strangely shaped mass, wider at the top, curving in at the middle and narrowing at the bottom.

"How do you know?"

"You can make out the letters if you look carefully. See here? A–F–R–I–C–A."

"That is my land? Who says it has that strange shape?"

"The cartographers who make the maps. The traders who sail the worlds. The British and the French and the Dutch and the others who go to Africa, sailing up and down the coast, mapping the shape of the continent."

On the map I paused over some squiggles in the form of baseless triangles. Lindo said they were meant to indicate mountains. I saw a lion and an elephant sketched in the middle of the land called Africa. I saw that it was mostly surrounded by seas. But the map told me nothing of where I came from. Nothing of Bayo, Segu, or the Joliba. Not a single thing that I recognized from my homeland.

"Here on this side of the water, in British North America," I said, pointing, "it says Charles Town. I can see where we are. But there are no towns written on Africa. Only these places along the water. Cape Verde. Cape Mesurado. Cape Palmas. How are we to know where the villages are?"

"The villages are unknown," Lindo said.

"I have walked through them. There are people everywhere."

"They are unknown to the people who made this map. Look here in the corner. It says *1690*. This is a copy of a map first made seventy-three years ago. They knew even less back then."

I felt cheated. Now that I could read so well, I had been excited by the prospect of finding my own village on a map. But there were no villages—not mine or anybody else's.

"Is there nothing more?" I asked.

Solomon Lindo looked at his watch, and said we had time for one more map.

Mapp of Africa, the second one said, *Corrected with the latest and the best observations*. I checked the date. *1729*. Perhaps it would be better than the first. The map showed land in the shape of a mushroom with the stem shoved to the right. Near the top, I saw the words *Desert of Barbary or Zaara*, and below that, *Negroland*, and below that, along the winding, curving coasts, sections named *Slave Coast, Gold Coast, Ivory Coast* and *Grain Coast*. There were tiny words scribbled where the land met the water, but inland was mostly sketchings of elephants, lions and bare-breasted women. In one corner of the map, I saw a sketch of an African child lying beside a lion under a tree. I had never seen such a ridiculous thing. No child would be foolish enough to sleep with a lion. In another corner of the map, I studied a sketch of a man with a long-tailed animal sitting on his shoulder.

"What's that?" I asked.

"It's a monkey," Lindo said.

This "Mapp of Africa" was not my homeland. It was a white man's fantasy.

"There is some lack of detail," Lindo said, "but now you see the shape of Africa."

I said I had seen enough. After all the books I had read, and all that I had learned about the ways of the white people in South Carolina, I now felt, more than ever before, that these people didn't know me at all. They knew how to bring ships to my land. They knew how to take me from it. But they had no idea at all what my land looked like or who lived there or how we lived.

As we walked home, I felt a sense of despair. Not only had I lost my son and husband, but it seemed that I would never find my way home. I did not want to take the route of runaway slaves, escaping to the Indians or the Spanish in the south. Hiding in swamps and forests would get me no closer to Africa. My only choice was to keep listening, learning and reading. Perhaps one day I would understand the world of the white man well enough to discover how to leave it.

Words come late from a wet-nurse

YEARS WENT BY AND MY WORK as a self-hire midwife stayed the same, but the losses of my life kept piling up. I never got to see Georgia again after I was sold to the Lindos in Charles Town, and one day final sad news came through the fishnet: Georgia had died in her sleep one night of no known ailment. And my fellow villager Fomba had been killed by a night patroller. Fomba had been fishing in his skiff at night when the buckra called out for him to identify himself. Fomba had never recovered the ability to speak, and the patroller shot him in the head. Rather than learning to feel less disappointment, I found that one insult to my heart just seemed to make the next one worse.

In the fall of 1774, nearly thirteen years after I had come to live with the Lindos, a smallpox epidemic took the lives of Mrs Lindo, Dolly, their sons and some two hundred other people in Charles Town. In our grief, Solomon Lindo and I barely spoke to each other. When he passed me coming in and out of the house, usually accompanied as he was by a man from his synagogue, it was as if he didn't see me.

Stumbling about in the fog of his sorrow, at least Solomon Lindo had friends to visit him and bring him food, but I had nobody to console me over my losses.

Negroes were not allowed to come visiting in the back-house, and most of the friends that I had made over the years were gone—they had left with owners who took them where they wanted, or they had died of fevers or the pox.

I could not stop thinking about Dolly and her son, who had been my most regular companions during the long years in Charles Town. She had fussed over me like a mother, cooking my meals and cleaning my clothes, and whenever I had given her some of the things that came from my work as a self-hire midwife—a miniature box made out of cherry wood, a small bottle of West Indian rum—her face had lit up like that of a child. She kept the bottle with her old buckled shoes, examining them from time to time as if she were checking in with old friends.

Dolly had been unbelievably proud to see me reading and writing. Sometimes while I read books in our back-house at night, she had lain next to me and fallen asleep with her hand resting on my arm. She never opened a book, but liked to sit near and watch while I taught her son Samuel to read. As a result of our late-night lessons, he had become a good reader by the age of ten.

"You done give him the one thing I ain't got to give," Dolly had said.

Losing Mrs Lindo was equally painful. She had never raised a hand against me in all my years of service. I had trusted her more than any other white person, and had come to care for her son David like a child of my own.

After Dolly, Samuel and David died, Mrs Lindo herself had taken the fever. Pustules broke out all over her body, causing unspeakable pain on her heels and palms. I was left to care for her, and I knew by the way the pustules all ran together, fusing on her face and neck and back, that she was not long for this world.

I had cried for a whole week after she died. I was not allowed to attend the shiva or speak to any of the people in the house about how much I had loved Mrs Lindo, so my only way of saying goodbye was to dust and stroke each of the books she had given me over the years. Long ago, she had settled into a pattern of giving me a gift of one book a month, along with a bottle of whale oil to refill my lamp. I kept the books stacked in thirteen columns—one for each year of my service with her—in a corner of the backhouse. It was safe up there, because no white folks ever came into my sleeping quarters. I had built my own little library up in that backhouse, and sometimes read halfway through my long, lonely nights while Dolly and Sam slept.

Until the moment that I excused myself for the last time from Mrs Lindo's bedroom, I had never imagined that I could lament the death of a white person. I would never have thought it possible for my insides to bleed for one.

Solomon Lindo had people from his synagogue in the house every day for a week, and people continued to come by almost daily for a month. Women from his synagogue brought food of every kind, and his sister—a short, severe woman named Leah who seemed offended by my very presence—often patrolled the house.

A few weeks after Mrs Lindo died, Mr Lindo and I found ourselves alone for a rare moment. "All these people around," he said. "It's suffocating."

At least he had his own people, with whom he could break bread and cry. I had nobody at all.

THE PEOPLE OF CHARLES TOWN had fallen on hard times. Coins were harder than ever to find, and the British government had passed laws preventing the use of paper currency in South Carolina. People were so angry about the way the British were controlling the shipping and sale of tea that huge quantities of the stuff had been allowed to rot on the docks of Charles Town, and the whites were refusing to drink it in their homes. Lindo and his friends blamed their problems on the British and warned of war if things did not improve. Lindo had told me that Carolina indigo could barely fetch half the price of Guatemalan and French West Indian indigo, and that plantation owners were talking about switching to other crops. To make matters worse, fever, syphilis and smallpox kept people in a constant state of fear and agitation. Charlestonians were often afraid to shake hands or leave their houses. For a time, town officials tried to prevent the spread of disease by barring slave ships from arriving at Sullivan's Island.

In January of 1775, some months after the smallpox epidemic swept through, Solomon Lindo told me that he would be leaving for a month to do business in New York City, where he hoped to convince British officials to protect the parliamentary bounty on Carolina indigo. He said the mud for dye was selling so poorly in international markets that production might grind to a halt in Carolina if the British subsidy were reduced or eliminated.

After Lindo left, his sister Leah moved into the house, but she took her meals alone and made no arrangements for mine. "There is no food," I told her the day after Lindo had sailed out of the harbour.

"Aren't you on self-hire?" she said.

"Yes."

"Then you can get your own meals too. I'm not wasting time or money on you, and if I have anything to say about it, my brother won't have anyone else doing it for you either."

When I tried to enter the house to find some of the books that Mrs Lindo had left behind, Lindo's sister refused to unlock the door. With nothing to read and no meals to eat, I wandered the streets every day, scrounging for fruit, peanuts and bits of cooked meat from women I had come to know in the markets. At night, I sometimes bought grilled fish sold behind a tavern where white men went looking for mulatto women.

Coins were almost impossible to come by, and in the markets even small goods were exchanged by means of trade. I thought ruefully of the lessons about money that Lindo had taught me years earlier. As it turned out, I had been right. Chickens were more reliable than silver. I rarely had chickens to trade, but exchanged whatever goods I received from the Jews and the Anglicans who had me catch their babies or the babies of their slaves.

Some of the new mothers gave me small quantities of rum, but one rich woman gave me a box filled with fifty glass bottles. At first, I felt cheated. What good was a box of empty bottles? But when I reopened the box at home, I found the glass to be of extraordinary beauty, coloured with swirling lines of blue. The tiny bottles had room for two or so ounces of liquid, but each was shaped differently, some cylindrical, others bulbous, some cube-like and still others faintly spherical. I filled each with two ounces of rum and stopped it with a cork.

For months, I used the smooth, slender bottles with swirling blue lines to make purchases in the market. The Negro hucksters loved the rum and kept the bottles because they considered it good luck to blow into blue glass. They called me Blue Glass Gal when they saw me coming, and the bottles that I traded changed hands among other buyers and sellers.

I slept at night in the backhouse, and felt terribly lonely without Dolly and her son. It seemed to me a violation of human nature to be made to sleep alone. Sometimes I comforted myself with thoughts of my parents in Bayo, or of Georgia warm and snoring in the bed we had shared on the Appleby plantation. When I couldn't sleep, I would stay up late into the night, re-reading books and thinking of the people—Georgia, Chekura, Mamed, Dolly, and Mrs Lindo—who had been in my life when I had first read them.

One night I heard footsteps downstairs. I jumped off the bed and covered myself with my cloth wrapper.

"Who is there?" I called out.

"Aminata?" It was a man's voice, whispering.

I stopped. When had someone last called me by my African name?

As Chekura reached the top step, I flew into his arms. When my hands pressed against his back and my toes rested above his, I felt my childhood in his flesh and my homeland in his voice. I clung to him for minutes, almost afraid to discover the man he had become. What if he was no longer the boy who had helped me stay alive in the long walk to the African coast, or the young man who had married me and given me a son?

His hair had fallen out, and he kept his bald head shining. He was still a slender man, barely heavier than I, and only a few inches taller. Half of the middle finger on his left hand was missing, but he still had the same smile he had worn almost everywhere in our homeland journey. I loved the light in his eyes and the way his lips turned up into a grin when he looked at me. We fell into conversation just as if we had been together the day before.

"How did you find me?"

"I asked for the home of Lindo the Jew," he said.

"How did you get to Charles Town?"

"A man who is taking a mess of tobacco and rum into the low-country has come to the Charles Town market, and I'm here with him."

"How long can you stay?"

"Just tonight. But I might be able to come back once or twice in a month or so."

"You might return once or twice," I said, letting go of his hand and sitting down on my bed.

He sat beside me and placed his hand on mine. I pushed it away. He took it again, but I shoved it away firmly.

"No," I said, "you can't do that. I've missed you more

than you could ever know. But you can't just climb into my bed with the promise that you might return 'once or twice.'"

"Do you have any food?"

"I eat in town. There's no eating here. Lindo is away."

He slid his curled fingers along my cheek. "Then you can come away with me and he won't know you're missing."

I turned my face away from him. "You want me to run into the low-country with you? And the man who owns you?"

"He might let me go for a day or two. I know places where we could be alone."

"A day or two is not what I want with you," I said.

"Sometimes a day or two is all we can get," Chekura said.

For some time, neither of us spoke.

"I married the man I loved," I said finally.

"And the man who loved you married you," he said.

"Do you still want me?" I said.

"Always did and never stopped."

"You didn't even come to see me after they took Mamadu."

Chekura stretched out on the bed, pulled me down beside him and whispered in my ear. "My master on Lady's Island sent me down to Georgia for three years. I was sent away before Mamadu was even stolen."

I pulled away to look into his eyes. He smiled at me and ran his fingers over my hair.

"My master and yours knew each other," he said. "They sent me away so there wouldn't be trouble."

I took his hands into mine. "All that time," I said, "I was sure that you blamed me."

"For what?" he said.

"For losing our child."

Chekura put his arms around me and brought me closer

237

to his body. "What mother is to blame for losing her child?"

We were lying side by side and my hand was on his hip. "What did they make you do down in Georgia?" I asked.

"Plant rice," he said. "Worse than indigo. Plenty worse, working in water all the time. If you didn't work hard enough, they whipped you. And if you did work hard enough, you died. I made it through three seasons."

Chekura brought my face to his chest and whispered, "When they sent me back to Lady's Island, I knew you were in Charles Town. But there was no more travelling and trading allowed. They used sentries to stop Negroes from moving about at night. I got past the sentries but fell into a man-trap."

I pulled away from his chest to look into his eyes. I took his hand and stroked it, and came across the half finger.

"My punishment," he said.

I kissed his nine good fingers and stayed much longer on his tenth, stroking and brushing my lips against the half that remained. I felt full of love for this man, but thought about how I would feel if he entered my body and then disappeared for another fourteen years.

"Your eyes are as round as acorns, and the moons on your face are beautiful," he said.

I thought of how good I had looked through my twenties, when I was fending off the drunken and obnoxious advances of Charles Town men—white and black—and suffering the stares of Solomon Lindo and the few friends he brought into the house to feast their eyes on me. Now I was thirty years old and had nothing to show for it. No son. No family. No homeland. And even my beauty would soon fade.

"Don't be sad," Chekura said, letting his fingers run up and down my arms. "No moons as beautiful as yours have crossed the Atlantic," he said. "All these years, when I was missing you, I would wait for the thinnest sliver of the crescent moon to come out at night. On those nights, just once or twice a month if the skies were clear, I felt that you were with me."

I burst into tears. Chekura took me in his arms and held me close, and as my sobbing ebbed to gentle weeping, I could feel his chest moving steadily in and out. I lay awake for a long time after Chekura began to snore, wondering if I would see him when the day broke. I was the first to awaken, and found him lying with his hand in mine. I pressed it to my breast. Once we had jumped the broom, once we had made a son, and once I had hoped that we would all stay together.

Chekura awoke and found our hands together. He turned his head my way. "A husband needs his wife," he said to me. "Would you love me now?"

The soft morning light bathed his face, and I noticed a wrinkle or two at the corners of his eyes. This man had once walked with me for three moons, all the way to the coast of our homeland. This man had risked his life time and again to visit me at night by the indigo fields of St. Helena Island. He had lost half a finger and all of his hair, but none of his love for me. A long-buried desire clicked at the back of my throat. I felt the same warmth and wetness that I had felt during the thousands of nights that I had missed Chekura, but this time he was here with me and he was mine.

I had no idea when I would see him again and wanted to savour every moment that we had. Licking and touching every inch of his skin, I basked in the smell and the sweat of him and felt my passion rising under his tongue and his fingers as they circled and teased and devoured me.

Our lips met. I brought just the very tip of him into me and we stayed like that, kissing and licking and slowly rocking. I moaned as his lips tickled my nipples and his thumb slid against the hard, extended ridge of my womanhood. Chekura arched and slid deep inside me and we inhaled life one from the other. The sound of his breathing and gasping brought me to the peak of my own pleasure. Once, twice, three times I shook and shuddered as my husband spilled himself deep inside me and we cried out together. We held on to each other long after we were both spent, and kissed once more before we fell asleep.

I awoke to find him tracing my cheeks with the fingers of one hand. He smiled at me faintly, and I knew that he had to leave soon.

"Do you know what happened to Mamadu?" I asked.

"He was sold down in Georgia," he said.

"Who told you?"

"Different folks. News came up from the fishnet."

"How come you heard if I never did?"

"I was working down in Georgia. Three long years I spent down there. I heard on the rice plantation that he had been sold off, and then later that you had been sent away. When I heard that, I thought about drowning myself."

I stroked the back of his hand. "You never know when you might see your wife again," I said.

"Maybe that's what stopped me," he said. Chekura sat up cross-legged on the bed. "I don't like this man Lindo. He keeps you here all alone and doesn't even leave food for you when he's gone."

"He's better than most," I said. "Never beat me, I can say that."

"I heard talk about Lindo in the fishnet."

"What sort of talk?"

"It came some time after Mamadu was sold. I knew your friends on St. Helena and the nearby islands were asking where he had gone. And in Georgia, I started asking after him everywhere I went. Every time I met a Negro who was coming or going, I sent out word in the fishnet.

240

Somebody, somewhere, had to know about my son. A year or two later, word came back: Mamadu had been sold to a family in Georgia. In Savannah. I would have kept on asking in the fishnet. I would have found that family and killed someone. But the pox came through the town and our baby died."

"He did?" I reached again for Chekura's hand and gripped it hard.

"About a year after he was sold."

"What family was this?" I asked.

"I don't know the name—but Solomon Lindo arranged the sale," Chekura said.

"How do you know it was him?"

"That's how it came up the fishnet. It was a rich white family in Savannah. They had a slave wet-nurse in the house. A wet-nurse born in Africa. When our dark-skinned baby arrived with no parents in sight, the wet-nurse sent out word through the fishnet."

"What, exactly, did she say?"

"The man who set up the sale was 'Lindo, the indigo Jew.' That's what I heard. The wet-nurse said 'the indigo Jew' was with the family when the baby arrived. He was paid a fee, and then he left."

I ran down the stairs and shut myself into the outhouse. I cried until I began to cough, and coughed until I vomited. Finally, emptied and numb, I returned upstairs. Chekura had not moved an inch.

"And the baby is dead?" I said. "You are sure he is dead?"

"Heard it three times in the fishnet. Three people brought me the news, and none of them knew the others. They knew I was the father of the baby who arrived with no parents in Savannah, and they knew the wet-nurse. She told each of them. She said pox carried off the baby in 1762."

I sat for a long while in silence. Finally, Chekura told me

he couldn't stay much longer. He had his man to meet at noon, on Broad Street.

We walked into town together. I used a blue glass with rum to buy two pieces of cooked sea bass, two buns and two oranges from a woman in the morning market. We ate them among the crowds of people—black, mulatto, mustee and white—coming and going in the morning.

"Do you want me to kill him?" Chekura said.

"Are you going to kill Appleby too? And every white man who brought us here?"

"It's just Lindo I want," he said. "Right here in town, he's one I could get. I could come at night and nobody would see me."

"They might not see you, but I would know," I said. "Killing him won't bring back our baby. I want you to stay alive, and I want you to stay good."

"You want me to stay good?"

"There's been enough killing in our lives. And you're no killer anyway. You're still the runt of a lad who was too foolish to run away before they chained you up and threw you in the ship."

"I would have run from the slavers, but I knew you were heading across the big river and I wanted to go with you."

I gave a tiny smile. "Nice try," I said. "You were a fool but you were good. If you stay good, come back and stick around a little longer next time—you never know what might happen. I might just marry you."

"And now you tell me," he said. He gave me a long, sweet look, holding me with his eyes just as deeply and as fiercely as any man could use his body.

It was time for Chekura to go. At noon he had a man to meet—the same man who had given him a night off and who now had to be guided through the low-country waterways. I spread my hands and brought my fingers to Chekura's. Together, our hands resembled the skeleton of a house. I pressed a little harder against the pads of his

242

fingertips, which were smooth and soft despite the years. When Chekura smiled, I could see deep creases at the corners of his mouth.

"Goodbye, my dear wife," he said.

A white man was watching us from across the street. It had to be the one who owned him.

I couldn't bring myself to smile, and I had no more words. I pressed Chekura's fingertips one last time, and then my man was gone.

SOLOMON LINDO RETURNED after being away for a month. I had caught two babies in his absence, but received nothing but a flask of rum, a pouch of tobacco and a yard of cloth dyed with indigo.

Lindo sent his sister home, spent a day doing business and then called me into his office.

"I have seen the accounts," he said. "You owe me two pounds."

I would not look at him.

"I expect an answer when I speak," he said.

In a low monotone, I said: "You owe me much more than silver."

"You're to pay me ten shillings a week, but in my absence you didn't leave a thing with my sister."

"I have nothing to give you. And there are other things on my mind."

Lindo snorted. "I have lost my position as the official indigo inspector—and would you like to know why?"

I ignored his question. What did I care about his indigo problems?

"Because," he continued, "there isn't enough being produced to merit my inspections. If I don't get the British to increase the bounty, and if we don't see the price rising on international markets, the Carolina indigo economy will collapse."

"And what does that have to do with me?"

He slammed his fist on the desk. "I keep you clothed and I keep you fed," he shouted. "You live better in this home than any servant in town. There will be no clothes, no meals, no benefits, and no support until you pay your way. Ten shillings a week, and not a penny less."

"I can't pay you money that is not paid to me," I said.

"Then you are not to go out, unless it is to do midwifery work or other tasks that I assign."

"So will you now start saying 'slave,' instead of 'servant'?"

He grabbed my wrist and pulled me to him. I could feel his breath on my forehead.

"You will cook and you will do as I say."

"I will not."

I tried to yank my wrist free but he held it firmly. With his other hand, he slapped me in the face. Then he let me go.

My cheek burned. I stared into his eyes until he turned his head.

"Forgive me," he said quietly, looking down. "I don't know what got into me. I am not myself now that Mrs Lindo is gone."

"You cannot blame everything on your grief," I said. When he looked up, I spoke once more. "You sold my son."

"I don't know what you are talking about. Robinson Appleby sold your son."

"You helped him. And you were paid to do it. You sold my son to a family in Savannah, Georgia."

"Who told you this?"

"Some Hebrew you are. And you say you're not a white man."

"Have you been going through my papers?"

I thought that he might strike me, or rip off my clothes and force himself on me. I thought that he might shove

244

me out the door and leave me to fend for myself on the streets of Charles Town. But Solomon Lindo did none of those things. He sat down heavily and asked me to join him. I refused, and stood with arms crossed.

"I do not expect you to understand, but there is more to the truth than you know." There was nothing more for me to say, because I did not care for Solomon Lindo and his truths.

OVER THE NEXT FEW WEEKS, Lindo moved at all times with reluctance and heaviness. We settled into an uneasy truce. I did not make any more payments to him, and he provided me neither food nor clothing nor whale oil nor assistance of any kind other than the right to sleep in his backhouse unmolested.

I received no more midwifery work from the Jews of Charles Town, and the Anglican slave owners would pay in nothing but the smallest quantities of rum and tobacco. I traded them with difficulty in the town markets. I had to start drawing my last good red wrap more tightly around my waist and hips, and it too started to fray.

Solomon Lindo cut me out of his bookkeeping work, and began to take meals in his sister's home. For the first time since I had come to Charles Town, I felt gnawing hunger every day. White people in the markets mumbled to each other about being enslaved by the King of England, but I had stopped listening to their complaints. *Liberty to the Americans. Down with slavery.* They weren't talking about the slavery I knew or the liberty I wanted, and it all seemed ludicrous to me.

Against all reason and logic, I waited and hoped for Chekura's return. He had said he might be coming back. But no voice called out my African name, and no feet climbed the steps to greet me in the night. I watched for him in the streets and the markets, but Chekura was not to be found. I even looked to the Charles Town newspapers, in case anyone was advertising for a runaway "servant" by the name of Chekura. But the papers said that the British had taken over the Spanish lands to the south. In a hostile town and with a highly patrolled low-country filled with sentries, guards, man-traps and plantation owners who shot Negro trespassers, I knew that he was as unlikely to make it safely to Charles Town again as I was to travel undetected to Lady's Island. There was nowhere to go and no place left to hide.

Three months after he had returned from New York City, Solomon Lindo told me to join him in his parlour. I hadn't set foot in his house in ages, and couldn't remember the last time I had eaten to my fill.

"It would appear that we are both suffering," Lindo said, "and I am going to end this standoff. I must travel again to New York City. I have one more opportunity to argue in favour of the indigo bounty." Lindo handed me a platter of bread, cheese and fruit, as well as a bundle of clothes. "Take this food and these things to cover yourself, for it is not right for me to let you wither away."

I thought he was going to sell me, but the man who claimed that he was not white surprised me one more time.

"The ship sails tomorrow at ten in the morning," he said. "Make yourself ready for eight o'clock sharp. I have decided to take you with me. We will be gone for a month. I will ensure that you are fed, and that you are clothed for the northern climate. You will write letters, do my books and run errands. Perhaps we can thus repair the damage between us. But go now, please, for I have work to finish."

I decided to travel with him in the morning. It would be my Exodus. With a bit of luck, I would never return to the Province of South Carolina.

Book Three

Nations not so blest as thee

{LONDON, 1804}

THE ABOLITIONISTS SUSPECT that my time left is limited, and I cannot deny it. It is as if my lungs have been granted a precise number of breaths. Now that the limit draws near, I can almost see the number written in the patterns of the clouds at sunset. In the morning, I awaken faintly troubled. The sunset remains in my mind at all times of day, but I try not to dwell on it, or to let it prevent me from taking each day as a new gift. I have not embraced a God as might be imagined by a Muslim, Jew or Christian, but in the mornings it comforts me to imagine a gentle voice saying, *Go ahead, that's it, take another day*.

I am no longer worked to the bone, nor do I struggle every hour to fill my belly or cover my head, and I find it easy to make one new discovery every day. Recently, I discovered that something happens when people realize they may never see you again. They expect wisdom from you. And they want you near to them during great moments.

Yesterday the jolly abolitionist—Sir Stanley Hastings, as the rest of the world knows him—finally prevailed upon me to accompany him to Sunday service. He had been at me for some time, and I could procrastinate no longer.

We attended his church, which, he said, was the only respectable house of worship in the city. True to his word,

249

he kept vigil over me throughout the ordeal, propping me up on every leaning side. On our way into the building, passing under an archway of timeless stones and echoes, men and women of every persuasion and under every imaginable wig or hat flocked toward me for an introduction.

"We have heard they will be bringing you out soon," one said.

"We hear the date is nearing for the parliamentary committee," another said.

"We hear that you can quote from Voltaire and Swift," a third said.

"Only when my own words fail me," I replied, which earned a round of laughter.

When the bishop stood, I finally got to rest my weary backside on a pew. The first pew, no less. Sir Stanley whispered that nearly a thousand people sat behind us, and I had the sensation of twice that number of eyes boring into the deep brown skin of my neck. Suffice it to say that mine was the only skin of that hue inside that sacred building. I found it enervating to be stared at by the bishop as he took to his pulpit, and by all the congregationists behind me. I sought nothing but sleep and the comfort of a quiet, solitary room. My eyelids dropped like bricks, and yet I strove to hold them up. I had no wish to disgrace my valiant host, so I sat as still and erect as the white Anglicans of London, dreaming with eyes open of a warm bed and a feather pillow.

The people of Great Britain and other seafaring nations have devised unspeakable punishments for the children of Ham, but in that moment and in that time, none seemed worse than their own self-inflicted torture: to sit, unmoving but forbidden to sleep, in a cavernous room with arching stone and forbidden windows while a small man adopted a monotone for the better part of a villainous hour.

I did my level best to remain upright. If I closed my eyes

only halfway, surely nobody could tell that I was escaping through dreams of other lands and other times. I thought of my mother, who had seemed so wise and old to me when I was but a child. Even as one takes the last steps of life, one seems still to long for the slow, rocking movement of a mother's arms. Rocking. My body was rocking. I had a moment of a nightmare, in which the rocking of a mother's arms turned into the rocking of a ship. I lurched in the pew. Sir Stanley's hand briefly touched my arm. I bolted up, hot, alarmed, embarrassed. My eyes lifted open. The bishop was still droning in a voice invented solely to tempt an old woman with sleep.

The mass of people rose about me, and I followed them. I stood when they prayed, waited while they sang, kneeled when they did, and sat back on the pew with what little grace I could muster. No wonder there wasn't a single solitary man or woman of African extraction in the church. If allowed to come, would they endure this hour of purgatory?

Could every Anglican ear possibly be tuned to the ever-mumbling bishop, who now offered words about resurrection and the everlasting? I heard something about the Israelites and the Promised Land, but my body ached for a horizontal position. One day soon I would tumble into that bed and from it rise no longer. But not yet. My eyes opened a little wider. *Not yet, please.*

I would need energy and vigour when speaking to the parliamentary committee. I would need lift in my legs, that day, and a whiff of my old passion. Alas, I had reached that fine age when it was easier to speak than to be spoken to. At that point in the service, it struck me that the last person on earth with a right to speak to any other was a diminutive Anglican bishop with no rolling of the eyes, no flailing of the hands, no kick in his legs and no crashing into the arms of Jesus. Come hell or high water, I would not be talked back into any Anglican church in this lifetime. If God had to be saluted, let it be among the Baptists of Birchtown or Freetown. At least they danced when they called out to Jesus, and hollered loud enough to keep the half-dead awake.

I managed to keep my chin up, and my eyelids sufficiently open to avoid detection. It was not pleasant to sit still in church, but that was no reason to embarrass Sir Stanley Hastings, his wife and five children.

Near the end of the service, I was shaken from my stupor one last time as the masses rose to sing. And I stood among them, fully awake this time. My heels were throbbing. They felt like they had been stripped of all padding, and now consisted of bone and bone only. As I stood righteously awake, with heels and every other part of me aching for the service to end, something happened to ease my discomfort and to prick up my ears. I heard voices. A thousand voices. The voices of all the good Anglicans were coming together.

When I caught the melody, it seemed faintly, distantly, impossibly familiar. Where had I heard it before?

> *When Britain first at Heav'n's command*
> *Arose from out the azure main;*
> *This was the charter of the land,*
> *And guardian angels sang this strain . . .*

The voices went on, and I dug deep into my memory. Was it in Charles Town that I had heard that song? No. New York? No, not there either. Where, then?

> *Rule, Britannia! Britannia, rule the waves:*
> *Britons never never never shall be slaves . . .*

Britons? Slaves? What nonsense was this? I listened again. The words were impossible. But it was not the lyrics I remembered. It was the music. What on blessed earth could this song be, and how was it that I somehow recognized its lift and its optimism?

> *The nations not so blest as thee,*
> *Shall in their turns to tyrants fall;*
> *While thou shalt flourish great and free,*
> *The dread and envy of them all . . .*

I tried to hold on to the words and turn them over in my mind. *Nations not so blest as thee, Shall in their turns to tyrants fall.* I glanced to my right. Sir Stanley Hastings was singing passionately, mouth like a baby robin in the spring. And then it came again. The chorus. The part that seemed most familiar of all. A sound that brought rousing passion to the good Anglican churchgoers and made them sing as lustily as I had ever heard white people sing.

> *Rule, Britannia! Britannia, rule the waves*
> *Britons never never never shall be slaves . . .*

That was it. There. Now I remembered. It wasn't New York. or Charles Town. It was earlier, much earlier. It was on the slave ship. In the cabin, beneath the decks, with the medicine man. He used to like to sing sometimes, and I had no idea whatsoever of his meaning. He was ailing, I supposed, and perhaps even mad, and sometimes in the middle of the night, when he had taken too much from the bottle and already soiled another woman from my homeland, he would lie in his bed, facing the low ceiling, and over the thrashing of the waves and the slapping of the sails he would shout out the chorus over and over again. For an audience, he had only the parrot in its covered cage, and me, lying rigidly beside him.

> *Rule, Britannia! Britannia, rule the waves*
> *Britons never never never shall be slaves . . .*

Unaware of English, and unaccustomed to white folk, and not even a woman yet but dangerously close to becoming one, I would lie as still as I could in the medicine man's bed and wonder what he was singing. Let him sing, I thought, because his hands don't touch me when he sings. Let him sing, I thought, hoping to spend just one more night out of reach of his thick, hairy fingers. Let him sing, I thought, ashamed that he spent himself on women from my land. The misfortune of those women was my good luck, their misery my escape.

> *Rule, Britannia! Britannia, rule the waves*
> *Britons never never never . . .*

Never never never were the last words I heard, until perceiving shouts of alarm from the men and women all around me. I must have fainted dead away. Sir Stanley Hastings had clearly caught me in my fall, for as I came to I was laid out straight on the wooden pew. Finally. The position I had sought for a full hour. *Never never never . . .* I was no longer with the medicine man, no longer a six-foot toss from the coldest grave on earth, but back in the Anglican church, stretched out on a hard wooden pew, under the protection of the most venerated abolitionist in England. Sir Stanley Hastings' firm hand kept me from sliding off the pew. I kept my eyes shut and wondered what to do. The Anglicans were in a state of vocal agitation, and Sir Stanley Hastings the most. *I plead with you, people, please stand back. Please. Back. Our noble visitor has fainted, surely due to the excitement of our faith, but fear not. We shall revive her. Here. She has a pulse. She is still breathing. Stand back please, and we shall aid her. All she needs is a little air.*

I kept my eyes closed until they carried me into the sun.

They come and go from holy ground

{MANHATTAN, 1775}

SOLOMON LINDO AND I SAILED from Charles Town on the *Queen Charlotte*. Through day after day of sailing, the waves rose and tumbled and foamed at the mouth as if calling out to me, *you will never see land again*. The water looked dark and menacing enough to kill a person with its chill. I dreaded retreating into my tiny apartment below deck, and would have stood day and night above water level had it not been for the air that grew increasingly cold as we sailed north. Lindo tried every day to speak with me, but I excused myself from any discussions about his correspondence.

Negro servants in white breeches and red vests served boiled crabs and roasted peanuts to Charles Town merchants who were happy enough to make friendly with them out on the open sea, but I wasn't allowed to enter the dining hall for white passengers and refused Lindo's invitations to join him in his private cabin. He seemed bent on taking the trip as a time to relax and socialize with me, and was miffed that I kept my distance from him.

On the third day of the voyage—the only mild and sunny part of the trip—men and women from planting or merchant families lounged in chairs on the deck, attended to by Negroes bringing Madeira, cigars and oranges. Lindo unpacked his portable chess set and asked me to sit with him, which I accepted only because my legs were too tired to stand any longer. People thought it a novelty that I could play. Lindo challenged a man in a straw hat and with red, sunburned forearms to play me, and they wagered two guineas on the outcome. Lindo had shown me all the strategies years ago, when our relations had still been cordial. Dominate the centre of the board, at first. Aim your bishops like cannons, and place your knights like spies. Leave the enemy no room to move. Control, attack and pin the king. It was an ugly game, I thought, but it kept me from having to chat with Lindo or to hear him drone on about the evaporating indigo market. The man with the sunburn was astonished to find himself check-mated and enraged to see Lindo turn the guineas over to me.

"She earned them," Lindo said, shrugging.

I knew better than to look into the eyes of my opponent, and slid the gold into my clothing.

We sailed into the harbour later the next morning. It was only upon approaching land that I saw that New York was an island, like a long leg with all the people shoved into the foot.

"They call it Manhattan," Lindo said, "after the Indian word for 'hilly island,' *Manna-hata*."

My spirits had been low during the entire trip over. However, as I looked out at the streets choked with build-ings and counted some fifteen church steeples—the tallest of which grew as high as a giant tree—the weight of the past began to lessen. *Mann-ahata* offered a comforting sort of chaos. Island or no island, perhaps it would be the sort of place in which I could take refuge.

On the wharf, we were swarmed by a shouting mob. A Negro threw my valise and Lindo's trunk on a cart and demanded a shilling from Lindo, who complied. Following the baggage man, we headed into streets packed with people, carts and horses. There were wooden buildings, but ones made of brick too. The buildings were sharp and rectangular, neat and trim. We hadn't travelled for long when we passed the outskirts of an area that had no proper buildings, but rather an odd collection of shanties, shacks and tents with corners poking out at all angles, like broken bones. Moving in and out of the mud alleys and paths were Negro men and women, some carrying scraps they must have pillaged from the shipyards: broken spars, ripped sails and long strips of wood bent like ribs.

"Canvas town," Lindo said. "Stay away from it, if you know what's good for you."

"Who are those people?" I asked.

"The Canvas town Negroes," he said. "A ne'er-do-well lot always willing to relieve you of your goods."

"Are they free?" I asked.

"The question is how they live," he replied.

I took another look in the direction of the Negroes entering and leaving their shacks, hauling canvas and water. One woman even had a pot cooking over a low fire. They appeared to move about unmolested.

"Let's not tarry now," Lindo said, and asked the baggage man to hurry up.

We left the edge of Canvas town and entered another built-up area. I read the names of every street. Broadway. Wall Street. William. We came to Broad Street, and then Pearl. Under a hanging sign that said THE FRAUNCES TAVERN, our porter opened the doors to a hotel.

A tall, well-built and light-skinned Negro with a blue chintz shirt and a watch on a chain stood behind the registration desk, smiling. "Welcome," he said, in a lilt that was neither American nor African. "Sam Fraunces," he said, shaking Lindo's hand, "but you can call me Black Sam or just Sam if you prefer. I know you haven't been here before, because I never forget a guest." He turned to me and shook my hand too. "And I know, without a shadow of a doubt, that I haven't seen you before. I've been wanting to meet you, though, for a long time. Yes I have."

I grinned.

West Indian, that's what he was. Probably Jamaican. I had heard Jamaican accents in Charles Town, but no Jamaican or other Negro could have owned a tavern there. And this wasn't just a tavern. It was a ten-room hotel in a two-storey red-brick building with a reputation for good food so widely established that people had mentioned it on the ship from Charles Town.

"I'm afraid I don't know your names," he said.

Lindo introduced only himself.

"From your bags, I surmise you have come a distance," Sam said.

"Charles Town," Lindo said.

I saw a smile tug at the corners of Sam's fine, wide-lipped mouth. Steady and solid, calm and confident. "Will the lady be requiring—"

"Yes," Lindo cut in, "separate rooms. I require a spacious room and please bring up a table and chair, as I have business to conduct."

"We'll see to that, sir," Sam said.

Lindo began to sign a registration book. He wrote, *Solomon Lindo and servant*, lost his patience, and said he had to get cleaned up and tend to some affairs in town before the close of business.

"But the form, sir, and the payment," Sam said. "Sorry, but no square money. I only take silver."

"She'll take care of it," Lindo said, handing me a pouch.

While Sam Fraunces arranged for a porter to escort Lindo to his room, I wrote my name into the registration book: *Aminata Diallo*. I took it as a good sign that I was free to write my own name in New York City. The mere act of writing it, moving smoothly, unerringly with the quill in the calligraphy that Mrs Lindo had so patiently taught me, sealed a private contract that I had made with myself. I had now written my name on a public document, and I was a person, with just as much right to life and liberty as the man who claimed to own me. I would not return to Charles Town. Never mind that April in New York felt as cold as December in Charles Town. Never mind the horse droppings and shouting porters and clamouring men pushing and shoving on the wharves. Never mind any of that. It was already clear to me that there were Negroes circulating freely in New York. I would somehow find my place among them. I would not submit again to ownership by any man.

Solomon Lindo and the porter went upstairs.

Sam retrieved the quill from me and placed it in its holder. "If you don't mind me saying, I have never seen a lady write so bold and pretty."

I smiled and met his dark, curious, dancing eyes.

Sam Fraunces folded his hands and glanced at the registration book again. "A most intriguing name," he said. "A-mee . . ."

"Meena," I said. "You can just call me Meena."

"That's easier than it looks," he said. "Is Mr Lindo your . . ."

"Owner," I said. I wanted him to know my situation. Something about this man's confidence suggested that he could help me. "But not for long," I added.

The tall man busied himself with his stack of registration papers and mumbled in a low voice, "New York is a place of opportunities."

I too lowered my voice. "Can you help?"

The boy who had taken Lindo's bags upstairs had returned for mine. Sam cleared his throat. "Room 4," he said, pointing to my bag. When the boy left, Sam said, "Have you eaten lunch?"

"No. We were four days at sea and I had no appetite."

"And how is your appetite now?" Sam said, grinning again.

"It has returned."

"Then I'll bring you something of my own making," he said.

Sam's porter showed me to my room. I opened the shutter and looked out the window at a sea of activity. A young Negro was playing a fiddle on the street. He spotted a well-to-do-looking white man, ran up to him and played the fiddle while walking alongside the gentleman, who finally parted with a coin. The fiddler glanced around, saw another white man in a waistcoat, and ran toward him.

I stepped back from the window, lay down on the soft bed and, listening to the pealing of church bells and the clattering of horses' hooves, fell asleep.

I HAD NEVER BEFORE HAD THE EXPERIENCE of watching a tall black man open my door, slip in with a tray of steaming food and set it down on a table near my bed.

"Apologies," he said, "but you did say that you were hungry."

I had fallen asleep dressed just the way I was, and felt a little awkward swinging my legs off the bed to stand and smooth the wrinkles from my clothing.

"Would you prefer to eat in solitude?" he asked.

"If you have the time, you may sit with me, for I have never cared to eat alone."

He smiled. "Most civilized, and I accept." He slid onto a chair across the table from me. "Mr Lindo departed while we were preparing your meal," he said. "What sort of business is he in?"

"Indigo," I told him.

"He said the two of you would be going to a concert this evening, and asked me to remind you to be ready for seven."

I sat at the table to eat. He had made bean soup with a dose of pepper hot enough to take me back home. On a side plate was cornbread, sweetened with honey and coconut milk. He also brought me fresh crab cakes. He said the way to make a decent crab cake was to roll just a touch of bread crumbs, melted butter and cream into the crabmeat. It was so good that you wanted to treat it tenderly.

"Crab is not something to overpower with energetic spicing," he said. "Crabmeat wants to melt quietly on the tongue."

I was ravenous. Between mouthfuls, I asked him questions. Sam Fraunces had been born and raised in Jamaica. His father was a slave owner and his mother a slave who had been set free by the father. Sam himself had been sent on his way when he was fifteen, with enough money to travel to New York and invest in a business. He had kept his money well guarded and had managed restaurants for two years until he understood the business in and out, and had made all the connections he needed with suppliers. He then got a mortgage to buy the current building and opened a restaurant called The Queen Charlotte.

"They say she's the Black Queen," I said.

"Some say that, and others dispute it," he said. "But nobody gives a fig about it around here. The British—the whole lot of them, King and Queen included—aren't exactly the best-loved people in New York."

Sam did not want his tavern and hotel to be associated with British royalty, so he renamed it the Fraunces Tavern.

"Better for business," he said. "The Tories can dine here, and feel fine. The Americans can dine here too. I say—you obliterated those crab cakes. I'll take that as a compliment. And let me return one: you are a very handsome woman."

I set my fork down gently. "I appreciate the meal and your company," I said, "and don't wish to be impolite, but . . ."

He put up his palm. "Let me spare you the indelicacy,"

he said, shifting in his seat. "One sort of appetite doesn't automatically lead to another."

"I'm sure a man in your position has many opportunities," I said.

He grinned and did not deny it. I thought he might turn to leave immediately, but he folded his hands one over the over, let his lips settle into a more tranquil pose and said, "From the moons on your face, I suspect that your journey began long before Charles Town. I can't help every person who walks in my doors, but I will do what I can for you."

"Is it possible to escape in New York?" I said.

"Canvas Town is where most go," he said, "but white men sometimes send in raiding parties and grab whoever they can—their own slaves or free Negroes."

Having found a sympathetic source of information, I brought out all my questions.

Yes, Sam said, I could most probably find a way to sustain myself in New York. He might have some work for me.

"What about a ship to Africa?" I asked.

"Impossible," Sam said.

"Are you sure?" I asked.

"To even dream of it is madness," he said.

"Why?"

"Ships don't sail from New York to Africa. They go to England first, unload sugar and rum and tobacco and the indigo that your Lindo so fancies, and then they sail to Africa."

"So from here it is possible for a person to get to Africa," I said.

"A shipper, merchant or slave-trader, yes. Via London. You? No. Never. What Liverpool ship captain would waste his time taking you to Africa? He would just sell you into slavery again, and you'd probably end up in Barbados or Virginia. And if you did somehow make it back to Africa, the slave-traders would just pack you up and send you right back over here."

I looked down at my hands.

"Don't lose faith," he said. "This is the best city for you. New York has places to hide, and offers many kinds of work. I made out just fine when I came here."

"But you came free."

"And you are already free where it matters most, in your mind. This is the best place in the Thirteen Colonies. It's the best place in the world. Forget London. New York is what you want."

I had a thousand more questions—where could I hide, how would I work and what would I do to feed myself?— but Sam Fraunces was out of time.

"I expect a full tavern at dinner," he said.

THAT NIGHT, SOLOMON LINDO TOOK ME to hear a cellist play a solo concerto by J.S. Bach in the Trinity Church—the one with the highest steeple in town.

"One hundred and seventy-five feet," Lindo said.

Climbing the steps, we passed black men, women and children with palms outstretched. I felt uncomfortable about having nothing to give them, and hoped that bad luck didn't drive me to join them anytime soon. Lindo fished six pence from his pocket, dropped them into a woman's hand and took my arm. His token gesture angered me. If he thought that it would lead me to write his letters dutifully the next day, he would soon discover his error. Inside the church, I saw a handwritten notice posted on a wall: *Volunteer needed, for teaching Negroes.*

We took seats in the first pew, and when the concert began, I sat close enough to the cellist to almost reach out and touch the hairs on his bow. He was a young black man with a neatly trimmed brown beard, and acorn-brown eyes that scoured my face as he played. He knew the music by heart, and instead of casting his eyes at the written sheets of music, this man, whose name was given on the program as Adonis Thomas, looked at me. As he leaned into his instrument, backed off, leaned into it again, dipped his head to punctuate a change in the music, I felt that he was speaking to me.

I have always had difficulty listening to the frenzied sound of many instruments together. In Charles Town, on occasion, I had heard flutes, oboes, horns and violins all rise together, but they always seemed like voices at war. Here, though, I could befriend the cellist, fall into his music, heed the melodic urgency, and be touched by the way it dipped low like the voices of village elders and skimmed high like singing children. Adonis Thomas's cello whispered to my soul. *Do not lose hope*, it said. *You too can make something beautiful, but first you must be free.*

LINDO HAD INSTRUCTED ME TO MEET HIM at eight o'clock the next morning in the hotel's breakfast room, but I arrived a few minutes early, to find Sam Fraunces.

"How was the concert?" he asked.

"Music to lift my spirits," I said.

"Let's hope it lifts his spirits too," Sam said.

"Whose spirits?"

"Why, those of Adonis Thomas, the cellist."

"What's wrong with him?"

"Didn't Mr Lindo tell you that he is the slave of a wealthy man in town?"

My jaw fell open. "He played so beautifully," I said.

"With real longing, I would expect," Sam said.

Lindo came down the stairs and took me into the dining room. I had never eaten with a white man in a public place, and was surprised that they let me in. But it was a Negro who came to take our orders, and he simply gave me a little smile. Lindo ordered buns and eggs for both of us, and asked for coffee.

I asked the waiter for tea with milk and sugar.

"We have coffee and beer this morning," the waiter said.

"Coffee with milk and sugar, then," I said.

"The patriots are furious at the British, and are weaning themselves from tea," Lindo whispered to me. "Now they say it weakens the tone of the stomach, inducing tremors and spasmodic affections. Can't say I blame them. The British have united the patriots in anger over the Tea Act and soon enough, if we lose the indigo bounty, they'll stir up even more resentment in South Carolina."

I wasn't hungry but felt that I should eat. I had to keep myself strong and healthy now, and sensed that soon I might spend a long time between meals.

Lindo said that he had prepared a letter to William Tryon, the governor of New York, about why the British bounty on indigo should be protected. Perhaps the governor could convince the right people in London.

"I have it in draft form, with corrections in the margins. I need you to write it properly so I can deliver it tomorrow," he said.

I didn't want to agree, but it didn't seem wise to refuse.

"Where is it?" I asked.

"In my room. I'll leave you the key. There is a large desk in there, with all the writing materials that you should need."

I nodded. "How long will you be out today?"

"I have meetings until the evening," he said. "It will take hours of persuasion to get an appointment with the governor. The man dines and golfs all day with the Anglicans."

I sipped my hot, sweet, milky coffee.

"Did you know that Adonis Thomas is a slave?"

"Who?"

"The cellist from last night."

"Of course. Do you think a Negro could learn to play like that without instruction? And where do you think he'd get such instruction? Living in Canvas Town?"

"I would have thought—"

"I don't have time for that right now," he said, getting up from the table. "Make sure that letter is ready by the end of the day. Somebody in London needs to know that indigo is rotting in barrels on the wharves of Charles Town."

After breakfast I could not bring myself to enter Lindo's room. I rested on my bed until the sounds through my window beckoned me out. My feet felt light, as if they were already touching free ground. People rushed in every direction, and nobody took objection to me. When I rounded a corner and the sun splashed on my face, I felt impossibly optimistic. I could walk in any direction I chose, so I headed over to Wall Street. When I got there, I heard shouting and looked up toward Broadway. Outside a fine, two-storey wooden home, I saw an odd crowd of white men, all agitating with arms raised: ruffians, labourers and well-dressed men too.

"We'll bust the door,"someone shouted. The crowd hummed with nasty energy.

The house was painted white, and had a neat stone path leading from the door to the street. A house like that in Charles Town might contain a man, a woman, their children, and one or two slaves. I wondered if slaves were in this house. I wondered if, for some reason, these angry men wanted to put their hands on Negroes.

"Down with the British," someone shouted.

A pack of men surged forward to kick and pound the door. Others began throwing rocks at the shuttered windows. The door opened. A white butler appeared. He was dragged out, struck in the face and knocked to the ground. The mob surged over him—bleeding nose and all—and into the house. I felt that I should run, in case they came for me next, but no other residents—white or Negro—emerged from the house. I saw only the rioting men, some still shoving in through the door and others struggling back out with vases, fine mahogany boxes, chairs and rugs. Inside, shutters were broken and silk curtains thrown out the windows. It was almost hypnotizing to witness their frenzied anger, but after a few minutes, when looters emerged with a cask of rum and sucked the liquor thirstily from their own palms, I couldn't help thinking about the horror that a person like Mrs Lindo or Dolly might feel to be trapped in a house with such livid men.

The butler managed to get up onto his feet. Rather than taking flight, he stood to the side with his fingers on his temples. More and more people surged up Wall Street, shouting news that I could not understand.

A white boy no more than seventeen stood next to me and hollered for the whole world to hear, "Blood spilt at Lexington and Concord."

In the excitement, I risked a question. "Whatever do you mean?"

"Rebels fought the Tories in Massachusetts, and the rebels won."

He was shouting so loud that I took a step back. He could see that I couldn't quite follow him, but all he really wanted was to be heard proclaiming himself in public.

"Rebels, that's me," he said. "Tories, that's . . . are you a Tory?"

"What precisely is that?"

"You talk fancy, for a nigger," he said. "You better not be a Tory. It's war now and we shall have freedom."

"Freedom? For the slaves?"

"Niggers, nothing. I'm talking about us. Rebels. Patriots. We shall be free of the British and their taxes. Never again shall we be slaves. Are you with the rebels or the Tories?"

"Does it matter?"

"Pick the rebels if you know what's good for you," he said, and ran off with his friends.

The streets were teeming with people who sang and shouted and shot muskets in the air. By the time I got back to the Fraunces Tavern, pandemonium had erupted inside. Men were drinking, falling down dead drunk, cursing the British and vowing that they would one day see freedom. They were eating, too, and Sam and his crew were busy serving them.

"What's happening, Sam?"

"If you help me get this mob fed and out of here," he said to me, "I'll pay you back."

I longed to get somewhere safe, away from the boiling anger, but the offer was too good to pass up.

I worked in the kitchen, pouring beer from kegs into pitchers, making punch with rum and lemonade and bits of orange, arranging plates of meats and cheeses and fruit, and passing it to the men who were serving. Customers were shouting so loud that I wondered if they would riot. But as wild as they had been on the street, they loved Sam Fraunces and his tavern and seemed at home. Drunk and boisterous though they were, they didn't break a thing.

Eventually the crowd thinned and the patriots headed back into the streets to celebrate. Sam took me by the arm.

"Meena, make a run for it," he said.

"Now?"

"War is inevitable, and the Brits are in for the surprise of their life. They have no idea how angry people are. If you flee now, Lindo won't have time to hunt you down."

"Why?"

"I've just heard that the British are talking of closing the harbour. Your man will want to return to his own home or business, because people could be rioting there too. If he doesn't get out today, he may not get out at all."

I never wanted to see Lindo again, but the idea of fleeing him terrified me.

"Where am I to hide?" I said.

"Go north for now. Go up Broadway and into the woods."

"What about Canvas Town?"

"No. Not yet. He may send an agent after you."

I felt paralyzed. What was I to do alone in the woods? But Fraunces was tossing apples, bread, a strip of salted beef and a small blanket into a sack.

"Take the bag. Go now. Do not return to your room, and do not wait any longer. North. Up Broadway. When you come to the end of town, keep walking deep into the woods." Out on Pearl Street, men were pouring more rum from another stolen cask into their palms. "Come see me in a few days," Fraunces whispered. "Come in the darkness. Tap three times at the door to the kitchen, in the alley out back."

Out I went into the insanity, venturing among the drunks and the laughing, cursing, brawling men who were breaking into all the fine houses on Wall Street. I got up to Broadway, passed the Trinity Church where I had been just the night before, and kept walking up Broadway to a smaller church called St. Paul's Chapel. Seeking a quiet place to think, I climbed the steps to peer inside and saw a few Negroes in a meeting. They turned around and stared at me. I turned and left the church. On the street, an old black man took my arm and said, "I wouldn't head that way if I were you."

"Which way?"

"That way you're going. Into Holy Ground."

"What's Holy Ground?"

"The church owns the land, but it's full of ladies of ill repute. You look like you're new in town, so you ought to know."

"Which way is safe?"

"Ain't nowhere safe these times," he said. "North you'll find woods. But be careful out there."

269

I changed direction and headed north as the man had suggested. The crowds thinned and the sounds of the revellers died down. After a time I crossed over the last street and entered a wooded area. I kept walking. I was frightened by the darkness and the lonely sound of my feet on dry leaves, but I kept on going. As I walked, I wondered if Solomon Lindo had ever imagined that I would escape.

Passing through a clearing, I noticed some whittled sticks pushed into a rectangular pattern on the ground, near a mound of stones in a perfect circle. Farther on, I saw more sticks and stones in the same pattern. When I finally believed that I had walked deeper into the wilderness than Lindo could ever imagine, I sat on the ground, laid the sack from Sam Fraunces by the thick trunk of a tree for a pillow and lay down to stretch out my legs. It was late in the afternoon of April 23, 1775, and I had taken back my freedom.

I visualized that sometime around that moment, Solomon Lindo would be arriving back at the Fraunces Tavern, expecting his revised letter to Governor Tryon. In the madness and revelry on the streets of New York, he would not find a soul to point to me. Indeed, if he stopped to ask anyone, he might be taken for one of the men who owned a fine house on Wall Street and put himself in danger. I wondered if Sam Fraunces was right—if Lindo would take the first ship sailing south from New York. If Fraunces was wrong, Lindo would look around town for me, but surely he would not come this far. Nearly twenty years had passed since I was seized in the woods outside Bayo, but here I was, all alone and surrounded by the trees of another continent—and I was free again.

I slept fitfully that night, huddled under my thin blanket. In my dreams, rabbits chased across paths and stopped in mid-flight, wide-eyed, to stare at me. There were two thin crescent moons in the sky. And I heard an owl calling for me. *Aminata Diallo*, it called over and over.

I awoke often and each time I fell back to sleep, the strange images resumed.

In the morning, I was aware of light touching my eyelids, and I heard voices calling again. Voices of Africa. Could they be calling my name? I opened my eyes. The ground was wet. The blanket was still over me, and the small sack of food sat against my belly. From where did those voices come? I got up, stuffed the blanket in the sack, shivered in the cold, damp morning, and stepped past a few trees, back in the direction of the city, toward those sounds.

They weren't voices of danger. They were voices of mourning, voices from my homeland. After another minute, I put my hand on the trunk of a tree at the edge of a small clearing and stared. There, near the sticks and the round mounds of rocks that I had passed the night before, was a small group of Negroes chanting African songs. It was no language that I knew, but it was from my homeland, deep and threaded with longing. The people had formed a circle, and they danced as I had seen before, arms raised, hips rotating, barely moving their feet. I drifted into their midst like a child drawn to her mother.

In the middle of the circle stood an African woman, wailing and holding the body of a child. The child's head was uncovered, but the body was wrapped in an indigo-coloured linen. Around its waist was a set of blue, green and white glass beads. The woman lowered the child into the ground, and a man with a shovel covered up the hole. Around it, other women arranged a perfect, circular mound of rocks, while more placed whittled sticks into the earth in a rectangular form the size of the child.

I moved forward with the wailing, and finally I was right up among the people, sobbing and moving with them. Some of the men and women had sculpted faces, but none had my moons, and none spoke Bamanankan or Fulfulde. They took me into their dancing, and did not ask where I

271

came from, for all they had to do was look at me and hear my own sobs in my maternal tongue and they knew that I was one of them. The dead infant was the child I had once been; it was my own lost Mamadu; it was every person who had been tossed into the unforgiving sea on the endless journey across the big river.

When the dancing was over, an older man turned back toward the city and the others walked behind in single file. I fell in with a woman at the back of the line.

"Where do you live?" I asked. She did not speak English, so I spoke to the woman ahead of her, repeating, "Where do you live?"

"Everywhere there are Africans," she said. "Some in Canvas Town, you know that?" she asked. I nodded. "Some with white folks who own us."

"Some free, and some not?" I asked.

"None of us are truly free, until we go back to our land," she said.

"And where is your land, in Africa?" I asked.

"We are from everywhere," she said, motioning at those walking ahead of her, "but I am Ashanti."

I did not know that word, so I repeated it.

"And you?" she said.

"Fula," I said, "and Bamana."

"Little bit of everything?" the woman said. "It like that over here."

"You live in Canvas Town?" I asked.

"No," she said. "I work in house for man from England who say he make me free one day. But there is no free in this land. There is only food in your belly and clothes on your back and roof to hold off the rain. Home is only place that's free. That baby we done buried is on her way home. You see the coloured glass?"

"The beads around her waist?"

"They bring her spirit clear across the water, and take her home where she belongs."

As I smiled at the woman, I stopped walking. We were coming closer to the edge of the city than I cared to go.

"Good place for hiding," she said. "The toubabu don't come to our burying ground."

She raised her fingers in salutation, and turned away. The Africans kept walking south through the woods, and none looked back at me.

AFTER TWO MORE DAYS AND NIGHTS in the woods, I knocked at the back of the Fraunces Tavern. I waited, knocked again, and Sam finally opened the kitchen door.

"Look at you," he said.

I was shivering, and my clothes were wet and filthy.

"Is he here?" I asked.

"Gone, the day of the outbreak," Sam said. "He came here an hour after you left, raged for a few minutes and then took the first ship south."

"Could I have something to drink and eat?"

"I'll get you something while you get into clean clothes."

"He didn't take my things with him?"

"I hid your bag and told him that you had taken it with you."

"I am in your debt," I said.

He put a hand on my shoulder. "You will no doubt sink a little deeper. But no worries. You will work it off."

I struck a deal with Sam Fraunces. He gave me five shillings a week, let me stay on a makeshift bed in a cramped storage room and take my meals with the kitchen staff, in exchange for working six hours a day for him. I washed dishes, swept floors, cleaned vegetables, emptied chamber pots and wrote invoices and receipts, but I knew that the arrangement was temporary. The Fraunces Tavern was hardly a safe place to hide from Lindo.

At the Trinity Church, I found out that the teaching of Negroes took place six blocks to the north, at St. Paul's

Chapel. The chapel was tiny in comparison to Trinity, but it was a charming place and more suitable to ordinary folks. The white minister clasped my hands when he heard that I could read and write.

"Just the person I've been looking for," he said.

He sent out word through some Negroes he knew, and that Tuesday evening I taught my first class. Six Negroes drifted into the sanctuary as darkness was falling. In a private room lit with lamps and candles, they told me their names, huddled around me, put their hands on my shoulders and arms and back, and peered at the words taking shape under my hand.

"What's that?" asked a tall thin man of about twenty.

"Your name," I said. "Claybourne Mitchell."

"Well, I can't read, so how do I know it from any other name?"

"I'll teach you," I said.

"I can cooper you a barrel of any size," he said, "but I ain't teachable."

"Sure you are," I said.

"Ain't not. My master saw to that. It's why I run from him."

"You can do it," I said.

Hand on my shoulder, he kept watching me write. "Claybourne the only name they done give me," he said. "Mitchell is a name I done took. Heard a man called that once, and liked it so much I decided when I got here I was gonna be a new man. Free man. With two names, both for myself."

Another woman of about the same age, much shorter than Claybourne but twice as wide, pushed in closer.

"Y'all giving that man too much time," she said. "What about my name? When you gonna write it down?"

"Right here," I said.

"Where?" she said.

"Here," I said, pointing down the list of names. "Bertilda Mathias."

"It's the name I done got, and I don't see no reason to change it like Claybourne. The man got a mouth the size of a drawbridge."

"Who you calling bridge mouth?" Claybourne said.

"Y'all think this here African woman just for you?" she shot back.

I got Bertilda to tell me a little more about herself, and wrote that down too for her to see. "Laundress at British barracks."

"Y'all not writing down how much they pay me," she said.

"No, you didn't tell me that."

"Good. 'Cause I want more. Write it down when I gets a shilling a day. That's what my mama got, till she up and died."

"How about if I write 'I want one shilling a day'?" I said.

"You do that, sister. Show me what that look like."

"You done run from the master too?" Claybourne asked her.

"No, I ain't," she answered. "Doan you call me no slave. Ain't never been, and ain't never gonna be. Mama got herself free before she had me, and she was laundressing for the British since my early days."

I wrote down a few more words—"I was born free"—while all six people jostled to get in closer.

After I wrote down the names and a few circumstances about each person, we practised repeating the sounds of each letter. Then I wrote a few other words: *New York. Canvas Town. Tories. Patriots. Negroes. Slaves. Free folks. White folks.* After two hours, the minister brought in bread, cheese and apples.

"Good bread," Claybourne said. "Fresh. Last bread I had was tougher than a rum barrel. Would have busted the teeth of a rat." Everybody laughed, including Bertilda. Claybourne told the minister I was a good teacher.

"You better treat her right, then," the minister said, "'cause she's teaching you for free."

"She the best teacher I ever done had," Claybourne said.

"Y'all ain't never had no teaching before," Bertilda shot back.

"Yes, but I can read my own name now," he said.

"Soon you'll learn to write your names," I said.

"How do you write 'no rats allowed here'?" Claybourne asked.

Everybody looked at him, uncomprehending.

"I'm gonna write a big fat sign and put it up in Canvas Town."

They laughed all the way out of the chapel. In the street, the group splintered and disappeared in the night.

After two more weeks of lessons, Claybourne offered to show me how to go about getting materials to build my own shack in Canvas Town. He said he would bring a hammer and crowbar, and told me to bring a few shillings and a lamp. We met at dusk one evening on Pearl Street, outside the Fraunces Tavern, Claybourne with a cloth sack hanging from his shoulder.

"Where are we going?" I said.

"Gonna find a house busting," he said.

We spent an hour or two walking up and down the streets, avoiding horses and their droppings. Each time we turned a corner, I noticed a group of young Negro men trailing a block behind us.

"Don't pay them no mind," Claybourne said.

We kept walking up and down the city streets until, up ahead, we saw a mob of white men running out of a two-storey house with lamps, silverware and casks of liquor.

"We waits till the bees leave the hive," Claybourne said.

We circled around and returned half an hour later. Darkness had fallen. The door was broken. The shutters had been kicked off the windows. Two barrels were turned over in the street, the last drops of spilled wine glistening in the moonlight.

"Our turn now," Claybourne said.

"What if someone's in there?"

"Mob like that come and go, ain't nobody left and hardly nothing left neither," he said.

I didn't want to break into somebody's home, even if it had already been damaged. I thought about my own mother. If she knew everything I had been through, what would she say right now? Claybourne saw me hesitating at the door.

"Everybody get their turn and the trick is knowing when to take it. Come on, girl, it's now or never."

I followed him in through the door. The house had been ransacked. I saw shattered vases and wine racks emptied and kicked into splinters. On the wall was a portrait of a man and a woman, each sitting in a fine chair. Someone had ripped through the canvas with a knife.

"Who lives here?" I asked.

"They gone now," Claybourne said.

"But who are they?"

"Tories, I suspect," Claybourne said. "Rebels been trashing Tory mansions ever since Lexington and Concord."

While I held the lamp, Claybourne slipped the sack off his shoulder, removed a crowbar and pried the legs off a fine table. In a closet with no clothes left, he found two woollen blankets. In a kitchen where the only food remaining had been strewn on the floor, he slid three drawers out of a counter. He moved quickly from room to room, prying posts off beds, gathering a cloth mattress stuffed with straw, and busting apart an odd green table with pockets along the sides and coloured balls inside the pockets.

"What's that?" I asked.

"Found one of these before," Claybourne said. "White folks' game is all I know."

"How are we going to carry all this stuff?" I asked.

"Did you bring your five shillings?"

"Yes."

"Good."

After we piled everything at the front door, Claybourne slid two fingers into his mouth and let out a piercing whistle. Four teenaged Negro boys came from around the corner and ran up to us.

"Canvas Town, and make it quick," Claybourne said.

They stood waiting.

"One shilling each," he said.

I dropped a coin in each of four hands. The boys grabbed everything they could and took off in the night. I had a bundle of table legs in my arms, and Claybourne had the tabletop balanced on his back. We struggled down the dark streets, but after a time were relieved by the boys, who ran back to help us lug the rest.

The next day, on Claybourne's instructions, I gave another shilling to a dock worker, who let me take away a roll of several yards of ripped canvas. With the help of three other men who had been learning to read and write at St. Paul's Chapel, Claybourne built me a little shack on the back edge of Canvas Town. It didn't seem possible that a home could be created out of the items we had stolen, but a few people brought extra wood from broken tables and from studs ripped out of walls, and in a matter of days I was able to move from the Fraunces Tavern into a lean-to shack just big enough for me. The legs of the green cloth-covered table with the hanging pockets were neatly sawn off, and it was laid down flat to keep my straw mattress off the ground. I had room enough for a chair, a lamp and the three drawers stacked one on another. If I managed to find a book or two, I would keep them there. Canvas was hung from the door for a bit of privacy, and Claybourne promised to build me a swinging door to help keep out the cold.

"But get yourself a man before the snow falls," he said.

"I've already got a man, and I hope he finds me," I said.

"And where's he at?"

"Can't say right now. Somewhere in South Carolina."

Claybourne shook his head, but said no more.

SOLOMON LINDO DID NOT RETURN to New York City and so it felt safe for me to keep returning to the Fraunces Tavern. Sam let me take my meals, relieved me from chamberpot duty, and gave me more work writing his letters and keeping his ledgers. He increased my pay to seven shillings a week, which was enough to keep me clothed. When travellers left books, clothes and old shoes in their rooms, Sam turned them over to me. Word got out that I knew how to catch babies, and I caught two of them at no charge in Canvas Town. As spring turned into summer, the group of Negroes attending my Tuesday evening classes grew from six to ten and then to fifteen. Sometimes, the minister watched for a few minutes from the back of the room, but then he retreated to let us have our lessons privately. Nobody paid me, but once every week or two somebody came by my little lean-to with more wood, nails or canvas.

"Gotta fix this shack up good and tight," Bertilda said, "to get our African teacher through the New York winter."

Under my instruction, a seventy-year-old white-haired Negro woman named Miss Betty learned the alphabet in three lessons, and was reading a month later. I asked if she was free, and she told me that she was too old for any of that foolery. She had belonged to the same white man for thirty years—a man, she said, who worshipped King George and had moved recently from Boston to New York. Now that she was old and useless, he didn't mind her learning to read.

"You need to get yourself free," Claybourne said to her.

"And live in that pigpen you call Canvas Town?" Miss Betty shot back.

"We's free," Claybourne said.

"Free with the fleas is what you is," she said. "I got me a clean bed under a roof that don't leak and I don't need no charity meals at St. Paul's Chapel."

"Good," Claybourne said. "Can I have your apple?"

Bertilda slapped the man playfully. "You is a right nasty cuss, you know that?"

"I'll keep my own apple, thank you very much, and just to spite you, Mr. Claybourne Know-It-All," Miss Betty said.

As the summer wore on, Miss Betty attended every class, even when I started teaching two evenings a week. She always sat beside Claybourne, and seemed to look forward to bickering with him. When she failed to show up for two lessons in a row, Bertilda put on her best clothes, asked me to come along to Miss Betty's owner's place, and we knocked on the door.

A white-haired white man opened the door, holding a gun. "If you're hooligans," he said, "I'll shoot holes through your hearts."

"We're here for Miss Betty," I said.

"Who are you?"

"I'm her teacher."

"Teacher? What foolishness is this?"

"Her teacher, at St. Paul's Chapel."

"Teaching her what?"

"To read and write."

"Silly bat. She didn't tell me anything about that. She said she was going for religion, and I had no objection. Well, she's taken ill and I don't expect you'll see much more of her."

We asked to visit with her. The man, who said his name was Mr Croft, let us into a room at the back of the house. Miss Betty was lying in bed under a thin red blanket and could barely whisper.

"Haven't had no visitors before," she said, gasping.

"What's the matter?" I said.

"Old and dying with no more to say," she said.

I felt her weak pulse and put a hand on her forehead. There was no fever. "Can we get you anything?"

"Teach me a lesson," she said.

I showed her a few lines from the *New Amsterdam Gazette*, and we read them together. It was a story about how rebels had raided an arsenal at City Hall and dumped provisions from a British ship straight into the river.

"Trouble coming," she said.

"Looks like it," I said. Mr Croft came to stand in the doorway. He wanted us to leave. Before we went, I made him promise that we could come back.

"Thank you, chile," Miss Betty said. "Your mama done raised you right."

I wished I could sit through the night with Miss Betty. I wished I could stay with her and hold her hand until she departed from this earth. But the best I could do was squeeze her arm and say that we would return soon.

BERTILDA AND I BROUGHT CLAYBOURNE to visit Miss Betty two days later, but we had to knock endlessly at the door before Mr Croft came to open it.

"How'd you know?" he said.

"What?"

"She died this afternoon. I went to the Trinity Church, but they don't take Negroes in their cemetery any more. I don't know what to do with her."

"We'll take her," Claybourne said.

Mr Croft clasped his hands together. "I'll give you something for this. You can fetch her in the backroom."

Bertilda and I dressed Miss Betty in her church clothes. Claybourne picked up the trunk with her belongings, but I made him put it down, opened it, and retrieved some beads and glass bottles that she had kept in a leather pouch.

"These are going with her," I said.

Mr Croft let us take the linens and blankets from her bed. We folded them into the trunk, except for the best one, which we used to wrap around the body. Claybourne carried the trunk to Canvas Town and returned later with a shovel, a lamp and several men and women.

Miss Betty hardly weighed a thing. Carrying her on our shoulders, we took the long walk north on Broadway, past Chambers Street and into the woods. On and on and on we walked until we reached the Negroes' burying ground. While the men dug the hole, Bertilda and I removed the linen cloth, arranged Miss Betty's hair and placed the beads and bottles on her belly.

None of us had really known Miss Betty, but we sang and held one another's hands and said goodbye to her as we hoped someone else would do for us, one day.

"*Our Lord and Saviour Jesus,*" Bertilda sang out, "*take this woman over those cold green waters, and take this woman home.*"

After we laid her into the shallow grave and covered her up with earth, Claybourne and the men scrounged for rocks in the moonlight, and clustered them into a round pile.

"Why do you do that?" I asked.

"I don't know, exactly," Claybourne said, "but I done seen it on all the other Negro graves, and it seem fitting and proper."

We walked back south into Manhattan, then broke into little groups and disappeared into the darkness.

That night, my bed seemed colder and lonelier than it had since I had come to New York. A year had passed since Chekura slipped in to visit me for one night in Charles Town. Had he ever come back to look for me? If so, any Negro fruiterer or huckster in the Charles Town market could have told him that Solomon Lindo had gone off with me to New York City.

By November, the weather had begun turning cold. I had a hat and mittens from Miss Betty's trunk and wore them day and night. I kept the hat on, even inside the tavern.

"You don't need that in here," Sam said, watching me sit on a stool with the *New Amsterdam Gazette*.

"I want to keep all the heat in, so it lasts longer when I go back out," I said.

He brought me a steaming coffee. According to the newspaper, war had broken out between the Tories and the rebels. What would happen to the Negroes in New York, I wondered, if the rebels chased out the British? Sam whispered that he believed the rebels were the better people. He didn't trust the British, even the ones who came to dine in the tavern. They were too friendly, too enthusiastic about his food, and half of them owned slaves, he said. For my part, I suspected it was best not to trust anybody.

I sipped my coffee, which was flavoured with molasses and milk, then put down the glass and stared at the paper. On the front page was a proclamation by Lord Dunmore, governor of Virginia, promising freedom for any Negroes who agreed to fight for the British in the war.

"To the end that peace and good order may the sooner be restored," Dunmore's proclamation said, "I do require every person capable of bearing arms to resort to His Majesty's standard . . . and I do hereby further declare all indented servants, Negroes, or others (appertaining to rebels) free, that are able and willing to bear arms, they joining His Majesty's troops, as soon as may be, for the more speedily reducing this Colony to a proper sense of their duty to his Majesty's crown and dignity."

The British were promising us freedom if we fought for

283

them. Questions flooded my mind. I wondered how they would make us free, and where, and how they would let us live. The proclamation spoke about people bearing arms. It looked like that meant only men. Surely they wouldn't let a Negro woman bear arms. And if all the Negroes who bore arms got themselves shot by rebel bullets, what good would freedom do them?

Sam came back into the kitchen.

"Did you see this?" I asked.

"It will get your Canvas Town crowd all worked up," he said, "but I wouldn't give it much mind. The British keep dying and need more men to fight, so they're calling on the slaves. It makes the rebels crazy. They are all fuming about it. They say it isn't fair, stealing Negroes from good men."

"But this offer of freedom," I said. "What about that?"

"Sooner or later the British are goners, and when they leave, do you think they'll be taking you?"

In the chapel that night, my students jumped up when I showed them the news from the *New Amsterdam Gazette*. They made me read the proclamation over and over again.

"What that-all mean?" Bertilda said.

"It means," one man said, "men that fights for the British, gets their freedom."

"It means men what fights for the British, dies with five bullets in the brain," Clayborne said.

"Why should we fight their fight?" another man asked.

"You want to be free, don't you?" Bertilda said.

"Free to die," Claybourne said. "Thanks very much, but I'm free already."

"You is free until some fat rice-growing white man show up here and place a ring round your neck," Bertilda said. "Get up off your bony butt and fight, man."

"Why don't you fight too?" Claybourne said.

"I would," Bertilda said, "if they let me. They give me a musket, and I would shoot down them plantation owners one after the other. I dead them faster than a voodoo chief."

"Take a shot for me too," Claybourne said.

A WEEK LATER, I WAS WALKING up Broadway on a cold, windy night, with Trinity Church behind me and St. Paul's a few blocks ahead, when a strong hand covered my mouth. I tried to look behind me, but my neck was seized and locked. My face was shoved into the crook of a big man's arm and I was dragged into a lane. I could hear no footsteps or voices, only the rough breathing of the man who flung me to the ground. Flat on my back with the breath knocked out of me, I saw a young white man, trousers already unbuttoned. I tried to roll to the side but he pounced on me.

I began to shout, but he clamped my mouth again and used the other hand to strike me. He dropped all of his weight onto me, and pinned me in the cold, wet mud. I spat at him and bit his hand but could not move under his weight and his force, even as I heard and felt my own clothes ripping.

Footsteps, finally, and then shouting. One man's angry voice in the night. "Hey! You. Ruffian lout! Let that woman up. Let her go, or I'll shoot."

Still my attacker pawed at me. He was hard and trying to find his way inside me.

Only when a pistol went off did he pause.

"Next one goes straight into your brain."

The weight rolled off me. My attacker got to his knees, scrambled to his feet, tugged his trousers up and ran away with them unbuttoned.

"What a disgrace," said the man with the pistol.

I didn't look at his face, but heard his British accent.

"One more instant and I would have shot him. Here. Let me help you up."

I was grateful he had warded off my attacker, but who-ever he was, I wished he would leave me alone. Skin was showing through my torn clothing. I just wanted to make it the last two blocks to the chapel, where someone could help me. I kept my face down.

"Thank you," I said, "but I'll be fine now. You can leave me—"

"You speak English very well. I've heard of you," he said. "You teach the Negroes in the chapel. You're the one they call Meena."

I looked up to see a young man in a British Army uniform. He reached out his hand, which I shook.

"Lieutenant Malcolm Waters," he said, releasing my hand. He had blond hair, cropped and pushed to one side, and a rugged face with staring eyes. "Believe it or not, I was speaking about you just the other day," he said.

"Thank you, but I really must go."

"I can't leave you alone like this. Were you on your way to the chapel?" I nodded. "Then I will accompany you there. And while your friends are helping you, I will get you a blanket."

I began walking with him.

"The minister at the chapel said you are the teacher, right? And a midwife too, I hear?"

I wondered why on earth he had been speaking with the minister about me, but I just nodded again and kept walk-ing. When we reached the chapel, he left me with my friends, who took me into their arms and cleaned the cuts on my face and clucked that I shouldn't be foolish enough to walk the streets alone at night. Claybourne wasn't there that night, but after an hour Lieutenant Waters showed up at the church with a blanket, which I wrapped around myself. He offered to walk me back to Canvas Town.

"You ain't taking her," Bertilda said. "White man like you, dressed up so fine. You can walk on into Canvas Town but you might not come back out."

"I'll walk with both of you for a spell," he said.

So Bertilda, Lieutenant Waters and I began the long walk back to Canvas Town.

"Who you is?" Bertilda asked.

"I'm a lieutenant with the British Navy," he said.

"What you want with my Meena?" she said.

"I have some things to ask her," he said.

"What sort?"

Quietly, he said, "It's a private matter."

"Humph. That man who messed with her had a private matter too."

"Well, it's not that sort. I'm an honourable man."

He had an odd sort of singsong voice, and he seemed amused, rather than offended, by Bertilda's questions. He offered to buy me dinner at the Fraunces Tavern the next day, then left us at the edge of Canvas Town and disappeared in the darkness.

"What kind of foolish white man want to walk into Canvas Town in the middle of the night?" Bertilda said.

"Same fools we are," I said, "to be walking around the streets of New York at night."

"That man Claybourne, always telling us not to walk at night, he's a fool hisself," Bertilda said. "How's a woman expected to get around, except on her own two feet? And I ain't got a man in my bed, or one to walk me home at night."

"Me neither," I said.

"Got your eye on Claybourne?" she asked.

"Nope, I've got my own man."

"Where he at?"

"I don't know. And you," I asked. "Do you have your eye on Claybourne?"

Bertilda's mouth curled up and her eyes widened in the darkness. "I been spending my nights waiting on him and wondering if the plain fool's ever gonna ask me for a little bit of loving."

"Maybe he needs to know you want it," I said.

"You ain't got nothing going on with him?" she asked.

"Nothing at all," I said.

"Good. Don't you go changing your mind on me, then."

ROASTED DUCK. BOILED POTATOES. String beans. Coffee with molasses. I ate a fine meal on Lieutenant Malcolm Waters' account, and he didn't come to any particular point during the whole time we ate. He had been stationed in New York for a year, he said, and was well regarded by his commanding officers. The war was proving difficult with the rebels, he acknowledged, but yes, absolutely, Lord Dunmore was perfectly serious in offering freedom to any Negro who would take up arms for them.

"Any Negro man?" I said.

He swallowed a sip of coffee. "Yes, well, there's that," he said. "Yes. Negro men is what he intended, for his fighting forces. But there are other ways to serve. There are other things a trained and trustworthy person might do."

I looked down at my glass of coffee and waited for him to continue.

"I need to speak with you in utmost privacy," he said.

The dining room was empty except for us. Sam Fraunces stepped in to check on us, and I asked if he could arrange to keep his workers out of the room for a while.

Sam raised his eyebrows and shot me a look that seemed to say, *I hope you know what you're doing.* But when Lieutenant Waters turned around to see him, Sam said, "Certainly," and left us.

Lieutenant Waters said, "Just the tact I need at this juncture."

"And what is particularly critical about this juncture?" I asked.

His mouth dropped open. "Has anybody told you that for an African woman, you have the most astonishing—"

288

"Diction."

He grinned. "I guess they have." He let a moment pass, and then began to speak again. "I've got myself in a bit of a pickle."

I sipped my coffee.

"You are a midwife," he said.

I nodded.

"Caught many babies?"

I nodded again.

"Have you heard of Holy Ground?" he said.

"I wasn't far from it when you saved me from that attacker," I said.

"Yes, there's that," he said. "A rough area. You will know that there are many ladies of the night in Holy Ground."

I looked at him calmly and let him go on. He leaned forward, elbows on the table, chin in cupped hands, face close to mine. "I've got myself in a little too thick with one of them."

"You have a lady friend," I said gently, "and she needs my services."

"I think the most of her, but she is . . . she is . . . how best to put this . . . a coloured girl. From Barbados, to be exact. Lovely girl, perfectly gentle, pretty as can be, and I'm afraid she is in need right now."

"How pressing is her need?"

"I was rather hoping you would come and judge for yourself."

"My fee is one pound in silver."

"That's a small fortune."

"It's my fee."

"You're not telling me that a Negro in Canvas Town coughs up a pound for you," he said.

"It's my fee," I said again, resisting the temptation to add the words "for you."

"Ten shillings," he said.

"It's my fee." I was already thinking of warm clothes that

I would buy. I needed thicker socks, a woollen sweater and a coat.

"Fifteen shillings," he said.

I met his eyes.

"Fine," he said. "One pound. Can we go?"

"When?"

"Well, now. The situation is pressing."

ROSETTA WALCOTT HAD A CREAMY COMPLEXION and dark brown freckles all over her cheeks and a huge, swollen belly to go with her thin arms and slender legs. She had come over from Barbados with the white family that owned her. Not long after they settled in New Jersey, she fled on foot one night and ended up in Holy Ground. She was thirteen years old and eight months pregnant, and she said she loved Lieutenant Malcolm Waters.

"He never beat me one single time," she said, "and he gave me clothes and food, but now he say I gots to go. I can come back when I'm skinny again, but I can't come back with any child."

"What do you want to do?" I asked.

"Drown this child in the river and come back for Lieutenant Waters," she said.

"That feeling may change when the baby is suckling you."

"The lieutenant loves me," she said.

"How do you know that?"

"All this time he took care of me. Set me up in this little room, and I didn't have to go with any of the other officers. He kept me for himself, and came to see me every week."

"If he loved you," I told her, "he wouldn't tell you to get rid of the baby."

"He said I couldn't come back with the baby. But I don't need no baby. I loves him and he loves me."

Lieutenant Waters offered to walk me back to Canvas Town. I refused. He tried to insist, but I told him to let me be if he wanted me to come back and deliver his child.

"Shh," he said, even though we were standing alone. "You are delivering *her* child, and that's all that needs to be said about it."

Wishing I had made him pay five pounds instead of one, I let him walk me back to Canvas Town. It had taken Solomon Lindo some time to reveal an uglier side, but the shine had worn off Lieutenant Malcolm Waters the very same day that we shared a meal.

"How old are you?" I asked.

"That's an impertinent question," he said.

"If you want me to help you, tell me your age."

"Twenty-two."

"Well, she's thirteen," I said.

"She's old enough."

"For what?"

"To know what she's doing."

"She thinks you love her and that you'll take care of her," I said.

"Holy Ground is no place for babies."

"You just don't want any baby around."

"Do you know a place where she can stay?" he said.

"Why don't you do something for her? Why don't you help her?"

A look of frustration came into his eyes. "I did grow fond of her. I wasn't thinking it would come to this."

"So why don't you help her now that it has come to this?"

"That's where you come in."

"One pound to catch the baby, and three more to move them both to Canvas Town."

"That's outrageous," he said.

"What's outrageous is that you're making her leave with

your baby. And I'd like to see you build them a shelter for three pounds."

A FEW WEEKS LATER A MESSENGER from the British barracks—a Negro lad who aroused no suspicions—tracked me down in Canvas Town and asked me to come with him immediately to Holy Ground. I caught Rosetta Walcott's baby, and used the money to pay Claybourne and a crew of men to steal, buy, carry and hammer together materials for a shack big enough for mother and daughter. There was no space next to my shack, as it was already taken. Fifteen more lean-to shelters had been built since I had moved in, so Rosetta and the baby were set up at the end of the haphazard block.

I caught another ten babies in Holy Ground over the next few months. I despised the British officers, but knew that their women would suffer without my help. Among the officers in the British barracks at Broadway and Chambers, I became known as "One-pound Meena." With the money, I bought food, clothing and scraps of lumber to make it through a long, cold winter.

In April of 1776, a year after I had arrived in New York, I returned from teaching at St. Paul's Chapel to find Rosetta Walcott weeping at my shelter.

"They're all gone," she told me.

"Who?"

"The Brits, that's who. Haven't you noticed? They've been rowing out to the ships for days, and the last ones left last night. I went up with the baby to see Lieutenant Waters."

"You call him 'Lieutenant'?"

Rosetta looked at me impatiently. "He's only seen her once before. But the barracks are empty. The Brits are all gone. Soldiers, officers, all of them. And he's gone with them."

The entire British military had retreated from New York City. The *New Amsterdam Gazette* said that even Governor William Tryon had taken refuge in a ship in the harbour. Rebels streamed down Broadway, shooting guns and tipping back bottles of gin.

Customers sang and cheered and drank until late in the night at the Fraunces Tavern. I felt lucky to have work in the kitchen, but now that the British were gone, I wondered how I would earn enough for food, clothes and repairs to my shelter.

"What?" Sam said. "You think the rebels don't have brothels? As long as there are fighting men, there will be work for girls like Rosetta—and work for you as well."

Negroes or other property

THE REBELS HELD MANHATTAN FOR SIX MONTHS. Then the British took it back and held it for seven years. There were no more English classes at St. Paul's Chapel, because the Tories locked rebel prisoners inside and left them there to starve. The cries of white men dying sounded so much like those of captives on the slave ship that I avoided walking anywhere near the chapel.

I was left with just three places to teach Negroes to read and to share news with them: the Negro burying ground for large gatherings; a room in the Fraunces Tavern (for twenty people at most), and a meeting circle in front of my shack.

Canvas Town had been attracting fugitives in twos and threes each day, especially after the Philipsburg Proclamation of 1779. Every Negro I taught learned the words of the proclamation, issued by Sir Henry Clinton, the British Commander-in-Chief: *To every Negro who shall desert the Rebel Standard, full security to follow within these lines, any occupation which he shall think proper.*

Every Negro who was capable took a job working for the British. This time, it wasn't just soldiers they wanted. They needed cooks, laundresses, blacksmiths and labourers. They needed coopers, rope makers, carpenters and night-soil men.

And they needed me.

Malcolm Waters returned to New York with captain's stripes on his shoulders. I told him his promotion probably had to do with his true calling in Holy Ground, and called him Captain Holiness. The British no longer kept their mistresses in separate houses in Holy Ground, since senior officers had commandeered homes throughout the city. But the flourishing brothels offered women of all types—Negroes in some houses, whites in others, and every kind going in still other places.

I wasn't just asked to catch babies. Often, I was called upon to give doses of tansy or cottonroot and to stay with the women as their pregnancies bled out of them. Men too sought me out for relief for the blisters and excretions on their penises. I kept a ready supply of bloodroot and aloe, and charged everyone who could pay the same one-pound fee. I needed the money and I needed it desperately. Prices were soaring and everyone was cheating—even the bakers. It got so bad that the British capped the price of bread at twenty-two coppers per loaf and ruled that each loaf had to weigh exactly two pounds. To prevent fraud, bakers stamped their initials into loaves.

Each time there were rumours of change, the people of Canvas Town assembled outside my shack, waiting for me to show up with the *New Amsterdam Gazette*. I read to them about Thomas Paine and his book *Common Sense*, which made most of the Canvas Town residents boo and hiss. They thought it absurd for any white man in the Thirteen Colonies to be complaining of slavery at the hands of the British.

Sam Fraunces had dropped by for that reading, and said that Thomas Paine had a point. "Say what you will, but the Americans are winning against King George and the English," he said. The rebels just wanted to control their own affairs, Sam argued, and that's all Paine meant when he went on about Americans being slaves in their own land.

The Negroes of Canvas Town adored Sam Fraunces for his donations of leftover food after parties and banquets, and they were proud to see one of their own running the most popular tavern in town. However, that day they shouted him down.

"What freedom they need, that they don't already got?" Claybourne called out.

Bertilda took Claybourne's hand and jumped in: "They is free enough to bust in here and lock us up by the neck and drag us right back out of here and all the way down south, right to the rice fields," she said. "Y'all know they's busting in here just as often as they can."

Some two hundred people roared in agreement.

"Nobody taking me down south," Claybourne said. "I up and dead first. Someone slap an iron around my neck, my heart up and stop. I looks down and I tells my own heart, you all can take a permanent rest now. Knock it off and go off to sleep."

Everybody laughed.

"Ain't no foolin'," Claybourne said. "All this time the rebels and the Tories been shooting each other up, I been teaching my mouth to run messages to my heart. I say stop, and it stop. I tell my heart it done lost its job. Time's up, baby, you out of work. You unemploy. You get quiet, now, and lie down and die. And my heart obey, just like a dog. And that's why nobody taking me back down south."

A man called out from the crowd, "Hey, Claybourne, what kind of dog you got for a heart?"

"It's a British retriever, that's what it is."

Sam Fraunces walked away in disgust. To him, Claybourne was nothing but a clown, and the kind of man who would never rise a step above slavery.

"It's only clowns and Claybournes who have reason to fear the Americans," Fraunces said. "The rebels demand their own freedom, and are more honest than the British.

Liberty is coming to this land. And soon enough, freedom for all Negroes will follow."

In 1782, I read to the people gathered around my door that the British had decided to end the war in surrender. It was a large crowd that night and people sat silent and thoughtful long after our talking was done. We clung to the words of the Philipsburg Proclamation: *To every Negro who shall desert the Rebel Standard, full security to follow.* Even I hoped against hope that they would take me to London. From there and only there, I imagined, would I have the chance to sail to Africa.

On March 26, 1783, the whole of Canvas Town ground to á halt. The people who had been washing clothes for the British wandered back home to their shacks. The three dishwashers and two assistant cooks working in the Fraunces Tavern walked off the job and camped out in front of my lean-to. Blacksmiths put down their metal, coopers abandoned their barrels, labourers left the wharves, and it seemed that every man, woman and child in our community huddled together in horror.

For those who hadn't already heard the rumours, I opened the *Royal Gazette* and read aloud the notice of the peace treaty from the commander-in-chief of all His Majesty's Forces in the Colonies.

In Canvas Town, the only part of the treaty that mattered was Section VII, which said:

All Hostillities both by Sea and Land shall from hence-forth cease all prisoners on both sides shall be set at Liberty and His Britannic Majesty shall with all convenient Speed and without Causing any destruction or carrying away any Negroes or other Property of the American Inhabitants withdraw all its Armies, Garrisons, and Fleets, from the said United States.

White people in New York exulted over the news, but for

anyone who had escaped slavery, the treaty spelled disaster. By agreeing not to take with them "Negroes or other Property," the british had betrayed us and condemned us to fall into the hands of American slaveholders.

Emboldened by the British capitulation, plantation owners began sending their men into Canvas Town on raids. We set up a system of men who took turns on guard duty to watch for strangers, white and black. Usually, our own patrols managed to catch the raiders and beat them and hold them until their arrest at the hands of the British. But slave owners and agents from Virginia to Georgia kept prowling the city, in larger numbers than ever before, grabbing fugitives whenever they could.

It was dangerous to stay in New York. But it was even more dangerous to leave. This was the last place in the Thirteen Colonies still run by the British, and until they left completely, we still had some measure of protection.

A few days after everyone began talking about the British betrayal, Waters came to see me as I was giving my regular Monday morning reading at the Fraunces Tavern. He had matured into a good-looking man, and was even more attractive dressed in full regalia, with epaulets, silver stripes, shining buttons and all. But on this day, I did not greet him as Captain Holiness. I was in no joking mood. The British had once before abandoned the people they had pledged to protect, and now it appeared that they would leave us again. I vowed to refuse to help Waters now, no matter how desperately he pleaded or how much money he offered. I was tired of making life easier for British officers by catching the babies of their mistresses.

Everyone seemed to share my disappointment and anger.

"What's the good of serving you?" Claybourne called out to Waters. "What kind of men are you, selling us to the rebels?"

"You're jumping to conclusions," said Waters. "Meena, could you come with me?"

"I'm not working today."

"It isn't what you think."

"I'm not working for you any more, Captain Waters."

Waters stepped closer and lowered his voice, so only I could hear. "This is not about Holy Ground. It's different and it's urgent."

"I'll be back shortly," I told my friends.

"Don't count on it," Waters said.

In an officers' room in the British military barracks, I was brought tea with milk and sugar, an apple, some fresh bread and a slice of Stilton cheese. I drank the tea and ate the bread and cheese but slipped the apple into my handbag.

Waters introduced me to a man named Colonel Baker, who had stripes all over his shoulders, a regal bearing, and enough confidence to swallow up both of us.

Colonel Baker shook my hand forcefully. "I'll skip to the point, as you have little time to waste and I have less," he said.

Following his example, I sat again, and waited for him to continue.

"Captain Waters says you are Guinea-born, correct?"

"I am from Bayo, in Africa."

"And that you are thoroughly literate and produce flawless handwriting."

I nodded.

"And that you have kept ledgers and understand how they work. Columns, rows, numbers and names in the right places, and all such details."

Once more, I indicated that his information was correct. I could only imagine that Waters had learned this last bit of information from Sam Fraunces, whose books I had kept over the years.

"Most important, I understand that you are said to know most of the coloured element of Canvas Town, and that most of them know you. And that you speak two African languages. And that, wherever you go, you have earned the respect of men and women in your community. Yes? Good. You are required for service to His Majesty the King. We must bring you into our employ, and haven't a day to waste."

For a moment, I wondered if this was an elaborate plan for me to catch babies of the mistresses of the most senior British military officials in New York.

Colonel Baker asked if I was familiar with Section VII of the Provisional Peace Treaty.

"I have taught half of Canvas Town to recite it from memory."

"I know the coloured element feels betrayed by it," Colonel Baker said, "but there is no cause for panic. You see, Section VII says that we agree not to make off with any Negroes or other property of the Americans. 'Property' is the operative word."

Colonel Baker paused for a moment and then leaned toward me. "Understand? The coloured element is not the 'property' of the Americans. If you have served the British for one year at minimum, you have already been liberated. You are no man's property."

That was easy for him to say, since he didn't have to fend off slave catchers in Canvas Town. But it didn't seem wise to challenge him, so I said, "You mean to say you're keeping your promises to the Negroes?"

"When we remove you to Nova Scotia, which is what we fully intend to do, we will not be violating any terms of the Peace Treaty."

"Nova Scotia?" I repeated. I hoped it wasn't a penal colony. "Not London?"

"Nova Scotia is a British colony, untouched and unsullied by the Americans, at a distance of two weeks by ship from the New York harbour. It is a fine colony indeed, on the Atlantic Ocean but north of here, with woods, fresh water, abundant animals and rich forest just begging to be converted to farmland. Nova Scotia, Miss Diallo, will be your promised land."

I had more questions to ask, but the colonel pressed forward. The British forces had agreed to vacate New York before the end of November. That left a scant eight months, and there was much work to do. Thousands of Loyalists would be moved to Nova Scotia, by dozens and dozens of frigates, transports, royal vessels and private ships. Property owners would be moving too, of course, and in far larger numbers than the Negroes.

"And in this place you call Nova Scotia," I said, "will we be free?"

"Entirely. You will be as free as any Loyalist. But be forewarned. It will be hard work. You will be given land and expected to farm it. You will need seeds and implements and provisions, and all of those things you shall have. There will be plenty for everyone in the vastness of Nova Scotia."

Like almost every Negro in Canvas Town, I was desperate to leave with the British before Americans—slave owners among them—took over New York City. I wondered if the things Colonel Baker promised were true. But when it came down to deciding whom I could trust with my tenuous liberty, my decision was already made.

"Why have you brought me here?" I asked. "Why are you telling—"

He cut me off again. "You will spread the word among your people. You will help us register them. In due time, you will collect names, ages, and how they came to serve the British. We can only help those who have been behind British lines for a year. We need to know how many wish to travel. And we need to begin embarkations almost immediately."

Colonel Baker stood up to leave the room but caught sight of my hand, index finger raised.

"Colonel, with due respect, I have not yet accepted your offer."

I heard the smallest exhalation from Captain Waters. I did not look his way but was certain he was stifling a laugh.

"I know you have a reputation for expecting fair pay, Miss Diallo. You will be compensated fairly."

"I too want to go to Nova Scotia," I said.

"You have my word," he said.

"Then I accept."

"Stupendous. Speak to Waters for details." Colonel Baker shook my hand once more and left the room.

I turned to Waters. "What about the others?"

"If they have served one full year behind our lines and if they can obtain a certificate to prove it, yes."

"How do they get a certificate? And what about the women in Holy—"

"Negroes who have served behind our lines and have the requisite certificate will be allowed to leave for the colonies," said Waters.

I hoped that meant the women could leave, but Waters was barely giving me any room to speak. "And my pay?"

"One pound per week, in silver. You will have to move into residence in our barracks, as there will be constant work. You will receive lodgings and food in addition to salary."

"All of this information about the Negroes," I said. "Where will it be kept?"

"In a special ledger," he said.

"What will it be called?"

Waters gave me a dry smile. "How about Exodus from Holy Ground?"

I folded my arms. "All of this amuses you," I said.

Waters checked his pocket watch, and his face became

serious. "It will be called the Book of Negroes. You are meeting the colonel and me for breakfast, seven a.m. tomorrow, Fraunces Tavern. We have logistics to review. It will be a long day of work. You will have eight months of long days."

"The Book of Negroes," I mumbled.

I nodded and got up to go. Waters put up his hand, told me to wait and left the room. Returning in a minute, he gave me a canvas sack. In it were apples, two loaves of bread, cheese and dried figs.

"Extras from the storeroom," he said. "I'm sure some-one can use them."

Within two hours of my return to Canvas Town, there wasn't a man or woman who hadn't heard the news. My friends gathered at the door to say goodbye.

"We'll keep this here shack for you, in case you get sick of the white folks," Claybourne said.

"He say that all pretty," Bertilda said, "but soon as you gone, he take all your wood. Licketysplit."

"I'm not taking nothing," he said, " 'cause I built her that shack. I built it before y'all moved in with me."

"He got a mouth like a drawbridge, but I do loves my man," Bertilda said, taking his hand.

I gave them half of the food and saved the rest for Rosetta.

Claybourne took the bread and judged its weight in his hand. "My wife got her own loaf in the oven."

Bertilda slapped his arm. "Shush," she laughed. "You wasn't supposed to tell."

I opened my eyes wider and smiled at the woman. She wasn't showing, yet.

"A loaf in the oven," Claybourne said, "and a right good one too."

Later that night, as I was packing up my possessions, two Canvas Town men rapped on my door.

"Meena," one said, "we got a man here."

"A man?"

"Says he wants to see you."

A knot formed in my stomach. They had found me. I imagined being pinned and tied inside my own tent. Outside, I knew, I could try to run. I stepped out into the night air.

"Meena, do you know this man?" one of the guards said.

It was a dark night with no moon. I stepped closer. A black man. Slender. Only a few inches taller than I. One of the guards struck a match and lit his lamp.

"Aminata Diallo!" said the man.

I threw my arms around my husband and smiled over his shoulder at the guards. "Yes, I do know this man. I know him in all ways and anywhere." I took Chekura's hands, feeling the space where one finger was missing and then feeling the absence of two more on the other hand.

"You're going to have to stop disappearing," I said. "Stick around me, and hang onto your fingers."

"I've still got enough left to hold you," he said.

"I've been waiting nine years for you," I said.

"Better than thirteen," he said, grinning. "I heard you came up here around the start of the war."

"That's right. And where were you?"

"In the low-country, as usual. All over Georgia, and then back to Lady's Island. When the British took Charles Town, they made me a river guide. So I could take them up and down the low-country streams without getting shot up. Don't know how much good it did. A few of them died of musket fire, but a lot more were taken by fever and the pox."

"Are you planning to stay for more than one night?" I asked.

"Your husband is a free man, Aminata Diallo. Free tonight, free tomorrow, free to stay right here with you."

"We aren't far from free, but we aren't there yet," I said. "Not until we leave the Thirteen Colonies."

It's not an easy thing to make love to a man you haven't seen in nine years. The last time I'd seen him, I was thirty years old. I feared I was less beautiful now. My breasts didn't lift the way they once had. Would the softness of my belly turn him away? I didn't find him any less beautiful than before. I didn't mind the silver-grey colouring by his temples, or the smooth baldness of his head. He was my man, just further along the road of life. I wanted to watch him grow older still. I wanted to note all of the changes, one day to the next, and I wanted to protect his hands, in mine.

I went to sleep that night confident that I would wake up with my husband. In the morning, after leaving Canvas Town, I would have one more thing to negotiate with Colonel Baker. Room and board for my husband, and his passage with me to Nova Scotia.

OVER BREAKFAST, I WAS GIVEN A MESSAGE to spread around Canvas Town. Starting the next day, from eight until eleven each morning, every Negro who had spent a year or more behind British lines was welcome to line up at the Fraunces Tavern. Every man and woman would be given two minutes to explain themselves. If they could satisfy the officers that they were of good moral character and that they had served the British for at least one year, they would be told which wharf to attend, on what day, in order to board what ship. There would be a more substantial inspection on the ships. Any person who presented himself fraudulently would be turned over to the Americans.

The next morning, four hundred people gathered outside the tavern. Colonel Baker took the first thirty, pushed them all inside, and told the others to return another day.

"We have months to do this," he shouted out. "We can't process all of you in one day."

My job was to interview the Negroes, and to relay answers to the officers. I met some people who came from places I had never heard of. Some of them, I couldn't understand. But for the most part, I was able to collect their information, and explain to them what was written on the tickets they received. The room was cramped and hot, and the days were long. But though I was eager to get back to Chekura's arms, I loved my new work. I felt that I was giving something special to the Negroes seeking asylum in Nova Scotia, and that they were giving something special to me. They were telling me that I was not alone.

I had imagined, somehow, that my life was unique in its unexpected migrations. I wasn't different at all, I learned. Each person who stood before me had a story every bit as unbelievable as mine. At the end of each of our encounters, I hastened to repeat the key details: the wharf where they were to go, the time to be there, the name of the ship they were to be rowed to, and the possessions they were allowed to bring: a barrel of food, a barrel of clean water and a chest of clothing. Colonel Baker insisted that I say all this, even though I told him that no Negroes in Canvas Town owned barrels of food or chests of clothes. But I did something else for the people who passed the first interview. I showed them their tickets, read out their names and made sure they saw that their names had been recorded.

Over the next two days, we processed sixty more emigrants. Then Baker told the mob of people waiting outside the Fraunces Tavern to go away and come back two weeks later. There would be no further tickets given out until mid-May.

They gave me a pleasant room in a house in Holy Ground. Chekura was allowed to stay with me, and he was promised passage to Nova Scotia. "We can offer him a job cleaning barracks, to keep him busy," Waters said. "He should take it, because he's not going to be seeing a lot of you."

AFTER THE FIRST NINETY NEGROES ASSEMBLED on Murray's Wharf first thing in the morning on April 21, 1783, my real work began. They were rowed out to a few ships anchored in the east River: the *Spring*, the *Aurora* and the *Spencer*, each bound for Saint John, and the *Peggy*, bound for Port Roseway. I knew that Saint John and Port Roseway were part of what was called Nova Scotia, and had been shown on a map where they were located.

Colonel Baker, Captain Waters and I were first rowed to the *Spring*. As soon as we boarded the ship, assistants set up a table for our use. We were joined by two officers from the American Army, who were there to ensure that no unauthorized Negroes were allowed to depart. Sailors and officers moved about on deck, but passengers were kept in a waiting area below. Also on board were dozens of white Loyalists who had been the first to embark. But they were not our concern. We were there to inspect the Negroes. My job was to listen to the officers interview the refugees and to enter details into a two-page ledger.

"Use your best scrivening skills," the colonel told me. "Neat, concise and precise."

These ledgers were to form part of a registration book listing all Negroes carried to the British colonies at the end of the war. If the Americans chose later to press for compensation, the colonel said, the Book of Negroes would show who had left New York.

A group of ten Negroes was called up to the deck. I had never seen them before.

"Who are they?" I asked Waters.

"Slaves and indentured servants," he said.

307

"But I thought . . ."

"We will get around to evacuating the refugees in Canvas Town," Waters said. "But first, we register the property of white Loyalists."

The colonel began to interview a Negro who stammered uncontrollably, but a white Loyalist stepped forward and said, "He's mine." The Loyalist, Lieutenant Colonel Isaac Allen, said he had acquired the Negro as an indentured servant and was taking him to Saint John.

Following the colonel's instructions, I began to write in the ledger. In the first column, *George Black*. Next to it, *35*. And then I wrote the name of the owner or indenturer, *Lt Colonel Isaac Allen*. In a final column, I wrote how he came to be freed before taken into indenture. *Freed by Lawrence Hartshorne, as certified.*

A girl appeared before me. From her disconsolate face, and from the white man who stood beside her, I could see that nothing about this trip suggested freedom.

Hana Palmer, I wrote, again taking down the colonel's words. *15, stout wench. Ben Palmer of Frog's Neck, Claimant.*

"Claimant?" I asked the colonel when the white man had taken away the girl.

"It means that he owns her," the colonel said.

We interviewed the other Negroes. None of the others were indentured or enslaved, and the questioning was more rigorous. How did they come to be free? Could they establish that they had served the British? Did they have a certificate from a British military official proving service behind His Majesty's lines? When the colonel grew impatient with the Negroes' accents, I took over the questioning and scrivening.

One young woman appeared before me with a baby in her arms. I remembered seeing her in Holy Ground.

Harriet Simpson, I wrote under the first column. *19*, I then wrote. Next came a column for a short physical description.

"Just a word or two," Baker told me. "Put 'stout wench.'"

Stout wench, I wrote, disgusted with the term. *Formerly the property of Winston Wakeman, Nancy Mum, Virginia.* Because she had proof of service to the British, I added *GBC*, for General Birch's Certificate.

While Baker busied himself by stuffing a pipe, Harriet whispered to me that her child had been sired by a British captain. *Sara, 2, healthy child. Daughter to Harriet Simpson and born within British lines.* I was relieved that Harriet owned the General Birch's Certificate—nobody found it necessary to ask exactly how she had served the British.

One man was eighty-nine years old. "Born 1694, Virginia," he told me, and so I wrote that down. As for how he had served the British, he said, "I deserted the Rebel Standard and that was service enough. Born a slave, but I will die free." The colonel was wearying of details and the American inspectors were growing bored, so I dashed out the entry as I saw fit.

John Cartwright, 89. Tired out & one eye milky. Formerly owned by George Haskins, Virginia. Says he came behind British lines three years ago.

The old man didn't have a certificate proving his service to the British, but no one asked for it, and he was allowed to stay.

We registered all the Negroes on the *Spring*.

"Only ten of them?" I asked Waters.

"Most of the space is for white Loyalists and their property," said Waters.

On the *Aurora* we inspected fourteen Negroes. I saw again that the British were indeed sending some fugitives to freedom, but were also allowing white Loyalists to bring along slaves.

Later that night, in bed with Chekura, I chattered on and on about what I had seen. But Chekura wasn't impressed.

"Slaves and free Negroes together in Nova Scotia?" he said, sucking his teeth. "Some promised land."

For four more days, we were rowed out to ships in the East River. In fifty ships, nearly six hundred men, women and children required inspection. Baker, Waters and I couldn't do all the work, so three other teams of inspectors were formed. I worked each day from dawn to sunset, and the time passed quickly. I liked writing names in the Book of Negroes, recording how people had obtained their freedom, how old they were and where they had been born: South Carolina, Georgia and Virginia; Madagascar, Angola and Bonny. I wanted to write more about them, but the ledger was cramped and Colonel Baker pressed me to rush through the lineups. The colonel was especially impatient over the descriptions and preferred short phrases such as *stout wench, marks on face, stout fellow, pitted with pox, likely fellow, ordinary fellow, worn out, one-eyed, lusty wench, incurably lame, little fellow, likely boy* and *fine child*. I didn't care for the descriptions, but I loved the way people followed the movement of my hand as I wrote down their names and the way they made me read them aloud once I was done. It excited me to imagine that fifty years later, someone might find an ancestor in the Book of Negroes and say, "That was my grandmother."

In June, I was sent down to Canvas Town to advise the Negroes that another seventeen ships were being made available to them in the North Hudson River.

On the *Free Briton*, which was inspected June 13, we registered thirty-four people, every one of whom was an indentured servant. One young woman looked terrified to be leaving with the man to whom she was indentured, but I could do nothing but enter the words that Colonel Baker dictated.

Sarah Johnson, 22, squat wench, quadroon. Ind to Donald Ross. Formerly slave to Burgess Smith, Lancaster County, left him with the above Thomas Johnson, her husband. The same Donald Ross brought five indentured servants with him on that ship.

When we left the *Free Briton*, I asked the colonel: "Is 'indentured' another word for slave?"

"No," he said, "you indenture yourself of your own free will. For a fixed period of time, in exchange for money, lodgings and food."

After such a long journey to freedom, I couldn't imagine agreeing to that.

In the month of July, another fifty ships sailed from New York Harbour, carrying more than eight hundred men, women and children. On a ship bound for Saint John, I looked up from my ledger to interview the next person waiting in line, and found myself face to face with Rosetta and her daughter. I knew that she had ended up working as a cook in the British barracks. I wanted to leap from my chair and throw my arms around them. But I was afraid that the colonel or one of the inspectors would get in the way if they thought I was helping my friends. I looked quickly into her eyes. She gave the tiniest shake of her head. She didn't want to be caught either. So I cleared my throat and got down to business. I looked at the certificate in her hand, asked her name and age, and turned back to the ledger.

"Hurry up, Miss Diallo," Baker told me. "If she's free, you can just put down that she's travelling on her own bottom."

Rosetta Walcott, 21, stout wench, on her own bottom. Said she came behind British lines six years ago. General Birch Certificate.

Adriana Walcott, 8, daughter of Rosetta. Fine girl.

From that point on, whenever I registered a woman who had come behind the British lines quite young and was now travelling alone with child, I wondered if she was escaping Holy Ground, and silently cheered for her.

We also inspected Negroes on ships bound for Quebec, Germany and England. At first, I envied the Negroes who were going to England, knowing that ships left from there to Africa. But it turned out that all of the Negroes heading to Europe were owned by British or Hessian military officers returning home after the war. Some of the Negroes had been owned by the officers for years, and others had been snatched from southern plantations and re-enslaved by the British for their own purposes. Quickly enough, my envy turned to pity.

David, 10, likely boy, Germany is residence of claimant, M. General Kospoth. The boy goes with the General who got him at Philadelphia. The boy can give no account with whom he formerly lived.

The colonel made me write it that way, but David had spoken with me briefly, on board the *Hind*, and he had told me that General Kospoth and his Hessians had made off with him and a number of other slaves belonging to a tobacco farmer. "Just keep it simple, Meena," Baker said, dictating the response.

CHEKURA WAS PATIENT THROUGH IT ALL. For five shillings a week, he swept the British barracks and hauled waste buckets to a rotting wharf on the river. Each day, we woke up two hours before dawn to hold each other, run our hands along each other's skin, and tell stories about our twenty-seven years in America. We never ran out of stories to tell. I wanted to know everything about him, and tell him everything that had happened to me, and I found great solace in knowing that my husband knew my whole life's story.

I believe that we conceived our child on August 15, 1783. I just knew by the way my man moved deeper and deeper inside me, and by the way we both quivered and shook and erupted together, that we had made another baby. It was early in the morning. The British soldiers had a pen of roosters and they weren't even crowing yet.

312

"I want to leave here with you just as soon as we can," I said, with my leg draped over his. "I want a real life with you, husband."

Chekura placed a hand on each of my cheeks, and traced the shape of my moons. "What we have right now is real," he said.

"But the British promise that we will be free in Nova Scotia," I said.

"Don't forget all the slaves and indentured folk you have put in that ledger. They were stolen from the rebels and re-enslaved by the British. We may get to the promised land and we may not, but wherever we are, life won't be easy. But that has never stopped us."

"Stopped us from what?"

"From this," he said, once more pressing his lips to mine.

BY AUGUST, SO MANY SHIPS had sailed that Canvas Town was beginning to thin out. It would have been an encouraging development if not for the fact that slave catchers were finding it easier to raid the area. There were fewer places to hide, smaller crowds to hide in and not as many Negroes left to protect one another. Bands of white men became increasingly bold about snatching up Negroes—escaped slaves or not. If Chekura and I hadn't been living in the British military barracks, we would have been at greater risk. Still, I felt uneasy. The longer we stayed behind to help others to freedom, the more likely we were to lose it ourselves.

In September, while I was being paid my weekly wage, I asked Colonel Baker if Chekura and I could leave.

Baker looked up from his account book. "He can leave any time he wishes," he said, nodding at Chekura. "But you have to stay to the end. We need you, Meena. That is the deal. We have hired you, but you stay to the end."

"When will the end be?"

"Before the year is out."

ANOTHER FIFTY OR SO SHIPS sailed out of New York in October. Without warning or explanation, I was assigned to a new team of inspectors. With them, I spent a long day registering Negroes on *La Aigle*, bound for Annapolis Royal, Nova Scotia. Many of them had papers proving service for a British military company called the Black Pioneers.

Joe Mason, 25, stout fellow, Black Pioneers. Formerly servant to Samuel Ash, Edisto, South Carolina; left him in April, 1780.

Prince, 30, ordinary fellow with a wooden leg, Black Pioneers. Formerly servant to Mr Spooner, Philadelphia, left him in 1777.

People showed up in bunches. All together in one family, or having served together as soldiers, cooks or laundresses in the same military regiment, or having run years ago from the same master in Charles Town, Edisto Island or Norfolk. There were people in their nineties, and new-born babies. There were healthy soldiers, and there were the dying. There were those who carried others, and others taken by hand.

Sarrah, 42, ordinary wench, stone blind, Black Pioneers. Formerly slave to Lord Dunmore, left him in 1776.

"How did you lose your eyes?" I asked her, whispering.

"Was mixing lye for soap, and a 'splosion went off," she said. "Man one foot over was handing me his redcoat, telling me to wash it soft and gentle. Kilt him lickety-split, so I reckon I was lucky."

"Must have hurt awful bad," I said.

"I've known worse," she said. "Say, you a Negro woman?"

"African."

"You writing this down?"

314

"That's my job," I said.

"Praise the Lord, girl. Praise the Lord. I always wanted to learn to read. Guess all I can do now is learn to sing."

"Lord Dunmore," I said. "He owned you?"

"Yes, ma'am."

"The same Lord Dunmore who issued the Proclamation? The first one, saying we'd be free if we fought for the British?"

"Same Lord Dunmore," she said. "Virginia governor got to have his slaves."

"You're free now, Sarrah, and going to Annapolis Royal."

"Don't know where it is, but it sure sound pretty."

"Up the coast, in Nova Scotia. Two weeks by ship."

"You sound so smart," Sarrah said. "Right pretty, I bet."

I leaned over to tell her something I hadn't told any other person, except my husband. I made sure that nobody could hear us. "I'm having a baby."

"A chile is a miracle, 'specially these days," Sarrah said. "Your man with you?"

"He is."

"Praise the Lord. You travelling with us, honey chile?"

"Not on this boat. Soon, I hope."

"Travel safe, girl, and watch your eyes."

ONE COLD OCTOBER MORNING, after we made love and were lying, fingers intertwined, Chekura told me how he had lost the tips of his fingers.

"I had been guiding the British through the low-country waterways. They raided every plantation they could find. They shot rebels. They stole knives, chickens, pigs and silver. They took some slaves as prizes and turned others into helpers like me. They promised to liberate all of us who helped them. But when the time came to evacuate Charles Town, the British only took some of the Negroes. They promised to take more, but, as usual, they lied. But I knew that if I didn't get out, a man in Beaufort County was just waiting to get his hands on me for trying to run with the British. The British soldiers started lifting the gang-plank. Another fellow and I jumped in the water, clothes and all. It was just a few feet to the boat. We tried to get up the ladder, but the men on board said they would fire if we didn't let go. I didn't believe them. I had served them for months. We kept climbing the ladder, even though two sailors on deck waved cutlasses. 'Let go,' they hollered, but we kept on. Turned out they didn't fire on us after all. But when my friend put his hand on the top rung, one of the soldiers cleaved off his fingers. He screamed as he fell into the water and kept screaming when his head came back up. I had both hands on the rail. One of the sailors slashed at my left hand. He took off two fingertips. But I hung on with my good hand. I would have sooner died in the water than go back to my owner.

"I caught the eye of another sailor. I had seen that man before. I had traded with him in the low-country. I saw his face change as he recognized me too. He yanked me up, gave me a cloth for my bleeding hand and shoved me behind him on the deck. I had a fever the whole time at sea, but I couldn't stop thinking of you. When we got to New York, I was let off in Brooklyn Heights. I stayed there until I heard about Canvas Town and went looking for you again."

I had been missing Chekura since our first days in America and I didn't want to spend one more day without him. Though I worked long days, the early mornings were ours and ours alone, for loving and talking.

"Let me talk to that baby inside you," he said, bringing his mouth to my navel.

"Get out of there," I said, laughing.

"No, let me say something. I have words for her."

I smiled at my man, remembering stories of how my father had done the same thing with me when I was in my mama's belly.

"Stick with your mother, little girl," Chekura whispered into my navel.

"You think it's a girl, do you?"

"Course it's a girl. Your papa is no good, so stick close to Mama."

"Papa just fine," I said, "just fine indeed."

"Papa is a travelling man," Chekura said.

"We are travelling peoples," I said, "all of us."

At the barracks the next day, I was told that Captain Waters and Colonel Baker had sailed for England. No goodbye. No thank you. No indication of who would keep paying my salary. And no word left of when I could leave.

I spoke to a deputy quartermaster general, who was fussy and impatient.

"We don't require your services any longer," he said. "We need the space in the barracks too. You'll have to move back to Canvas Town."

"And my ship? What ship can I take with my husband?"

He fumbled about on his desk and shoved something toward me without looking up. "Take these," he said, and dismissed me from the room.

Our tickets said, "*Joseph*, boarding November 7 for Annapolis Royal."

Chekura and I stood with a crowd of two hundred Negroes on Murray's Wharf. Huddling together under a freezing rain, we hoped that Annapolis Royal would offer gentler winters than the biting cold and snow of Manhattan. Under my heavy coat, I had the certificate that had been issued when I began my work on the Book of Negroes.

On a small square of paper with lines in flowing ink, it said:

New York, 21st April, 1783. THIS is to certify to whomever it may concern, that the bearer hereof, Meena

Dee, a Negro of Mandingo extraction, resorted to the British lines, in consequence of the Proclamations of Lord Dunmore, Governor of Virginia and Sir Henry Clinton, late Commander in Chief in America; and that the said Negro hereby has His Excellency Sir Guy Carleton's Permission to go to Nova-Scotia, or wherever else she may think proper. By Order of Brigadier General Birch.

I also had crab cakes, hard cheese, two loaves of bread, six fresh apples and four bottles of beer, all of which had been donated and wrapped in newspaper by Sam Fraunces, who had come down to the wharf to see us off. All of my friends had gone by then—some to Saint John, others to Annapolis Royal, and still others to Quebec. I knew none of the people crowded onto the pier. Sam Fraunces shook Chekura's hand and hugged me. I didn't know how to thank him. After Chekura and I had been made to leave the British barracks, Sam had let us stay in his tavern. Canvas Town was just too dangerous, he had told us, because white men were prowling the area every night. People were now saying that George Washington would ride into town before the end of November.

Just as Chekura and I were leaving, Sam leaned closer and whispered to me that George Washington had promised him a job when the war was over. Sam was to become the head cook at the general's residence in Mount Vernon, Virginia.

"When the Tories pull their last anchor, the Americans will prove to be the better people. You never gave them their due."

"I'll take my chances with the British," I said.

Sam clasped my hand. "Write to me care of General Washington, Mount Vernon."

We were rowed out in the rain, mustered on the *Joseph* and sent below to await our interviews. For two days, the ship was loaded with salt beef, dried peas, suet, wine and water. Finally, three British men began inspections for the Book of Negroes. I didn't know any of them. Two American officers were watching our every step. They took Chekura before me.

Chekura, 41, little fellow, says he served the British in Charles Town, left his owner, Mr Smith, Beaufort, 1779. In possession of General Birch Certificate.

It seemed to me that the less I told them, the better. I even gave them my Anglicized name, to keep things simple.

Meena Dee, 38, Guinea born, served behind British Lines in New York since 1777, previously owned by Mr Lindo of Charles Town. In Possession of General Birch Certificate.

With a few businesslike scratches of the quill on paper, we were free. Chekura and I moved below deck with the last of the inspected Negroes. But just as the *Joseph* was preparing to lift anchor, a loud voice called out: *"Meena Dee. Return here please."*

The British and American officials conferred in whispers. The Americans produced a slip of paper, and were pointing out details to the deputy quartermaster.

Finally, the deputy quartermaster spoke. "Meena Dee, there is a claim against you. We cannot allow you to leave at this time. You must go with these men."

"But—"

"There will be no discussion."

"But I have a General Birch Certificate. I served the British for years. I worked from April to a week ago on this very Book of Negroes, under Colonel Baker."

"You will be allowed to respond to the allegations of your claimant."

"What claimant?"

"Gentlemen, please remove this woman."

Chekura took my hand. "I am her husband, and I go with her."

The deputy quartermaster frowned. "Look here, boy. If you get off this ship, I can guarantee you that you will board no other. If she prevails over her claimant, she may board another vessel. But if you leave this ship, you stay in New York. I will personally see to that. I have no time for this."

"Stay on the ship, Chekura," I said. "I will be back."

"I can't leave you, wife."

"Go with the ship. It's the only way. We will find each other in Nova Scotia. Send out word for me, and I will, for you."

He hugged me. I held his hands. His fingers slid away as I was pulled off the deck, down the ladder and into a boat that rowed me back to Murray's Wharf. The whole way back, I kept my eyes on the *Joseph*. I knew Solomon Lindo had put in a claim for me. He had helped separate me from my son more than twenty years ago, and now he had just separated me from my husband. I didn't like the feeling of hatred in my heart, so I tried to put Lindo out of my mind and to think instead of Chekura's arms around my body.

I spent the night in jail. They took my bag, which contained some spare clothes and all my savings. I didn't even have a few shillings to bribe the Negro jail guard. But I whispered to him anyway and pleaded with him to go tell Sam Fraunces of my fate. If he could do that for me, I promised, Sam would surely reward him in some way.

The guard smiled at me. "I was going to do it for you anyway," he said. "I know who you are."

"You do?" I said.

"You taught my daughter at St. Paul's Chapel, and she reads fine now. She taught me some reading too, after you taught her."

* * *

THE NEXT MORNING, Sam Fraunces came to see me. At other times, he had always been impossibly optimistic. But now, he wasn't smiling at all.

"I trusted the British," I said. "They said they would protect us, and I believed them."

Sam took my hand. He said that some of the plantation men who showed up with proof were being allowed to claim their runaways.

"I can't promise to get you out of here, though I'm going to do everything I can," he said. "But I do have some bad news."

"What?"

"I've just heard that Solomon Lindo is in town."

I cupped my face in my palms. "I'm done for now."

"Don't give up," Sam said. "I'll see what I can find out."

The guard escorted Sam from my cell. I rubbed my belly and whispered the songs of my childhood to soothe the baby inside me. I didn't want to be afraid. I didn't want that baby to learn fear from me. To stave off my anguish, I tried to imagine the shape of my baby's mouth and the sound of her first cries.

AFTER TWO DAYS IN JAIL, I was taken—wrists tied and legs shackled—to the Fraunces Tavern, whose meeting room had been converted into a court for claims.

I waited with the jailor and a justice of the peace, who would not even name the man who claimed me.

The door swung open, and into the room stepped Robinson Appleby. My mouth fell open. I hadn't seen Appleby since leaving St. Helena Island twenty-one years earlier. He was bald now and had a bulging belly, but his confidence had grown over the years. He had a huge smile on his face.

"Meena, what a pleasant surprise," he said.

"How dare you?"

"Careful how you speak to the one who owns you."

"You own nothing but your own conscience," I said.

"You made quite the name for yourself in New York," he said. "It was easy to track you down."

Appleby told the justice of the peace that he still owned me. He said that I had only been loaned out to Solomon Lindo, that Lindo had absconded with me and that I had run from Lindo. Therefore, Appleby said, I had never been freed, was illegally in New York and still belonged to him.

Appleby unfolded a worn-out piece of paper. "This, sir, indicates that I purchased this woman from Mr. William King in Charles Town in 1757."

"What is your response to this?" the justice of the peace asked me.

"That part is true," I said. "But he sold me in 1762 to Solomon Lindo." And then I had no choice but to go on with a lie: "Mr. Lindo manumitted me in 1775."

"Where are your papers?" asked the justice of the peace.

"I lost them," I said.

"She claims to have had papers, but she has lost them," Appleby said. "I make my claim with documentation."

"Have you anything else to say for yourself?" the justice asked me.

"He is lying."

Just then, Sam Fraunces slipped into the room.

"Mr Fraunces," the justice said. "Have you something to contribute to this process?"

"You know me to be an upstanding businessman," Sam said.

"Your reputation is steady," said the justice.

"Then I ask for a brief delay. I need two hours. I am in the process of obtaining proof on behalf of the woman."

The justice sighed. "I have three more cases today," he said. "I shall hear them. Afterwards, if you have not brought forth your proof, I will have no choice but to decide this matter."

I sat under guard, still shackled, while Appleby stepped out to lunch. At the back of the room, I heard claims against two other Negroes who, like me, had been pulled off ships in the harbour. Both—one man, and one woman—were given over to men who said they owned them. I despised the Americans for taking these Negroes, but my greatest contempt was for the British. They had used us in every way in their war. Cooks. Whores. Midwives. Soldiers. We had given them our food, our beds, our blood and our lives. And when slave owners showed up with their stories and their paperwork, the British turned their backs and allowed us to be seized like chattels. Our humiliation meant nothing to them, nor did our lives.

Appleby waited with two strong aides. The better, I feared, for carrying me off. Finally Sam Fraunces came into the room.

"Mr Fraunces," said the justice, "have you made progress?"

"I have."

"Submit it, then."

"I will."

Sam opened the door, and into the room stepped Solomon Lindo.

Solomon Lindo? Sam had to be out of his mind. Had he turned traitor? Was he now sealing my fate? Perhaps Lindo had offered him money. Perhaps times were so bad that Sam needed it. But it didn't seem possible. Unlike Appleby, who stared with his lips pressed together, Lindo walked with a shuffle and kept his head down. He did not look at me.

"Please identify yourself," the justice of the peace said.

"Solomon Lindo."

"Place of residence?"

"Charles Town."

"Type of business?"

"Merchant."

"Do you own property?"

"I own property, yes," Lindo said, "a house in Charles Town, and an indigo plantation on Edisto Island."

His indigo grading must have slipped during the war years. He must have been running the plantation out of desperation. I couldn't imagine how I could go on living if he made me oversee his indigo production or do his books again.

"Have you come to New York to claim this woman?"

"I came to discuss indigo trade with the governor of New York. But I knew she was here."

"What stake have you in this case?" the justice of the peace asked.

"This man," Lindo said, nodding in Appleby's direction, "sold Meena Dee to me in 1762. I have the papers here."

"So you are saying that she belongs to you? You are claiming her for yourself?"

"Mr Appleby does not own her," Lindo said. "I do."

"Mr Appleby has already shown his papers," the justice said. "Do you have more recent proof of purchase?"

"Yes. Shall I show it to you?"

"Mr Lindo, this has been a long day. Just read it out."

"I would prefer—"

"Just read it, Mr Lindo."

Lindo cleared his throat and removed a paper from his pocket. He unfolded it carefully, scratched his chin, cleared his throat and began to read.

"'Bill of sale between Robinson Appleby of St Helena Island and Solomon Lindo of Charles Town. Dated February 1, 1762. Terms of sale of Meena, a Guinea wench.' Will that suffice?"

"Read on," the justice said.

"'Solomon Lindo agrees to purchase the said wench Meena for sixty pounds sterling, and—'"

Lindo paused at this point. I could see the paper rustling in his hand.

"We don't have all day, Mr Lindo. Please go on."

Lindo continued reading: "'. . . and to arrange the sale of Mamadu, son of Meena. Said sale to be effected in Savannah, Georgia, on terms suitable to Robinson Appleby. Proceeds of sale of son to be divided, three quarters to Mr Appleby and one quarter to Mr Lindo.'"

Three-quarters of the profits to one man, and one-quarter to the other. I didn't want to poison my own heart with hatred, because I had another little one inside me now. For that baby, I wanted to be as calm as a Bayo villager walking with a bundle on her head. I placed my palm on my own belly and waited for the men to finish talking.

"Was that contract signed and executed?" asked the justice.

"Yes."

"And you call yourselves gentlemen?"

Appleby said nothing. But Lindo raised his hand to speak.

"Sir, I am not proud of the things I did, but I wish to correct the record. Mr Appleby was determined to sell the baby to one owner and the mother to another. He was obsessed with a desire to punish his slave because she had resisted his authority. I could not persuade him to let me buy the two of them. But, with a substantial sum of money—much more than the usual fee, at the time—I finally persuaded him to sell Meena to me. Even this, he allowed only if I served as a broker for the child. I did my best to place the boy in the hands of a man who was respected as a gentleman. And as for Meena, it is true that I wanted to buy her, and that I planned to make use of her labour. But I also felt it would be better to take her with me than to let her go to a rice plantation in Georgia."

The justice of the peace shook his head. "Mr Appleby, do you care to reply?"

"I have nothing to say to the Jew," Appleby said.

"Let me see the contract," the justice of the peace said. He accepted it, smoothed the crease in the paper, looked at it carefully, then handed it back and turned to Appleby. "Mr Appleby, you give white men a bad name. You have one day to leave New York. If at noon tomorrow you are still in this city, I will have you arrested. And if you are not out of this room within thirty seconds, I will arrest you right now for perjury. Now get out."

Appleby passed through the door without looking at Lindo or me.

"Mr Lindo, you may take your property," the justice said.

"She is free to go," Lindo said.

"You came all this way to manumit your slave?"

"It is a matter of making peace with my past," Lindo said.

"Set this woman loose," the justice told the jailer, "and let her go."

I was released from my shackles by the smiling guard whose daughter I had once taught. He touched my shoulder, then left the room behind the justice of the peace and the court clerk.

Lindo looked at me with a mixture of reverence and shame. "Meena," he said, "may I have a word with you?"

I wasn't ready to receive Lindo's sorrow, or to thank him for giving back what had always been mine. I could see that Solomon Lindo was a better class of man than Robinson Appleby. But he was tainted by the very world in which he lived, and from which he too richly profited. I did not want to hate him, but neither could I forgive him.

Suddenly, a new fear erupted inside me and engulfed my thoughts like flowing lava. What if the baby growing inside my own body had just heard the evilness of these men and all their manoeuvrings?

"Meena," Lindo repeated. "May I—"

"No," I said, "I can't." I grabbed Sam Fraunces's a
ran from the room.

No more ships left New York City until the final day of the
British occupation. On November 30, 1783, I was rowed
out to the *George III*, inspected for the Book of Negroes by
men who did not know me, and allowed to leave the
Thirteen Colonies. I knew that it would be called the
United States. But I refused to speak that name. There was
nothing united about a nation that said all men were
created equal, but that kept my people in chains.

I had lost my belongings in jail and there would be no
husband to meet me in Port Roseway. Annapolis Royal
had been my hope, since that was where Chekura's ship
was heading, but there was no ship leaving for that
location and I was given no choice in the matter. I had my
legs, which were still in working order, and my hands,
which could still catch babies, and I had the little one
growing inside me. I wondered who would catch the baby
for me, when its day dawned bright in Nova Scotia.

I hoped it would be Chekura.

Gone missing with my most recent exhalation

{Birchtown, 1783}

Sailing into the port at the end of a nine-mile bay, I felt the snow on my face and a film of ice gathering above my lips, and I saw the granite spilling onto the shores. There were mammoth pines and thick forests, and in this brand-new town, hundreds of people walked about. I had been told that we were sailing to Port Roseway, but the sign on the pier said Shelburne.

I paid two prices for taking the last ship carrying Loyalists from New York City: my husband had gone before me, and so had every other free Negro who was allowed to leave with the British. Six other Negroes disembarked from the *George III*, but they were all enslaved or indentured and were led off by the men who owned them.

Was this the promised land?

I stepped off the pier and walked about town, looking everywhere for Chekura. Maybe he had found out where the last ships from New York had sailed. Maybe he had come for me to place his hand on my growing belly and greet the child we had made. But I saw no familiar faces. Most of the people were white, and they walked past as if I didn't exist.

A white woman in a cap and a long coat approached me on Water Street.

"Is this Port Roseway?" I asked. She walked right by without stopping to look at me.

Nova Scotia was colder than Charles Town, and even colder than New York.

In that moment, I buried my thoughts of Chekura and set about finding a place to sleep and food to sustain the little person growing inside me.

Inside the Merchant's Coffee House, I asked for information about lodgings and work. A big man took me by the arm and pulled me to the door. "We don't serve niggers," he said.

"I'm not asking to be served," I said. "All I want—"

"Move along," he said. "Birchtown is the place for your kind."

Outside, standing again on Water Street, I looked left and right, wondering where I could get help. I had not thought about where to sleep or eat when I was first brought to St. Helena, Charles Town or even to New York. Here, I had nothing and knew no one to ask for assistance. But I had chosen freedom, with all its insecurities, and nothing in the world would make me turn away from it.

Something with the weight of a June bug struck me on the back of the head. But the December snow was swirling in the wind, so it was too cold for insects. I turned—and was struck again, twice in the face. I caught something on my cheek and held it in my palm. It was a peanut. And then I heard laughter. Two white men in the ragged remains of the British Redcoats were passing a bottle back and forth. When I stared at them directly, they stopped pitching peanuts in my direction, but spat, one after the other.

Two doors down, I passed under a sign for THE SHELBURNE CRIER and opened the door. A short white man was arranging letters on a metal stick.

"Morning," he said, eyes fixed on his labours.

"And good morning to you," I said.

He looked up immediately and gave me a little smile. "I thought I detected an accent from a place much warmer than this."

It occurred to me then that nobody in the world had my exact accent, because nobody had lived with the same people in villages, towns and cities on two continents. I liked having my accent, whatever it was, and wanted to keep it.

"Is this Port Roseway?" I asked.

"Shelburne," he said. "Are you just off the boat?" He didn't seem to mind that I was black and unknown to him.

"Yes. But I thought we were sailing to Port Roseway."

"You did. Recently, the name changed to Shelburne."

"Those letters," I said, nodding at his work. "They're all upside down. Looks like a child tried to write them and got them wrong."

"You have a sharp eye. The letters are made to go in that way, but when the machine is done, the words come out properly. Except for the mistakes."

"I can catch mistakes. Do you need any help?"

He smiled. "I could use help of all kinds, but I can't pay you anything. Where on earth did you learn to read?"

"Long story," I said.

"I have time," he said. "Some people will give you the cold shoulder in Shelburne, but I believe in treating each person on his merits. Can I offer you some tea?"

A gust of cold wind battered the door. "Thank you, but I can't stay long. I'm looking for shelter and must find work."

His name was Theo McArdle, and I drank his sweetened tea with gratitude. He offered to let me return to proofread the first impressions that came off his printer, in exchange for biscuits, tea, free newspapers and whatever information he could share with me. And a helpful detail came with that first tea, even before I had done any work for him: free Negroes mostly lived in Birchtown, three miles around the bay, and I could find out more at the Land Registry Office. I thanked Theo McArdle for the tea and promised I would be back.

The only person in the Land Registry Office was an old Negro sitting on a stool near a sign that said OUT FOR TEA. His cheeks were pitted with scars from the pox, and he wore spectacles with only the frames—no glass. One of his eyes was milky, but the other was clear. In a hand that was creased and thick and thrice the size of mine, he held a white cane made of knotted birch. With this cane, he tapped my foot gently.

"Won't you say hello to a broken-down old man?" he said.

"You're not so old," I said.

His lips turned up in a smile. "That's mighty Christian of you. Call out another phrase or two, so this lame and blind man can hear your voice again."

"Is this where they distribute land?" I said.

"That depends."

"On what?"

He leaned forward and took my hand in his palm, which was dried and cracked. It was the widest palm I had ever seen.

"On a whole mess of things," he said. "Have you come in from New York?"

"I have."

"And are you of African persuasion?" he said.

"I am persuaded," I said with a smile.

The man guffawed. "I like a sense of humour in a woman."

"I've got a little person to worry about, so I'll be in better humour when we find a warm place to sleep," I said.

"I didn't hear anyone come in with you."

"The little one is growing inside me."

"Hallelujah, sister," he said. "Don't fritter away your

morning. You don't have time to waste. The man you want isn't here and wouldn't help you if he was. But you're in luck, sister, because I am Moses Wilkinson. Some folks call me Preacher Man, but most just call me Daddy Moses. Have you been saved?"

"That depends," I said.

"On what?" he said, grinning.

"Do you know where I can stay?"

"I surely do," he said. "You've come to the right man."

"Then I have been saved, Daddy Moses."

I spoke with the preacher until a strong young man came by, said "I'm back, Daddy Moses," and picked him up like a baby in his arms.

"Grab my stool," Daddy Moses called out to me.

I picked it up and followed the two of them outside. The young man set Daddy Moses down on a two-wheeled cart.

"You can come along, but you'll have to walk," Daddy Moses said.

The young man hitched himself to the front of the cart and began pulling Daddy Moses. I walked beside the preacher as he bumped forward.

"Are we going to Birchtown?" I asked.

"Heard of it, did you?" Daddy Moses said. "It's three miles that way, in the dog's ass of the harbour."

Along the way, he explained that slaves and indentured servants stayed in town with the white Loyalists who owned them. But if you were coloured and on your own bottom, he said, Birchtown was where you belonged. Nova Scotia had more land than God could sneeze at, Daddy Moses said, but hardly any of it was being parcelled out to black folks.

"But the British said we would have land," I said.

"Get good and comfortable at the back of the line," he said. "There are a thousand coloured folks waiting before you. And, ahead of them, a few thousand white people.

They call this place Nova Scotia, but folks in Birchtown have another name for it."

"What's that?" I asked.

"Nova Scarcity."

I thought of Chekura warning me to be realistic about the promised land. I wondered where he was at that moment, and if he had food and shelter.

"We have to go out hunting for you," he said.

"Hunting?"

"We must get some furs for you. Good thing for deer, moose and bear, young lady, because the Loyalist office won't save your soul or warm your back." While we walked, Daddy Moses explained that the people of Birchtown were divided into companies, each having a leader to distribute rations from the British and—when they came—land allotments.

Daddy Moses led the Methodist church, which was also one of the companies. "Have you taken Jesus into your arms?" he asked me.

"My arms have been busy, and Jesus hasn't come looking."

"The good thing about arms," he said, "is that you only have to open them. I lost my eyes and my ability to walk four years ago."

"Smallpox?"

"That's right. But I've still got my heart and my arms, and that's good enough for Jesus. That boy right here? The one who is pulling me? I tend to his soul, and he and the others get me from here to there. Jesus tells us to take care of each other."

Two poles stuck out from the cart. The young man stood between them, pulling one in each hand. He was about sixteen, already tall and muscled, and he was barely breaking a sweat.

"Hello," I said to him.

He turned with a big smile, as if he had been waiting for

permission to do so. "Good morning, ma'am, and welcome to Nova Scotia."

"Thank you," I said. "It's good of you to pull the preacher."

"Daddy Moses and me, we pulls each other."

"We are travelling peoples," I said.

"Amen," Daddy Moses called out.

I looked again at the boy, and thought about how good it would have felt to have my own son alive and strong and taller than me, and to watch him helping another person. I wondered what Mamadu would have looked like, if he had been allowed to stay with me. If he had lived this long, he would have been just over twenty years old.

"What's your name, son?"

"Jason Wood. And how do they call you, ma'am?"

"Aminata."

"Ah—ah—ah. Sounds like one of them big words in the Bible."

"Aminata," I said again. "But you may call me Meena."

Daddy Moses found the small of my back with the tip of his cane. He prodded me there, ever so gently.

"For a gal without Jesus, you talk like a preacher," he said. "Your words sound like they were spoken five hundred years ago, and that you're reading them off holy walls. I could do with a voice like yours in my church. You got rhythm and cadence, Meena, but as Jason here would say, 'a right funny sound jump out yo' mout.' We've got time right here and right now, so tell me all about yourself and where you done come from."

Among strangers in the Thirteen Colonies, I had kept my heart and my soul cautiously locked. But Daddy Moses had an understanding, solicitous voice that slid like a key into that lock. I sensed that he would not hold me in judgment, and perhaps it helped that he was stone blind. For the first time since leaving my friend Georgia, I began to speak to a stranger about my mother and father and the things I had learned from them in Bayo. I explained how I had been walked to the coast, and spoke of crossing the sea. While he murmured "amen" occasionally, or gently called out, "God has sent us on a long migration and he has seen to our survival," I told him about how I had been taken to South Carolina, and what I had done there, and how I had come to lose my son Mamadu. I didn't want Daddy Moses to expect that I would give something that wasn't within me to give, so I explained that mine wasn't a Christian soul, although I had seen a little of the Qur'an and the Torah and had many times read parts of the Bible.

"We are travelling peoples, as you say so well, and you are one of the travellest of them all," Daddy Moses said.

"Amen," Jason called out.

"Even travelling peoples need homes, and failing that they need hosts," Daddy Moses said. "My wife and I live simply, but we will be honoured to have you stay with us until other arrangements have been made."

"Thank you, Daddy Moses."

His cane came to rest gently on my shoulder. "I'm not asking you to take Jesus in your arms," he said. "Let's just call your soul a work-in-progress."

"With all that you're doing for me, you can call my soul anything you want," I said.

"It doesn't matter what we call your soul," Daddy Moses said, smiling at me. "What matters is where it travels and who it uplifts."

After moving along in silence for a spell, we passed through a long corridor of fir trees. To my right, the forest seemed thick and impenetrable. To my left there were fewer trees, and in the spaces between them I could see the cold, grey waters of the nine-mile bay.

After walking a good distance, I asked Daddy Moses, "How long does it take to walk to Annapolis Royal?"

"We don't even have you dressed for the winter, and you're already talking about leaving."

"My husband is there."

"Perhaps when the winter is out, we can help you find him."

"Can't I go sooner?" I asked.

"It's not walkable, girl."

"I will walk as far as it takes to find my husband."

"It's not walkable. Not in the winter, for sure, and not with a baby. You would both perish. To get to Annapolis Royal, you have to take a ship. And if you're like the rest of us, you don't have money for ships. Right now you just need to keep yourself and that baby alive. Your husband will take care of himself until the two of you can catch up."

I tried to ask if he had heard whether the *Joseph* had sailed into Annapolis Royal, but he got impatient.

"I don't know about any ships coming and going elsewhere in Nova Scotia," he said. "It's the most I can do to tend to my own flock."

WHEN WE ARRIVED IN BIRCHTOWN, I found a dusting of snow on the ground, and much more swirling about in the cold wind. About a thousand free Negroes lived in the area. Some had shacks, but others dug deep pits in the ground, covered them up with logs and evergreen boughs, and huddled together to stay alive through the winter.

Daddy Moses and his wife, Evangeline, had a one-room shack with a curtain down the middle. They slept in the back. The front half was where parishioners met privately with Daddy Moses. It also became my temporary sleeping quarters.

Theo McArdle employed me to write advertisements for importers selling silk, tobacco, molasses, fruits, flour, duck and rum. He gave me food to share with my hosts in Birchtown, but what I most liked was the chance to read the *Shelburne Crier*. I scoured the pages for news from other places, hoping to catch some word about Annapolis

Royal or the Negroes there. But I saw no notices at all about free Negroes. Just about the only news that I read about my own people had to do with runaway slaves. In an old issue of the *Nova Scotia Packet and General Advertiser*, which Theo McArdle also sold in his shop, I found such an advertisement:

FIVE DOLLARS REWARD.

Runaway from the Subscriber, on Saturday, the 22nd . . . , a NEGRO WENCH, named DINAH, about twenty five Years of Age: had on when she went away, a blue and white Ticking Petticoat, a purple and white Callico short Gown, and an old blue Cloak. Whoever will apprehend and secure said Wench, so that the Owner may have her again, shall receive the above Reward, with reasonable Charges. Robert Sadler, Shelburne, Mowat Street, July 24, 1783. Makers of Vessels and Others are hereby forbid to carry off or harbour said Wench, at their Peril.

BACK IN BIRCHTOWN, people told me that Dinah had indeed been caught and returned to her owner, who then whipped her. I came to understand that if you had come to Nova Scotia free, you stayed free—although that didn't prevent American slave owners from sailing into town and attempting to snatch back their property. However, if you came to Nova Scotia as a slave, you were bound just as fast as our brothers and sisters in the United States.

Within my first month in Birchtown, I caught two babies and was hired by a British group called the Society for the Propagation of the Gospel in Foreign Parts. They paid me three shillings a week to teach people in Birchtown how to read. I gave lessons in the Methodist church, huddled around a stove with my students. I worked as much as I could to buy warmer clothes and to purchase a bear hide for my bed. I didn't have much. I had less food and fewer comforts than at any other time in my life. But I was in Nova Scotia and I was free.

When Daddy Moses didn't need it for his own transportation, we all shared the cart that had been used to pull him from Shelburne to Birchtown. With my savings, I managed to cover that cart with three loads of old lumber, nails, tree trunks and scraps of canvas sail. With the help of Jason and three other young men that I taught, I erected a shack. We pounded poles into the ground, bound crossbeams to them, filled the gaps with moss and scraps of wood, wrapped canvas around the whole thing to break the wind, and lugged a potbellied stove in through the door. There was just room in that shack for a bed, a chair and table, the stove and me. The stove made me something of a curiosity. I was one of the few people in Birchtown to own one, and that was only because Theo McArdle knew a white Loyalist who didn't need his any more, having just received a shipment of supplies from England.

While Daddy Moses tended to our souls, his wife Evangeline looked after our stomachs. When I was settled in my own shack, I went to see her for provisions supplied by the British. Evangeline was a big woman who carried a hatchet on her belt. Anybody who even dreamed about breaking into her supply shed would have to face her wrath. She counted her supplies daily and itemized the goods that she gave to me. A saw. A hammer. A sack of nails. A pound of dried beans, a lick of salt pork, and a sack of rice or potatoes.

I hesitated. "I don't want the salt pork," I said. "Can I have something else?" She gave me salt fish, instead. I asked if it was better to take the potatoes or rice.

"Take the rice," she said. "Easier to keep, easier to stretch out. Rice, you can add to. Get some pepper, toss it in. Find

338

some greens, toss that in. Dice up chicken livers or a hog's ear and toss that in. Folks round here find bitter apples off the tree or on the ground and cook them up too. If you dress it up with condiments, rice stands up and talks right back at you. But potato is the same, day in and day out. Take the rice, I say, and watch it like your own baby. Wrap it good and keep it out of the rain."

Evangeline was a pious woman who believed that whatever trouble Negroes got into at night was their own fault. She attended every sermon her husband gave and called for swift punishment for any coloured people caught drinking and dancing in violation of Shelburne's official ban on "Negro frolicks."

In the Shelburne Sessions Court, people from Birchtown were sentenced once a month to a variety of punishments: a flogging here for dancing in a Negro frolick, a lashing there for drunkenness and vagrancy. One Negro who stole a loaf of bread and punched the store owner who tried to stop him was lashed twenty times at each of three intersections along Water Street. At whipping posts stationed at the corners of William, Charlotte and Edward streets, crowds formed to cheer and throw peanuts as the man's back was whipped to all corruption. A woman was hanged at the gallows at the foot of Charlotte Street for stealing silverware from a man to whom she had been apprenticed. The runaway slaves who were caught were brought into the court session and always returned to their owners, although we in Birchtown were adept at concealing fugitives and blending them in among us as if they were family.

Nobody had a thing in Birchtown, in our first months. Never a coin was passed among us. I helped one man write a letter to his wife in Boston, and he helped shore up one of the rusting iron legs of my potbellied stove. I caught the twin sons of an eighteen-year-old girl from Georgia, whom I remembered registering in the Book of Negroes in

New York, and her husband hacked down and sawed up four trees in the forest to enlarge and reinforce my shack. The people of Shelburne paid me when I worked for them, and I needed their money to buy other goods in town. But the Birchtown residents had so little that some of them traded their own clothes for food. The mother of Jason—the one who had pulled Daddy Moses in the cart to Birchtown—had to kill her own dog after going two days without eating. A woman who had boasted to me about coming to Nova Scotia on her own bottom found herself so hungry and cold that she placed her x mark on indenture papers, giving up her freedom for two years in exchange for the promise of room and board and—when she finished her contract—a payment of five pounds.

I talked to the baby growing inside my belly of my trials and tribulations. "Child of mine," I said, "I will never indenture you or me to live. I am just getting enough to keep you and me alive these days. The first thing you're going to learn from me is where your mama comes from and who your people are. The second thing you're going to learn from me is how to read and write. Think you can learn that round about the same time you start to walk?"

Whenever I heard that someone from Annapolis Royal was visiting Shelburne, I asked if they had heard of the *Joseph*, or met Chekura. Nobody could help me. I sent letters with two or three people who were travelling by ship to the town, and asked them to hand them out at taverns frequented by the Black Loyalists. but nothing ever came back to me. It was too far to walk, I had no money to pay for ship's passage, and I was busy trying to stay alive and healthy for the baby growing in me. Wherever he was, I knew that Chekura would want me to take care of our baby, first.

* * *

BIRCHTOWN WAS A LONG, HARD, MUDDY WALK from Shelburne. It took a good two hours if you were "on the hoof," moving as quickly as two legs went. We had no horses or wagons—nothing but our own calloused soles to carry us back and forth. In Birchtown, apart from the cabins and the tents and the holes in the ground, we had music and laughter in our churches. We took rum and rye, when we could get them. It was dangerous to drink in Shelburne taverns, but no white person would object to a frolic in Birchtown. White people rarely set foot in our community.

At night in Birchtown, many of the men and women roamed from bed to bed. Despite the clucking of Evangeline Wilkinson, who muttered about the sin of fornication, couples formed and split up and switched partners and reassembled. Wandering about the muddy laneways of Birchtown, I heard deep-chested moans and high-pitched wails coming from the shacks at night and chapels in the day. At his pulpit, Daddy Moses sometimes asked—but always in vain—for people to conduct themselves with more daytime modesty and to offer up more *silent nights* to Jesus.

MY FIRST WINTER IN NOVA SCOTIA, disease streaked through Birchtown. When the land was too frozen to dig, the dead went straight into the bog. The living took the clothes of the dead, and prayed that when their own time was up, it would come in the warmer months when soft ground would permit a decent burial.

I caught four more babies, but two of them died in their first month. I wondered how any baby could survive infancy in such weather, and felt fortunate that my own child was not due until the spring. People in Birchtown had no money or goods to pay for my help, but they would give me a rabbit and potato stew, because there were always a few bushels of potatoes and some of the youngsters were adept at trapping snow-coloured hares.

In Shelburne, for catching the baby of a white woman who declared that the doctor in town was a quack with a two-pound fee, I received two loaves of bread, twenty apples, a bag of rice and an old toboggan. I put the food on the toboggan and hauled it back to Birchtown. Jason fortified the toboggan and attached a stronger rope, which gave him a better way to haul Daddy Moses over deep snow.

Twice a week, I attended Daddy Moses's services. While leaning on his pulpit so that he could stand unassisted, he thundered and wailed until his voice grew hoarse. Sometimes his eyes rolled back in his head and he fell back into the arms of two waiting deacons. In the pews, worshippers jumped up, thrashed about and collapsed. I never found myself born again like that, but while others were in the throes of ecstasy, I thought of my father reading the Qur'an and wondered what he would think about such fits of piety. Thoughts of my father led to thoughts of my mother, and while the people of Birchtown sagged in one another's arms and sang out to Jesus, I sat on the pew and let my sadness erupt. To the sounds of "Praise the Lord" and "Hallelujah, sister," I drew from my own well of tears, confident that nobody would embarrass me with solicitude. Many times that winter, I slid onto my knees and called out the names of my parents, my son and my husband, crying for them as if they had just gone missing with my most recent exhalation. Arms around my belly, rocking back and forth, I prayed for the gift of a healthy child.

On the spring day that my labour began, most of the people in Birchtown had left to meet a ship on the wharf in Shelburne. Every man and woman with a strong back and good arms could earn two shillings for carting boxes and crates from morning to night.

I didn't want to have my baby all alone. What if

something went wrong? What if I needed help? Back when I was a child in Bayo, people used to say that bad luck befell any baby who was caught by his own mother.

Nobody answered when I banged on the preacher's door. I pulled it open and watched it swing on its rusty hinge.

"Daddy Moses! Evangeline!"

Evangeline, who dressed and shaved her husband each morning, was not in the front room. In the back, Daddy Moses was snoring.

"Daddy Moses. Evangeline!"

I pulled back the curtain. The preacher was lying fully clothed on his bed, on top of his blankets. He was alone. There was a cup of tea on a table by his bed. It was luke-warm. I concluded that Evangeline had dressed her husband, made tea and then left to spend the day working in Shelburne.

"Daddy Moses!"

He sat up with a start. "Who's that?"

"It's Meena."

"What time of day is it?"

"Morning."

"What you doing in my bedchamber, woman?"

"My time has come, Daddy Moses."

He didn't appear to hear me, or to understand. "Where is my wife?"

"Looks like she already got you dressed and fixed you tea, Daddy Moses."

"Yes, yes, that's right. She's in Shelburne today. Where are my glasses?" he said.

I grabbed the spectacles off a crate and placed them in his hand. He adjusted them on the bridge of his nose.

"Say again why you've come this morning?"

"I'm ready to have my baby."

In church, the man was so vivid and alive that people could not contain themselves when he thumped the

343

pulpit and carried on about Moses taking the Hebrews to freedom. *They were chosen to settle in Palestine, and we too are the chosen people. We too, brothers and sisters, are chosen for freedom, right here in Birchtown, Nova Scotia.* But without his wife to take care of him, the man who made so many parishioners jump up and shout seemed vulnerable at home.

"If you've got a baby coming, we have things to do." Daddy Moses sat up and swung his legs off the bed. "Go find some boys to lift me up."

I left, and returned in a few minutes with four boys who had been left behind in Birchtown to care for younger siblings. They carried Daddy Moses out of the shack and onto the community cart. After pulling him to my cabin, they lifted him inside and sat him down on the stool that I had brought along.

When we were alone again, I said: "I don't know if I can do this all by myself."

"Let not your heart be troubled, and neither be afraid."

I chuckled. "The whole time I'm having this baby, you're not going to carry on like we're in church, are you?"

Daddy Moses stretched out his legs and tapped his cane on a wall. "Suppose not. Don't worry, girl. You're sturdy like a ten-foot tree."

"I'd feel much better if the women came back from Shelburne soon."

"I'm been meaning for some time to ask you a question."

"Well, go ahead and ask, then."

Daddy Moses turned his face toward mine, as if he could really see me. "Were you married when this child seeded up in your belly?"

"I sure was. My man is Chekura. Like I told you before, I was supposed to sail with him to Annapolis Royal, but I got pulled off the boat and he had to go on. I don't know where he is. I don't even know if he made it to

Annapolis Royal. But I was hoping he'd show up today."

"Today?"

"Yes, that's what I was hoping."

"If he was coming, he'd be here already. Take it from me. I know the ways of men."

"He's coming," I said. "I just know it."

"Why are you so sure?"

"I've got to believe in something," I told him.

"Amen," Daddy Moses said.

"And now, I have a question for you."

"Let me hear it, then."

"If you are stone blind, why do you wear spectacles?"

"I like the way they rest on my nose, and they give me a certain dignity."

"But the glass is gone."

"Fell out after I had the pox. I never bothered to replace it."

"What does it look like inside your eyes?"

"It looks like nothing at all," he said. "I see nothing. No light. No darkness. It is as if I have no eyes whatsoever, but I remember what things look like."

We sat in silence for a while. Then I put some water in an old iron pot on top of the stove.

"What that water heats up," Daddy Moses said, "can you put some kick in it?"

"I have some lemon, rum and sugar."

"Here in Birchtown, we call that preacher's lemonade."

"Why?"

"The sheriff stopped one of our men at a frolic in Shelburne and asked what he was drinking," Daddy Moses said. "And our man said, 'Ain't nothing but the preacher's lemonade.'"

Daddy Moses and I took our hot drinks and spent hours talking while my contractions grew more intense. Finally, when my body felt ready, I pushed over and over and over again, but I could feel no head with my hand. I didn't even know how close I was, and I started to fear having that baby stuck forever in me, plugged up and suffocating and killing both of us.

I took another sip of preacher's lemonade and suddenly my body heaved.

While the reverend held my hand, I pushed and I grunted one more time. Seated with my back propped up and my legs wide open, I pushed for all the life inside me. I felt the head slide through me, and on the next wave I pushed out the rest of my baby.

Looking down, I reached for the newest person in the world and lay back with her planted flat on my chest.

"Land sakes, good woman, tell me what you've brought into this world."

But in that moment I wasn't thinking of Daddy Moses or of the sex of my child. I felt the heart pounding against my baby's chest, let my hand drape softly on her back and covered us both with a dry blanket that I had kept ready beside the bed. That little heart hammered right against mine.

My children were like phantom limbs

I NAMED MY DAUGHTER MAY, after her month of birth. When she had her little fits—perhaps I took too long to bring her to my nipple, or to mash boiled potatoes and greens as she grew older—I called her Little May First, after the very day she was born. I didn't know what to make of the girl's temper. Sometimes it seemed that all the wrongs of the world were pent up in her soul, waiting for any excuse to erupt. Before she turned one, she howled and pounded my back to be let down and allowed to stumble about on her own. She loved being held by the other women in Birchtown and especially by Mrs Alverna Witherspoon, a white Loyalist who came to our aid not long after my daughter was born. But when May had enough of substitute mothers and wanted to get back in my arms, she raised the roof if she met with delays.

Wherever I went—teaching, working in the print shop and catching babies—I kept her swaddled to my back with a fine yard of indigo-coloured cloth. I talked to her about everything, even before she could understand. I felt that the sound of my voice had to make up for all the things she lacked—a father, and the traditions of my native village. I even explained to her that I had bought the cloth that kept her close to me at Everything in the World in

Shelburne and that only a few shops in town welcomed Negroes. "You need to know where it's safe to go, and where it isn't," I said to her.

Alverna Witherspoon came into Theo McArdle's print shop many times before we got know each other. Her husband ran a whaling business, and Mrs Witherspoon brought in his advertisements twice a month. McArdle always dealt with her while I remained at the back of the shop, minding misplaced p's and q's and other spelling mistakes in beds of upside-down letters being readied for printing. But one day I was setting type alone in the store when Mrs Witherspoon came in.

"Is Mr McArdle here?" she said.

"He has gone out on an errand, Mrs Witherspoon," I said.

"How did you know my name?"

"You come in every week."

"I've seen you in here with that baby, but I'm afraid I don't know either of your names."

"Well, this little one who likes to try to grab letters out of the composing stick is May. And I'm Meena."

"I gave Theo an advertisement this morning."

"Yes, for whale oil. I was just setting the letters."

"I gave him the wrong price. For a firkin of oil, it's not two pounds six shillings. It's three pounds six."

"I can fix that," I said.

"Can you correct it before printing?"

"Just a minute," I said. I removed a few pieces from a bed of letters, let May hold one—she liked to run her fingers over the ridged lines—and replaced them. "Done," I said.

"Done?" Mrs Witherspoon said. "Can I see that?"

"It's rather complicated. The letters are upside down and in a big tray, and I'm rushing to finish up before printing. I can show you another time if you wish."

She smiled at me brightly. "No, that's just fine. Tell Mr McArdle I said hello. You are quite a sight, looking just like an apprentice printer in that lovely African garb, and with a well-behaved toddler beside you to boot."

"I was an apprentice last year. Theo doesn't consider me an apprentice any longer. I set the type for him on Mondays, without supervision."

"Please tell Mr McArdle that I was by, and that I was taken care of wonderfully."

May suddenly slipped away from me, ran to Mrs Witherspoon and put in her hand the upside down letter M from my composing stick.

"She's normally more shy than that, with strangers," I said.

"Thank you, dear," Mrs Witherspoon said to May. She winked at me and quickly put the letter back in my hand.

"No," May shouted, pulling at my hand.

Finally, when I relented, she pried open my fingers, retrieved the M and gave it back to Mrs Witherspoon.

Mrs. Witherspoon blew May a kiss, waited till she turned back to me, set the letter down on the counter and sailed out the door.

The following Monday, Mrs Witherspoon returned and asked, "How many days a week do you work for Mr McArdle?"

"Mondays and Tuesdays," I said.

"How would you like to work Wednesdays through Saturdays for me?"

Mrs Witherspoon and her husband hired me the next day. I did whatever they needed—cleaning their large house on Charlotte Street, ironing, hauling water and wood, setting fires, cleaning the fireplace, buying food and running other errands in town. I even cooked. They paid me a shilling a day to work from dawn to dusk. I preferred McArdle's print shop to the physical labour in the Witherspoon household, but the job offered certain advantages. I was allowed to take May with me, and to let her walk about and explore the house as long as she remained well behaved. The Witherspoons had no children but they frequently entertained and had leftover food. May and I were allowed to eat whatever was left or take it with us back to Birchtown. Mrs Witherspoon showed me any household items that she was planning to throw out—old chairs, tables, buckets and rope. If I couldn't use them, somebody else in Birchtown could.

My good terms with the Witherspoons left me envied in Birchtown. Many Negroes had indentured themselves to the Shelburne Loyalists for three-year periods. It was better than starving or freezing to death, but not much. A white Loyalist had every motivation to push an indentured Negro to the point of collapse by the end of the period. And some indentured Negroes who had become injured or ill were thrown out when they were no longer useful—with their salaries withheld.

"Don't get too close to white folks," Daddy Moses would warn me. "They can be fair-weathered friends." Fair weathered or not, salaries paid by McArdle and the Witherspoons helped keep my daughter and me alive and often went to support others, such as Daddy Moses. I was still delivering babies in Birchtown, but it had been a long time since anyone could pay me.

May loved coming along when I worked in Shelburne. By the time she was three, she would receive biscuits and milk every week from Mrs Witherspoon, who would sit with my daughter while she ate and played. One day, Mrs Witherspoon wrote the letters *M–A–Y* on a sheet of paper.

"Do you know what—?"

"May," my child said.

"How did you know that?" Mrs Witherspoon asked.

"It's my name. *M–A–Y*. May. Mama told me."

"What about this?" Mrs Witherspoon said, writing again.

"Mama," May said.

"And this?"

"Papa," May said. "He is missing some fingers and he loves me."

Mrs Witherspoon glanced up at me. She knew that with McArdle's help, I had long ago arranged for newspaper advertisements to be placed in Annapolis Royal, asking information about the whereabouts of Chekura. Nothing came back. Mrs Witherspoon also knew that when May was one year old, I had enough money to take her along with me on a summer trip to Annapolis Royal, but we took the next ship back home: I hadn't been able to find a single Negro who had heard of Chekura or knew anything about a ship called the *Joseph* having arrived in the fall of 1783. I had no idea what had become of my husband or where he was, but I still believed that if he was alive and if he was able, he would one day find me. I made sure that every Negro in Birchtown and every friendly white person in Shelburne knew I was waiting for Chekura, so that anybody meeting him or hearing about him could help us find each other.

A few weeks after May's third birthday, when I was telling her about her father and our homeland, she said, "Don't worry Mama, we will go back there one day." I asked her how we would do that. "We will go for a long walk and take along lots of food in case we need to eat lunch and when we get to the end of the woods, we will find Africa."

Soon after that conversation, my daughter developed a fever and diarrhea that had been circulating in Birchtown. I had to miss two days of working for McArdle, but could not afford to miss more days with the Witherspoons. I decided to take May along, thinking that Mrs Witherspoon might let me fold up an old blanket so May could sleep while I worked. I carried May on my shoulders, but she was too weak to bend forward and place her hands around my forehead for balance. For the entire walk into Shelburne, I had to keep my arms up to hold onto her

351

hands. When we got to the household, my arms were exhausted and my daughter's forehead was burning.

"Goodness' sakes," Mrs Witherspoon said, "what have you done to our lovely May? Hello, May. Can you see me? Can you look at me? Here, dear. Look this way."

May could barely keep her eyes open, and when I tried to put her down, she could not stand without help.

"Shall I call a doctor?"

"No," I said, rather sharply. Then I tried to soften my words, because I needed her help and did not want to offend her. "I'm sorry but I don't trust doctors. May just needs a little rest while I work."

In a spare room on the main floor, close to where I worked, we put May in a bed, covered her up and brought her water every hour. At the end of the day, Mrs Witherspoon offered to let us stay the night. I was deeply grateful, and even more so over the three days that it took before May's fever broke and diarrhea ended and she began to eat again. Mrs Witherspoon insisted that we spend a fourth night, to give May every chance to recover before the return to Birchtown. By that final day, May had made a full recovery and played with Mr Witherspoon by trying to tug at his beard. I watched their tender play and wished again that my daughter could see her father. Chekura, I was sure, would have been like that with her. I loved every inch of my daughter and worshipped every beat of her heart, but I was not a playful mother. I did not have a lot of fun in me. I fed her, clothed her, taught her to read before her third birthday and took her everywhere I went, but I was too busy and too tired for games.

The experience of bringing May through the illness brought both of us closer to the Witherspoons. They gave us old blankets to take back to Birchtown, and even let me take an old wooden bed frame so that May and I wouldn't have to sleep so close to the ground. Now, each time I came to work, May was greeted at the door by Mrs

Witherspoon, who often entertained May while I worked. Mr Witherspoon gave me whale lamp-oil until the summer of 1787, when his whaling business closed for lack of markets. The day the business closed, he and Mrs Witherspoon insisted that we have supper with them and stay the night. I spoke about the long months of waiting before leaving New York, and they talked about having lost land and a good home when they left Boston and sailed to Shelburne during the Revolutionary War.

"Why are so many businesses closing?" I asked Mr Witherspoon.

"They built this port in too much of a hurry," Mr Witherspoon said. "Everybody was convinced it would become the next New York. But the jobs never came. The people have no money to spend, and the businesses can't sell their goods. This town will collapse nearly as quickly as it was built."

An unusual heat wave settled over Shelburne and Birchtown in the month of July. The mosquitoes were meaner than any I had met in South Carolina, and bears came to the edge of town to eat berries off the bushes and to root through our garbage. Few of the Negroes had received land, and the British had cut off our provisions. Men hunted deer and moose to salt as much meat as they could for the winter. Most of the healthy men and women of Birchtown looked every day for work in Shelburne, but jobs were becoming harder to find. Mr Witherspoon's whaling operation was just one of many businesses to close. Wages were dropping—especially for the Negroes. At nine pence a day, Negroes carrying crates on the wharves made less than one-third the pay of whites. Businesses that did have work were often happy to hire the Negroes at the cheaper rate, but that left growing groups of white labourers—many of them disbanded soldiers who, like the Negroes, had come to Shelburne after serving the British in the war in the Colonies—gathering angrily in the alehouses. From their ragged clothing and worn faces, I could see that many of the white men endured difficulties too, and I knew that for the Negroes, these were the most dangerous people of all.

One evening in late July, May and I had finished at the Witherspoons' house and were walking down Charlotte to Water Street. May would usually walk until she was too tired; then I would swing her up on my hip for the rest of the way home.

"How far would you like to walk this evening?" I asked, holding her hand.

"To the first ale," she said.

"The first 'ale' sign? That's not far enough. How about to the end of Water Street?"

"No, Mama. Too many men. Up, Mama. Up now."

I picked up my daughter and looked down the street. Near a sign that said MILLIGAN'S ALE, a group of white men tormented a Negro labourer on a ladder.

"What you doing up there, boy?" one of the men shouted.

"Fixing the roof," the labourer said, reaching for a hammer hanging off his work belt.

I pulled May out of sight between two stores, and peered around the corner of the building. I could see the men trying to shake the carpenter off the ladder. He grabbed the eavestrough to keep from falling. The men ripped the ladder away, leaving him dangling in the air.

A man in a white smock came out of the tavern. "Hey! Give that ladder back. This boy works for me, and he's got a job to do."

Two of the men shoved the tavern keeper back inside. The others taunted the dangling worker until he dropped to the ground. Then the men fell upon him with kicks and blows, carried him over to the wharf and threw him into the harbour.

The carpenter struggled out of the cold water, but they

threw him in again and again. The men shouted that they would kill him if he got out one more time. When he did, moving slowly under his wet clothing, the men beat him until he lay still. When they threw him once more off the pier, he did not come back out.

"Mama, what are they doing?"

"They're hurting people," I said. I wanted to hurry back to Birchtown. But the angry mob was growing outside the alehouse to my right, and another crowd was forming to my left on Water Street. I pressed May flat against the side of the building.

"Let's burn their homes," one man shouted.

"Let's torch Birchtown," another said.

"It's time to teach the niggers a lesson," said one man. "Let's start with that big bastard down there."

Many of the men were drinking beer, and others carried muskets. The two groups of white men merged as they moved away from May and me, crossed Water Street and headed toward a Negro who was well known in Birchtown. Ben Henson, a tall, thick-set man, was stationed at his usual post to the side of Water Street, sawing logs at the rate of one penny a foot. Ben had the biggest arms in Birchtown, but I wished that he would take off and run before they got to him. I didn't want him to prove his strength. I wanted him to be safe. But as the men advanced, Ben kept working on his thick log.

"Why don't you haul them logs back to Nigger town?" a man leading the crowd called out.

Ben did not look up from his sawing. The leader walked closer to him, musket pointed at Ben's waist. Ben kept working until the man was within reach. In a flash, Ben grabbed the musket, seized the man and flung him to the ground. Two more men jumped him, but Ben tossed them off like cats. While he was dodging the knife of a fourth man, yet another slid behind him, raised a musket and shot him through the head. Big Ben Henson dropped like a sack of hammers. I felt nauseated at the sight of blood pooling around Ben's shoulders.

Then the men turned away from Ben Henson and saw me.

I grabbed May in my arms, turned back to Charlotte Street and ran up the hill to pound on the Witherspoons' door.

"Who's there?" Mrs Witherspoon called out.

"Meena and May."

She opened the door, hurried us in and slid the bolt behind us. "I've been watching through the window. I was worried they had you too."

"They're killing folks," I said.

"They've gone crazy," Mrs Witherspoon said. She led my daughter to the kitchen to distract her with ginger and molasses cookies. I looked out through the window toward the harbour. I could see Ben Henson, lying by his broken sawing tripods. From a distance, it looked like he was napping. There were no other black people in the street. The band of white men had moved on.

"I saw two men killed," I whispered, when Mrs Witherspoon brought me a shot of rum.

"Take this," she said. "And stay with us until this madness ends."

Mrs Witherspoon fed us and put us up for the next three days. Her husband brought more news: the white men were still rampaging. Roaming bands of unemployed workers had killed at least four Negroes and beaten many others. There was talk of rape. When the whites descended on Birchtown, they had been beaten back, but they had only returned in larger numbers to tear down some houses and set fire to others, attacking anyone who resisted.

Throughout the days we stayed with the Witherspoons, I kept to my regular duties while May played. Each night, I climbed into bed with my daughter and tried to calm myself by following the rise and fall of her breathing. How would I take care of us if our cabin had been destroyed? What if all of Birchtown had been torched? And what about Daddy Moses and other people who needed me?

Every evening, I asked Mr Witherspoon for a report. Four days after the riots began, he told me that they had stopped. There were no more bands of men roaming the streets, he said, and no more reports of violence in Birchtown. I wanted to be sure that it was safe to take May back to Birchtown, and thought it would be best if I first went there alone.

I arranged to leave May in the Witherspoons' care for two days. In that time, I planned to find out if my home still stood, fix it if I could, help Daddy Moses and my other friends, and then rush back to Shelburne for my daughter.

I slipped down Charlotte Street early in the morning, turned onto Water Street and saw no Negroes working in the town. A ship was at a wharf, but only white labourers moved about the docks. Some men stopped working, put down their loads of lumber and glared at me, but nobody approached me or said a word. I got out of town without incident. Usually I passed four or five people on the way between Shelburne and Birchtown, but on this day I saw only one Negro, and he was dead—hanging from a tree to the side of the path. He had on a pair of breeches but no shirt and no shoes. I shuddered, yet did not feel that I could keep going without stopping to see if it was someone I knew. I spun the feet and looked up at the face, but the man had been so badly beaten and bloodied that I could not recognize him.

Daddy Moses had arranged to have his Methodist chapel built on the east end of town; no visitor could arrive from Shelburne without taking notice of it. As I rounded the bay and crossed the bridge over a creek, the charred remains of the chapel came into view. It had been burnt to the ground. Three old women stood outside praying, and another was cooking over a fire near the ruins. As

I headed into town, I could see that many of the shacks had been torched or knocked over. Gardens had been trampled, and people walked about ragged and bent. I found Daddy Moses sitting on his cart at the graveyard. His glasses were missing, and I saw a welt on his cheek. I put my hand in his.

"I'm glad you're alive, sister," he said. "Nobody knew where you were."

I pulled Daddy Moses to his own cabin. The door was gone, a wall had been bashed in and the roof looked like it would cave.

"Were you there when they attacked your house?" I asked.

"Sitting on the front step, waiting for them. I heard them drinking and laughing and carrying on, so I looked straight in their direction as they came my way. I told them, 'If the Lord wants me, the Lord will come get me. So go ahead and shoot an old blind man, if killing is in your blood.' Somebody hit me with a gun butt. Another man kicked at my ribs. 'I can't see you,' I told them, 'but I know you. I know each of your voices, and when I meet your Maker, I'm going to tell Him of your carnage. Shoot me if you are so brave.' But they didn't. Cowards, all of them. 'Blind man,' somebody called out to me, 'tell your people to keep out of Shelburne. Stay in your place and there won't be no more trouble.'"

In my own cabin, someone had kicked the door off its hinges and thrown all my things to the floor. I thought of the men who had surrounded Ben Henson, and shuddered to imagine them tearing apart my home. Outside the cabin, Daddy Moses and I met with a group from his chapel. We agreed to first fix up the houses that had been least damaged. People who needed their cabins mostly or completely rebuilt moved in with others.

I spent that day and night in Birchtown and much of the next morning, working with a group of ten people to fix up two other cabins and mine. I helped move Daddy Moses into a spare bed in my front room, and at noon, promising to return before dark with my daughter, I headed back to Shelburne.

I passed the burned remains of the chapel, crossed over the bridge and set out on the path back to town. It was a long way to be walking alone. The wind whipped through the trees to my left, and out on the bay to my right, white-caps lifted and crashed over and over. Up ahead around a bend in the trail, I heard the loud voices of men. I ran into the forest, and moved quietly forward until I saw saw five men with knives, guns, rope and liquor walking toward Birchtown. There was no point in going back, because they would find me there. But it was dangerous to go on, because they might hear me thrashing through the woods. So I climbed high into a pine tree, pulling myself up onto one sticky branch after another. Then I sat perfectly still. My heart pounded in my chest. My fast breathing, at least, was drowned out by the shouting and laughter of the men.

They were talking about "shack busting in Nigger town," when Jason rounded the curve in the trail and found himself surrounded.

"Where you going, boy?" one of the white men said.

"I am going to Shelburne."

"Birchtown where you belong."

"My mama is in Shelburne. I am going to fetch her."

"Why is your mama in Shelburne?"

"Taking in laundry."

"Taking a white person's job, is she?"

"She is just washing clothes."

Another man smacked Jason in the head with a rifle butt.

"You've gone and spoiled my fun," said the first man.

"What fun?"

"I was gonna play with him a little. Teach him a lesson.

Kill him slow. Now you gone and knocked him clean out and spoilt my fun."

"Let's tie him up and have our fun with him later."

The men dragged Jason off the path, tied him up to a tree close to mine and continued on the path to Birchtown.

I waited a few minutes to see if anybody else was coming. Jason slowly came to and started moaning. I climbed down, ran to him and hurried to loosen the knots binding his wrists to the tree.

"Are you okay?"

"Yes. Good thing you're here," he said.

"So you're going to see your mama?"

"Mama died in the riots. She just up and died, without anybody even beating on her."

As he got up from the ground, I gave him a hug. "That's awful news," I said. "Is there anybody else at home?"

"No. It was just Mama and me."

"Why are you going to Shelburne?"

"Need food. Need work. Need a place to sleep. My mama's dead and gone and our shack's too tore up for living."

"Those men will kill you if you go back to Birchtown. Come along with me and see what you can find in town."

We began walking together to Shelburne.

"All the time we been in Birchtown, you never talked about writing me up in the Book of Negroes."

"Heavens," I said. "Did I write you up too? I'm sorry, Jason—I worked on so many ships and wrote down so many names that I've just forgotten some of them."

"I was in an all-day line-up on that ship, and all the coloured folks knew who you were. Little bitty pint-sized fast-talking African woman writing down the names of half the Negroes in Manhattan. You didn't know all of us, but we all loved you."

"You did?"

360

"Because you were taking care of us."

"And you say I wrote you up in the Book of Negroes?"

"You did, missus."

"What did I write?"

"Don't know, missus. Couldn't read then and still can't now."

"Why didn't you come to my reading classes in Shelburne?"

"I'm already nineteen," he said. "It's too late now."

"It's never too late," I said.

When we got into Shelburne, I noticed that the ship had left. Jason went to look for a man who had hired him before, and I turned up Charlotte Street.

I knocked on the Witherspoons' door. Nothing. I knocked again. I tried the door. It didn't budge. I wandered from window to window, to the wood shed, to the well, to the back door, but saw no signs of activity or people inside. I pounded again on the front door, until the woman in the nearest house opened hers and asked me what in tarnation I thought I was doing.

"I want my daughter, but nobody's home," I shouted.

"Would you calm down?" the woman whispered. "Hasn't there been enough trouble lately?"

"The Witherspoons have my daughter, but nobody is home. Do you know where they are?"

"Goodness, woman, stop all that racket."

I tried to contain myself. Perhaps if I could control my breathing, the woman would tell me what she knew. "Where," I sobbed, "is my daughter? She's three. This high. Named May."

"That little thing is yours?"

I crossed the street and brought my face within inches of the woman's. In my terror and anger, I wanted in the same instant to throttle her and to get down on my knees and beg for help.

"Where is May?"

The woman stepped back and cleared her throat. "The Witherspoons left on a ship. You and that girl are none of my business."

She closed the door in my face. I heard the bolt sliding.

I crossed the street again, found a rock, and smashed open the shutters covering a window of the Witherspoons' house. I crawled inside. Every room was empty. The tables, dressers and beds were all gone.

"May!" I screamed over and over again. But no one answered.

I stumbled down to Water Street. A number of white workers moved about the docks. I marched up to them.

"I'm looking for my daughter. Three years old. Named May. Have you seen a little Negro girl? Perhaps with some white people?"

One of the labourers spat near my feet. Others kept working.

"Please. I just want my daughter. Can anyone say if they've seen a little Negro girl?"

None of them would speak to me. I wandered out on the pier toward a young man working with rope.

"Please," I said. "I am looking for my daughter. A little girl. Three years old."

"I haven't seen any Negro girl," he said.

"Have you seen the Witherspoons? A man and a woman, who lived on Charlotte Street?"

"I don't know any of those rich people," he said. "But some sailed out this morning, on the ship. There were three or four families on it. That's all I know."

I ran off the pier and burst into Theo McArdle's shop. McArdle looked up from his printer.

"Meena!"

"Where is my daughter?"

"Did anyone see you come in? It isn't safe for you here."

"I can't find my daughter. The Witherspoons are gone."

"If anyone thinks I am paying you, they—"

362

I picked up one of his newspapers and threw it at him. I grabbed a bundle of papers, opened the door and hurled them out into the street. "What happened to my daughter?"

McArdle rushed past me to bolt the door and lower the curtain. He brought me a chair and motioned for me to sit, which I did, and he stood with his back to the door.

"The Witherspoons were preparing to leave for some time," he said. "I thought you knew. And as soon as the riots ended, they decided to get out."

"But where is my daughter?"

"When the disturbances settled down, they hired twenty porters to carry their things to the water. Within an hour or two they were gone."

"White porters, or black?" I asked. Negroes, at least, would be able to tell me something about May.

"White."

"Was May with the Witherspoons?"

He could not speak, but nodded slowly.

"Tell me," I screamed. "Tell me with words. Did my daughter go on that ship?"

He turned away and looked to the floor. "Yes."

"Where did they go?" I whispered. He did not hear me, so I repeated the question.

"Boston."

"And you did not stop them."

"I tried," he said.

"What happened?" I said. "Tell me!"

"I left the store and followed them down to the docks."

"My daughter, was she crying?"

"No."

"Was Mrs Witherspoon talking to her?"

"Yes, she was saying that you'd be along soon. I tried to speak to Mr Witherspoon."

"What did you say?"

"I asked if it wouldn't be better to leave the child with

me. Until you could come back to get her. There were guards on the docks, because of all the riots. Mr Witherspoon told them I was causing a disturbance. I backed away then, Meena. I shouldn't have done it, I should have complained louder. But I backed off the pier when the guards came my way, and the Witherspoons left with your daughter."

"Were there any Negroes by the docks? Any people who could speak to me?"

"No," he said.

"And my daughter all this time?"

"In Mrs Witherspoon's arms."

"Not crying or upset?"

"No. She had a tiny abacus—just a toy—and was pushing all the pieces."

I could think of no more questions, and Theo McArdle had no more to say.

"I have barely eaten in days," I said, "and I have friends in Birchtown with nowhere to live. Give me some food and I will leave you in peace."

"I don't have much."

"Give me something to eat, Mr McArdle. You let them take my daughter, and I need something to eat."

From the back of his shop, McArdle brought me a two-pound bag of rice, a ham hock, a bag of peas and a loaf of bread. I took the food and left.

JASON WAS WAITING FOR ME at the edge of town. He had no food, but he did have a cut on his face. There was no work in town for him and no place to stay. Nobody but disbanded soldiers with guns ready, fists clenched, boots for kicking. Jason asked where my daughter was. I couldn't answer. He didn't ask again.

We trudged through the mud back to Birchtown. The woods were eerily silent, and free of marauding men.

"I have lost my daughter," I whispered finally. "My last child."

"Never say last," Jason said. "Don't say that, Missus Dee."

"She *was* my last, Jason, and I am saying it because it is true. Don't look for me to keep you alive again when we set foot in Birchtown. Because I am in the mood for dying."

Jason slipped the load off my shoulder and hoisted up my sacks of peas and rice. I didn't even think to protest, and I don't know where the next thirty minutes went, except to disappear into a fog of despair. When we arrived we saw that more homes had been destroyed in Birchtown, but at least the white raiders were gone. Daddy Moses was sitting outside my cabin on a fallen log, waiting for me. Jason raised the old man up and we went back to my shack. Miraculously, it was still standing. The shack had more strength than I did.

For the next few weeks I was in such agony that I could barely speak. I tolerated Jason and Daddy Moses staying in my shack until they had their own place built, but I couldn't think of teaching the Birchtown children, or catching any babies, or working again for Theo McArdle, or doing anything at all. I feared that if I expressed my feelings, so much pain would erupt from within that I'd lash out and kill somebody. I had no money to pay for a trip to Boston, and when I finally asked McArdle or any other whites in town about going there, they insisted that I could be arrested—and possibly enslaved—if I showed up in that city with no money and no person to stand up for me.

"We don't know that they stayed in Boston," McArdle said. "They could have gone to Philadelphia, New York or Savannah. They could have gone to Jamaica, Barbados, St. Domingue or England."

With McArdle's help, I placed newspaper advertisements in Boston, Philadelphia and New York, offering a small reward for any information about the whereabouts of the Witherspoons, formerly of Shelburne, Nova Scotia. I asked every white person who would speak to me in town, but not one of them had any details about what had become of the Witherspoons. I even wrote to Sam Fraunces, care of President George Washington, Mount Vernon, Virginia. After six months, I got a friendly letter back, but Sam Fraunces hadn't been able to find out anything, either.

My children were like phantom limbs, lost but still attached to me, gone but still painful. I stopped cooking, working and eating. For the first time in my life, I had no desire to read. I even stopped thinking about Chekura. Perhaps Daddy Moses was right. If Chekura had meant to come back, he would have returned long ago.

Daddy Moses asked if I was ready to let Jesus into my heart. I told him that I had had a faith when I was a young girl, that I had had to give it up, and that I wasn't thirsting for another God in my life. He took my hands and turned to me as if he could see deep into my eyes. "But you are good, Meena. So many people love you." Perhaps that was true, but I couldn't see it and couldn't feel it. All I knew was that the people I had loved more than anything else in life had all been torn from me.

I started attending Daddy Moses's services again. I can't say that they changed a great deal. People were kind, bringing me food, sitting to eat with me when they noticed that I would never eat alone, bringing by fresh lumber and branches and nails, when they could, to help fix up my little place. Jason and Daddy Moses dropped in on me every day. When they set up a class for me, I resumed teaching, and even though I didn't really feel it, I tried to act like I loved the children I was showing how to read.

Eventually Theo McArdle persuaded me to come back to work for him, and I tried to be interested in the copy I wrote. When I was alone, I read whatever books McArdle could get for me. He found me a map of Africa, but in the interior there were only sketches of hills, lions, elephants and monkeys.

About a year after I lost May, I got a little lamp and a gallon of whale oil in exchange for catching a white woman's baby in Shelburne. It was the first baby I had caught since losing my own. The pain of my losses never really went away. The limbs had been severed, and they would forever after be missing. But I kept going. Somehow, I just kept going.

Elephants for want of towns

OVER THE NEXT FOUR YEARS, I could find no information about May. I believed that she was alive, but had no more idea about where she or the Witherspoons had gone than I did about the whereabouts of Chekura. Shelburne's heyday had come and gone, and many Loyalists closed their businesses and returned to the United States. The blacks of Birchtown stayed, however, and I stayed with them.

Nearing what I assumed was my forty-fifth year, I had no objection to the silver threads slowly taking over my hair, and wasn't embarrassed to be seen using spectacles with blue-tinted glass that I now needed to read newspapers and books. Theo McArdle had helped me order the spectacles from England, after explaining that they were double-hinged and contrived to press neither upon the nose nor upon the temples. The spectacles cost me two months of savings, but I had little else to do with extra money. I had no husband, no children, and no home other than the cabin in Birchtown that I fortified each summer against the coming winter. Twice I had the opportunity to visit other churches in Nova Scotia with Daddy Moses and members of the congregation, but each time I refused. I lived in hope that my daughter and my husband would return, and did not want to be away on the day that they came looking for me.

In the spring of 1790, the Methodists crammed into Daddy Moses' chapel to listen to a visitor from Annapolis Royal. He was a short, stocky fellow who looked a little older than me, and he spoke in a tone so flat that some parishioners fell asleep. But he seemed to have something urgent to say, so I slipped into the first pew to hear him better.

"My name is Thomas Peters," he said. "Fourteen years ago I ran from the man who owned me in North Carolina. During the war I served the British in the Black Pioneers, and anybody who doesn't believe me can come on up here and see my regimental papers. I'm just the same as the rest of you: I came to Nova Scotia seven years ago and I'm still waiting for my land. But now I'm tired of waiting and I'm going to do something about it."

Thomas Peters said he was taking up a collection to travel to England. There, he said, he hoped to speak to members of the British Parliament about the landless Black Loyalists and the perpetuation of slavery in Nova Scotia. None of us imagined that anything would come of it, but contributed what we could. I admired Peters' determination, and gave him ten shillings. After the meeting, I helped him write the conclusion to what he called his Memorial. "The poor friendless Slaves have no more Protection by the Laws of the Colony . . . . than the mere Cattel or brute beasts . . . and . . . the oppressive Cruelty and Brutality of their Bondage is particularly shocking, irritating and obnoxious to . . . the free People of Colour who cannot conceive that it is really the Intention of the British Government to favour Injustice, or tolerate Slavery in Nova Scotia."

"Make no mistake about it," Thomas Peters said as he thanked me. "I am going to England. And while I am there, I will not for one day forget the situation of our people."

Peters' boldness and ambition made me aware of how much my own will had weakened. There had been a time when I wanted nothing more than to go to England, and from there to find a way back to Africa. But now I would not travel. I stuffed moss in the spaces between logs to protect my cabin from the wind, and hauled wood from the forests to keep my stove burning through the nights. I had little left but the cabin, and worked each day to keep it clean and dry for Chekura and May. If they ever returned, I wanted the comforts of home to hold them forever. I tried to distract myself with work, but memories of Chekura and May shadowed me.

In Birchtown, we soon forgot about Thomas Peters. But the next year, he returned to our church to say that he had been to England and had met some white folks who were prepared to send us to Africa. It seemed ludicrous. He had no details to back up his story, and none of us believed him. Before he left, however, Peters promised that more information would come to us soon.

A few days later, while reading the *Royal Gazette*, I came across a notice from the chairman and twelve directors of the Sierra Leone Company in London, England: FREE SETTLEMENT ON THE COAST OF AFRICA.

The notice claimed that the Sierra Leone Company was willing to receive into its African colony Free Negroes who could produce testimonials of their character, "more particularly as to their honesty, sobriety and industry." It said that every "Free black" who could produce such a written testimonial would have a grant of twenty acres of land in Sierra Leone for himself, ten for his wife and five for every child. Blacks and whites would have the same civil, military, personal and commercial rights and duties in Sierra Leone, and it would not be lawful for the Sierra Leone Company to hold any person in slavery or to traffic in the buying or selling of slaves.

Once I started reading the notice to people in

Birchtown, others asked me to read it over and over again. I read it in Daddy Moses' Methodist chapel. I read it in the Baptist church. I read it anywhere and everywhere that folks wanted to hear about it. I read the document aloud enough times to memorize it. Still, I could not understand who would be allowed to travel to Africa, how they would get there, how they could pay for the journey, or who was behind this scheme and why they were offering it. Everybody asked me where Sierra Leone was, but I did not know.

We soon discovered that it was unsafe to discuss the scheme publicly. In Shelburne, three men beat up a Negro cooper who stepped into a coffee house with a copy of the *Gazette* in his hand. Some people in Birchtown worried that all the talk of moving to Africa would amount to nothing more than an excuse for white people to riot against the Negroes again.

A few days later, an Englishman named John Clarkson rode into Birchtown on his horse, wearing his full uniform as a lieutenant in the Royal Navy. He was a young-looking man. I was about 46 that year, and he appeared to be half my age. Young, but earnest. He had a boy's face, small nose, pursed lips. He was clean shaven but with wildly bushy sideburns. He asked to address Daddy Moses' congregation. Hundreds of people crammed into Daddy Moses' chapel and just as many crowded outside the doors, so we all moved outside. John Clarkson stood with his back to the ocean, brushing the hair out of his eyes. We gathered around him in a giant horseshoe shape, looking out at the bay.

John Clarkson had a high-pitched voice but it carried well. We stood motionless and silent so as not to miss a word.

"Reverend Moses, ladies and gentlemen, my name is John Clarkson, and I am a lieutenant with the British Navy. I am not here, however, on a military mission. I am

371

here on a civilian purpose, which is to offer those of you who are interested and eligible passage to Sierra Leone, in Africa."

The people cheered so loudly that Lieutenant Clarkson had to wait for the roar to subside. I was stuck by his paleness, and could see a blue vein near his temple. His eyes were lively, however, and appeared to study all the people before him while waiting for them to settle down. His gaze fell on me. I imagined that his eyes were lingering on the orange scarf wrapped around my head. John Clarkson's own hair was blond and receding. Bald spots extended back from the top of his forehead. He wiped sweat from his brow and buried his eyes in his palms, like a man who was fighting sleep because he had too much work to do.

When the crowd had grown quiet once again, Clarkson said that he had been born in Wisbech, a small port some ninety miles from London. He and his relations believed that the slave trade was a stain on Christianity. He said that he had become acquainted with the fact that Negroes who had served the British in the war against the rebellious Colonies had been denied land and opportunities in Nova Scotia and New Brunswick.

"I am here to tell you today that I have been authorized by the proper authorities in England to offer loyal Negroes passage to a new life in Africa."

Clarkson went on to issue numerous promises to those who wished to found a new British colony in Sierra Leone. "Adventurers," as he called them, would have the freedom to govern their own affairs. They would enjoy political and racial equality. They would have seeds for crops, implements to tend to them, and land to call their own.

"We don't even have our own land here," someone yelled.

"I cannot alter your circumstances in Nova Scotia," Clarkson said, but the Sierra Leone Company would give free passage to the colony and land to all who went there.

"Where is this place you call Sierra Leone?" Daddy Moses called out.

Clarkson asked if he should draw a map. Everybody demanded one. "You realize," he said with a grin, "that I failed all art classes in school."

"So did we," Daddy Moses said, to loud laughter.

Clarkson removed a quill and some paper from his carrying bag, and quickly sketched the contours of Africa. He drew it like a long oval, with the bottom left corner chopped out. North of a spot where the continent bulged to the west, he drew in a big dot and called it Sierra Leone. To the west, he said, was the Atlantic Ocean. To the northwest, something he called Wolof country. To the southeast, areas known as the Grain, Ivory, Gold and Slave coasts. When he had finished, he passed the paper through the crowd.

Clarkson said, "I did fail art, but I had to learn a little about maps in the Navy."

I liked the warmth with which Clarkson spoke, and I liked that he said that many of us could teach him a lot more than he could teach us about Africa.

"Draw us a lion," someone yelled.

"But it might look like an elephant," he said.

When the laughter died down, Clarkson grew serious again. He said that all adventurers to Sierra Leone would have to refrain from dishonest, disagreeable, unchristian, and immoral behaviour. And reading from his notes, he said, "Criminality, drunkenness, violence, theft, licentiousness, adultery, fornication, bawdiness, dancing and any other displays of uninhibited emotion will be strictly forbidden."

A few groans went up in the audience. One man standing near to me muttered, "Hell, man, we go all the way back home and can't dance about it?" A few people sniggered, but Clarkson ignored them and continued.

Criminals and disreputable people would not be

allowed to join the trip. Single women would not be permitted to journey alone, unless a man could vouchsafe for the integrity of their character and promise to ensure their welfare.

Clarkson asked for an assistant to take minutes of the meeting. Several people shouted my name.

"And who is this Meena?" Clarkson asked.

I stepped forward, so he asked me also, "Would you point me to Mr Meena?"

"I am Aminata Diallo."

He scratched his sideburns and looked bemused.

"My name is Meena, for short," I said. "You wanted a note taker, and I can help."

"You can?" John Clarkson lowered his hand.

His face lifted into a smile the likes of which I hadn't seen in years. It was an *I am so indescribably happy to meet you* sort of smile. It was an *I think the two of us could be friends* sort of smile. To my great surprise, I felt the same way. I liked the man from the instant I met him.

I was given writing materials and a stool to sit on, and I took notes as the meeting continued.

Clarkson asked for the names of the leaders of the community, so that he could quickly obtain and relay information in the coming weeks. He was given the names of three ministers. He asked if anyone was opposed to the idea. One Birchtown resident named Stephen Blucke argued that Negroes should make the most of what they had in Nova Scotia. Why risk losing everything on a dangerous journey to an unknown land?

Rather than taking offence, Clarkson merely urged Blucke and any others who felt they were doing well to stay put in Nova Scotia. I liked the way Clarkson was confident enough to let folks speak their minds.

Clarkson took pains to answer every question. Word by word, he gained my respect. No, he said, the ships would not be slave vessels.

He raised his finger to emphasize a point. "Slavers of many nations still trade in men on the coast of Africa. Some of them do their vile work in Sierra Leone. But there will be no question of slavery in the colony we create."

The Sierra Leone Company was directed by men whose life's passion was to abolish slavery, he said. The ship or ships would be outfitted with modern conveniences and stocked with proper food so that every man, woman and child could cross the ocean in decent conditions.

Clarkson said he hoped that the adventurers would be on their way within two months, and said that it would take about nine weeks to sail from Halifax to Sierra Leone.

The Sierra Leone Company, he continued, would spare no expense in removing us from Nova Scotia, out of the twin sentiments of duty and patriotism. Duty, because black people had a right to live free of slavery and oppression, and what better way to set them on the right footing than to send them back to Africa, where they could civilize the natives with literacy and Christianity. Patriotism, because we, the black colonists of Sierra Leone, would help Great Britain establish trading interests on the coast of Africa. No longer would the empire have to depend on slavery for enrichment. The land was so fertile, Clarkson said, that figs, oranges, coffee and cane would leap from our farmlands. We would meet our own needs easily and help the British Empire bring to market all the rich resources of Africa.

There was the small matter of those who had gone before us, Clarkson said. Some black people from London had settled five years earlier in Sierra Leone, but their colony had failed to prosper. However, we would have use of their old townsite, on which we could expand and make improvements.

I found myself believing that Clarkson's promises were real, but felt that I could not go with him. If I travelled back to Africa, I would never see my daughter or husband again. And so, as Clarkson held forth, I found my attention wandering a little and I missed one or two of the questions and answers that I was supposed to be writing down. The dream of my lifetime was finally within reach, and yet it didn't seem right to take it.

After the meeting, the lieutenant hoisted Daddy Moses onto his cart and the two men came to my cabin for a visit. We ate apples, buttered bread and cheese that Theo McArdle had given me for the occasion, and we drank my own hot libation of mint, ginger and honey.

"My stars," Clarkson said, "this sure clears out the nasal passages, doesn't it?" He peered at the stove rigged up for cooking and heating, looked over the utensils hanging on the wall and bent over to examine the books on my shelves.

"They look well read," he said.

I told him that I had read each book many times.

"Isn't reading a fabulous escape from the world?" he said.

I laughed, surprised at his directness.

"Don't tell me you've read *Gulliver's Travels*?" he said.

"Many times," I said.

"Don't you just love that term 'Lilliputians'?" he said. "Where on earth did Swift come up with the word?"

"They may be small but they do wreak havoc," I said.

"Sounds like the English," he said.

Daddy Moses and I laughed, and I served Clarkson another hot drink.

"How would you like to be my assistant?" Clarkson asked me. "I need someone to take notes, communicate with the Negroes and help me organize the adventure."

"I will help, but I cannot go with you," I said.

"Perhaps I can help if you are indentured or in debt," Clarkson said.

"I am free and have no debts," I said. "But I am waiting

for my husband and daughter and could not leave without them."

Clarkson asked what I meant. He listened carefully and tapped his fingers together while I told him about Chekura and May.

"I don't know what to say about your daughter," he said. "Given that the Witherspoons are wealthy, they could have taken her to any number of cities or countries. But let's talk about your husband. You say that his ship was called the *Joseph*?"

"Yes."

"And that it was bound for Annapolis Royal?"

"Yes."

"And that it left New York City on November 10, 1783?"

"That's right."

"Then I should be able to dig up some naval records. When I'm back in Halifax, I'll see what I can do."

I agreed to work for Clarkson for three shillings a day, plus room and board. Clarkson said that he would be needing me night and day until the departure for Africa. He would get a room for me at the Water's Edge Inn in Shelburne, and after a few days of work we would sail to Halifax to finish the job.

"Could I have another spot of that tea?" he said. "It is the most marvellous drink."

Perhaps one day, I thought, I would tell him about drinking mint tea with my father in Bayo. But for now, I wanted to know more about the men who directed the Sierra Leone Company.

He said the Company included some of the leading abolitionists in London, his brother Thomas Clarkson among them. They wanted to create a profitable colony in Africa, where liberated blacks could live productively and in dignity, and from where Great Britain could build a profitable trade with the rest of the world—trade, he said, that did not rely on the evils of slavery.

* * *

JOHN CLARKSON APPLIED HIMSELF EVERY WAKING HOUR to the details of registration. "Necessary civilities," he called it when we paid a courtesy trip to the Shelburne mayor, knowing that he opposed the adventure. The mayor predicted that the Negroes would die en route, or be consumed by tropical diseases, or cannibalize the naive Europeans who took them to Guinea.

John Clarkson heard every imaginable objection in the five days that we registered Birchtown residents for the trip, and I heard every term under the sun for people from my homeland. People called us Ethiopians, darkies, and those of the "sable race." They called our land Sierra Leone, Serra Lyoa, Negritia, Negroland, Guinea, and the dark continent. They called us ingrates for wanting to leave Nova Scotia. Knowing that slaves, indentured workers and debtors would not be allowed to sail with Clarkson, some people accused Negroes of having debts or of being indentured to them. My job was to ensure that every Birchtown resident who wanted to leave showed up to register at the Water's Edge Inn, and to find evidence to disprove false allegations.

Although we had to rush through our work, Clarkson always took a few moments to ask if I needed anything—food, drink, ink or quills. When I was tired, he told me that he felt the same way. And when we had a few minutes alone to eat at the end of our long hours of work, Clarkson entertained me by mimicking some of the people we had met that day. The man could pick up any person's accent. But ultimately he was completely serious about his assignment, and I liked the fact he respected my efforts to help him.

The nights, however, were difficult for Clarkson. I don't know how he had survived naval battles with his mind intact. The slightest insult or provocation set his anger simmering for the rest of the day and night, and either pre-vented him from sleeping or plunged him into nightmares. The walls at the Water's Edge Inn were as thin as parchment and each night his screams awoke me. "*No,*" he would shout out, "*I said, let her go right now.*" After the first eruption, I understood that these were merely nocturnal anxieties. I had had my share of nightmares too, so I did not judge him.

Over tea in the morning, he would tap the table, ask me to remind him to write a letter to his fiancée that night, and fuss over the Negroes who were being prevented from leaving for Africa. When a tavern owner claimed that one Negro still owed him five pounds for unpaid beer and fish, Clarkson paid the debt himself and warned the adventurer not to set foot in any more taverns for the rest of his stay in Nova Scotia. Clarkson wore his worries on his face, and sometimes dissolved into tears while we were discussing unfinished work. But neither Clarkson's tears in the day nor his outbursts at night prevented him from carrying out his long hours of work. I admired him for persevering in the face of his own struggles, and I made a private vow to support him to the best of my abilities.

When we finished the registration process in Shelburne, Clarkson advised the six hundred adventurers who had been accepted for the journey to Africa that he would send ships to bring them to Halifax. After reminding Daddy Moses and Theo McArdle to keep their eyes open for Chekura or May, I set sail with Clarkson.

I had a cabin of my own on the two-day trip to Halifax, and felt an odd sense of relief to be leaving the place I had inhabited for eight years. I had time to think during the long nights alone, and it struck me that good white men weren't likely to stay sane for very long in this world. Any white man who wanted to help Negroes "raise themselves up," as Clarkson liked to say, would be an unpopular man indeed among his peers. I hoped that Clarkson would retain his faculties long enough to get us safely to Africa. His tantrums and outbursts worried me. He was just too concerned about Negroes. It didn't seem natural.

HALIFAX WAS A FLEDGLING TOWN when I arrived in November 1791. It was not as attractive or meticulously laid-out as Shelburne. It lacked the array of storehouses and public buildings that the black people of Birchtown had built in Shelburne, but it was a gentler place to be, and far less menacing for Negroes.

I moved into a room at The King's Inn, among a set of ramshackle wooden buildings along a busy street by the water. I had only a few minutes of free time every day, and liked to start my mornings in solitude by eating breakfast in my room while I read the newspapers. Henry Millstone, who ran the tavern in the hotel, brought me the *Royal Gazette* and a bowl of fish chowder at seven o'clock every morning. He always liked to pause and chat.

"Lieutenant Clarkson tells me that you are the most literate Negro he has ever met," Mr Millstone said. "Is that true?"

I was discovering something intriguing about white people. It seemed that they wanted either to sing my praises or to run me out of town. But sometimes it was difficult for me to make the transition from one sort of person to the other.

"There are some literate Negroes, Mr Millstone, and over time there will be many more in Nova Scotia, where they are not prevented from reading."

"I wouldn't mind learning with them," he said with a laugh. "So are you going with the others to Guinea?"

"Africa," I said.

"Yes, that's what I meant."

"For the time being I am just helping the lieutenant," I said.

"Dangerous place, Africa is," he said.

I put down my soup spoon and looked him in the eye. "So is Nova Scotia."

A few days after I arrived in Halifax, three Negroes pounded on the door of my room at ten in the evening. They had just spent fifteen days walking through the woods from Saint John. An agent in that town had refused to register them for the departure, or to allow them to embark on a ship bound for Halifax, so they had no choice but to set out overland for the city, hoping to arrive before the ships departed. Clarkson agreed to admit the men.

Within a week, another hundred cold and hungry Negroes drifted by foot into Halifax. I saw men without coats, women with nothing but ragged blankets around their shoulders, and children without any clothes at all. By mid-December, boats from Shelburne and Annapolis Royal had transported more people to town, bringing the total of Negro adventurers to more than one thousand.

Clarkson lodged people in warehouses by the water, brought blankets so they wouldn't freeze at night and hired dozens of women to boil up cauldrons of food every evening. He worked all day and through half the nights, buying clothes for the naked and arranging medical care for the sick between his long hours at the docks. While I spread the word about what the Nova Scotians were allowed to take to Sierra Leone—no more than one dog for every six families, fowls but not pigs, a trunk of clothing but no tables or chairs—Clarkson oversaw the provisioning of ships. He spoke daily of the health of the travelling Negroes, and in each ship ordered pitch boiled, decks scrubbed with vinegar, and all sleeping quarters refitted to allow for a minimum height of five feet. He even posted a Bill of Fare to reassure travellers that they would be properly fed. At breakfast and supper, we would eat Indian meal with molasses or brown sugar. At dinner, we would have salt fish days, pork days or beef days, and eat turnips, peas or potatoes.

Clarkson arranged to have nearly two hundred turkeys slaughtered, dressed and cooked for a feast on Christmas Day, and for each man or woman to have one cup of beer or wine. During the course of the meal, he took me along as he walked from warehouse to warehouse to address the adventurers. He prayed with each group and repeated his "Rules and Regulations for the Free Black People embarking for Sierra Leone." He usually dealt respectfully with individuals, but had a tendency to speak to groups as if they were children. I flinched when he instructed the assembled travellers to pay attention to divine worship, to use soft words to prevent broils and not to make friendly with the seamen. However, none of the Negroes objected to his lectures. They venerated the man who was leading them to Africa.

The Governor and his wife invited Clarkson and me to dine with them for Christmas. As we entered their palatial home, Clarkson whispered to me that Government House had been built at a cost of twenty thousand pounds, and that the same amount would have employed one thousand Negro labourers for a year. Clarkson and I joined sixteen other guests in the dining room. Mrs Wentworth was a loud, cigar-smoking woman, and we were barely into the meal when she turned the conversation to the migration.

"I'll say, Lieutenant, it's quite the voyage you are cooking up."

"It means a great deal to the Negroes," Clarkson said.

"Do you honestly believe they'll have a better go of things in the tropics?" she asked.

I was tired of letting them debate as if I wasn't there, so I added a comment of my own: "We have waited eight years for land, and most of us still don't have it."

"Every Nova Scotian can tell stories of delays in getting

their land," she said. "It's not just blacks who are clamouring for acreage."

"It's about more than land," I said. "It's about freedom. Negroes want to make our own lives. But we are wilting here."

"You take our provisions and our handouts when it suits you," she said. "That doesn't sound like wilting to me—"

Governor Wentworth cut in. "Speaking of freedom, may I propose a toast to His Majesty the King?"

After fruit and cheese were served, a butler showed up to offer guests a tour of Government House. Clarkson and I followed some of the others up and down endless flights of stairs and in and out of rooms full of portraits, but only the map room caught my attention. The butler said there were maps from every conceivable place in the world. When the tour left the room, Clarkson and I stayed behind. I thumbed through a thick wad of maps while Clarkson complained that the dinner had wasted his time.

"It's doubtful that you could get much work done on Christmas," I said.

Clarkson said he still had to finish outfitting the ships and look into finding another ship's surgeon. He had asked Wentworth if he could take one of the royal surgeons from Halifax on the mission to Sierra Leone, but the governor had refused. Clarkson nearly choked with anger as he described the situation. One surgeon for a flotilla of fifteen ships was grossly inadequate, he said. What if the ships got separated on the voyage? What good was a surgeon on one ship if somebody was dying on another?

"Plainly," Clarkson said, "he doesn't want me to succeed in my business. He would prefer that the free blacks stay right here to prove that they are content in Nova Scotia and that their complaints of ill treatment are groundless."

Clarkson was breathing heavily and starting to wave his hands wildly. I sat with him for a minute and managed to calm him down by urging him to take steady, regular breaths, and breathing along with him. When he settled down to join the other guests for a drink, I had the maps to myself.

Somebody had taken the trouble to organize them into categories: British North America, Nova Scotia, the Thirteen Colonies, England, Jamaica and Barbados, and Guinea.

From the portfolio marked GUINEA, I removed the first map and spread it out on a table with two burning candles. It showed the typical paintings of half-dressed African men and naked African women, usually with baboons and elephants nearby.

Reaching again into the Guinea portfolio, I pulled out a piece of paper with flowery handwriting: "Copied from *On Poetry: A Rhapsody*, by Jonathan Swift, 1733." And then I found the lines:

> *So geographers, in Afric-maps,*
> *With savage-pictures fill their gaps;*
> *And o'er unhabitable downs*
> *Place elephants for want of towns.*

Elephants for want of towns. I found it comforting to know that nearly sixty years earlier, before I was even born, Swift had expressed the very thing I was feeling now. These weren't maps of Africa. In the ornate cartouches of elephants and of women with huge breasts that rose in unlikely salute, every stroke of paint told me that the map-makers had little to say about my land.

I pulled out the next map, and the next, and the next, but they were old maps with no details that I hadn't already discovered. They listed the Grain Coast, the Gold Coast, the Slave Coast, and they showed some of the major ports, such as Bonny and Elmina. I always remembered that last one, because it sounded like my name. Finally, I pulled out the most recent map that I had ever seen of Africa. It was dated 1789, and printed in London. I saw slave ports again, such as Wydah and Elmina. But much farther to the northwest, I saw another slave port: Bance Island. I remembered that William King, the slave trader in South Carolina, had told me that I had been shipped from Bance Island. I could not tell if Bance Island belonged to a particular country, but the words "Sierra Leone" appeared slightly to the southeast. I studied the map more closely. Although there were still the obligatory naked African women with children on their backs, and monkeys and elephants—especially in the so-called "Zarra or Desert of Barbary"—I also found the names of a few inland towns. This map had the coastal ports—most of them, it seemed—but also a few villages. From my childhood, I remembered my father promising to take me one day to the town of Segu. He had said it was about four days by foot from our village. And now I saw the name appearing a few inches north of Bance Island. I was puzzling over what four inches meant in real distance, when John Clarkson came back for me.

"Could we sit?" he said. "I want to have a word with you."

I sat facing him, imagining that he had come to speak about all the work remaining.

"You asked me to look into your husband's ship," Clarkson said. "The *Joseph*, which sailed from New York when you were being evacuated."

"That's right." I put my hands together, formed my fingers into a steeple. Sitting my chin in the crook of my thumbs, I pressed my nose with my index fingers.

Clarkson cleared his throat. "The ship went down."

I sat there, motionless.

"I checked with the British naval authorities," he said, then coughed. "They have an office down the street. Manifests, records, ships logs—they keep all that." I couldn't move or speak.

"The *Joseph* went down," he said again. "It was blown off course in high winds. It was blown so far off course that it almost made it to Bermuda. But then, in a huge storm, it sank. Everybody on board was lost. The captain, the crew, the Loyalists white and black. I'm so sorry. But you did ask me to find out."

"When did you hear about it?" I asked.

"Today."

John Clarkson reached out to put his hand on my shoulder, but I recoiled from him and ran from Government House. I didn't want to be seen or touched. I wanted only to be alone with the news. *Chekura*. My husband. After such a long journey. Gone, on the very vessel that I should have taken.

I wondered how the ship had gone down. Perhaps it had been struck by lightning, or had flipped in the churning sea. Had my husband died quickly, or had he had time to think of me as the water swallowed up his body? I consoled myself by imagining that he had probably been helping somebody else. Holding a child, perhaps. So very many Africans had been lost at sea, and many more again had been lost on the way to and from the slave ships. And now . . . this.

Many times I could have died, yet I was here still, now on the precipice of yet another journey across the water. The first one had been involuntary. This one was my choice. Chekura was dead. Mamadu was dead. May had been gone for five years. If she was still alive, she probably didn't remember me, and most certainly wasn't coming back. I missed all three of my loved ones so terribly that my body, it seemed, was half missing.

I spent a morning in my room in the King's Inn, emptying my grief into a pillow. Then I returned to help John Clarkson. I would take what was left of my body and spirit and join the exodus to Africa. There was nothing left for me in Nova Scotia. I imagined May showing up at

Shelburne and asking for me, and this gave me trouble breathing. I tried to calm myself by holding a book, stroking its cover and opening to a random passage, which I read over and over until I was able to speak the words. No matter what the book or the passage, the matter of reading it out loud brought me to a simple truth that I had denied for years in Birchtown: I would never see May again, and it was time to move on.

WE FORMED QUIET, ORDERLY LINES on the docks in the Halifax harbour. Huddled in the wind and the rain, waiting our turn to be rowed to the ships, we spoke in whispers. One out of every three men and women had, like me, been born in Africa. Including children, there were 1,200 of us. It took five days for the storm to subside. I boarded the *Lucretia* with John Clarkson, the ship surgeon and all the pregnant women and ailing adventurers. On January 15, 1792, our fifteen ships lifted anchor and set sail for Sierra Leone.

Book Four

Toubab with black face
{FREETOWN, 1792}

IN MY OWN SHIP, THE *LUCRETIA*, seven out of the 150 passengers died during the ocean crossing. John Clarkson himself nearly succumbed, choking on his own vomit during a storm, but was rescued. He remained bedridden for most of our journey, though he rallied as our ship sailed into St. George's Bay on March 9, 1792. I scoured the green mountains. From my childhood, I remembered the profile of the lion's back and head. Sierra Leone—Lion Mountain—rose up so sharply on the peninsula that I wanted to reach out and touch it.

I knew now that I had come, some thirty-six years earlier, from a slave ship that had left Bance Island. I had found the island on a map, and Clarkson had told me that it was in Sierra Leone. But until the coast with the lion-shaped mountain came into sight, I had doubted that I would truly return to the place of my departure. It had seemed too much to hope for.

The Nova Scotians hugged one another on the deck of the *Lucretia* and shouted praise to Jesus and to John Clarkson.

"Please, that's enough," Clarkson said, laughing but embarrassed.

"Tell us more about this land you've taken us to," a woman called out.

391

"I'm afraid I'm like most of you," Clarkson said, fixing his eyes on the coast. "I've never been to Africa before."

I stared at him, and noticed others doing the same. It had never occurred to me that the man who had led our exodus from Nova Scotia had never seen my homeland.

To break the silence, one of Clarkson's officers tipped a barrel and poured rum into glasses for the men and the women. I wanted no drink, felt no need for laughter, and preferred to stand alone at the ship's railing. I pressed my hands to the wooden bar, felt the humid breeze on my face, and wondered what would become of me now. I had expected to be overjoyed, but instead felt deflated. Waves crashed up against the shores of Africa, yet my true homeland was still far from sight. If I ever did make it home, I knew the one question that people would ask: *Where are your husband and children?* I would have to confess that in the land of the toubabu, I had managed to save only myself.

The crossing had taken nearly two months, but our waiting was not over yet. While the fifteen ships in our flotilla from Halifax dropped their anchors and baked for three days in the African sun, Clarkson was rowed back and forth between our ships and a handful of others already in the harbour. I could see that they too flew the flag of the Sierra Leone Company—two clasped hands, one black and the other white.

I felt relieved, seeing that they were friendly ships, but Thomas Peters ranted about them to me and to any other passengers who would listen. Peters was fond of reminding us that he had been the one to make the migration possible, by travelling to London two years earlier to complain that the black Loyalists were still without land in Nova Scotia.

But now Peters had something new to say: "What are all those ships from London doing here? This was supposed to be our colony. Our new life. And all decisions in our hands. But what are we doing? Waiting while Lieutenant Clarkson discusses our fate with other white men."

Clarkson had hired a group of African men to row him about St. George's Bay. We all stood on deck, admiring the rowers' muscles and their sleek, smooth paddling, until Peters had a chance to put his questions to Clarkson.

"And who are those men?" Peters asked.

"They are the Temne, and they belong to King Jimmy," Clarkson said.

"And who is he?"

"The local ruler."

"And these men, what do they normally do?" Peters asked.

"They are rowing men, for carrying goods and people."

"What kinds of people? Slaves?"

Clarkson's face began to redden.

Peters raised his palm. "No disrespect intended. Just tell us. Do those men row slaves in these waters?"

Clarkson coughed, and took a moment to compose his answer. While he was thinking, we slowly gathered around him.

"Thomas," I said to Peters, "why don't we all stand back a little and give the man room to breathe?"

"Thank you, Meena," Clarkson said. "I have already told you that there are slavery operations in Sierra Leone."

"But on our doorstep?" Peters said.

"Hardly," Clarkson said. "On Bance Island, eighteen miles down the bay."

"But Mr Clarkson," I said. Many heads turned to watch, because everybody knew that Clarkson and I got along well. "How," I continued, "could you put us anywhere near a hive of slave trading?"

"It's not as if we had twenty choices," Clarkson said. "This is where we have operations. This is where we have negotiated with the locals. And this, at least, is removed from the activities of the slavers."

I heard a few people cursing. I was happy that we had sailed close enough to Bance Island for me to see the shore and be sure that this was the land from which I had been taken. But I wished right now that we could drift another two hundred miles along the coast, in any direction.

Clarkson seemed to guess my thoughts. "At any place where Europeans have established themselves on the Guinea coast, you will find slave-trading factories. Nowhere is safer than this. Our mission is special, and our colony will be different. We will thrive with farming, industry and trade, and find our own ways to serve the British empire."

"We didn't leave our homes in Nova Scotia to serve the British," Peters said. "We came to Africa to be free."

"That you shall be," Clarkson said. "I have given you my word. Is this perfectly clear? None of you shall be taken as slaves."

Peters fell silent. He had echoed my very concerns, but I reasoned that Bance Island was far enough away. If I could go where I pleased, I would never even have to see it.

"When shall we disembark?" I asked.

"Tomorrow," Clarkson said.

We spent the rest of that day and all the next morning looking out at the lush green land in the distance, and were at the ship's railing when we saw a new vessel drawing near. Clarkson stared through his looking glass and groaned.

"What is it?" I asked.

He handed me the looking glass, which I lengthened and adjusted. Peering through it, I spotted naked home-landers on deck. And then the stench engulfed the *Lucretia*. The stink grew as the ship drew closer. Some of the Nova Scotians went below to their rooms, but I was transfixed. I didn't want to see it, but could not turn my eyes away.

Clarkson headed for his cabin and returned to the deck dressed in his uniform as a naval lieutenant. The approaching ship had also prepared for the meeting: all captives had been sent below decks. The true nature of the ship could not be disguised, however, because the stink made us choke and gag. I knew exactly how the captives were chained in the belly of the ship, and I could imagine the running sores on their legs and the moans leaking from their lips. A white man was rowed from his ship to ours and allowed to climb aboard.

Clarkson exchanged handshakes, pleasantries and goods with the man. The lieutenant gave him three barrels of dried meats, and the slaver gave Clarkson barrels of fresh water and oranges. They shook hands as if they were friends. Later, when the man was being rowed back to his ship, Clarkson saw me staring at him.

"It's best to remain cordial with the enemy," he said.

"Why did you let that vessel go?" Peters asked him.

"Mr Peters, I do not control these matters."

"You are sanctioning the trade of men."

"I received water and oranges from them—things that you and your fellow adventurers badly need," Clarkson said. "Do you think I took those supplies for my own consumption?"

"Why did you not stop that ship?"

"Mr Peters, this vessel is not a warship. Do you see any cannons or soldiers with muskets? Everything about me opposes the trade in slaves, but we have to pick our battles. We have come to establish a free colony—not to start a war with the slave-traders."

I had not even set foot back on land and I already could see that nothing would be simple. I admired Peters for objecting to the slave trade. But for the time being, I felt that Clarkson was right. I had learned that there were times when fighting was impossible, when the best thing to do was to wait and to learn. First we had to get off our ships, build shelters and find food.

That night, while I watched from the *Lucretia*, dark

clouds rolled in over the mountain. The skies grew black and starless. Lightning sawed through the clouds, illuminating the ships in the harbour and sending waves of thunder crashing across the bay. From the caves in the mountain, the thunder shot back at us, echoing over and over like cannons in the night. Many of the people on the ship were terrified, but I had not forgotten the storms, even after all these years, and I knew that they would pass.

BY THE THIRD DAY OF BAKING IN THE SUN, it became clear that the Sierra Leone Company had no plan for getting us off the boats. With just one rowboat per ship, it would have taken an eternity to move a thousand passengers and our belongings to shore. While I stood on the deck with the others, feeling that the *Lucretia* was less a liberating vessel than a prison at sea, I watched sixteen oarsmen row a massive canoe carrying a straight-backed homelander in a regal English chair. Behind him sat a coxswain, and ahead, a beating drummer. We heard the tamtam rhythm skimming over the harbour waters before we could make out the faces of the men. King Jimmy was coming to pay tribute to John Clarkson, who ordered his sailors to fire twenty guns in salute and told us to address the chief as "Your Excellency."

"Not on your life," Peters muttered.

Thomas Peters stood erect beside John Clarkson at the top of the ship's ladder, but the chief brushed past him, reaching out his arms to embrace Clarkson. King Jimmy greeted the white soldiers in English and shook their hands, but he refused, in his first moments, to even look at us. King Jimmy gave Clarkson fifteen pineapples and an elephant tooth in exchange for unwatered rum.

He looked at me and asked the lieutenant: "Your mistress?"

"I am old enough to be his mother," I said.

396

King Jimmy guffawed, motioned at the Nova Scotians assembled on deck, and said, "King John Clarkson have many servants."

Thomas Peters spoke up. "We are the Nova Scotians and we come as equals."

The Temne chief wasn't paying attention. Turning again to Clarkson, King Jimmy pointed to me and said, "Is she the one you tell me about? The African who knows more books than the Englishmen?"

John Clarkson frowned. I could see that he did not want King Jimmy to mock me.

King Jimmy looked me up and down and then sent a torrent of African words my way. I had no idea what he was saying. He burst into laughter and disappeared into Clarkson's cabin to drink rum. Later, he bowed to me on his way out.

"One day you come to my village. How are you named?"

"Aminata."

"One day you be Queen Aminata, wife of King Jimmy."

"Thank you, but I am already married."

"Where your husband?"

When I paused, King Jimmy laughed again.

"If he on other side," he said, gesturing west across the water, "you free now."

With that, he climbed over the side of our ship and down a ladder, got into his canoe and was rowed away.

It seemed absurd that my first conversation as an adult with an African in my own homeland should take place in English. Something about his bombastic nature, expressed in the broken language of the toubabu, made him appear to me more as a buffoon than a threat.

Within a few hours, King Jimmy sent men in thirty canoes to fetch the Nova Scotians. Pulling steadily toward us, they resembled an army of rowers. I was glad that they were coming to help, but aware of how easy it would have been for them to wage war on us. When my turn came to climb into a canoe, I tried to speak to the young rower who sat closest to me. But he stared blankly ahead, would not even turn his head toward me. He did his job and nothing else—working with his mates to pull us smoothly and quickly to shore. And so it happened that the same men who rowed slaves to Bance Island carried us over the waters of St. George's Bay and onto the shores of Sierra Leone.

JOHN CLARKSON STOOD UNDER A SHELTER erected out of old canvas sails, with twelve representatives from the Sierra Leone Company behind him and all of us gathered around him. Staying in one spot, I lifted my feet up and down, over and over, to feel the land under my heels. I pulled off my shoes to let the sand of my homeland slide between my toes. I was thinking that I never wanted to set foot again on a ship, and that I had just one journey remaining in my life—a long trip overland.

"Ladies and gentlemen," Clarkson said, "we shall call our new colony Freetown. My orders were to bring you here and then return to London, but the Company directors have sent a note from London, asking me to remain with you for a short time."

Most of the Nova Scotians broke into applause, and I joined them. I trusted Clarkson more than any other white person, and I believed that he would do his best to help us in our new life.

Clarkson introduced the men behind him, explaining that the Company had sent them from London to manage the colony in Freetown.

"Can we not govern our own affairs?" Peters asked.

"Eventually, of course," Clarkson said. "But the Company has invested a fortune to bring you here and intends to govern the colony to ensure its success."

Peters groaned. "We didn't come all this way for more white man's rules."

Daddy Moses was sitting on a cart that had crossed the ocean with him. "Mr Peters," he said, "give the lieutenant a chance to say his piece."

"Thank you," Clarkson said. "Each one of you will have to give to the best of your labour. I must warn you that shirkers will not receive food, water, building supplies or anything else from the Company." Clarkson instructed us to place our temporary shelters far back from the water, because prime land was reserved for wharves, stores, warehouses and company residences and offices.

Peters and a few men who were close to him shouted that they had not come to Freetown to build homes for Englishmen.

But Daddy Moses spoke up again. "Brothers and sisters," he said, "this is not the time to argue. You all have eyes, and you see for me, so tell me this: Can anyone see five hundred homes already built for our weary bones? Do we have a house of worship? Do we have a system for gathering food and hunting game and sharing among ourselves until we are all self-sufficient?"

Nobody said a word.

Over the next weeks, we cleared trees and bushes, split wood for fires, emptied supplies from fifteen ships, rowboat by rowboat, ripped up spare canvas, and built simple homes out of mud, clay and thatch.

We depended on the Company for everything. Did we need a hammer? A bit of canvas sail for cloth? Salt pork? Molasses? Bread? Everything came from the Company, which owned the resources, the food, the means to build proper shelters—and which even seemed to own us. When we ached from the hours of working in the sun or were soaked by the sudden storms, Daddy Moses reminded us that there were times to fight, but this was a time to survive.

For the time being, we had food. The Company had brought supplies in ships from England, and much was left over from our trip from Halifax. However, the cheese had turned foul, the butter rancid, and molasses had leaked out of rotting barrels and covered the floor of our warehouse.

Daddy Moses couldn't do much work, but he sat where we congregated and threw out suggestions. We divided ourselves into work crews, and set out to collect drinking water, hunt, make meals, and erect temporary buildings. We also built a sick house. People caught fevers left and right, and in our first two weeks in Freetown, ten Nova Scotians and three Company men died. For a time, we had a person dying every day or two. In the mornings, it wasn't uncommon for us to ask each other, "How many died last night?"

Clarkson warned us repeatedly not to leave Freetown. Outside the town limits, we were told, the Company could not protect us from slavers or potentially hostile Africans. Many of the Nova Scotians seemed content to build their homes and work for the Company, but I felt that being obliged to stay within town was like staying on an island off the coast: I wasn't yet free to reclaim my homeland. Between building churches, houses, granaries and roads, we had no lack of work to keep us busy. But to me, all the sawing and hammering seemed designed to create barriers between Nova Scotians and the Temne people inhabiting the coastal region of Sierra Leone. We were no longer in Nova Scotia, but we were transplanting a good part of it. I felt that the colony we were establishing was neither one thing nor the other. But if Freetown was not what I had come to find in Africa, it was only right to devote myself to it for the time being, and to support the dreams of my Nova Scotian friends. For now, my own dreams would have to wait.

I managed to avoid the illnesses and fevers that took so

many lives, and made myself useful by caring for the sick, catching babies and working sometimes for Clarkson. I slept in dampness at night, and was tired all day. My bones ached and called out at night for a soft feather bed. I thought sometimes of the angry voices of white Nova Scotians warning, *"You have no idea how good you have it here."* It was true that life was hard for us in those early days in Freetown—our shelters, churches, food and clothes were as rude, or ruder, than they had been in Birchtown. The Nova Scotians grumbled about the poor quality of supplies and our utter dependency on the British, and they appointed sentries and guards to watch out for possible attacks by slave-traders. Still, the colonists felt a quiet optimism about the new lives they were building, and that their security was less tenuous in Freetown than it had been in Nova Scotia or New York. Personally, I concluded that no place in the world was entirely safe for an African, and that for many of us, survival depended on perpetual migration. Now that I had finally returned to my homeland, I had no thoughts of leaving. But I didn't know how long I would be able to live next door to a slave-trading post.

Although I had lived among the Nova Scotians for ten years in Birchtown, I no longer felt entirely at home with them. I sought out the community of the Temne, though many Nova Scotians called them "heathens" and said that they should not be allowed to trade inside our settlement. Some Nova Scotians seemed intent on taking all of the contempt that they had endured in North America and redirecting it at the Africans. I heard from John Clarkson that two Nova Scotians were so disgusted at having to live under the rules and regulations of the Sierra Leone Company that they ran off to work with the slave traders at Bance Island.

In South Carolina, I had been an African. In Nova Scotia, I had become known as a Loyalist, or a Negro, or both. And now, finally back in Africa, I was seen as a Nova Scotian, and in some respects thought of myself that way too. I certainly felt more Nova Scotian than African when the Temne women clustered around me, grains and bound fowl and fruits balanced on huge platters on their heads. They knew that I had come with Clarkson and the white sailors, and by the way they squeezed my hands and arms, they seemed to think that I was just as foreign as the British.

I tried to speak to them in Fulfulde and Bamanankan, but they laughed and had no idea what I was saying. I couldn't wait to learn their language well enough to say that I too had been born in Africa. I knew that the Temne did not see me as one of them and that they never would. Still, I felt a certain connection to them, and the easiest and most natural way to feed that sense of kinship was to learn their language. I memorized new Temne words every day and used them constantly in conversation. I began by learning the Temne words for the oranges, water, fowl, salt and rice that they gave me, as well as words for the knives, pots, beads, cloth and rum that I collected from the Nova Scotians to trade.

I learned how to count to a hundred, and how to greet a person in the morning, at noon and at night. I learned to ask, *How are your children? How goes the work? How stands the house?* and *It all goes well* and *Thank you very much*. I needed to learn those words. It would be impossible to travel inland without speaking to the local people.

But even as I learned new words and phrases each day, I wondered just who exactly I was and what I had become, after more than thirty years in the Colonies. Without my parents, my husband, my children or any people with whom I could speak the languages of my childhood, what part of me was still African? I would never feel truly at home again until I found my way back to Bayo.

*   *   *

WITHIN A MONTH, we had cleared the land for a townsite, erected tents or huts for all of the Nova Scotians, erected a few key Company buildings and finished a basic church, which became our community centre. For a time, we took turns in the church. The Baptists had it first thing Sunday morning, the Methodists at noon, and the Huntingdonians later in the afternoon.

Within two months, we had hewed out four streets running parallel to the river and three streets perpendicular.

The Nova Scotians, led by Thomas Peters, asked repeatedly for land grants so that we could begin farming. But the surveyor died, succumbing like so many people—white and black—to this new climate. The Company used this misfortune to insist that the Nova Scotians devote ourselves entirely to fortifying the town and building company structures.

Thomas Peters tried in vain to rally the Nova Scotians against the Company. I admired him for trying. The British had given false promises to the Loyalists who fought in the Revolutionary War and travelled to Nova Scotia, and they had lied once again about what we would receive in Sierra Leone. They did not attempt to enslave us, but nor did they set us free. They did not give us the promised tracts of land or any other means of becoming self-sufficient in Freetown. We depended on them for our work, our sustenance and even the materials and tools to build our homes. And they set the rules by which we lived.

"They betrayed us in Nova Scotia and again right here in the land of our ancestors," Peters said to a group assembled in Daddy Moses' church.

"Give it time," Daddy Moses said. "We are not yet free, but we are moving in that direction."

I shared Peters' disappointment that we found ourselves once again under British control, but anger did not burn in my heart. I believed that Daddy Moses was right—

freedom would come to us, one day at a time. But I also had other things on my mind. Freetown, for me, was nothing more than a stepping stone.

Before leaving Halifax, I had imagined that the colony we set up in Freetown would blend in with African settlements, and that I would rarely see Europeans again. As it turned out, the Temne people came daily to trade with us, but did not invite us to join them in their villages. And a steady stream of commercial, supply and military vessels plied the African coasts and brought sailors every week to Freetown. They stopped for provisions, trade and simply to rest, drink and eat, and thus our new colony in Sierra Leone became an unlikely mix of Nova Scotians, Africans, British officials, and sailors on leave from their ships.

As well, the captains and crew of slave vessels regularly took time out from buying slaves at Bance Island to come drinking and looking for women in Freetown. I worried, initially, that the visiting slave-traders might try to re-enslave the Nova Scotians in Freetown, and spoke to Clarkson about it.

"We're better to let them have their fun than to try to bar them from town and incur their wrath," he said.

"It makes the Nova Scotians uncomfortable," I said, "and it puts me ill at ease too."

"What are we going to do?" he said. "Identify every visiting sailor by ship?"

"They trade in slaves," I said.

"Not here in Freetown."

"What makes you so sure?"

"They can get all the slaves they want at Bance Island," Clarkson said. "Trying to take people here would be messy, and cause problems, and they don't want that. All they want is to drink and carouse. Bance Island is where the slavers go to work. This is where they come to play."

* * *

FOR A TIME, I LIVED WITH A WOMAN named Debra Stockman, who had been pregnant on the trip from Halifax and whose husband died en route. I caught Debra's baby several months after we arrived, and taught her to wrap the baby around her back in the African style. I taught her to feel the straining in the baby's legs and backside, so she could loosen the infant from her back, remove her waist clothes, and let her do her business.

Debra soon set up her own business—a curio shop for visiting sailors. With my help as an interpreter, Debra bought sculptures, masks, ceremonial knives, little wood carvings of elephants, necklaces and ivory bracelets from the Temne traders, and sold them at a profit to sailors who wanted to take trinkets back to England. The fastest-selling items were tiny sculptures carved out of camwood. The deep reddish brown colour of the wood appealed to the sailors. Debra polished the sculptures with palm oil—little elephants, alligators and monkeys. But sailors couldn't resist the sculptures of young, bare-breasted women. They could rarely pay in silver, but they gave Debra rum, iron pots, small cauldrons, iron bars, or clothing from England, and Debra was always able to give these to the Temne in exchange for food, or firewood or building services. The Temne were quick learners in the art of building the wooden, often elevated houses that pleased the settlers so much—and as a result Debra and her daughter, Caroline, were soon established in their own house and they lived in it well.

Apart from trading with the Temne and visiting sailors, we also depended on supplies from the *Sierra Leone Packet*, a Company vessel that sailed back and forth between Freetown and England.

One day, a few hundred of us gathered by the wharf to watch a ship unload. We had been hoping for boxes of hammers and nails, but in the crates we found three hundred clay watering pots.

"What's this?" Daddy Moses asked, when I put one in his hands.

"A clay pot," I said.

"Pardon me?"

"A watering pot. We just got three hundred of them. No hammers, though, and no nails either."

"Girl, you need to write those white folks a letter. Tell them we don't have any gardens, just yet, and that with all the rain we don't need their clay watering pots."

I never wrote to the Company, but I did write to Sam Fraunces and Theo McArdle, when Clarkson explained that the letters would be sent to America after reaching England. I liked to imagine my words travelling across the seas, and I hoped that one day a letter might come back for me.

THE COMPANY HIRED ME TO TEACH CHILDREN and adults how to read and write, and Clarkson—who said writing brought on his headaches— gave me extra work preparing reports to the directors in London. As his occasional secretary, I was sometimes rowed out to his ship to work with him in a large cabin that had been turned into an office.

"Would you not rather live on land?" I asked him one day.

"I am a Navy man," he said, "and I find it more peaceful out here on the water. I have time to think, and people cannot just bang on my door and barge in while I'm concentrating."

"If the Company asked you to be superintendent of the colony, why do you let the other managers take over almost everything?"

"I am happy to leave them to it," Clarkson said. "And it would strain my good relations with the Nova Scotians if I had to enforce all of the Company rules."

"They are not the rules you had anticipated?"

Clarkson lifted his palms in the air, but would only say, "One can't anticipate everything."

When my writing work was done, Clarkson invited me to sit with him for tea.

"It must be lonely for you, without your fiancée," I said.

Cracking his knuckles, he acknowledged that it was true. He encouraged me to read some of his London newspapers, and while I did that, he read a book. It was the first time in my life that I had felt connected to another person, merely by dint of our sitting in the same space and reading together. I felt that I shared a good moment with him, even though we didn't speak much. Actually, I appreciated that he did not enquire into the state of my own heart. Returning to Africa could not bring back all the people I had lost. But in Sierra Leone, I found myself less burned by longing for my daughter, perhaps because I had stopped looking for her in every child I saw. Wherever May was, she certainly wasn't in Africa.

IN THE EARLY MONTHS, the only way that most settlers could survive was to work for the Company, and thereby receive wages and provisions. Although the Company had promised that our provisions would be free for the first months, within a month or two we were brought down to half rations. And soon enough, if we wanted food, we had to draw it at the company store in exchange for labour. But there was never work, every day, for every person in the colony. And although a skilled labourer could make two shillings a day, he had to pay four shillings a week for provisions. The Company infuriated the Nova Scotians by charging exorbitant rates for salt fish, beef and poultry, and by watering down its alcohol. Nonetheless, drink and religion shot up side by side in our colony.

Within months of arriving, six different religious

denominations had established their own meeting houses—at first tents, then huts, then wooden chapels. They rang with singing and praying through the night. The people of Freetown knew nothing of sleep, or else learned to sleep through pandemonium. In any given night, you could hear the tamtams beating from King Jimmy's town half a mile away, and you could hear visiting sailors staggering and singing and falling down in the streets, and arguments and palavers between settlers—who killed whose duck, for example, or who made eyes at whose woman. You could hear men beating men, men beating women, and yes, women beating men. And through it all rang the amens and the hallelujahs of the churchgoers.

One Nova Scotian by the name of Cummings Shackspear had brought supplies with him from Halifax, including seven barrels of rum. I never learned how he managed to accumulate all that rum before sailing, or under what false pretenses he got it loaded on board his ship in Halifax, but he had the barrels sealed by the most able coopers of Halifax, and was still in possession of his huge store of drink by the time he opened a tavern two blocks back from the water. Some parishioners would emerge from church sweating and exhausted, and get straight to drinking. Fewer taverngoers left off their drinking to go straight to church.

Cummings watered down his rum—no worse than the Company—and sold it by the glassful. He raked in enough money to keep up his supply and he gave up on the Company goods. They tried to extract exorbitant dues and didn't like selling to him anyway, but there were enough passing ships—trading vessels, slaving vessels, British military vessels—and Cummings was usually able to buy a few barrels of rum in exchange for goods he was able to obtain, sometimes, from Temne traders: ivory, camwood, or even occasionally large stores of pineapple, puncheons of fresh water, goats, poultry and the like. He built a storehouse for his goods directly behind his tavern, and hired a Temne native to guard it at night. His place of drink became known as Shackspear's Book. Sailors knew its reputation and went looking for it the moment they got off their yawls.

Cummings did such a business that he soon no longer depended on the goodwill of the Company, and divorced himself from the politics of the struggles between the settlers and the Company. Few, however, could afford such a luxury.

I never had a mind for business, and the services that I offered—reading and writing lessons by evening in the backroom of my house, medical care for the sick, who needed me especially because Company doctors were generally drunk or dying—never brought many rewards, but kept me from depending totally on the British for my survival. During the mornings, I continued to teach at the Company school.

King Jimmy and his people lived just a mile or two away, and by the time I'd been in Freetown for a year I had come to understand that he was pressuring John Clarkson to pay him for the use of Temne lands. Nobody had told us prior to arriving in Sierra Leone, but it gradually dawned on us that King Jimmy's men had raided and sacked the earlier colony of black settlers from England, and that they did not accept the terms under which the British claimed they had purchased the African land. King Jimmy's favourite method of pressure was to send dozens of canoes full of warriors past our shores at night, whooping and hollering and beating drums as they went. It frightened the daylights out of the Nova Scotians, who pleaded with Clarkson to provide them with more guns. I liked the sound of the drums. I liked the way they sang over St. George's Bay and vibrated within my very body. They made me feel closer to home. *Go find your village*, they seemed to be telling me, *go see your people.*

Nestled on the slopes between sandy shores and inland mountains, our new community of Freetown was exactly where most of the Nova Scotians wanted to stay. It was the only place they felt safe, and the only place they felt they could prosper. For me, however, Freetown was only a bridge. As I traded with the Temne and learned their language, I dreamed only of my first home. And I planned my overland journey, walking three revolutions of the moon to reach my native village.

A YOUNG TEMNE WOMAN NAMED FATIMA traded with me several times a week, but each time, she made me work her down to an acceptable price. She would always insist on three yards of cloth for twenty-five oranges, but at the end of each negotiation, she would accept a single yard. Before we concluded the deal, we had to pass through a labyrinth of discussion. And the more Temne I mastered, the longer the detours before I could take the oranges for the cloth. One day, as part of a detour, Fatima asked me a dozen questions about my husband, my children, and how I had lost them. After answering them all truthfully, I asked Fatima the one thing I really wanted to know.

"You have strong legs, yes?"

"I do, thank God."

"And you can walk great distances, yes?"

"I can, thank God."

"Then tell me how to find my way inland, going toward the river Joliba."

Fatima started picking up her oranges and stacking them on her platter. "That is our secret."

"Why?" I asked.

Now she lifted the platter up on her head. "We must not let you into our lands."

"Me?"

"Any of the toubabu from the ships."

410

"You call me a toubab? Did you not hear my story about my husband and my children? I am born in this land."

"That is a story, and a very good one. And I will tell you a story too, if you want one. But you are not asking for a story now. You are asking about my land."

"I am asking about *my* land. The land where I was born."

"You have the face of someone born in this land, but you come with the toubabu. You are a toubab with a black face."

"I was born in the village of Bayo, to Mamadu Diallo the jeweller and Sira Kulibali the midwife. I would still be there, but I was stolen away."

Fatima turned away from me. "One yard for the oranges, please. Story time is over."

For days afterwards, I felt a loneliness that I remembered from my earliest time in the Colonies. I was now standing on the continent of my birth, but as lost as I had been across the ocean. In the end, I decided that Fatima's rejection didn't matter. I knew who I was, and where I was from. The fact that the Temne wouldn't accept my story didn't change a thing about my life. It just meant that I was going to have to go elsewhere for information. I thought again of the lines by Jonathan Swift:

> *So geographers, in Afric-maps,*
> *With savage-pictures fill their gaps;*
> *And o'er inhabitable downs*
> *Place elephants for want of towns.*

It was true that mapmakers placed elephants for want of towns. But now I understood how hard it must have been for them to penetrate the interior of Africa.

WHEN RAIN CAME TO FREETOWN, it came down in sheets. The skies hurled water as if from puncheons. We built our

411

houses on stakes to avoid the rivers of mud. We learned to hang valuable dry goods from the ceilings. The roof became one of the most important features of our houses. We borrowed thatch techniques from the Temne, and then, when supplies allowed, constructed wooden roofs and even painted them with tar. We cooked in front of our humble dwellings, and we learned to share, to take turns, to build little shelters above our cooking stations, and to use Temne cooks. The first rainy season began in May and lasted until September, and in that time, if your beans or cassava did not have strong roots, they had no hope of withstanding the wind and the water. When the first rainy season ended and the sun emerged again, the slaving vessels began to show up more frequently in the Sierra Leone River, and the Bance Island factory became even more active.

One day in October, while Debra and I were boiling up a pepper-pot chicken gumbo, I heard footsteps, grunts, low moans and laboured breathing. It sounded like a whole village on the move, and transported me immediately back to the last day of my childhood in Bayo. Turning, I saw thirty people yoked around the neck, mostly or entirely naked, marching in line toward the river. They were being driven by tall, dark men in flowing robes with tight caps on their heads and sticks and whips in their hands. Every woman in the coffle carried a big chunk of salt or a bulging leather bag—likely filled with rice or millet—on her head. The male slaves carried bundles for their captors. One man with vacant eyes and mouth hanging open carried a bundle of spears. If his neck had been free, perhaps he could have used the weapons. But I knew that he had likely been yoked for weeks, and that his neck was sore and blistering.

I dropped my stirring spoon straight into the cooking pot and ran to King Street before they reached it. I watched them coming, captives of all ages and sizes, and wondered how I could set them free. A girl in the coffle looked at me pleadingly. She wasn't a woman yet, but she was close to becoming one. As she came near, I could see the traces of blue dye in two vertical lines carved high up on her cheeks. Looking at me directly, she called out a few words. She had the low, hoarse voice of an old woman. I saw the flash of her teeth, and although I did not know her language, I knew what she wanted: water, food, and most of all, help getting back to her family. Around her neck sat a tight-fitting wooden ring; from it ran chains connecting her to the yokes of men before and behind her. She appeared to belong to nobody but her captors. I took the girl's hand as she crossed the road. Her skin was dry and cracked; I longed to give her water but had nothing with me but the clothes on my body. She mumbled again three words. It sounded like a prayer. Perhaps the words were *food*, *water*, *help*. Perhaps they were please save me. I tugged at her yoke, but it was bound fast.

"Don't give up, child," I said as gently as I could, because I wanted to give her the sound of a mother's voice. In one motion, I slipped the red scarf off my head and tied it quickly around the girl's wrist. I was going to say some other kind words to her, but in that moment a coffle driver came up from behind and shoved me to the side as if I were nothing more than a goat in his path. He stayed next to the girl as she trudged forward with the coffle, and from that point the drivers stuck close to their captives. The girl was already five, ten, fifteen steps ahead, and I could not get back to her.

I looked around for help, and saw many Nova Scotians gathering by the harbour. A Nova Scotian pushed Daddy Moses onto a cart to confront the head slave-drivers, but they marched past him. Thomas Peters ran up behind me, took my arm and pulled me as we fell in behind the coffle and walked toward the water.

"Where is Clarkson when we need him?" Peters said.

413

"Away on business with King Jimmy," I said.

Debra led Clarkson's second-in-command—a Company man named Neil Park—to the waterfront. We all stopped there—the thirty captives, six captors, a growing crowd of Nova Scotians and a number of armed Company men. To our dismay, we saw six large canoes with Temne oarsmen ready to row.

Daddy Moses, on his cart, was having trouble reaching the edge of the water. While he struggled, Peters' angry voice rang out.

"Free these people now," he called out to a tall African in a flowing robe who stood at the front of the coffle.

The lead coffle driver ignored Peters and began to negotiate with a coxswain in charge of the canoes. Peters, enraged at the snub, reached out to grab the coffle driver. Three coffle drivers seized Peters, and one held a knife to his neck. The girl with the lines of blue on her cheeks looked at Peters and then looked at me and at the dozens of Nova Scotians behind me. I imagined that she felt that we could save her if we truly wanted to do so.

Neil Park stepped into the fray, flanked by his Temne translator. The slave-drivers didn't speak Temne either, but communicated through an interpreter of their own.

"Step back so no one gets hurt," Park said to us. Nobody moved.

Park was the king of our people, the translator said. The chief slave-driver turned, smiled, gave a slight bow, and removed a small pouch of kola nuts from inside his robes. He presented them to Park, who held them lamely in one hand.

Park kept talking and managed to get the drivers to release Peters. He ordered Peters back, but the man wouldn't move. The drivers raised knives again. Peters stepped back a few feet.

"This is not your business," a translator told Park. "The coffle drivers have paid for passage through this territory. King Jimmy himself authorized the passage."

"We do not allow slavery in Freetown," Park said.

Park was told that this was Temne territory, shared with the white man but not owned by him, and that other white men at Bance Island were expecting them.

Park dropped his hands and turned to us. "We must let them through and leave them be, and take this matter up with King Jimmy."

"We will not let them take these captives," said Peters.

Park signalled to his Company men. Five officers of the Sierra Leone Company raised their guns. "It is my order," Park said, "and I shall enforce it."

"We shall not leave, and they shall not go," said Peters.

"Step back," Park said. "You cannot save the slaves. But if you cause trouble now, you could start a war with the Temne."

"They wouldn't dare," Peters said.

"They already did," said Park.

I remembered hearing that the Temne had sacked the first settlement of blacks from London.

The lead coffle driver unyoked the first captive—a young boy of about fifteen who looked as frightened of the Nova Scotians as he was of his captors—and began to steer him into a canoe. Peters dove forward, grabbed the boy and tried to pull him back onto land. The Company men raised their muskets. Park held up his hand to prevent them from shooting. Two other traders grabbed Peters, who flung them off and grabbed the captive once more. Just when I thought that Peters might prevail, pull the first boy free and trigger a full-fledged surge from the Nova Scotians, one of the slave-traders drew a sabre from a sheath and plunged it deep into Peters' chest. He grunted, tottered, dribbling frothy blood from his mouth, and dropped to the ground. The Nova Scotians began pressing forward to the water, but Park and his men sent a volley of shots above our heads.

"Last warning," Park cried out.

One settler aimed his own musket at the African traders. Park's men let fly a volley of shots, and the settler fell. No other settlers moved forward, but I ran to Peters, who lay by the water's edge, just a few feet from the captives, who were being loaded into canoes. I knelt beside him and put my hand on his shoulder. His brown eyes widened, as if to absorb all the life that he was about to lose.

I kept my hand on him. "You are a good man, Thomas," I said, "and a good leader."

Peters seemed barely able to comprehend his fate. He lifted his hand an inch and I took it. Then he stopped breathing, his fingers went limp and the light left his eyes. I kept talking to him. I wanted his spirit to hear what I told him. "You led us to freedom, Thomas Peters. You led us to Africa."

Suddenly I became aware of the hollering and the orders. Scott Wilson, the Nova Scotian who had raised his own musket against the Temne, was lying dead just a few yards away. The others were being held back at gunpoint by Park's men. Park was urging the traders to get the captives into the canoes and away from land before things got worse. The canoes pulled away from the shore in the direction of Bance Island. The slave-traders did not look back, but the girl did.

I waved my hand, to let the child know that someone in the world still wished her well. She raised her hand in return, my red scarf still on her wrist.

Help from the saints

OUR COMMUNITY WAS CAST INTO DESPAIR at the loss of Peters and Wilson. We spoke of how to honour them, and I was asked to write the epitaph for Peters' tombstone: *Thomas Peters, leader of Nova Scotian settlers. Fought for freedom, and is free at last.*

When Daddy Moses began to plan a "family meeting" at which only the Nova Scotians would be welcome, Clarkson privately complained to me that we were creating a barrier between ourselves and the Englishmen.

"But Nova Scotians can't attend Company meetings," I said.

"Running a company is one thing, running a community quite another," Clarkson said.

We agreed to disagree on that point. But on Clarkson's request, I did ask Daddy Moses if the Nova Scotians could first gather privately, and then invite Company officials into the meeting. Daddy Moses agreed.

When we met in the church, speaker after speaker condemned the Company for siding with the slave-traders in Freetown. Some called for an armed rebellion, insisting that the few dozen Company men would be no match for a revolt by one thousand settlers. I didn't want the Company to condone any more visits by slavers in

Freetown, but I did not believe that more violence would improve our situation. Every time I had seen men rise up, they had not prevailed and innocent people had died.

Daddy Moses managed to conclude the private meeting without any general commitment to armed revolt. When the church doors were opened to Company officials, we were joined by Clarkson as well as Alexander Falconbridge, who was another governor of the Freetown colony. Falconbridge stood at the back of the room quietly to observe the proceedings, while Clarkson took to the pulpit.

I felt impatient at hearing Clarkson repeat that "terrible, tragic circumstances led to the deaths of two respected Nova Scotians," but relieved when he promised that the Company would pay for their funerals and offer support to their widows.

When Daddy Moses raised the matter of traders bringing slaves through Freetown, Clarkson could only say what he had told us before: "We will not sanction slavery in Freetown. On that point every one of the Company directors in London is united."

Clarkson's words had the effect of making us all feel more vulnerable. I wondered how vigorously the Company would protest if slavers attacked Freetown and tried to whisk us away to Bance Island. Even if twenty Company men brought out their muskets, they would be in no position to resist waves of attacks from the Temne.

As we left the church, Alexander Falconbridge came to speak with me. "I have heard all about you, Meena," he said, extending his hand.

"Hello, Dr Falconbridge," I said. I knew that Falconbridge had once worked as a surgeon on a slave ship, only to turn around later and publicly denounce the slave trade. He was a tall man, and broad about the shoulders, and big in the stomach in ways that made his breathing laboured. From his bushy eyebrows, hairs spiralled out madly. His pupils were dilated and his breath smelled of rum, but I saw kindness in his eyes.

"I am sorry for your loss," Falconbridge said. "Peters and Wilson were good men who wanted the best for their people."

"We wouldn't be here if it were not for Peters," I said. We were out on the street and Falconbridge was still walking with me. I stopped so as not to oblige the man to follow me all the way home.

"John Clarkson respected him, even though they argued," he said.

I nodded again.

"John Clarkson is also full of admiration for you."

"He too is a good man," I said.

"The last decent toubab," Falconbridge said, chuckling.

I knew that Falconbridge had spent time in Sierra Leone well before Clarkson or any of us settled here. "Lieutenant Clarkson tells me that you were once involved in the slave trade, and that you later denounced it."

"Yes, I was. I could have been the doctor on the vessel that took you to America," he said.

"There was but one doctor on that vessel, and I saw him die."

"Well, the surgeons do what they can for the slaves. They are one cut above the rest." He paused for a moment. When he spoke again, his voice was barely audible. "But no matter. They participate. They perpetuate the sin. I did myself. But no longer."

I allowed as how Clarkson had told me as much.

"You must also know that I am married, and that my wife is aboard the ship right now."

I did know that.

"Then you know that my intentions are honourable. Come with me aboard the *King George* this evening, and let us speak more."

* * *

419

FALCONBRIDGE KEPT SEVERAL ROOMS on the *King George*. That evening, he sent his Temne cook off to make a fresh chicken stew and he offered me a glass of rum.

"I'll take a small one," I said.

"Small for you, not so small for me," he said, smiling.

He sat back and exhaled, took a sip of his rum and exhaled again. "Life is short, and we must take our pleasures where we can find them."

I nodded.

"I don't expect to make it out of this place alive, so I'll be damned if I'll be denied the comforts of drink."

We spoke of all the different places that the Nova Scotians had lived before arriving in Sierra Leone: Africa, Georgia, South Carolina, Virginia, New York, Nova Scotia and New Brunswick, to name a few.

"Englishmen are born to sail," Falconbridge said, "but few of them know of all the places you Nova Scotians have been."

"We are travelling peoples," I said.

In the midst of our conversation, the meal arrived. When we had finished, Falconbridge lifted his napkin from his lap, pushed back his chair and sighed.

"Do you hate me?" he asked.

"Should I?"

"Might you not hate all white men indiscriminately? You would have good reason."

I poured myself more water from the carafe. "If I spent my time hating, my emotions would have been spent long ago, and I would be nothing more than an empty cowrie shell."

Falconbridge scratched his elbow—he was sweating profusely. I wondered where a white man bathed when he lived on a crowded ship no longer fit to sail. At least in Freetown, we Nova Scotians bathed. We set up bathhouses for men and women separately, and you would be hard pressed to find a settler who didn't bathe at least weekly.

Those of us who had been born in Africa did so more often—daily, even. Sometimes, late at night when I had trouble sleeping, I would lug a bucket of water up to the woods. I would find a quiet spot under the trees and the stars, and stare up at the same drinking gourd I had admired as a child. In the cool night air I would enjoy splashing the warm water on my skin and wonder, sometimes, if anybody from Bayo had survived on the night I was stolen.

The voice of Falconbridge shook me from my reverie. "You would have reason for hating me. Do you believe in redemption?"

Sometimes it amazed me how direct white people could be. "I don't know," I said. "I was born three revolutions of the moon northeast of here. In my village, we had various beliefs. My father was a Muslim, and had studied the Qur'an. Others in our village said that animals and sometimes even vegetables contained spirits. We believed in helping one another at harvest time. We worked together. Ate together. Pounded millet together. We believed that we would gather when we died, return to those ancestors who had brought us to life. But nobody spoke of redemption."

"Redemption is invented by the sinner," he said. "I have sinned, but I have also changed. It was my job to go down into the holds, and to examine men to determine if they were breathing, or if they were not. I saw monstrous abuses. My soul died in those slave vessels."

"I know what went on in the holds of those ships," I said.

Falconbridge pressed his fingers against his temples. "Do you know that I could not do a single, solitary thing for those men? Put on a plaster, they would rip it off. Treat a wound, it would grow redder and run with pus, and likely as not they would die anyway. The only good thing I ever did was to fight with the captain for cleaner water, better food and more frequent cleaning of the slave quarters."

Falconbridge and I were both survivors of the ocean crossing, but it seemed that his suffering had only grown since his time on the ship.

"I can see that you are ill at ease," I said, as gently as I could. "Why don't you tell me more about your life those days?"

"I got out of it," he said. "And I wrote about it."

"You did?"

"I am not much of a writer. Clarkson tells me you are a scribe."

I nodded.

"You are surely more lettered than I, and I admire that. But yes, I did write about my work as a surgeon on slave vessels, with much help from the saints over there in England."

"The saints?"

"The people like your John Clarkson here. There's a whole crew of them in London. Whenever they can trap an unsuspecting audience in a church, they beat on their drums of sainthood good and long."

"They do?"

"They tried to abolish the slave trade. Are you familiar with the word 'abolish'?"

"End. Terminate. Be rid of. Eradicate. Is that about right?"

"Are you quite sure you were not born in England?"

I smiled. "Do I look like I was born in England?"

"You'd be surprised by the odd-looking ducks who have been born in my country."

"I've been called many things," I said, "but never a duck."

Falconbridge laughed and sipped from his rum. "I hear that you want to go home."

I nodded, and waited for him to continue.

"I could help you, but it would involve returning to Bance Island," he said.

"Why?" I asked.

"The only men around here who know their way along the inland routes are the traders who show up at Bance Island," he said. "The ones who work in the fort are decent fellows."

I stared at him.

"What I mean to say," Falconbridge said, "is that if you meet them directly—say, with me along to make an introduction—I can guarantee that they will treat you with civility. Shake your hand, give you a drink, laugh a little, trade food for rum, or rum for food, give you a newspaper from London."

I sighed. I couldn't imagine voluntarily taking myself to the slave factory on Bance Island.

"It's true that they do the work of the devil," Falconbridge said. "But one of them might put me in touch with somebody who could take you inland. And then you'd get your wish."

After a year of trading with the Temne, I had been unable to get a single detail about how to travel to Bayo. And now it seemed that a white man might open the door for me.

"I will think about it," I said.

His wife, Anna Maria, came into our mess room.

"My goodness alive, you surprised me," she said.

"I was just readying to leave," I said.

"My husband is a complex man," she said. "Aren't you, dear."

"I am a complex failure," he said. With that, he slipped me the tract that he had prepared for the men in England who, he said, had tried but failed to abolish the slave trade.

The tract was about forty pages. I looked at the cover. *An Account of the Slave Trade on the Coast of Africa, by Alexander Falconbridge. Late Surgeon in the African Trade. London, 1788.*

"What, exactly, does 'Late Surgeon' mean?" I asked.

"It means that I quit when I couldn't stomach the work any longer."

"He likes you," Anna Maria said.

"Don't start," Falconbridge said.

"When he hands out his precious little tract, he likes you, and he wants you to like him," she said. She pointed to an open page and asked me to read.

I took it, held it six inches from my eyes, and said I needed to have two or three candles lit. They indulged me. I brought out my blue-tinged spectacles and slid them on my face. I knew that some white people in Nova Scotia would use them privately but never if others were watching. But I was too old to worry about whether Anna Maria and her husband found me unattractive. And I couldn't read without the spectacles, anyway.

I opened the tract and read aloud: "'It frequently happens that the Negroes, on being purchased by the Europeans, become raving mad; and many of them die in that state; particularly the women.'"

I put the book down and told them that in my experience the men went mad more readily than the women. The men, who felt an obligation to change their situation, could go mad in the face of their own powerlessness. But the women's obligation was to help people. And there were always little ways to help, even if the situation could not be altered.

Anna Maria opened the tract to another page and handed it back to me. I read once more: "'The diet of the Negroes, while on board, consists chiefly of horsebeans, boiled to the consistency of a pulp; of boiled yams and rice, and sometimes, of a small quantity of beef or pork . . .'"

I closed the book. It seemed like only yesterday that I had eaten such foods to stay alive, on a ship that smelled like death itself. Captives had squatted around buckets of slop, desperate for the biscuits and peanuts I smuggled from the medicine man's cabin.

Anna Maria squeezed my elbow. "I can see that the reading is traumatic," she said. "Leave it for another time, if you'd like. But I would like to get to know you better. Would you come for tea tomorrow?"

ANNA MARIA FALCONBRIDGE AND I BEGAN TO VISIT. She said there was hardly anyone interesting in the Company to talk to. She sometimes invited me on board to sip rum with her, and she was the only Company person who ever came to my home.

On one occasion, she complained about Company men who were constantly giving dashes—grandiose gifts—to King Jimmy. "In Africa, bringing gifts—even small ones— is a sign of respect," I said.

"One bottle of rum, perhaps. But an entire barrel?"

I said nothing.

She looked me over carefully. "With your obvious literacy and experiences, you should write about your life," she said. "Others have turned out such accounts to great personal advantage. Have you heard of Olaudah Equiano? He is an African, and formerly a slave, just like you. He wrote a book about his life, and became famous. I have no idea if his account is entirely true. But no matter. His book has sold everywhere in England. There is many a white Englishman poorer than he."

"I have not seen his account," I said.

Anna Maria said that she had brought along a modest personal library. "I have no one to share it with, Meena. Most of the Company men know no more of reading and literature than asses know of astronomy. I would be pleased to let you have my copy."

Outside, Temne builders were putting a new roof on my friend Debra's house next door. I saw Anna Maria eyeing the sweat glistening on their chests, and said, "Better that they be building houses than rowing slaves."

Anna Maria chuckled. "I'm for humanity and all that rot," she said, "but many people more intelligent than I have argued that the slave trade saves Africans from barbarity. Are you aware of that?"

"The English just say that to justify their own devilry," I said.

"What about you?" she said. "Worldly. Intelligent. Literate."

"So the fact that I can read justifies the theft of men and women?"

"Theft? The traders on Bance Island pay dearly for their acquisitions."

"It is theft nonetheless."

"But, Meena, theft begins right on this continent with the Africans, stealing and plundering each other."

"For whom do you think they are stealing each other?"

"Africans were dealing in slaves long before the first ones were sent to the Americas," she said.

"We had an expression in my village. 'Beware the clever man who makes wrong look right.'"

"I can just imagine how the Liverpool businessmen would reply to that," she said.

"Liverpool?"

"It's where many slave-traders run their affairs in England. They would ask if you could be debating with me or if you could have read hundreds of books, had you not first been taken as a slave. Was that not your salvation? And are you not a Christian?"

"Not really," I said, welcome for a change of topic. "I go to church to be with my people, but I can't say that I'm a Christian."

Anna Maria fell into an uncomfortable silence. I expected her to praise the civilizing influence of Anglicanism, but she leaned forward, touched my hand

426

and said, "I don't believe there is a single senior Company man here, or a senior officer at Bance Island, who does not have his own African mistress. Or two. Or more."

"I have noticed," I said.

Leaning against my shoulder, she said, her voice barely audible, "Of course, for the Company women it never works that way. You have no idea how complicated it is."

"When it comes to understanding others," I said, "we rarely tax our imaginations."

Anna Maria sighed and touched my arm.

It seemed that I would disagree with her often, but I liked the way she spoke so openly and sought my opinions.

Before Anna Maria Falconbridge could go on, a Company messenger came around to say that a rower was ready to take her back to the *King George*. On her way out, she took another look at the Temne roof workers next door.

G is for Grant, and O for Oswald

FOR ANOTHER YEAR, I TRIED IN VAIN to find a Temne who would agree to talk to me about travelling inland. And then, finally, I accepted Alexander Falconbridge's offer to take me to Bance Island. All the while, I dreamed of Bayo, my memories more brilliant than on the slave ship or during my earliest days in the Colonies. I felt that I would give anything at all to be home.

I put on my best clothes for that trip—a yellow hat with a peacock feather, an English dress instead of my usual African wrap, and my red shoes with gleaming silver buckles. The clothing helped me feel as far removed as possible from the skinny, naked girl who had been penned and branded in the Bance Island slave pen some forty years earlier.

I was told that the best time to visit was just after the rainy season, when the traders from inland started bringing their goods to market. Falconbridge arranged for a team of Temne oarsmen to row us to the island.

It took us all morning to row eighteen miles upstream. The water was as smooth as glass, and they pulled us, steadily and unerringly, to the place I had never wanted to see again. We didn't talk much. While the sun beat down and the rowers strained against the current, Falconbridge said only one thing: "Sometimes a deal with the devil is better than no deal at all."

As the white castle came into view atop the hill, I noticed how small the island was—only a few hundred yards long, and oval. A whiskered, big-bellied man dressed all in white greeted us on the wharf. In his left hand, he held two polished canes of solid wood, each about four feet long with a thick club at the foot. They looked like tools for a beating, but the man held them like toys. The same hand held a wooden sphere, a little smaller than my fist.

With his free hand, he shook hands with Falconbridge. I made a point of extending my hand, onto which I had slipped one of the gloves I'd borrowed from Anna Maria.

"William Armstrong," he said. He had a firm shake. He did not seem like the sort of man who would press a band of red-hot metal into my chest.

"Armstrong is second-in-command of the forts," Falconbridge told me.

"*Aminata Diallo*," I said. The formal name made me feel safer.

"Armstrong, old boy," Falconbridge said, "this is the woman about whom I sent you the message. Brilliant. She is African, American, and Nova Scotian—a cocktail of travel lies in her wake, and not all of it voluntary. And let me tell you, she is better read than nine out of ten Englishmen."

I had imagined that Falconbridge would see this trip to Bance Island as something of a chore. It bothered me to see him so relaxed in Armstrong's company.

Armstrong smiled. "I like a woman who's a bit of an enigma. I've had my boys get some lunch together. Hungry? That's a long ride upriver, isn't it."

Falconbridge gave Armstrong a bottle of rum from Barbados. "Good man," Armstrong said, clapping him on the back. "A round of golf, just for a few minutes before we sit down to eat?"

"Why not?" said Falconbridge.

"Come along to watch?" Armstrong asked me.

It didn't seem that I had any choice, and for the time being, I wanted to stick close to Falconbridge.

We walked up the many steps to the fortress. Six cannons faced the sea. The Union Jack waved in the wind. There were guards on the docks, on the roof, and at the door, keeping an eye out for strangers and ships appearing on the horizon.

Behind the castle, the men took turns using the clubs to bash a small wooden ball back and forth between two holes. Each time the ball fell in a hole, one of the men would fish it out and knock it back to the other hole. Englishmen amused themselves in the strangest ways. I thought back to my own time on the slave ship, and of how the medicine man had loved his parrot. Lucky for me, Armstrong and Falconbridge tired fast of their game. They gave the clubs to a little Temne boy dressed in a cap, shirt and breeches, and we stepped into the castle.

In its size and ornamentation, the Bance Island castle rivalled Government House in Halifax. We ascended marble steps and entered a dining hall on the second floor. It had a table made of the red-tinged camwood, and gleaming chairs of the same construction, and paintings of King George III and Queen Charlotte on the walls. I paused to look at her for a minute. I couldn't understand why anyone had called her black: her skin looked light, and her features white. I turned away from the painting. Candles in elegant silver holders sat on tables throughout the room. There were large, shuttered windows on two opposite walls. On one side, the windows were opened and gave a view of the Sierra Leone River. There were windows on the other side too, facing the back of the building, but the shutters were drawn and I couldn't see through them.

Armstrong gave Falconbridge some sherry.

"Does she drink?" he said.

"Ask her," Falconbridge said. "She has a mind of her own, that one."

Armstrong turned to me. "A drink?"

While I considered an answer, the two men clinked glasses. Something about the sound reminded me of tapping chains. I fell into a moment of utter dread. Here on Bance Island, these two men could do whatever they wanted with me. Had I been insane to come in the first place? If for any reason they turned against me, within days or hours I could find myself chained in a slave vessel.

"Are you quite all right?" Armstrong asked.

"Yes, thank you," I said. "And I will please have that drink."

Armstrong nodded to a Temne dressed up as an English butler, who brought me some sherry. It came as a relief to put my hand around the stem of the glass. I took a deep breath, and then a tiny sip.

It tasted like what I could only imagine to be a mixture of molasses and urine. I did my best not to frown, and held the glass steadily. It cost me a great effort to appear so calm.

I was seated next to Falconbridge, and opposite Armstrong. African servants brought us bread, cheese, fruit, wine, water and steaming platters of cassava, fish and pork. The food was fresh and it smelled delicious, but I barely touched mine. My appetite had disappeared. I wanted to tend to our business and leave the island as soon as possible. But Armstrong and Falconbridge lingered over their drinks.

"Would you look at this?" Armstrong showed us a silver coin. It was a Spanish dollar, also known as an eight reales piece.

I remembered them well, from the years that I worked for Solomon Lindo in Charles Town. But this coin looked a little different. The back of the coin showed the head of

King Charles III of Spain, but stamped into his neck I could make out the tiny image of King George III.

I looked at Armstrong and decided that speaking a little more to him would help restore my confidence. If he heard my voice and witnessed my mind at work, it would be difficult for him to see me as a potential slave.

"I know the eight reales piece," I finally said. "But what is King George doing on the neck of King Charles?"

"One of my men brought this over from London," said Armstrong.

"They're short of silver coins, so they're using Spanish currency too."

"But making it English," Falconbridge added.

Armstrong said he had heard a silly limerick on the subject. When Falconbridge asked to hear it, Armstrong sang out: *The Bank, in order to make its money pass, stamped the head of a fool on the neck of an ass.*

Falconbridge laughed, but then said, "Do you really think he's such a fool? Could he allow the American Colonies to just declare independence and walk away without a war?"

"He fought too long," Armstrong said. "And yes, he's a fool. Didn't you hear about what he did to his son?"

"I know, I know," said Falconbridge, shaking his head. "In one of his mad spells, he tried to smash the prince's head against a wall. They say he was foaming at the mouth, like a racehorse."

"I rest my case," Armstrong said. "Head of a fool on the neck of an ass."

While the men smoked and debated about whether the King was truly mad, I excused myself from their company and wandered over to look once more at the portraits of the King and the Queen. I stroked the candle holders, sat in a comfortable chair and read an article in an English newspaper about the composer Mozart, and finally approached the shuttered windows giving onto the back of the building. The men were still busy drinking and smoking and laughing. I touched the shutters, saw they were not locked, and cautiously opened them. I looked up at the blue skies, but heard the sounds of human groans. My gaze dropped. On the grounds behind the stone fortress, inside a fenced pen, I saw forty naked men. They sat, crouched and stood. They bled and they coughed. Each man was shackled to another, at the ankle. For a moment, I forgot how long it had been since I lived in Bayo, and I strained to see if I could recognize any of the faces of the men. I shook my head at my own foolishness, but could not stop staring down at the captives.

A Temne who was dressed properly and who had a large clubbing stick tied to his hip brought out a cauldron of watery gruel and dumped it in a trough. Some captives hobbled toward it and had to kneel in the mud and lower their faces to sip and slurp at the trough. These men were divided, by a stone wall some seven feet high, from a group of ten or so women who were not shackled but who were also captives. Two men lay motionless in the mud while others walked around them. One woman lay just as still on the other side. I hated myself for doing nothing to help the captives escape their wretched confines. I tried to tell myself I was powerless to free them, but in truth, the mere sight of them made me feel complicit and guilty. The only moral course of action was to lay down my life to stop the theft of men. But how exactly could I lay down my life, and what, in the end, would it stop at all?

Fingers touched my shoulder. I turned to see Falconbridge.

"Don't torment yourself," he said. "We both know what goes on here."

Armstrong came from behind and gently closed the window shutters. "So sorry about that," he said. "I hadn't intended for you to see that."

I could not bring myself to speak.

"Falconbridge tells me you are an amateur of books and maps," said Armstrong. "How about if we retire to my study?" He led me to a room lined with shelves and books.

"Tea?" Armstrong asked. "Shall I ring for a servant?" Before I could answer, he rang a bell.

A Temne man appeared, and made a point of not looking at me. He took Armstrong's orders and returned minutes later with a tray. I didn't want to drink it, taste a bite of food or spend another minute in the castle, but I was trapped. I took the tea and tried to hold the saucer steady in my lap.

"Falconbridge told me a bit about you—hope you don't mind," Armstrong said.

"Not at all."

"And are you quite all right just now?"

"Yes," I said. But my hands were shaking and the cup rattled against the saucer. "I mean no. But I will be fine."

"Is it the sight of the slaves?"

I gave him a steady look.

"Falconbridge told me that as a child, you were taken from a village far inland."

"That's true."

"Hard to believe, really. That you were there, and taken overseas, and are back here now . . . You must understand, it's unusual."

I let him chew on his own thoughts.

"He says that you want to go back home."

"I do."

"May I speak candidly?"

I nodded.

Armstrong sipped his tea, then placed his china mug on the polished side table, and said, "Fat lot of good it would do you."

"It's not about whether it will do me good. It's that I want to go home."

"You'll be sold back into slavery," he said.

"How do you know that?"

"Because men are wicked."

I couldn't sit any longer in the chair. I got up, walked over to Armstrong's shelves, and picked off a book: *Journal of a Slave Trader (John Newton), 1750–1754*. I put it back on the shelf and turned back to Armstrong. "I was born here, but not here. I was born to the northeast, one long journey by foot. I have crossed the ocean to go home. Do you think I'm going to stop because you say it's dangerous?"

"How do you know that you were shipped from here?"

"A slave owner told me, in South Carolina. But I remember this place."

"What do you remember?"

"During night storms, after the lightning flashed, thunder echoed out of the mountain caves."

"There are storms all along the coast," said Armstrong.

"I remember this castle and the slave pens. I even remember that ridiculous game you play with those sticks and the ball."

"You remember golf?"

I nodded.

"When you were shipped from Bance, where did you go?"

"Charles Town."

"And where, precisely, did you arrive in Charles Town?"

"Sullivan's Island. We stayed a week or two in quarantine."

"You certainly have the details right."

"There is no need to test a woman about her own life," I said.

"And this was forty years ago, you say?"

"I arrived in Charles Town in 1757, and I was about twelve at the time."

"And now you want to go home?" he said.

"It's what I have always wanted, from the moment I was taken."

"What on earth for?"

"Before you die, do you want to see England again?"

"When I sail home, I will arrive in England. But if you travel inland, you will not find your village. You either won't find it, or you will find it destroyed. Thousands of slaves have been pulled from the interior. Whole communities have been sacked. I doubt your village still stands. Take my word for it."

"I cannot take your word for it. I have to find out for myself."

"The traders are rough men."

"They are the only ones who know the routes inland."

He sighed, sipped his tea again and said that he hoped I wouldn't object to staying the night. I raised my eyebrows.

"There are no traders here today, but I expect them tomorrow."

Armstrong said that he would see to it that I was made comfortable. He glanced at a watch on a chain, and stood. He seemed to want to go. But a question burst from me before I could contain it.

"Why do you do this?"

"What?"

I gestured at the windows, bookshelves and ceiling. "This. All this."

Armstrong cleared his throat and folded his arms. When he spoke, his voice was softer, less boisterous. "It's all I know. I love Africa. Wish it didn't have to be this way, but if we weren't here, the French would take over this fortress in the blink of an eye. And everybody's doing it. The British. The French. The Dutch. The Americans. Even the bloody Africans have been mixed up in the trade for an eternity."

"That doesn't make it right."

"If we didn't take the slaves, other Africans would kill them. Butcher them live. At least we provide a market, and keep them alive."

"If you stopped, the market would wither."

"You have not been to England, so let me tell you something. Ninety-nine Englishmen out of one hundred take their tea with sugar. We live for our tea, cakes, pies and candies. We live for the stuff, and we will not be deprived."

"But you don't need slaves to make sugar," I said.

"In the West Indies, only the blacks work in the cane fields. Only the blacks can stand it."

"You could do something else with this fortress."

"What, like your beloved John Clarkson in Freetown?"

I nodded.

Armstrong pounded his fist on a table. "Has the Colony in Freetown produced a single export? Where is the sugar cane? Where is the coffee? Are you exporting boatloads of elephant teeth or camwood? You're not even growing corn, or rice. You have no farms under cultivation. You aren't even self-sufficient."

I wasn't ready for this argument. My mind circled around, looking for a response.

"There is no profit in benevolence," Armstrong said. "None. The colony in Freetown is child's play, financed by the deep pockets of rich abolitionists who don't know a thing about Africa."

I didn't know what to tell him. It was true that the colony hadn't produced any exports, but its problems did not justify the slave trade.

"Look," said Armstrong, "was the experience so terrible for you? Here you are, a picture of health, comfortable clothes, food in your belly, with a roof over your head and abolitionists fending for you in Freetown. Most of the world doesn't live that well."

I had no words. I didn't know where to start. I felt exhausted. Suddenly, I wanted that bed I had been offered, and a place to be alone to sort out Armstrong's arguments.

"We feed the slaves here, I'll have you know," Armstrong said. "It's not in our interests to starve the very people who have to fetch a profit. And I'm sick and tired of abolitionists claiming that we brand our captives. In all my years here I have never seen such a thing. It's nothing more than propaganda to excite society ladies to the cause."

I hesitated. I didn't care if he was second-in-command of the slave fortress. I didn't care that I could not leave Bance Island without his say-so. "Would you turn your back for a moment?"

"I beg your pardon?"

"Please just turn around. Just for a moment."

He turned. I unfastened a clasp, undid three buttons, and pulled down a portion of my dress to reveal the raised welt above my breast. "You may turn around."

He turned around and let out a shout.

"This is what I remember about Bance Island," I said.

William Armstrong stepped closer and peered carefully at my exposed flesh. A whisper trickled from his lips: "Do you know what that is?"

"It's the mark I was branded with, out back in your own slave pen, when I was eleven years old."

Blood rose to Armstrong's face, and he stepped back. "Two letters," he said quietly. "Do you know what they represent?"

"It's a G and an O," I said. "Never knew what they meant."

"Grant, Oswald," he said, his voice flat and emotionless.

"What?"

"The company that runs Bance Island. *Grant, Oswald*. Richard Oswald is a Scotsman. This is his company. His associates—"

William Armstrong retreated to his chair, sat down and stretched his hand over his brow. I let him sit quietly for a moment while I turned away and did up the buttons and

438

the clasp of my dress. And then I took three steps in his direction, looking straight into his eyes.

"You have no idea what I have lived through. Every waking moment is a nightmare for the captives you hold right now, on the other side of these stone walls. You have no idea what they endure, if they will even survive in the ships, no idea of the thousands of humiliations and horrors waiting at their destinations."

"Some things are better not to think about," he said.

"Tell that to your captives," I said.

Armstrong rose from his chair and said that he would see to it that I wanted for nothing. Tomorrow, he would take me to meet the traders.

THE NEXT MORNING, heavy fog blanketed the waters. I took coffee and bread alone in my room, and then followed Armstrong out of the building, past the cookhouse, past the thatched huts where African workers slept, to a two-storey building. Inside, I found three rooms full of imported goods: cowrie shells from the Maldive Islands, iron bars from England, perfumed soaps from the Netherlands, and rum. There were pistols, rifles and shot. I saw huge bolts of cloth in an array of colours, which Armstrong said had been bought from the East India Company in London. There were also knives and sabres, iron pots, iron cauldrons, and scarves, trousers and dresses.

As the sun rose, African slave-traders began arriving in the Palaver House, shaking hands with Armstrong and inspecting the samples of goods that they might accept in exchange for slaves. I saw Fulbe in white robes and white caps, and Temne men in their own clothing, and Maninkau traders from inland. I heard Temne, Arabic, Fulfulde, Maninka and English, and a litany of other languages I did not know.

Armstrong and the principal Fula, whose name was Alassane, began negotiating. Alassane spoke in Temne to an aide who translated the words into English for Armstrong. Alassane wanted twenty iron bars, one barrel of rum, one bolt of cloth, six rifles, two boxes of shot, two iron cauldrons and two sabres for every healthy adult male. Armstrong offered him half of that. They finally settled on a price—about halfway between the two starting positions—and agreed that a healthy woman would go for half the price of a man, and a healthy child one quarter. As the men launched into endless discussions about the relative values of ivory, camwood, rum and guns, I stopped listening to the details and thought about how I had once been traded for these very goods. I would have been worth about five iron bars, a quarter of a barrel of rum, one or two rifles, and fractions of a few other goods. Surely when I was abducted on the path outside Bayo, the men who seized me had also estimated my worth. Maybe, to them, I was worth a few rabbits and a goat. In South Carolina, the first time I had been sold as a refuse slave, I was worth only a pound or two at most. I suppose in a way I was lucky to have been sold at all, for if I had not, I might well have been killed. The last time I was sold in South Carolina, Solomon Lindo had judged me to be worth sixty pounds. Who was to blame for all this evil, and who had started it? If I ever got home to Bayo again, would people in the village still be at risk of being valued, and stolen? Would my own villagers still keep *woloso*—second-generation slaves—as we had done in my own childhood? It seemed to me that the trading in men would continue for as long as some people were free to take others as their property.

William Armstrong was calling my name. A number of people were looking at me. Perhaps he had called to me several times. Now it was time, he said, to come forward and address Alassane.

I had heard Alassane speaking in Fulfulde, the language of my father, to his aides, but I didn't want him to know that I spoke that language too. So I spoke in Temne, saying that I wanted to travel far inland, to a village called Bayo, some three revolutions of the moon by foot northeast of here, not far from Segu on the Joliba River.

The tall Fula raised his eyebrows and said, "I don't trade with women."

"One barrel of rum," I said, "if you take me inland."

"One thousand barrels of rum," he said.

"One barrel of rum," I said, "with not a drop of water in it."

"You negotiate like a man," he said. "We will meet again, one day."

"When?" I asked.

"The next time I come."

"When will that be?"

Alassane smiled. "I will return when I return. I am known here. I am Alassane, the great Fula trader."

I didn't trust the great Fula trader. But he was my only hope.

THREE WEEKS PASSED before I was able to speak to John Clarkson. He had been away negotiating land claims with King Jimmy, but when he returned to Freetown, he paid a visit to my home. I offered him a hot drink. He said that he had always enjoyed coming to where I lived, ever since the day I had given him mint and ginger tea in Birchtown.

"There's nothing like a visit with you, Meena, to take my mind off the Company men."

We settled into chairs with our tea.

"I return to England in a fortnight," Clarkson said.

I nearly dropped my teacup on the saucer. "The Nova Scotians will be devastated," I said. "You are the only Company man they trust."

"It's time for me to go home. I don't wish to keep my fiancée waiting any longer."

I could understand that. I would have crossed the seas to be with my husband too—or asked him to come find me.

"I have a proposal to make," said Clarkson. "Come to England with me. I can arrange for your travel."

When enslaved in South Carolina, I had hoped many times to sail to England—but only as a means of moving on to Africa.

"Leave the colony?" I asked.

"Yes."

"For how long?"

"Forever," he said, "or for as long as you would like."

"And why on earth would I want to leave Africa, now that I have finally come home?"

"We need you, Meena. The abolitionist movement needs you. We need your story and we need your voice."

It seemed inconceivable to me that people should need me in a place I had never seen. I asked what he meant.

"My brother Thomas and a group of like-minded men—Anglicans and Quakers—have recently come close to persuading Parliament to abandon this barbaric practice."

"Falconbridge told me that some men had tried to abolish slavery," I said.

"Not slavery. The trade in slaves. There is a great difference. By trade, I mean buying slaves on the African coast, carrying them across the seas and selling them in the Americas. It is not the best we can do, but rather a first step. Slavery would still exist, yes, but no more men, women and children would be taken away in slave ships."

"How could I possibly help your cause in England?"

"I said that the abolitionists have come close, Meena, but they have never succeeded. Something was always missing. But you have survived slavery, and you can tell Britons what you went through. Your voice could move thousands of people. And when it comes time for

Parliament to deliberate on the matter, your voice could swing the vote."

I was touched that Clarkson was reaching out to me, but it was hard to imagine that I could affect public thinking in England. I could count on the fingers of one hand the number of white people I had influenced thus far in my life.

"Lieutenant Clarkson," I said.

"You may call me John."

No white man had ever invited me to do such a thing. And from what I had seen, white men used titles such as "Mister" or "Captain" even in addressing each other.

"Mr Clarkson," I said.

He smiled.

"John," I said. "You must understand that I have my own plans. Recently, I travelled with Mr Falconbridge to Bance Island."

"You did? For what possible reason?"

"To look into finding an African to take me inland."

"A trader? A slave-trader?" Clarkson jumped up from his chair. "You can't be serious." Now he was shouting. "It was men working for slave-traders who killed Thomas Peters. And the same sort of thugs stole you away from your own family. You are a fool to be thinking about this, and you must remember who you are consorting with."

"That's what Armstrong said," I said.

"As far as slave-traders go, William Armstrong is an honourable sort," Clarkson said. "If he told you it was dangerous, I would believe him."

"I don't govern my life according to danger," I answered. "Otherwise, I would not have fled from the man who owned me in New York. I would not have travelled to Nova Scotia—a land where I had no friends, no land, no home and no work—in the month of December. And I certainly never would have joined your mission to Freetown."

443

Clarkson sat down again, smiling and shaking his head.

"Did danger prevent you from joining the British Navy?" I said. "Would danger prevent you from doing everything in your power to return home to your loved ones?"

Clarkson rubbed his palms together and looked into my eyes. "Well, Meena, you do know your own mind. No one could know it better. You have been a world of help to me. So if I can help you, I would like to do so."

I told him that I had offered the slave-trader one barrel of rum, but that he would surely ask for more. Clarkson said he would use some funds at his discretion to procure, for me and me alone, three barrels of rum. This would be his gift to me. I had served him long and well, he said, and if this rum allowed me to make my journey home, then so be it.

"Just make sure you cling to your offer of one barrel for the longest possible time," Clarkson said. "Because eventually, he will drive you up. The Africans are skilled traders."

"Lieutenant Clarkson, please remember that you are speaking to an African."

He smiled and shook my hand. "Best British luck," he said. "And if you should return from your mission, perhaps you will consider England."

"If I go home," I said, "I expect to stay."

God willing

IN SEPTEMBER OF 1800, just a month or so after the tornadoes and hurricanes of the rainy season had ceased, I prepared for the long voyage inland. I had a strong pouch of goat intestine, big enough for two pints of water, and it sat inside a pouch of antelope leather, just a little bigger, that I slung around my neck. This way, whenever I came upon fresh water, I could fill my bag. In another leather pouch, I brought along a sleeping mat, a pair of comfortable leather sandals, one change of clothing, and ten brightly coloured silk scarves from India, which I had purchased at the Company store. I expected that I might have to part with one from time to time, to pay for a favour. I had a pouch of chinchona bark, ready to boil in case I met with fever, as well as the leaves of a plant known to the Temne as tooma, which, when pounded, boiled and mixed with lime juice, was used to treat gonorrhea. This might increase my value to any suffering male who happened to be travelling with me for a spell. I wasn't sure what value coins might have inland, but I also brought along five gold guineas. If payment was required and the guinea was accepted, at least it wasn't heavy carrying. The guineas I interspersed in the clothing in my bag, so that the coins could not be heard tinkling against each other as I walked.

I had hoped to travel inland within a few months of my first visit to Bance Island, but my waiting turned into six long years. In those years, the colony had been bombarded once by French warships, and had brought another wave of Negroes—hundreds of Jamaican Maroons who sailed from Halifax—just in time to use them to put down an armed rebellion by disgruntled Nova Scotians who still had no land and little say in the affairs of the colony. Still, somehow, Freetown lived on and attracted an increasing number of Africans—Temne and others—who settled on the outskirts, found work in town and eventually began moving into the town itself. The Nova Scotians of Freetown were never abducted as slaves, but over the years a few captives managed to escape coffles and canoes and find refuge in our midst.

The Fula trader Alassane showed up at Bance Island only once every year or two, and I had to negotiate on and off with him for years before he agreed—for three barrels of rum—to take me to Segu, a town on the river Joliba that was only a few days by foot from Bayo.

The Company governor sent me in a small shallop, together with a group of friends to see me off. In the trip across the bay and upstream to the island, I was accompanied by Debra, her daughter Caroline, Daddy Moses and by Anna Maria and Alexander Falconbridge.

"If I were to offer you a British newspaper and a new book every week," Anna Maria said to me on the journey in the shallop, "would that persuade you to abandon this idea?"

"No," I said, smiling.

"Whatever you find," Anna Maria said, "you can't expect to find civilization on the scale of England."

"If I were looking for England," I told her, "I would have gone with John Clarkson. I am looking for my people. I am looking for my home."

Debra put her arms around me, as did Caroline, who

446

was now seven years old and made me think daily of the children I had lost. I wondered if May were still alive, and what her smile looked like. I would have given my life and my future and even this journey home, just to put my arms around her, to see her face. But that was impossible now, and there was only one place left for me to go.

Daddy Moses hugged me before I stepped off the shallop.

"I am not long for this world, Meena. I bid you a fine journey home. I, too, will be going home soon. But I believe my journey will be less eventful than yours."

"Say a prayer for me," I said.

As I left the boat, Caroline, representing all my friends, gave me a wild straw hat with a blue peacock feather rising straight skyward. We all laughed, because everybody knew about my penchant for hats and scarves.

Debra said, "It's so your dignity will remain intact as you journey inland."

Caroline made me bend down so she could whisper something in my ear. "Inside the hat, toward the back, Mama and I sewed five gold guinea coins. In case you need them."

I stepped off the shallop and waved to them all until they were out of sight. I believed I would never see them again, and spent a moment remembering all the people I had left behind in my migrations—enforced and elected. Then I walked up onto the slave island from which I had been shipped forty-three years earlier.

Alassane arrived with ten canoes and fifty slaves. He unloaded the captives, negotiated with Armstrong and drank tea with him, then shook hands and stood up.

"We leave," he said to me in Temne.

"And I return home, God willing," I said.

"*Alhamdidilay*," he said. God willing.

My stomach stirred, and I wished I were twenty years younger.

Alassane beckoned for me to sit in his lead canoe. Oarsmen rowed us upriver, past two slave factories run as Bance Island outposts. There were eighty paddlers in the ten canoes, with a coxswain in each. There was one drummer for the entire group, and a guide who consulted with Alassane. Before night fell, the canoes were emptied of rum, guns, shot, iron bars, cotton cloth and India silk. Alassane's men passed my payment of rum on to a local chief who met us at the shore. Alassane and the chief negotiated about the rum, and appeared satisfied with their agreement. The rum that Alassane had obtained from Bance Island came in smaller quantities—flat-bottomed firkins that could be balanced atop the head. Twenty of his paddlers became porters of rum, each covering his head with a thick woven mat and balancing a firkin on top. The guns, shot, silk cloth and other goods had been strung together, or wrapped in large plant leaves, and they were carried overhead by twenty other paddlers.

Alassane was a tall, thin, serious man. His age, I suppose like mine, was hard to guess. If he had been a young man, capable of being my grandson, say, twenty or so, I would have worried about his honesty. But he was older— perhaps forty. I hoped that he had seen enough of life to want to honour his promises.

Alassane wore a loose shirt hanging down past his waist and a thin, tight cap on his head and baggy trousers of white India silk. He stepped into sandals when preparing to trade with people or meet dignitaries, but at other times walked barefoot. The skin on his feet was orange and dusty, cracked in places but as tough as leather.

He led the procession northeast through the wooded hills, and kept a team of scouts and hunters ahead on the trail to deal with snakes, leopards and other tribes. Alassane kept another five men around him—three in front, and two behind—who were also armed. Other than a knife sheathed to his hip, and a Qur'an hanging in a leather pouch from his shoulder, Alassane carried nothing. He indicated for me to walk behind the two armed men who followed him, making me the last person in the head group of travellers, before the eighty or so porters. The porters, too, were armed with knives and sabres, and some with guns.

On the first day, Alassane gave me no opportunity to talk to him. He spoke from time to time with the men around him, and at one point I heard him mention me, in Fulfulde, to one of the men.

"She wants to go to her village," he told the aide. "She says it is near Segu."

I missed a bit of the conversation, and then picked it up again.

"Stupid?" Alassane said. "No. She is clever. She counts and reasons and argues like a man. Be careful. She speaks Temne, English and Bamanankan."

I had not told Alassane that I spoke Fulfulde, and had no plans to.

Two hours before darkness fell, the procession stepped off the worn trail we were ascending in the hilly country, and set up a circular camp. A group of six men—three with whips and canes, three with cutlasses—beat the grasses to flush out snakes. They let out a roar of pleasure when a long snake slipped out of the bushes, coiling and hissing for the few seconds it took a cutlassman to lop off its head. Eight men scoured the land for wood, brought back armfuls, and within minutes had fires burning.

From out of the woods, villagers brought a goat to Alassane. He inspected it before it was held down, sliced at the jugular, bled to death, and then skinned and butchered. I had never seen men prepare animals that quickly for consumption—Alassane's men were practised butchers and cooks. Villagers brought mangoes, oranges, millet flour, onions, malaguetta peppers and iron cauldrons. The cauldrons were suspended in the most ingenious manner from square iron grates built like tables with strong legs that sat over the fire. The stew bubbled for an hour in each of the cooking pots. I saw one of Alassane's aides oversee the process of draining about one-third of a firkin of rum into a huge calabash brought forward by a head villager. Payment, I supposed, for food and for the right of passage.

About half of the men—Alassane and all of his leading group of men included—prayed, kneeling in the dust, all facing east, before they ate. Many of the porters did not pray, but remained silent during the prayers. The last time I had seen Fulbe praying as a group was in my own village of Bayo, and it made me feel ill to think that men who shared the religion of my father made their fortunes from trading in slaves. I wondered for a time how a person who considered himself a good Muslim could treat other humans in such a way, but it occurred to me that the same question could be asked of Christians and Jews.

Having nothing better to do while Alassane and his men prayed, I climbed a tree, sat on a branch and pulled out the one book I had brought along—Olaudah Equiano's account of his own life—and read for a time. Shortly before the meal, Alassane walked over to the tree. I slid down to the ground to meet him.

"Go there," he said. His men had erected a small canvas tent in the shape of a pyramid. They had spread a mat inside it for sleeping, and a mat behind it for eating. "You will eat there. And sleep there. Every night, this you will do."

I didn't like the way Alassane issued orders. It made me wonder if men would try to speak to me like that when I got home, and if all my time of living independently had made me unfit for village life in Bayo.

I ate alone that night, and for the next ten nights, each time we made camp. The men huddled in their groups of ten around their cooking pots, and I was brought a generous portion of food. That was my only meal, although village children and women brought platters of fruit on their heads to the procession, and whenever oranges or pineapples were offered, I received my due. We were in a dense forest, and I was pleased to be behind the first ten men in the procession because of all the snakes and rodents that were flushed from the trail as we walked. We climbed in the direction of the mountains, and although we passed many groups on the way, Alassane and his men rarely stopped to address them.

The first time we passed a slave coffle, I counted forty-eight captives. The men were yoked about the necks and shackled at the feet. The women and children walked free, but were burdened with loads of food and salt on their heads. Male slaves carried ivory, camwood, ebony sculptures, water skins. I rarely saw a captive not required to carry, in his arms or on her head, a heavy burden. Some captives had eyes that were downturned and dead; others looked constantly to one side or the other, still hoping to come upon some means of escape. I could not look away from them, or stop wondering about the wives and husbands and children and parents that they had lost, for-ever, in this steady march to the sea. Terrified as they already were, I could imagine their tension boiling over into hysteria, wordlessness and in some cases madness when they were stuffed into slave ships like fish into buckets, hauled across the seas and sold—if they survived—at auctions. As a child, I had believed that any decent adult would not let any slave coffle pass un-molested. Yet here I was, silent and unable to act. I had no words of comfort to offer the men, women and children who passed me on the way to the sea, and there was nothing to do as our shoulders brushed on the narrow footpaths.

I dared not speak a word of Fulfulde to captors or captives. I did not want Alassane to know that I understood his language. Alassane kept a deliberate, quick pace. My legs were sore and I had one or two cuts on my feet, but in the first ten days I held up well, even as we ascended the hills.

I had time to let my mind wander during the long days of walking, and found myself thinking about what I would do when I returned home. I had spent more than forty years thinking about Bayo, but not about what I would do when I got there. Now I stopped to wonder who would greet me in the village and if anybody would remember my name, or my parents. Perhaps the people of Bayo would honour me for returning home to talk about life among the toubabu. Surely I would be the first to come back with such a tale. I realized that I wasn't concerned any longer with the things I wanted to do, but rather, with the place I wanted to be. All I really wanted to do was return to the place where my life began.

Occasionally, during the days, we stopped so that the porters could rest and drink water, and so that the Muslims could pray. One day, after the rest and the prayers, Alassane signalled for me to walk with him as we continued our trek in a northeasterly direction.

"You pray to Allah?" he asked.

"No," I said. I did not want Alassane to know that I had once been a Muslim, because I feared he would judge me, and perhaps punish me, for having left the faith. In my heart, I didn't feel that I had truly left the spiritual beliefs of my father—I had simply grown accustomed to letting them sit quietly at the back of my soul.

"You do not pray at all?" he said.

"I have my own prayers."

"To whom do you pray?"

I wanted to reinforce my connection to the English at Bance Island, so I said, "I pray to the God I discovered among the toubabu."

452

"You have walked with men for twelve days," he said. "Are you not tired?"

"My legs are sometimes heavy," I said. "But I want to go home."

"Home. Segu on the river."

"Bayo," I said, "near Segu on the river."

"How big is Bayo?"

"It had twenty families when I was last there."

"And you say this was your home, and where you once lived?"

"Yes."

"Then why do you not know where it is?"

I did not want to speak to him about once having been a captive, so I said nothing.

"It is not correct for an old woman to walk this far. Where is your husband? Where are your children? Where are your grandchildren?"

I imagined it would be inconceivable for him to think that I did not have a family. "They are waiting for me," I said, "in Bayo."

He laughed. That made me worry. He did not believe me, after all.

"Go back now," he said.

I dropped into position, stuck behind the men who guarded his back but ahead of his porters. I wished there were another woman on the trip, in the same way I had wished for children on my journey to the coast long ago.

Fifteen days into the trip north, my bones began to ache and my skin felt cold. As I struggled to keep up, I thought I saw my father ahead on the trail, his arms stretched out in greeting. I believed I could see Fomba skinning rabbits and goats for all the people of Bayo. I knew they were not there, but still I kept seeing them.

On the sixteenth day, I could barely walk. We had ascended the mountains and come down the other side, and we were now entering much less densely wooded forests, with more grasses, fewer trees, and more open spaces. This looked more like the land from which I had come, but I remembered that as a child I had walked endlessly through these lands before reaching the mountains. Two hours into the morning's walk, I dropped. I heard shouting, and the commotion of feet all around me. Someone carried me under a tree and tried to pour water into my open mouth, which made me choke. Next, I was carried into a tent. As I was laid down, I could make out Alassane's angry voice in a heated discussion. I gave a man chinchona bark to boil into an infusion of tea.

By the next day, I was able to walk again. It felt as if half the strength had drained from my legs, and I was grateful that I had no load to bear on my head. I saw Alassane watching me for signs of faltering, but my legs gradually regained their strength as my stomach and bowels settled. I remembered feeling confusion as a child when older people just couldn't keep up with the coffle. I had thought back then that they would avoid all sorts of trouble simply by speeding up. But now, walking with just a fraction of the strength that I had once had, I looked back with admiration at all the vulnerable people—pregnant women, old women and old men—who had survived the long walk to the coast. Most people I had met in the Colonies—any people at all, who had not themselves been stolen from Africa—imagined that captives had been scooped up on the coast. It made me think once more of the men who had drawn elephants and lions on their maps of Africa. They had no idea who we were, how we lived, or how strong we had been just to make it to the Colonies.

When we were twenty-one days into the journey, I asked Alassane how much progress we had made toward Segu.

"It is very far," was all he would say.

After another ten days of walking, I awoke in the night to the sound of men talking and arguing. Alassane and his advisers were sitting at a fire nearby; I remained perfectly still in my tent.

"She sleeps," one man said in Temne.

"Use Fulfulde, to be safe," Alassane said.

"She was as stupid as a mule to make this trip with us, and she slows us down," one man complained. "She is not stupid, but she is a woman." That was Alassane speaking. "Quiet now."

I heard Alassane say that in two days, we would be arriving at the village of Kassam, a place where slaves were sold. A route south from there led to the coast, far east of Bance Island.

"When we get there," Alassane said, "I will sell the woman."

"What will you sell her for?"

"It doesn't matter. We shall see. Five bolts of cloth, perhaps. She is old. But she speaks many languages. The toubabu at Bance say that she catches babies with great facility. We must sell her now, while she is still healthy. It will soon be hot, and she will soon be ill. And then nobody will buy her."

For a moment, I could not believe the words. Surely Alassane would honour his promises to me. Surely he would not forget that he had already accepted my three barrels of rum.

The men in the tent laughed; I heard Alassane join in. It was almost inconceivable. Goosebumps rose all over my arms. I could not go on living if all my years of longing for liberty and homeland were to lead me back to the neck yokes and ankle chains of my childhood abduction.

I put my palm over my mouth, to calm myself with the warmth of my own breath, but also to stifle any cry that might escape my lips.

The man-stealers planned to sell me after all.

I knew in that moment that I would never make it back home, and I began to plan my escape.

All of the next day, as we walked northeast, I sucked at a chunk of salt and drank as frequently as I could. Every cluster of homes that we walked past, every village that I saw off in the distance, I tried to burn into my memory. Every group of people we passed on the trail—and we were constantly passing villagers, hunters, slavers with their coffles—I studied, and listened as hard as I could. I checked to see if I could understand their language, or determine if they were friendly, or figure out if they lived nearby.

I felt shivers and shakes in my bones again. The fever was returning. I slid once into the woods, on a water break, and felt that half of my body flooded out of me as I crouched and emptied my bowels. But I focused on what I had to do, struggled to show no sign of discomfort, and prayed and prayed for the late afternoon. As always, two hours before the sun set, Alassane's procession stopped and set up camp, and I ate because I did not know when I might eat again. What I could not eat, I buried in a hole that I dug behind my tent, so that no person could report to Alassane that I had not finished my meal.

As soon as night fell and the men were sleeping, I gathered my belongings—the pouch for the water, which I had filled before dark, and the dried bark for the fever, and my leather pouch of scarves and coins—and I slipped directly into the woods behind my tent.

I walked for a mile or two southwest, back by the trail we had taken that day, but when I came to the creek I had seen that afternoon, I slipped into it and walked barefoot on the bed, over the stones, for as long as I could endure. Now I was travelling northwest, but the men would try to overtake me by turning back and going southwest. They would look for my footprints and scour the forests near the trail. They would be better at tracking me than I would be at hiding. I could not beat them in the game they knew best, and could only avoid them by outwitting them entirely.

I walked as far as I could in the night, stopping frequently to empty my bowels. Each time, I drank water, sucked a chunk of salt and then walked on. Finally, around daybreak, I came across a cave and climbed far into it, feeling at that moment that I would sooner confront any beast than a man. I slept all day. When I woke, night was falling and I headed out again. For three nights, I struggled forward, hiding during the day until I was weak with illness and lack of food. I had cut my foot too, on a sharp branch, and the redness was worsening around the source of the cut, though I bathed it as frequently as possible in river streams.

Late one afternoon, I saw a man tending goats on a hill. He stood motionless, watching as I struggled uphill toward him. Halfway up the rise to him, I slipped and fell, and exhaustion sank over me as surely as the sun sets. I could not get up. He came to me tentatively, beating the grasses as he walked. I tried Bamanankan. He said something that I could not understand. I tried to get up, but he motioned for me to stay there and brought me a leather skin of water. I drank of it freely, and vomited. I tried Temne. No answer. I tried Fulfulde, and he understood my words: "Help me. Hide me. Take me to your women, please."

He was young and he was wiry, but he was strong enough to carry me easily. He took me to the shade of a tree, gave me his water pouch and told me to wait. He returned with three men, four women and a cot made of saplings and rope. It looked like something for carrying injured warriors. On I was loaded, as the women fussed and asked me questions—who was I and where was I from?—and we walked, it seemed, for hours. Every time we hit a bump, my bones shouted with pain. Fever crawled through them all: my neck, back, knees and ankles. We came to a village of mud homes and thatched roofs. I was relieved it was so small; no slavers would look there. I was carried into the shade of one home. I slept and drank water for days before I could stir from the bed.

As I entered into consciousness, I noticed a small form drifting in and out of my room. I blinked. The face of a mule was peering at me. Then a bright little voice criticized it, and a young girl with a wooden stick entered, and smacked the animal with her switch, and it retreated. She brought me water. She was perhaps eight years old.

"What is your name?" I asked in Fulfulde.

"Aminata," she said.

"I too am Aminata," I said, pointing at my chest and repeating my name.

Her face lit up in a smile as wide as the day.

"Aminata," she said, pointing to herself and to me, and saying the name again.

"Food," I said.

"Later," she said.

She looked at me for a time, and then asked, "Are you a toubab?"

"Do I look like one?" I asked.

"I have not seen a toubab."

"Toubabu are the colour of pink and white, or the colour of a certain pale calabash," I said.

"Toubabu eat people like we eat goats," she said.

"Not the ones I know," I said.

"You have seen them?"

"I have lived among them. In their land."

"You lie," she said. With that, she giggled and danced out of the hut.

I slept again, drank more, sucked at some salt and ate a mango. As I licked and sucked at the stringy pit, not knowing when I might eat again, I understood what I had to do. If I managed to escape Alassane and his men, I would do whatever I could so that nobody else fell into his hands—or those of any other slave-trader.

Most of my lifetime had passed since I had last seen

458

Bayo, and I was not even sure I would recognize it. Would it still have a mud wall bordering the houses? Would the chief still have four small round houses, one for each wife? Would I hear the pounding of millet and shea nuts as I entered the village? Perhaps there would be no village at all, or perhaps it had survived and expanded to ten times its original size. If Bayo was still there, I could not be sure that one person would recognize my face.

From the day I was stolen, thoughts of home had made it impossible for me to feel I belonged anywhere I lived. Perhaps if I had been able to keep my husband and to live for years with him and our children, I would have learned to feel settled in a new place. But my family never settled in its nest. We never had any nest at all. But after I heard Alassane's words, I felt no more longing for Bayo—only a determination to stay free. And now, as I waited for my strength to return in a hut belonging to people I didn't even know, I let go of my greatest desire. I would never go back home.

Falconbridge had called my bargain with the slavers "a deal with the devil." He was right, but he was wrong to say that it was better than no deal at all. I had entrusted my life to a man who sold people in the same way that he sold goats. He would sell me as he had bought and sold so many others. And I had helped him in his work. I had offered myself to him and paid him for the privilege. Who knew how many people my three barrels of rum might purchase? I would sooner swallow poison than live twenty more years as the property of another man—African or toubab. Bayo, I could live without. But for freedom, I would die.

A FEW DAYS AFTER I BEGAN EATING AGAIN, the villagers brought me to a meeting area, and introduced a headman from another village.

459

"Is it true, that you have crossed the ocean in a toubabu canoe, and that you have lived among them?" The man seemed to speak for them all.

"Yes."

"Can you prove it?"

"How would I do such a thing?" I asked.

"Let us hear you speak the language of the toubabu," he said.

I pulled out Olaudah Equiano's book, and read a passage from it.

"'That part of Africa, known by the name of Guinea, in which the trade of slaves is carried on, extends along the coast about 3,400 miles, from Senegal to Angola, and includes a variety of kingdoms. Of these the most considerable is the kingdom of Benin . . . I was born (in this kingdom) in the year 1745. The distance . . . [to] the sea coast must be very considerable: for I had never heard of white men or Europeans, nor of the sea . . .'"

A murmur spread through the crowd. People pushed closer to me. The man held up his hand. "Now tell us what that means," he said.

I told them that Equiano was an African, kidnapped and taken to the land of the toubabu, and that he had survived and recaptured his freedom and written a book about his life.

"Did he go home to kill the people who captured and sold him?" one man asked.

"No," I said.

"Then what kind of man was he?"

"A man in a difficult life, travelling many oceans and lands, with no time to kill his enemies, as they were far away. He was too busy surviving to go back and kill his enemies."

The headman was humming, which I knew was a sign of satisfaction, and the children behind him shoved each other as they tried to get closer to me.

I was asked where my husband and children were. It hadn't worked to tell Alassane that they were in Bayo, so this time I spoke the truth. I said that the toubabu had taken my children away, and that my husband had drowned at sea.

"And what does this sea look like, exactly?" asked the headman.

"Like a river that never ends."

"And what were the names of your husband and children?"

"Chekura, Mamadu and May," I said.

"And what were the names of your parents in this place you call Bayo?"

"Mamadu Diallo the jeweller and Sira Kulibali the midwife."

The people laughed and shouted when they heard the names. At first I was taken aback, and then I realized that they were expressing their pleasure at hearing the sort of names they recognized.

The headman had many other questions. What did I mean by the statement that not all toubabu were devils, and how could it be possible to see good in some of them?

I replied with a question of my own: "Do you not know the human heart?"

After an evening of conversation, I was exhausted. But I stayed to speak with a village elder named Youssouf. I told him that I wanted to go to the coast.

"No," he said, "you must stay. You will be a good wife to me."

"But I am an old woman."

"But you are a brave and a wise woman, and you would bring me great respect."

"How many wives do you have?" I asked.

"Four," he said.

"I can't be the fifth," I said. "I can only be the first, and the only."

461

"The only? What good, strong man has only one wife?"

"My father did. My husband did. Some toubabu do."

"Toubabu," he spat, "are animals. They steal our men and women and children and take them off and eat them or work them to death."

"They do work them to death, and beat them and starve them, but I have never seen them eat one," I said.

"Stay here, among us. You will do us all honour. All the villagers nearby will come to us to hear your stories."

I knew that Youssouf and his people had saved my life, and that without them I could never escape the slavers. But I had somewhere to go, and other things to do, so I would give them the very best of myself for the time that it took me to regain my strength. And then I would leave.

"I will stay for one moon, if you will feed me and keep me safe from the man-stealers. I will repay you by bringing honour to your village. But I cannot marry you because there is a man waiting for me, and I must go to him."

"Another man awaits you?" he said. "Why did you not tell me that earlier?"

"I'm telling you now," I said, and left it at that. It was not necessary to explain that the man was not an African but a toubab, and not a husband but an abolitionist. I thought of Georgia, my protector and friend, and how she had told me years ago on St. Helena Island, "Men don't need to know everything, and sometimes it's best if they know nothing at all."

"So what honour can you bring me without becoming my wife?" Youssouf asked.

"Take care of me and let me get my strength back," I said, "and every night for one revolution of the moon, I will tell stories of all the places I have been and all that I have seen in the toubabu's land. I will tell these stories to you and any visitors that you invite to your village."

For one revolution of the moon, I told my stories each night to people who had come from other villages, sometimes walking hours to hear me. They brought food and kola nuts as gifts, and they left thinking and talking and satisfied.

I told my stories to people who were willing to sit half the night, listening to me and asking questions. I was asked to speak to men, alone. I was asked to speak to women and children. Sometimes I spoke to anyone who assembled, while the drums beat and the people danced and the musicians played their balafons and their stringed guitars and sang.

I told the story of my youth, the story of my trek to Bance Island and how I had caught babies along the way. Always, with each story, I was asked for names.

"Who was the woman who had the baby and kept walking with her to the ship?" one woman asked.

"Her name was Sanu, and she was most gentle," I said.

"And what was the name of her child?"

"Aminata."

"But that is your name."

"So it is."

"Did she name her after you?"

I smiled, and the woman smiled, and four people called out to me to keep talking. I told the story of the ship's passage, the revolt on the ocean, the conditions on board the ships, and of Sullivan's Island. I told of growing indigo, and harvesting it, and the Negroes enslaved in America regardless of where they were born. I told about how the toubabu would rather have pieces of silver than chickens or rum. Especially popular were the descriptions of the rich white men's homes, and of their women, and of how their women carried themselves, and gave birth, and cooked. They laughed until they cried when they heard that no white man who was wealthy would do without an African cook. And they rolled on the ground in laughter when I spoke about the medicine man on the ship who had kept a bird as a pet, fed it good food and

463

taught it to speak the language of the toubabu. I told of the wars between the white men in America, and our betrayal in Nova Scotia, and, ultimately, of our passage to Sierra Leone and my futile search for my home.

I never managed to return home to Bayo, but for one month in a tiny village of strangers, I became the story-teller—the *djeli*—that I had always hoped to be.

Eventually, I found my energy again. I walked with the women to the millet fields, and pounded the grain with a pestle. I sat with other women while they extracted indigo from plants, stirring it in large vats just as I had done in St. Helena Island. They coloured their cloth shades of blue and purple. When the time came for me to leave, I took some of the cloth as a gift and dressed myself as they were dressed. I asked how to get back to the coast, and discovered that it was not difficult to find a guide. And thus, I made one last discovery.

It was almost impossible to get into Africa, but easy to be taken out.

Grand djeli of the academy

{LONDON, 1802}

CLOUDS DARKENED THE SKIES INCREASINGLY as we approached England, and high winds and ugly seas battered the ship and all of us in it. I lost my appetite and didn't eat for days. I felt a singular absence of courage, perhaps because I had no determination to go somewhere else. All I truly felt was that I had grown tired and old.

I could have stayed in Freetown, where—although some Nova Scotians had taken up arms against the Company to fight for their land and the right to self-government—at least the weather was warm and where friends had offered to care for me. But to assist the abolitionists, I was crossing the ocean one last time. During my years in America, I had often longed to go to London—but only as a stepping-stone to Africa. Never had it occurred to me that Africa would be my pathway to London. With me on board the *Sierra Leone Packet* was a botanist named Hector Smithers, who brought crates of insects, reptiles and animals preserved in rum, as well as diverse living species: one caged serpent, two rats, a box full of sand and termites, an antelope, a boar and an infant leopard.

I took to my bed for the final weeks of the voyage, but Smithers' caged creatures fared even worse. In the end, all but the termites met their Maker over the Atlantic Ocean.

Smithers pressed five sailors into duty as he raced to eviscerate the animals and preserve them in giant puncheons of rum. As the botanist scrambled to save what he could for an exhibition in London, I found myself hoping that when my time came, I would be laid gently into the earth. Neither ocean waters nor rum would do for my grave.

I HAD FORGOTTEN ABOUT THE WHITE POOR. The long years in Sierra Leone had done that to me. The whites in Freetown had been Company men and their wives, living in the best houses, drawing the best salaries, eating the tastiest provisions. But England. Oh, England. I saw a crippled man, hobbling about on rough sticks for crutches, holding his hand out for money. I saw blind men begging, and lame women with their snotty-nosed children at all corners. It seemed that half of all Englishmen had at least one rotting, blackened, abscessed tooth. I saw the people shivering, ill-dressed for the cold, coughing, sneezing, sputtering and dying. Men in torn clothes had to jump— sometimes into foul ditches—when horses and carriages bore down on them. Shouts, claims and counter-accusations filled my ears. The air was acrid with burning wood and rotting vegetables and meat tossed out of shop doors. There were vendors everywhere selling newspapers, tobacco, pipes, tea, snuff, wine and hard loaves of sugar.

In Gravesend, I was met by John Clarkson and his brother Thomas. I had not seen John in eight years. The two brothers shook my hand fiercely, put me in a horse-drawn carriage and spirited me to London. I was offered rum in the carriage, and bread, and a bit of cheese, and we stopped in a coffee house for a hot drink and a look at the newspapers.

The coffee house was thick with tobacco smoke that burned my eyes. We had coffee sweetened with honey because the owners were boycotting sugar to support the abolitionist movement. I sipped this drink in the company of men who smoked, read, and drank coffee and tea. They spoke volubly but peaceably and peered over their newspapers at me. One bald old man seemed unable to keep himself from staring, so finally, I got up from my chair and asked if I might borrow his newspaper since he wasn't looking at it.

"What?"

I repeated my request.

The man let out a guffaw. "You kin read, kin ya? I'll buy ya coffee with my own wages, and one for each of the gentlemen what brung ya, if ya can read me a piece from this newspaper."

I took the newspaper. In Sierra Leone, I had been accustomed to reading newspapers that had been printed three or six months earlier. But this one bore the current date: October 4, 1802. I flipped through the pages and came, sure enough, to an article of interest.

"Slavery Hearings Again," the article announced. I read aloud: "'William Wilberforce is demanding that Parliament convene another committee to investigate the alleged abuses of the slave trade.'"

I WAS LED TO THE OFFICES of the Committee for the Abolition of the Slave trade, at 18 old Jewry Street, in a part of the city where boys were hawking newspapers, men were calling out for passersby to enter their coffee houses, and vendors were standing outside minuscule shops, prepared to hack a side off a lamb or a chunk from a block of sugar. Horses and carriages clattered by constantly. It was noisier and more active than anything I had ever seen in Shelburne or New York, and after almost ten years in Freetown, it felt like an assault on my senses. I was led into a small, tight building and up to a room where a stove burned and candles flickered. Awaiting me were twelve men, all eager to shake my hand and welcome me to England.

How pleased they were that John Clarkson had finally prevailed in his attempts to bring me, they said. John Clarkson did not speak, but listened while older men took over. I was accustomed to seeing him in charge in Nova Scotia and in Freetown. But here in England, Clarkson sat in the shadows of his brother and the others.

A tall man pumped my hand, introduced himself as Stanley Hastings and began to tell me all the great plans they had in store for me. "With delicacy and all meticulous care," he said, "we will interview you and write a short account of your life, including the abuses you suffered in the slave trade."

I cleared my throat. "You will write an account of my life?"

"It's so important that I may take on this task myself," said Hastings. He cracked his knuckles, making each one pop, and busied himself by stuffing a pipe. "We need to arrange the account just so. The slightest inaccuracy or inattention to detail could be fatal to our cause."

I listened warily to Hastings' plans to write about my life. The man had the energy of a workhorse, but such a thick beast had no business breaking the soil of my own private garden.

Twelve attentive white men laced their fingers together and trained their eyes on me, but their very faces began to swirl around and around. My fever had returned. Heat and chills rolled through my body like waves on the ocean. The abolitionists kept their fire burning, but their room felt cold and unwelcoming and so very distant from the warmth of my homeland. In the absence of a husband, a son or a daughter, I longed for the African sun to envelop me in its own kind of benevolence. But I found no warmth now, just the rattling of my teeth and the familiar agony stirring in my bones.

I raised a finger, because it was all I could lift. I wanted just three things: a blanket, a glass of water, and nobody but me writing my life story. But I was unable to ask for any of them. The next thing I knew, men with big jowls, sideburns and solicitous eyes were perched over me.

"Are you all right?" Hastings asked.

I closed my eyes and heard the voice of John Clarkson.

"Of course she is not," he answered. "I told you before that this meeting was premature, and I'm afraid that I must now insist. She is my guest, under my care, and she will not face this committee again until given every opportunity to recover in my home."

I was carried down the stairs from the room at 18 Old Jewry Street, lifted into a carriage and taken to Clarkson's home on the same street. A black butler met us at the door. He caught me when my knees buckled and took me to a private room where I was given hot broth, tea, a bed and blankets. When fever brought my bone marrow to a boiling pitch, a second black servant named Betty Ann bathed me and applied wet cloths to my forehead.

In time, I was able to stand unassisted, empty my own chamber pot and take my first meal with John Clarkson and his wife, Susannah. Afterwards, the three of us sat together, drinking tea in a cold room with blankets over our laps and legs. Outside, a few flakes of snow had fallen, and it was damp and cold and windy. I resolved that even with the wicked British climate, I should begin to stir again and get outside if I wished to stay alive a little longer.

Despite my life of losses, the loneliness I felt in London rivalled anything I had felt before. I was too weak to write, get up, explore the streets of London or meet with the committee. But finally, as winter turned to spring and the chill fell off the London damp, I began moving about again and gained confidence that I would not yet perish.

In the endless grey of London, I missed the colours and tastes of my homeland. I found bread and meat uninteresting and unpalatable, and I wondered how it was that people who sailed the oceans and ruled the world cared nothing for food and how to prepare it.

Londoners ate hardly any fruit at all. I missed the bananas, limes, oranges and pineapples of Sierra Leone. I especially missed the malaguetta peppers, and found myself writing to Debra, pleading with her to send me a shipment of spices for cooking.

I saw almost nothing of black people, apart from the occasional quick conversation with Clarkson's butler and maidservant, and neither of them would stop for more than exchanges about the weather or my health. I meant to ask the butler, a short man with a shaven head who went by the name of Dante, how I might be introduced to the black people of London, but he kept slipping away from me. When I was better able to spend more time out of bed and around the house, I sought him out and found him in the Clarksons' kitchen.

"May we have a word?" I asked.

"Pardon me, madam, but I was just on my way out."

"Meena," I said. "You can call me Meena."

He cleared his throat and looked toward the door.

"Why are you avoiding me?" I asked.

"No desire to offend, madam."

"But you never stop to answer my questions."

"It's just my orders, that's all."

"Orders?"

"Mr Clarkson says I'm not to speak with you."

"Why ever not?"

"You are to be allowed to regain your health and prepare your account for the committee, without interference."

"What interference?"

Dante removed his hat, rubbed a spot on it and put it back on his head.

"The time is late, madam."

"What interference?" I asked again.

Dante looked once more to the door. It was just the two of us, alone in the kitchen. He spoke so quietly that I could barely hear his next words.

"From the blacks of London."

"How can anyone interfere with my account, if I am to write it myself?"

"My feelings exactly, madam. But they want your story to be pure. 'Straight from Africa' was what Mr Clarkson said. The committee men don't want Londoners saying that the blacks of London made up your story."

"Dante, I do not wish to get you into trouble. But please, just tell me this: Are there many of us here?"

He exhaled audibly and broke into a broad smile. "Thousands," he said.

"In Sierra Leone, I read a book by an African who was living in London."

"Olaudah Equiano," Dante said.

"So you too have heard of him?"

Dante smiled. "We all know of Equiano," he said. "Any one of us who succeeds among the Englishmen lives on the lips of every black in London."

"Do you think I could meet him?"

"He died a few years ago."

I felt deflated. Equiano was one man I would have liked to meet. I felt I already knew him after reading his story, and had hoped to ask how he had gone about writing the account of his life.

I MET THE SAME WEEK with the abolitionists' committee. Stanley Hastings began with a long preamble about how pleased he was to see that I had regained my health.

"Hear hear," the men called out.

I told them that I would sooner expire in the streets of

London than be told whom I could and could not see, or where I could go, or what I could do. I believe they must have worried that my heart would give out on me, because all twelve abolitionists leapt from their chairs.

"I am feeling fine now, so you may all sit down."

Hesitatingly, they took their seats.

"I have made a decision," I said.

"Please, continue," said Hastings.

"I have decided to write the story of my life."

"Certainly," Hastings said, "but you will require our guidance to ensure—"

"Without guidance, thank you very much," I said. "My life. My words. My pen. I am capable of writing."

A slender, well-dressed man stood and introduced himself as William Wilberforce, member of Parliament. He asked if he might clarify the matter.

"Please do," I said.

"This is not a question of your literacy," Wilberforce said. "It is rather an issue of ensuring its authenticity."

"That is precisely why nobody will tell my story but me."

"It must cover your childhood," Thomas Clarkson jumped in, "and how you were marched to the sea. It must explicate your enslavement in the ship, and your time in South Carolina. It must . . ."

John Clarkson rested a palm on his brother's shoulder. "She is aware of what her own story should say."

I said I would begin immediately, provided that nobody interfered with my right to speak to any person, John Clarkson's butler included.

"Meena, I want you to know that it was not my plan to prevent you from getting to know Dante," John Clarkson said.

Wilberforce leaned toward me. "Blame it on me, if you like. But please understand. There can't be a whiff of suggestion that your story has been influenced by the blacks of London. This would do our cause great damage, as they are not well regarded here."

"If I give my account, you will have all of it. But it will be on my terms and my terms only, coloured neither by you nor the blacks of London."

"If we proceed in this way," Hastings said, "will you promise to share your account with us, allow us to introduce it as evidence in the parliamentary hearings, and not speak in public about it until that is done?"

I nodded in consent.

"Fine," Wilberforce said. "Wonderful. We do need to proceed, so how soon can it be done?"

"We will have to see," I said.

"Just let us handle the newspapers, all right?" he said.

"What do you mean?"

"It will be your story, through and through, but for God's sake let us manage how and when it gets out."

I saw no reason to disagree.

THE NEXT DAY, DANTE TOLD ME his salary had been increased. "What did you do to those abolitionists?" he asked.

"African witchcraft," I said, with a smile.

That evening, when he had finished working, Dante took me to the back of the house, to the servants' quarters. I was greeted by Betty Ann, who had helped me through my illness, and I thus discovered that the two were a couple. Betty Ann was a young woman born in Jamaica who had been transported to London as a domestic slave to a rich planter, and had liberated herself by running away.

"They didn't try to take you back?" I asked.

"They dare not. The courts won't let them. These days in London, if a black walks out the door of his master, he will be free."

I knew it was a big city and an even bigger world, but I had to ask if they had heard of a wealthy white family named Witherspoon. They hadn't. I felt a little foolish, and told myself not to drain my limited energies by dreaming of the impossible. London had a million people. And if my daughter was still alive, she could be in any number of villages, towns or cities on either side of the Atlantic Ocean.

Dante and Betty Ann offered to take me to a part of London where other black people lived, but I had little strength for excursions and chose to devote my remaining energies to writing the report for the parliamentary committee.

Supplied with food, and quills and ink and paper, kept warm about the legs by blankets, sitting at a comfortable table with candles burning, I began to relate the story of my life. Once I began writing, I could not stop. My childhood erupted on the page, and then my young womanhood, and then my experiences in catching children and bringing my own into the world. On and on I wrote, with no end in sight.

The abolitionists fussed.

"It is wonderful that you have so much to communicate, Miss Dee," Thomas Clarkson said during another meeting with the abolitionists. "But it will be worth nothing if the parliamentary committee does not hear it."

"He has a point," Wilberforce said. "The slavers made excellent presentations to the committee. Every newspaper is reporting their justifications for continuing the trade."

The men around the table rustled nervously in their chairs. I had read the accounts. The pro-slavery men had claimed that slavery was a humane institution that rescued Africans from barbarity in their homelands. Africans would simply kill each other in tribal wars if they were not liberated in the Americas, where they enjoyed the civilizing influence of Christianity. The papers reported that shipping was clean and as safe as possible, and that Africans succumbed to the voyage in no greater proportion than English seamen on the same vessels.

But Hastings spoke calmly. "Gentlemen, Miss Dee will tell her story and when she does, all of England will be listening."

Wilberforce arranged to delay my appearance before the parliamentary committee. In the meantime, he urged the press to play close attention to the testimony of the slavers. Soon, he said, he would offer evidence to refute their testimony. And then he persuaded me to give him fifty pages he could use for my report.

THE MORNING THAT I WAS TO SPEAK to the parliamentary committee, the front page of the *Times* told readers about Hector Smithers, the botanist who had mounted an exhibition of dead but well-preserved African rodents, bats, butterflies, termites, leopards and alligators. The exhibition had drawn so many people on its opening day that it had been obliged to shut its doors to prevent over-crowding. The *Times* called it "a spectacular showing of the frightful, lush, colourful barbarity of the animal kingdom in darkest Africa," and noted that entrance cost six pence. A small article inside the newspaper noted that the parliamentary committee would soon receive a report from a woman "fresh from Africa" who had survived slavery.

I stood outside the doors of the parliamentary committee room, waiting with Hastings. I had no idea what to expect, or how I would be treated. I could feel my pulse pounding in my throat, and tried to calm myself by thinking of my father and how—even when making tea or jewellery—his hands moved with confidence. I imagined his voice, deep and musical, reaching out across the ocean to soothe me now: *Just be who you are, and speak of the life you have lived.*

The door opened and I was summoned. Along the walls of the rectangular room, ten chairs had been set up for newspaper men, and another thirty chairs for visitors. Every chair was taken. I sat alone on one side of a long table, facing all the committee members seated across from me. There were ten committee members, and William Wilberforce was one of them. He smiled and began his official explanation of what I already knew: he would ask me questions and I was to answer them.

Wilberforce asked me to state my name, date of birth and place of birth. I did so.

"Could you please give the committee an indication of the conditions of your childhood, Miss Dee?"

He asked how I came to be stolen, at the age of eleven, and marched three months overland to the sea. I gave as many details as possible. I explained that men had been yoked about the neck in the slave coffles. I said the dead, the near-dead and the rebellious were thrown overboard to the sharks. Whispers rose in the room when I told the committee that seamen made free with the African women on the ship, and that even I, as a child, had been required to stay in the ship surgeon's bed.

"And what do you say to earlier testimony that men and women are not branded in the slave factories on the coast of Africa?" Wilberforce asked.

"It's not true," I said.

"And how would you know that?"

"Because I was held in one of those factories, and I was branded."

"Which factory, and when?"

"It was around 1756, and I was branded on Bance Island off the coast of Sierra Leone." I heard murmurings in the room. Wilberforce asked me to repeat those details for the record, and I did so.

"And how do you know the name of this island, because surely you did not speak English at the time?"

"I returned a few years ago, with the assistance of an official with the Sierra Leone Company."

"If it is not too indelicate, may the committee hear how you were branded?"

"A hot iron was pressed into my flesh."

A woman left the committee room.

"Shall I show you the mark?" I asked, for the abolitionists had instructed me earlier to make this offer.

"Where is it located?" Wilberforce asked.

"Above my right breast, sir."

A collective gasp went up in the room. I heard the sounds of quills scratching paper.

"Am I required to show it, sir?"

"That will not be necessary, as she is under oath," the clerk said.

I described how I had come to be sold in Charles Town, and how my son had been taken from me. I spoke of the birth of May in 1784, and how, in Shelburne, Nova Scotia, she had been abducted.

I gave testimony for two hours. When asked if I had prepared anything for the committee to consult at its leisure, I tabled a copy of my life story.

The meeting over, the abolitionists led me into a private room where I was asked to reveal my branding scar to the newspaper reporters. Ten men stepped up, one after the other, to examine the proof on my flesh. They wanted to ask questions, but Wilberforce insisted that I had had enough for the day and directed them to consult their notes of my testimony.

When it was all over, and Wilberforce and Hastings had climbed into a carriage with me, I felt suddenly exhausted. Just a few years ago, when I had told my stories night after night in the village far in the interior of Sierra Leone, the people had made me feel admired. With their laughter and interjections, and with the drinks and the food that they urged me to take, they had made me feel as if I were surrounded by family. Here, it was different, for when I spoke to the committee, apart from the occasional groans and the sound of quills, it felt like I was speaking to a wall. I had no idea what the parliamentarians thought of me or my words, because they sat as still as owls and offered nothing but questions.

The next day, John Clarkson brought me the *Times*, the *Morning Chronicle*, the *Gazette*, the *Morning Post* and *Lloyd's List*. Every single newspaper carried the story of my presentation, and each one began with the scar. Over the next weeks, the papers continued to run new reports about what I had told the committee. Every day, people asked to speak to me. When the reporters had had their fill, I began to receive requests to speak to school children and to literary and historical societies. I accepted a number of such requests, and found that people in these groups had much more to say to me.

One evening, John Clarkson tapped on my bedroom door.

"A letter for you," he said. "And let me say that insofar as public recognition, you have just eclipsed every member of the abolition committee, with perhaps the sole exception of William Wilberforce."

He smiled as I took the envelope, and asked if he could watch me open it.

"Yes, Lieutenant," I said.

"John," he said.

I nodded and studied the envelope. It bore the seal of King George III. Inside, I found a card requesting the pleasure of my company for tea.

"Stupendous," Clarkson kept saying. "The King would never meet Olaudah Equiano. This is better than any of us had hoped for."

When the abolitionists spread the word that the King and Queen were prepared to receive an African for the first time, the newspapers carried another round of stories. For the *Morning Post*, the artist James Gillray had drawn a caricature of me plucking a cube of sugar from the fingers of King George III. In the caricature, the King is skeletally thin and I am obese and the words *I'll take that* appear in a bubble at my lips.

William Wilberforce, being the sole parliamentarian in the abolitionist committee, was chosen to escort me to tea with the King. A line of people waited outside the committee offices, hoping to meet me. For weeks, they had been queuing up daily. It seemed that half of London wanted to have words with me. I saw Hector Smithers in line and waved, but could not stop. And then I looked again.

I noticed a black face in a sea of white people. It belonged to a beautiful young African woman of about eighteen years. Amid all those people she kept her dignity and an upright bearing. Our eyes met, and I wondered if I had seen her before. Her lips moved, but I could not hear the words above the din of the crowd.

"Who are you?" I tried to call back, but she could not hear me either.

Silly me. After all these years, I sometimes still caught myself scanning faces in crowds, hoping for the impossible.

I had lost many loved ones in my life, and none had ever come back to me. Still, I couldn't prevent myself from wondering why this young woman had stood with the others in the rain, only to catch a glimpse of me. But I could give it no more thought, because I was put in a carriage and whisked away toward Buckingham Palace.

I HAD ANTICIPATED A PRIVATE MEETING with the royal couple, but as Wilberforce and I were led into a parlour the size of a house, I saw a dozen servants and just as many men and women in wigs and gowns. One wigged parliamentarian after another strode up and seized my hand and asked if it was true that I had just arrived "fresh from Africa." To ward off the interviews, Wilberforce took my arm and steered me to a table where a maid served biscuits and tea.

"Notice the absence of sugar, out of deference to you," Wilberforce whispered.

He was right. On the table, I saw three pots of honey. The maid spooned the thick fluid into my tea. It was an odd feeling to be served by a white person, and I struggled to keep the teacup from rattling on its saucer.

A man introduced himself as an aide to the Royal Family, and asked me to sign a guest book. As he peered intently, I wrote: *For a woman who has journeyed from freedom to slavery and back, it is a true honour to meet the King and Queen, and it is my hope that liberty will prevail for all.*

The aide stared with his mouth fully open, as if he had just witnessed a zebra reading a book.

Wilberforce received the signal he had been anticipating, so he excused us from the aide, set my tea down on a table and led me through some doors into another room.

The King and Queen were seated in broad red chairs. Their ample robes spilled onto the floor, but I caught sight of polished camwood on one arm of the King's chair. I wondered if he knew his armrest was made of the red wood from my homeland.

"Slowly, surely," Wilberforce whispered. "Curtsy but do not offer your hand."

We moved first toward Queen Charlotte Sophia.

She was the one I most wished to meet, for I wanted to see for myself if she appeared to be a daughter of Africa. The portraits I had seen had drawn her delicately, giving her face a porcelain composure. But seated before me was a woman with a broad nose and full lips, and skin much richer than in any painter's rendition.

Queen Charlotte held out a gloved hand, and I shook it.

"Welcome, Aminata," said the Queen. "Welcome to England."

"Your Highness," I said.

I was touched that she had taken the trouble to learn my real name, and I believed that she was the first white person to use it on first greeting. But then again, perhaps she wasn't white after all. I resolved then and there that since the Queen of England could pronounce my name, so could the rest of the country.

"I am honoured, as I have been hearing about you for so many years," I said.

"That's quite a statement, considering the breadth of your travels."

The Queen gave a crisp smile, and I could see in her eyes the desire to end the conversation. "I have arranged for you to receive a little gift from my library," she said. "Thank you," I said. I wanted to tell the Queen of England how profoundly I wished for her country's leadership in ending the traffic of men, women and children. But an aide took my arm and guided me gently but unerringly a step or two away, allowing the Queen to address Wilberforce.

I now stood facing King George III. I curtsied. He nodded. I waited, as instructed, for the King of England to reach out his hand or to speak, but he did neither.

He nodded several times, and opened his mouth to speak. But then he turned his head slightly and his eyes opened wider. He did not appear to know what he had meant to say, or who I was, or where we were.

I gazed calmly at the large, round, reddish face and the glassy eyes of the man who presided over the greatest slaving nation in the world, and I understood that there would be no conversation between us. I was led away, but I was not troubled. For all I knew, the King could have been on the verge of one of his fits. I had read all about them. The Bank of England had even issued a coin, years earlier, to celebrate the King's return to sanity. I wondered what the people of my homeland would ask if they knew that I had met with the *toubabu faama*—the grand chief of England. Never in a million years would they believe that he suffered from an illness in his head and had chosen an African queen.

As I was leaving Buckingham Palace, the same aide who had shown me the guest book now pressed into my hand a leatherbound volume. The Queen of England had given me *On Poetry: A Rhapsody* by Jonathan Swift.

THE TESTIMONY IN PARLIAMENT and the visit to Buckingham Palace had drained me again. I sought quiet and solitude and my best comfort, literature. I was rereading Swift's book when John Clarkson tapped lightly on my door.

"There is somebody here who wishes to see you."

"But I am not dressed to see anybody this evening," I said.

"I do not think the lady is concerned with your attire. She reports that she has been waiting a long time to meet you."

And then I saw an African woman—a girl, really—step into my room. Cheeks smooth like ebony. No moons and no scarification, but she looked like somebody from my village of Bayo.

"I am sorry," I said, my mind turning. "I know I saw you today in the rain. I could not stop to greet you then."

"The rain did not bother me. What were a few hours of standing in line? Mama, I have been waiting for years."

She stepped forward and threw herself into me with such vigour that she nearly knocked me over. It was the embrace for which I had been praying for fifteen years. We rocked on our heels, and clung to each other. I couldn't speak, so I just kept squeezing until my muscles grew tired.

We parted enough to look into each other's eyes, but our hands remained locked.

MAY AND I DID NOT LEAVE each other for two full days. We slept in the same bed, ate at the same table, and walked hand in hand by the Thames. The mere sight of the woman made me want to keep on living. Her lips brushed my cheeks every hour. I wanted to live on and on so that I could see her, and soak up her beauty, and love my own flesh and blood just a while longer.

I had little need to tell her what had happened to me, as she had read reports of it in the newspapers. Over the hours and the days, I came to learn what had happened to her.

The Witherspoons had never changed her name from May, or hidden from her that she had been "adopted"—as they put it—in Shelburne, Nova Scotia. They claimed, however, that they had saved May after she was abandoned by an African woman.

But May had been old enough to remember our life together, and from the very start she had questioned the story. The Witherspoons had taken her from Shelburne to Boston and sailed promptly to England. They doted on her at first but grew impatient and then angry when she refused to stop asking where I had gone.

"I had a terrible will," she said, "and they did not appreciate the tantrums in which I screamed for my mother."

The Witherspoons kept May as a house servant. She was locked in her room at night. She was not allowed to walk about London on her own. She had been taught to read and write and serve tables and perform domestic tasks, all of which she had to do daily. She had never been called a slave. Nor had she been paid.

At the age of eleven, she asked to go free, and they

refused. One night she wriggled out of her bedroom window, dropped into the street and ran until a black preacher swept her up in his arms and asked why she was fleeing barefoot. The preacher let her stay with him and his wife until he could find a family in his own congregation to take her in. The woman of the family washed houses and the father sold newspapers and they squeezed May into the room with their own two children. May worked with the woman, washing houses, for three years, until she was able to get work teaching at a school for the black poor in London.

"You learned to read and write," I said.

May said she remembered me scratching out words for her to practise. "I knew how much you loved words, Mama, and I wanted to love them too."

"What happened to the Witherspoons?" I asked.

They had come after May. But the family that had taken her in sought the help of an abolitionist named Granville Sharpe, and he had "fierce words" with the Witherspoons and reminded them that they had no right to detain a Negro who had liberated herself from their possession. He said that he would humiliate them in court if they persisted. The Witherspoons moved to Montreal to open a shipping business, and May remained in London.

The next day, May took me to the school where she taught. Reporters followed us all the way there, and watched for hours as I spent the day with thirty African children who were learning to read and write. The conditions were crude and they had few resources, but May told me that it was much better than what others had. Many white children did not even attend school. When the papers wrote about my visit, I began to be asked every week to speak in a school, library or church. I addressed black people and I addressed whites. I would speak about my life to anyone who cared to listen. The more people who knew about it, the more would press for abolition.

* * *

WHEN THE CHILLS RETURNED TO MY FLESH, nobody in London had Peruvian bark. The fevers nearly swept me away, but May tended to me in my illness for months. Soup and bread, soup and bread, soup and bread, rice and a bit of mutton, when I was able to hold it down. I looked more and more like a skeleton. But I had a reason to live, so once more I clawed my way back to health.

May and I moved into lodgings paid for by the abolitionists. They rented two pleasant rooms for us at the rate of fifteen pounds a year, and hired a cook to make our meals.

In 1805, John Clarkson paid a visit to our new home, bringing me a new map of Africa. The cause of abolition was advancing steadily, he said, and the committee was endlessly grateful for my work.

"Is there anything at all that you need?" he asked.

I asked May to let us have a moment alone.

"You won't have to feed me much longer," I told Clarkson, "but I ask you to take care of my daughter." I secured his promise that the abolitionists would support May until she reached the age of twenty-five and see that she received any additional education that she wanted.

"She is an eminently capable young woman, and we will do our best to put her on a solid footing in life," Clarkson said.

"Good," I said.

"I hope that's my last contest with you," he said, "because you're some negotiator."

I smiled. "It's in my blood."

WHEN I URGED THE ABOLITIONISTS to donate to May's school, they complied. When we set up once-a-week church meals for the black poor, they gave food. But as they prepared to pounce with a motion in Parliament, they would consider only the slave trade.

"One step at a time," John Clarkson told me.

"Hop with two steps," I said. "Children do it. So can you."

May's school expanded to include forty and eventually fifty students. It did so well, and received so many materials and donations from the abolitionists that some white students began to attend as well. May renamed it the Aminata Academy, and I became known as the school's grand *djeli*. Every student in the school knew that the word meant storyteller, and each one looked forward to my Friday morning tales. I always began the same way. Unrolling a map of the world, I would put one finger on a dot I had drawn to represent my village of Bayo, put another finger on London and say: "I was born there, and we are here now, and I'm going to tell you all about what happened in between."

I AM FINALLY DONE. MY STORY IS TOLD. My daughter sleeps in the room next to mine. At first, I objected to being left alone at night. But May softly tells me that she has a man in her life now, and that they are planning to have a baby. Get yourself a good midwife, I say, because my hands tend to shake these days. And she says, Don't you worry, Mama, all that will be done.

May tells me that she has found a publisher for my story. But the abolitionists have their own publisher and insist on correcting "allegations that cannot be proved" and she doesn't know whether to give in or to use the man she has chosen. Does your man know the story of our people? I ask. Yes, May says. Then look him in the eye and see if he's a good man, I say. She has done that, she says, and she knows he's a good man—the publisher is her fiancé. But, she says, the abolitionists claim that they have earned the right to publish my story. I stamp my foot. It hurts. The fevers are back and my bones burn. Next time, if there is a next time, I will put my foot down gently. I tell my daughter, in a voice that even I can barely hear, to thank the abolitionists for their food and shelter, and for the contributions to May's school, because without education our children's hopes are drowned, but that my story is my story and it will be published by the one who lets my words stand.

"This man who is going to marry you," I say. "When do I get to meet him?"

"You've met him, Mama, but you keep forgetting."

Write to my friend Debra in Freetown, I tell May. Tell her to come. Tell her to put Caroline in your school. May tells me that maybe Debra should stay in Sierra Leone, that maybe Sierra Leone needs her. Write to Debra anyway, I say, and pass on my love.

I would like to draw a map of the places I have lived. I would put Bayo on the map, and trace in red my long path to the sea. Blue lines would show the ocean voyages. Cartouches would decorate the margins. There would be no elephants for want of towns, but rather paintings of guineas made from the gold mines of Africa, a woman balancing fruit on her head, another with blue pouches for medicine, a child reading, and the green hills of Sierra Leone, land of my arrivals and embarkations.

They bring me the newspapers as well as tea with honey, because I don't get out any more. I seem to be napping so much of the time, and can't keep track of the days. May says she has news about the publisher and a cartographer. They will work together, she says, and include a map with my memoir. May and her new man are dressing up to go and hear William Wilberforce make his motion in Parliament. They say he is going to win this time. He'd better. I have helped him all I can.

May kisses me on the forehead and is gone. The girl has

487

young legs and moves like a cyclone. I, with bones afire, have no more tolerance for walking. I will cross no bridges and board no ships, but stay here on solid land and take my tea with honey and lie back on this bed of straw. It is not such a bad bed. I have known worse. They can wake me with the news, when they come home.

THE END

A word about history

THE BOOK OF NEGROES is a work of my imagination, but it does reflect my understanding of the Black Loyalists and their history.

In terms of the sheer number of people recorded and described, the actual Book of Negroes is the largest single document about black people in North America up until the end of the eighteenth century. It contains the names and details of 3,000 black men, women and children, who, after serving or living behind British lines during the American Revolutionary War, sailed from New York City to various British colonies. Although a few went to England, Germany and Quebec, most of the people whose names appear in the book landed in Nova Scotia and settled in the areas of Birchtown, Shelburne, Port Mouton, Annapolis Royal, Digby, Weymouth, Preston, Halifax, Sydney and other places. It should be noted that some Loyalists sailed from South Carolina, and many are likely to have escaped by other means to the British colonies, away from the prying eyes of the inspectors registering names in the Book of Negroes.

In this novel, some of the excerpts from the book of Negroes are real, and others have been invented or altered. Readers who wish to see the Book of Negroes can find it, or parts of it, in the Nova Scotia Public Archives, the National Archives of the United States and in the National Archives (Public Records Office) in Kew, England. It can also be found on microfilm at the National Archives of Canada and, through an electronic link provided by Library and Archives Canada, at: *http://epe.lac-bac.gc.ca/100/200/301/ic/can_digital_collections/blackloyalists/index.htm*. As well, the Book of Negroes is reproduced in *The Black Loyalist Directory: African Americans in Exile After the American Revolution*, edited and with an introduction by Graham Russell Hodges, Garland Publishing Inc., 1996.

Some 3,000 Black Loyalists arrived in Nova Scotia in 1783, and about 1,200 of them gave up on Nova Scotia after ten years of miserable treatment in the British colony. From the shores of Halifax, they formed the first major "back to Africa" exodus in the history of the Americas, sailing to found the colony of Freetown in Sierra Leone. To this day, the Black Loyalists of Nova Scotia are still known as some of the founders of the modern state of Sierra Leone. Like my protagonist Aminata Diallo, some of the Nova Scotian "adventurers," as they were known, were born in Africa. Their return en masse to the mother continent in 1792 took place decades before former American slaves founded Liberia, and more than one hundred years before Marcus Garvey of Jamaica became famous for urging blacks in the Americas to move "back" to Africa.

Readers might like to know that in 1807, the British Parliament passed legislation to abolish the slave trade the following year. In the United States, abolition of the slave trade also took effect in 1808. It was not until August 1, 1834, that slavery itself was finally abolished in Canada and in the rest of the British Empire. Another thirty-one years passed before the Thirteenth Amendment of the United States Constitution officially abolished slavery in the USA in 1865.

Though this work is built on the foundations of history, in some instances I have knowingly bent facts to suit the purposes of the novel. I will cite four key examples. First, my protagonist Aminata Diallo is paid by the British government to record the names of thousands of blacks into the book of Negroes in New York City in 1783. My understanding is that the British did not hire private scribes for the Book of Negroes, but simply used officers from within their ranks. Second, Canada's first race riot—in which disbanded white soldiers took out their frustrations on the blacks of Birchtown and Shelburne, Nova Scotia—actually took place in 1783, but I have set it in 1787. Third, Thomas Peters—the Loyalist who helped set the exodus from Halifax to Freetown in motion by travelling to England to complain about the ill treatment of blacks in Nova Scotia— travelled to Sierra Leone and died soon after his arrival, but not at the hands of slave traders, as happens in this novel. And finally, although the British Navy lieutenant John Clarkson organized the exodus from Halifax to Sierra Leone and sailed to Freetown with the black "adventurers," he did not stay in Africa as long as I have him there.

John Clarkson and Thomas Peters are two of a number of fictional characters who are drawn from real people having the same names. Others are Clarkson's brother Thomas Clarkson; the slave-ship surgeon and subsequent abolitionist Alexander Falconbridge; his wife Anna Maria Falconbridge; King George III and his wife Queen Charlotte Sophia of Mecklenberg–Strelitz; Nova Scotia governor John Wentworth and his wife Frances Wentworth; as well as Sam Fraunces, the tavern owner who fed George Washington and other patriots and went to work as a cook for the president after the Revolutionary War.

Moses Lindo was a Sephardic Jew from London, England who arrived in South Carolina in 1756. In

Charles Town, Lindo became a member of the Kahal Kadosh Beth Elohim—one of the oldest Jewish congregations in the United States. Eventually, Lindo became the official indigo inspector for the Province of South Carolina. For this novel, I have borrowed Lindo's last name and his interest in indigo, but everything else about my fictional character Solomon Lindo is invented. In the case of Solomon Lindo and all other characters in *The Book of Negroes*, I have taken complete liberties, creating imaginary dialogue, actions, events and circumstances.

For further reading

FOR READERS WHO WISH TO KNOW MORE about the history
behind *The Book of Negroes*, I will mention some of the
books that I came across in my research. (Other titles are
noted in my acknowledgments.)

Novelists may forever be trying to make sense of the
transatlantic slave trade, but in my view a good way to
begin to appreciate its impact on ordinary people is by
reading the memoirs of freedom seekers. As the editor of
The Classic Slave Narratives, Henry Louis Gates, Jr.,
assembled four key slave narratives, including memoirs by
Frederick Douglass, Olaudah Equiano, Harriet Jacobs and
Mary Prince.

First-hand accounts reflecting the experiences of the
Black Loyalists of Nova Scotia can be found in George
Elliott Clarke's *Fire on the Water: An Anthology of Black Nova
Scotian Writing, Vol. 1*, which contains memoirs by David
George, Boston King and John Marrant, among others.

Europeans have left accounts of their experiences with
the Black Loyalists, travels in West Africa or participation
in the slave trade in the eighteenth century. I am especially
indebted to John Clarkson, whose personal journal
documenting his work in organizing the exodus of the
Black Loyalists from Nova Scotia to Sierra Leone in 1792

was ably introduced and edited by Charles Bruce Fergusson in *Clarkson's Mission to America, 1791–1792*. Also indispensable were *An Account of the Slave Trade on the Coast of Africa* by the slave-ship surgeon Alexander Falconbridge and the letters written by his wife Anna Maria Falconbridge in *Narrative of Two Voyages to the River Sierra Leone During the Years 1791–1792–1793*. These two accounts can be found independently in libraries or joined together in one book with the same titles, introduced and footnoted by historian Christopher Fyfe. I relied on *The Journal of a Slave Trader (John Newton), 1750–1754; With Newton's Thoughts Upon the African Slave Trade*, edited by Bernard Martin and Mark Spurrell; and on *Journal of a Slave-Dealer: A View of Some Remarkable Axcedents in the Life of Nics. Owen on the Coast of Africa and America from the Year 1746 to the Year 1757*, edited by Eveline Martin. The historian Alexander Peter Kup edited the diary by the Swedish botanist *Adam Afzelius: Sierra Leone Journals, 1795–96*. Dr Thomas Winterbottom provides many details in his two-volume *An Account of the Native Africans in the Neighbourhood of Sierra Leone*. Finally, in *Travels in the Interior of Africa*, the Scottish doctor Mungo Park describes his trip from Gambia through what are now Senegal and Mali in the years 1795–1797.

I found many books about the people of Africa. Some of the books about Sierra Leone were *A History of Sierra Leone* by Christopher Fyfe and *A History of Sierra Leone, 1400–1787* by Alexander Peter Kup. To learn more about Mali, I consulted *Groupes ethniques au Mali* by Bokar N'Diayé; *The Heart of the Ngoni: Heroes of the African Kingdom of Segu* by Harold Courlander with Ousmae Sako; and *The Bamana Empire by the Niger: Kingdom, Jihad and Colonization 1712–1920* by Sundiata D. Djata.

There are many books about the transatlantic slave trade. Most helpful for my purposes were *Black Cargoes: A History of the Atlantic Slave Trade 1518–1865* by Daniel P.

Mannix and Malcolm Cowley; *Citizens of the World: London Merchants and the Integration of the British Atlantic Community, 1735–1785* by David Hancock; and *The Slave Trade: The Story of the Atlantic Slave Trade: 1440–1870* by Hugh Thomas.

For old maps of Africa, I studied the *Historical Atlas of Africa* by J. F. Ade Ajayi and Michael Crowder; *Blaeu's The Grand Atlas of the 17th Century World* by John Goss; and *Norwich's Maps of Africa: An Illustrated and Annotated Cartobibliography*, revised and edited by Jeffrey C. Stone.

For information about slave vessels and life on board eighteenth-century ships, I looked carefully at *Scurvy: How a Surgeon, a Mariner, and a Gentleman Solved the Greatest Medical Mystery of the Age of Sail* by Stephen R. Bown; *Slave Ships and Slaving* compiled by George Francis Dow; *The Wooden World: An Anatomy of the Georgian Navy* by N. A. M. Rodger; and in *The Journal for Maritime Research*, Jane Webster's article "Looking for the Material Culture of the Middle Passage."

A number of books introduced me to the history of South Carolina— particularly the history of black people in Sea Islands and in Charleston (or Charles Town, as it was spelled before the American Revolution). Some were: *Slave Badges and the Slave-Hire System in Charleston, South Carolina, 1783–1865* by Harlan Greene, Harry S. Hutchins, Jr., and Brian E. Hutchins; *Charleston in the Age of the Pinckneys* by George C. Rogers, Jr.; and *A Short History of Charleston* by Robert N. Rosen.

The literature on the history of South Carolina is vast, but some books of great help to me were *Slave Counterpoint: Black Culture in the Eighteenth-Century Chesapeake and Low Country* by Philip Morgan and *Africanisms in the Gullah Dialect* by Lorenzo Dow Turner. I also read *Pox Americana: The Great Smallpox Epidemic of 1775–82* by Elizabeth A. Fenn; *Masters, Slaves, and Subjects: The Culture of Power in the South Carolina Low Country,*

1740–1790 by Robert Olwell; and *Black Majority: Negroes in Colonial South Carolina from 1670 Through the Stono Rebellion* by Peter Woods. Other helpful books were *Reminiscences of Sea Island Heritage: Legacy of Freedmen on St Helena Island* by Ronald Daise; *Gullah Fuh Ooonuh (Gullah For You): A Guide to the Gullah Language* by Virginia Mixson Geraty; and *The Gullah People and Their African Heritage* by William S. Pollitzer.

I also came across articles and books about slave hair and clothing. Shane White and Graham White wrote *Stylin': African American Expressive Culture from Its Beginnings to the Zoot Suit*, as well as the article "Slave Hair and African American Culture in the Eighteenth and Nineteenth Centuries," which appeared in the *Journal of Southern History*. In the *Journal of American History*, Jonathan Prude wrote "To Look upon the 'Lower Sort': Runaway Ads and the Appearance of Unfree Laborers in America, 1750–1800."

I drew additional information about South Carolina history and details about indigo from *South Carolina: A History* by Walter Edgar; *The History of Beaufort County, South Carolina, Volume 1, 1514–1861* by Lawrence S. Rowland, Alexander Moore and George C. Rogers, Jr.; and the booklet "Indigo in America" produced by BASF Wyandotte Corporation.

Two books offered herbal remedies and details about the care of pregnant women in the South: *Hoodoo Medicine: Gullah Herbal Remedies* by Faith Mitchell and *Southern Folk Medicine 1750–1820* by Kay K. Moss.

Various books describe Jews in South Carolina in the eighteenth century. Among others, I relied on *This Happy Land: The Jews of Colonial and Antebellum Charleston* by James William Hagy; *The Jews of South Carolina Prior to 1800* by Cyrus Adler Hühner; and *A Portion of the People: Three Hundred Years of Southern Jewish Life* edited by Theodore Rosengarten and Dale Rosengarten.

For details about New York City in the eighteenth century, I consulted *New York Burning: Liberty, Slavery, and Conspiracy in Eighteenth-Century Manhattan* by Jill Lepore; *The Epic of New York City* by Edward Robb Ellis; *The Battle for New York: The City at the Heart of the American Revolution* by Barnet Schecter; *Gotham: A History of New York City to 1898* by Edwin Burrows and Mike Wallace; *The Loyal Blacks* by Ellen Gibson Wilson; and *Somewhat More Independent: The End of Slavery in New York City, 1770–1810* by Shane White. To learn about the African Burial Ground in Manhattan, I read "Historic background of the African Burial Ground," a chapter in the *Draft Management Recommendations for the African Burial Ground*, produced by the United States National Park Service.

As for the lives of the Black Loyalists in Nova Scotia, I read *King's Bounty: A History of Early Shelburne, Nova Scotia*, by Marion Robertson; *The Life of Boston King: Black Loyalist, Minister and Master Carpenter* edited by Ruth Holmes Whitehead and Carmelita A. M. Robertson and the Nova Scotia Museum curatorial report "The Shelburne Black Loyalists: A Short Bibliography of All Blacks Emigrating to Shelburne County, Nova Scotia after the American Revolution, 1783," by Ruth Holmes Whitehead.

To learn about the abolitionist movement in Britain and to imagine the lives of blacks in London at the turn of the nineteenth century, I consulted *Hogarth's Blacks: Images of Blacks in Eighteenth-Century English Art* by David Dabydeen; *Staying Power: The History of Black People in Britain* by Peter Fryer; *Black England: Life Before Emancipation* by Gretchen Gerzina; *Bury the Chains: Prophets and Rebels in the Fight to Free an Empire's Slaves* by Adam Hoshschild; and *Reconstructing the Black Past: Blacks in Britain, 1780–1830* by Norma Myers.

I could never have written *The Book of Negroes* without the work of all the diarists, memoir writers and historians who went before me, but I alone am responsible for any intentional or accidental deviations from history in this novel.

Acknowledgments

I CAN'T BEGIN TO ACKNOWLEDGE ALL OF THE PEOPLE—some living, and others who wrote diaries, travel accounts and slave narratives more than two hundred years ago—on whose shoulders I climbed to write *The Book of Negroes*. But I do wish to thank the people, books and institutions that helped me the most.

I came across the idea for *The Book of Negroes* while reading a book that I had stolen, so I will begin by acknowledging what I took and where I found it. The book was *The Black Loyalists: The Search for a Promised Land in Nova Scotia and Sierra Leone, 1783–1870*, and the author was James W. St. G. Walker, a history professor at the University of Waterloo in Ontario. I took it from the Toronto home of my parents, Donna Hill and Daniel G. Hill. Dad scribbled his name inside the front cover before I went out the door, but it did him no good, because that was twenty years ago and I still have the book.

Dr Walker was a good friend to my father and mother— they all wrote books about the history of blacks in Canada—and later he became a friend and steady adviser to me, as well. He answered numerous questions as I researched *The Book of Negroes*, introduced me to other scholars and commented on an early draft. Out of respect for Dr Walker and all of the other scholars who advised me, I must emphasize that any historical inaccuracies in this novel—intentional or otherwise—are my responsibility and mine only.

Paul E. Lovejoy, Distinguished Research Professor in the Department of History at York University and author of *Transformations in Slavery: A History of Slavery in Africa* and many other books, shared with me some of his scholarly articles dealing with scarification, enslavement and Muslims in West Africa. Dr Lovejoy commented on scenes set in Africa, suggested other books and articles, and provided details about British parliamentary hearings into the abolition of the slave trade.

Valentin Vydrine, author of the *Manding–English Dictionary* and head of the African Department, St. Petersburg Museum of Anthropology and Ethnography, answered many questions to do with languages and ethnic groups in the West African country now known as Mali.

Gordon Laco, a ship expert who acts as a consultant to filmmakers, was kind enough to offer advice for the novel, as was my friend Chris Ralph, who has spent years working on ships performing scientific missions.

Nicholas Butler, Special Collections Manager of the Charleston County Public Library, suggested and helped me find many books and articles about colonial Charleston. Dr Butler took the trouble to send me a good dozen letters, assisting—and correcting—me on matters such as identification tags worn by slaves, travel by small craft in the low-country waterways, the Gullah language, coin usage, slave clothing, slave auctions, street life and so forth. He must have answered one hundred questions, and every one patiently and kindly.

I wish to acknowledge assistance from the Penn Center on St Helena Island. Located on the site of one of the first schools for freed American slaves, the Penn Center is a museum and cultural centre exploring the history and culture of Gullah people in the Sea Islands. Staff at the Penn Centre introduced me to the video *Family Across the Sea* produced by South Carolina ETV, which documents the connection between the Gullah people and their ancestors in Sierra Leone.

Throughout revisions of the novel, I was lucky to have a steady stream of advice, encouragement and corrections from Ruth Holmes Whitehead, Curator Emerita of the Nova Scotia Museum, and Co-curator of its virtual exhibit *Remembering Black Loyalists, Black Communities in Nova Scotia*. Dr Whitehead has spent the past ten years researching a forthcoming book on the black Loyalists of South Carolina.

Cassandra Pybus, Australian Research Council Professor of History at the University of Sydney and author of *Epic Journeys of Freedom: Runaway Slaves of the American Revolution and Their Global Quest for Liberty*, answered my questions about blacks in Manhattan in the eighteenth century and led me to scholarly articles.

In Nova Scotia, Elizabeth Cromwell and Debra Hill of the Black-Loyalist Heritage Society gave me access to their resource centre in Shelburne and introduced me to descendants of Loyalists, and Debra Hill took me on a walking tour in the old black settlement of Birchtown on the south shore of Nova Scotia. In my endeavours to learn more about the Black Loyalists and their first ten years in Nova Scotia, I was also assisted by Henry Bishop of the Black Cultural Centre for Nova Scotia, who gave me a copy of John Clarkson's journal *Clarkson's Mission to America 1791–1792*, and by Finn Bower, Doris Swain and Betty Stoddard in the Shelburne County Museum, who steered me to numerous books and old newspaper clippings.

David Bergeron and Sophie Drakich, curators of the Currency Museum of the Bank of Canada, shared reference texts and answered my questions about eighteenth-century coins and other media of exchange—both African and

European—and Yann Girard gave me a personal tour of the museum.

Librarians working in the University of toronto Robarts Library led me to atlases, maps and other references. Staff at the Burlington Public Library helped me find scholarly articles about the living conditions of slaves in South Carolina.

I wish to thank the Canada Council and the Ontario Arts Council for their financial assistance.

I thank my literary agents, Dean Cooke (in Canada) and Denise Bukowski (international markets), for supporting this novel and bringing it to market with both enthusiasm and professionalism.

I am grateful to my editor, Iris Tupholme, and all of her wonderful colleagues at HarperCollins Canada. Iris wanted this novel before it was written, waited patiently for the first draft, advised me on revisions and—in her notes and our conversations—always found a way to be both exacting and encouraging. I also wish to thank Lorissa Sengara for additional editorial advice and Allyson Latta for her diligent work as copy editor.

Many friends helped me in this long project. Agnès Van't Bosch prompted me nearly thirty years ago to begin a series of trips to West African countries as a volunteer with Canadian Crossroads International. A walking encyclopedia of knowledge about African cultures, languages and books, Agnès made suggestions about the novel and gave me a place to write in solitude. Charles Tysoe read early drafts, made suggestions about religious matters, directed me to helpful books and planted an idea that led me to write the chapter "Nations Not So blest as Thee." Jack Veugelers, an old friend and a sociology professor at the University of Toronto, brought scholarly articles to my attention and expressed belief in the book throughout its long gestation. Judith Major, Rosalyn Krieger and Sandra Hardie advised me on early drafts.

Barbara and John McCowan, Deborah Windsor and Ray Argyle, Michael and Cara Peterman, Laura Robinson and John Cameron, Conny Steenman-Marcusse and Al and Mary Lou Keith offered me keys to their homes—all well stocked with food, coffee and good writing chairs—so that I could work for long periods of time in solitude. Randy Weir shared with me his extensive knowledge and collection of books about eighteenth-century coins in the British colonies, and Peter Haase helped with details about traditional printing presses. The novelist Lauren B. Davis and her husband Ron Davis offered perspective and personal encouragement as this story was settling into its final form.

And now I come to my family. This is the first book I've written without advice from my father, Daniel G. Hill. He died before I had made much headway on the novel, but his love of story and passion for history inspired me to keep at it. My mother, Donna Hill, was finally able to offer her own insights into one of my books without fending off interruptions from her beloved husband. Sandy Hawkins, my mother-in-law, assisted me with proof-reading and a considerable amount of research. Sandy and my father-in-law, William Hawkins, helped look after my children when I was writing and let me use their house for long spells of concentrated work. My sister, Karen Hill, also helped with research, and she and my brother, Dan Hill, read drafts and offered suggestions. The first person to offer comments on the initial draft of the novel was my stepdaughter Evie Freedman, who, by the age of ten, had already read more books than most adults in her life—myself included. Evie encouraged me to fill in the story about Aminata's childhood in Bayo, and I followed her advice. Geneviève Hill, my eldest child and an enthusiastic reader in her own right, commented on a later draft.

In this loving madhouse we call home, my other children—Beatrice Freedman, and Andrew and Caroline

Hill—not only endured my disappearances into *The Book of Negroes*, but also proved to be terrific listeners and conversationalists around the dinner table. I admire the energy that all of my children bring to the business of living, and hope that my own passions have inspired them.

I would not have found the strength, courage, and time to complete this novel without loving assistance on every front from my wife, Miranda Hill. Spending years inside one's own head—with no guarantee of emerging with a finished book—can be a lonely way to live. Miranda was the one person with whom I could speak at all times about where the book was moving—forward, backward, sideways or nowhere at all. She told me she loved me every day of every year that I gave to the novel, and fed and cared for the children and me while I pounded away on the keyboard. When I was ready to share my drafts, Miranda made practical suggestions on every page. Miranda was my first editor, my first critic, my biggest supporter and my great woman . . . so I thank her with everything I have.

Overleaf, page from *The Book of Negroes*, the historical document, which is kept at the National Archives in Kew.

Vessels Names and their Commanders	Where Bound	Negros Names	Age	Descriptio
Ship Hope	St Johns River	Jack Hyde	50	Almost past
Robt. Peacock Mr.	"	Dick	38	Stout Fell
Ship Sovereign	St Johns River	Corn. Moss	30	Do. likely
Wm. Stewart Mr.	"	Tho. Brinkerhoof	34	Very short bre
"	"	Peter Bean	32	Likely fello
"	"	Arth. Gillman	46	Stout short
"	"	George Black	40	Stout fello
"	"	Betsy Black	35	Ordinary
"	"	Wm. Black	11	Fine boy
"	"	Sam	30	Stout Bl
"	"	Luke Spencer	25	Do.
"	"	Abigail his Wife	26	Stout Wench
"	"	Bill Pigott	28	Stout fellow
"	"	Pompey Chase	28	Do.
"	"	John Voice	36	Do. B
"	"	Dran	20	Stout squat
Ship Ann & Elizabeth	Port Roseway	Peter Johnson	35	Stout Fellow
Ben. Fowler, Mas.	"	Judith Johnson	27	Ordinary
"	"	Tho. Danvers	45	Do.

	Claiments		Names of the Persons in whose Possession they now are.
	Names.	Places of Residence.	
Sabour			John Ketchum
			Capt. Peacock
			Capt. Rd. Ellison
a. Man			James Petters
			James Travess
llow			Hilliard
			Jore. Sketcham
nch			D.o
			D.o
			James Sayre
			Dr. Stevens
mall Child			D.o
			Geo: Harding
	Reuben Chase	River St. Johns	Reuben Chase
mall Child			Capt. Stewart, St. Sovery
			Geo: Harding
			Stepn. Shakspeare
ch			D.o
now			Arch.d Clarke

Remarks.

Formerly Slave to Joseph Hyde, Fairfield New England left him

D.° . . . to Jn.° Jones Savannah left him 5 Y. past, Indented

D.° . . . to Dan.° Moore Woodbridge N. Jersey left him 7 Years ag.°

D.° . . . to Corn.° Boggard near Hackinsack N. Jersey left him

D.° . . . to Dav.d Davis White Plains left him 2 Years past say

D.° . . . to Major Gillman Plaso N. England left him ab.t 3 Y.

D.° . . . to Jos.° Portress, Petersburg Virg.° left him 4 Years pa

D.° . . . to . . . D.° . . . D.°

D.° . . . to . . . D.° . . . D.°

D.° . . . to Henry Bracy, Great Bridge Virg.° left him ab.t 2

D.° . . . to Oliver Spencer, Elizabeth Town N. Jersey left him

Served her time out with Jos: Graham of Boston . . .

Formerly Slave to Gabriel Jones, Augusta Co.y Virginia left him

Property of Reuben Chace as p.r Bill of Sale from Jacob Sharp

Free born at Fonta Hill Barbadoes . . . .

Formerly Slave to Jn.° Scull Philadelphia left him 4 Years ago

Says he got his freedome from Selo.° Brindly Quaker N. Jersey that

Formerly Slave to Garret Langston, Shrewsbury left him 3 Years pa

D.° . . . to Tho.° Brown Savannah left him 5 Years past G.

Years past G. B. C . . . .

7 Years with s.d Capt.n . . . .

G. B. C . . . .

Years past G. B. C . . . .

has since been Sold by his Mr.s to s.d Travers . . . .

s past . . . .

G. B. C . . . .

. . . .

ars ago G. B. C . . . .

Years ago D.o . . . .

. . . .

ears ago . . . .

Boston . . . .

. . . .

. . . .

has liv'd in New York y.se 6 Years past G. B. C . . .

G. B. C . . . .

. . . .